W9-CNU-630

ELIZABETH'S WOLF

LORA LEIGH

BERKLEY
New York

BERKLEY
An imprint of Penguin Random House LLC
375 Hudson Street, New York, New York 10014

Copyright © 2004, 2018 by Lora Leigh
Excerpt from *Cross Breed* copyright © 2018 by Lora Leigh
Penguin Random House supports copyright. Copyright fuels creativity, encourages diverse
voices, promotes free speech, and creates a vibrant culture. Thank you for buying an authorized
edition of this book and for complying with copyright laws by not reproducing, scanning, or
distributing any part of it in any form without permission. You are supporting writers and
allowing Penguin Random House to continue to publish books for every reader.

BERKLEY is a registered trademark and the B colophon is a trademark of
Penguin Random House LLC.

ISBN: 9780399587887

Library of Congress Cataloging-in-Publication Data

Names: Leigh, Lora, author.
Title: Elizabeth's wolf / Lora Leigh.
Description: First edition. | New York : Berkley, 2018. | Series: A novel of the breeds ; 3
Identifiers: LCCN 2017036490 (print) | LCCN 2017040289 (ebook) | ISBN 9780399587894
(ebook) | ISBN 9780399587887 (softcover)
Subjects: LCSH: Genetic engineering—Fiction. | Paranormal romance stories. |
GSAFD: Fantasy fiction. | Erotic fiction.
Classification: LCC PS3612.E357 (ebook) | LCC PS3612.E357 E45 2018 (print) |
DDC 813/.6—dc23
LC record available at https://lccn.loc.gov/2017036490

PUBLISHING HISTORY
Ellora's Cave ebook edition / February 2004
Ellora's Cave trade paperback edition / June 2005
Berkley trade paperback edition / January 2018

Printed in the United States of America
1   3   5   7   9   10   8   6   4   2

Cover photo by Claudio Marinesco
Cover design by Rita Frangie

ELIZABETH'S WOLF

I woke about two o'clock in the morning. I was restless and not ready to return to bed, so I opened my email. I found the letter within minutes.

A list of military personnel overseas who had signed up to receive mail from those willing to write to them. Most of the names were men; many notations next to their names said that they received no mail and no care packages from home.

I read over this letter several times.

No mail? No care packages? Nothing?

And suddenly Dash Sinclair was there, filling my imagination.

I didn't have time for another book, I told myself. But he refused to step back, refused to wait his turn.

He was a man alone. A man who received no letters or packages, but one willing to give his life at any moment to save those who had no idea he even existed. Until one little girl's letter arrived and touched his soul.

This book is dedicated to all those men and women in our armed services who make our lives safe and protect us, often with their own lives. It's most especially dedicated to those who do so without a letter from home, without anyone to write and tell them what their sacrifices and their lives mean to us. How much it means to me.

God bless and keep all of you safe.

✦ PROLOGUE ✦

CASSIE AT SEVEN

Dash Sinclair. That's the name you want, Cassie. Choose Dash.

Seven-year-old Cassie Colder stared at the name that the pale, translucent finger pointed to. Her heart raced, fear was an ugly taste in her mouth and desperation had the tears she couldn't shed threatening to well in her eyes. But when the fairy pointed to the name, all she could do was hope.

Dash Sinclair sounded like such a nice daddy's name. She bet Dash Sinclair didn't hit his little girl or scream at her. She bet he loved her and he took care of her like a daddy was supposed to do.

No, Dash Sinclair would never hit his little girl or scream at her, the fairy that always followed her whispered in her ear. *He will love his little girl. But he has to find her first.*

Cassie looked up from the paper cautiously, her gaze going around the schoolroom just to make certain no one else could see or hear her fairy.

Raise your hand, Cassie, before someone else chooses his name, her fairy demanded gently. *He's the one we've searched for. The only one that can help your momma . . .*

Her hand shot up.

That mention of her momma had her heart racing, had the fear returning. Someone had to help her momma. She was determined to save Cassie. And the bad men who kept chasing them would kill her momma if someone didn't help them.

"Cassie, do you have a name?" Ms. Davies asked, her voice nice but not as gentle and filled with warmth as the fairy's.

"I have a name, Ms. Davies." She nodded quickly. "Dash Sinclair. Can I write to him?"

Ms. Davies lifted the list in her hand, her dark eyes going over it before a small smile tugged at her lips.

"I liked his name myself, Cassie. You can have Dash Sinclair, then," the teacher agreed.

Hope grew stronger within her.

It was a wonderful daddy name and if she was really lucky, then he didn't have any other little girls and he would like her enough that he would come help her momma.

Very good, Cassie. Her fairy bent next to her, her pretty face gentle and approving, her blue eyes filled with warmth. *Now, remember the rules. You can't tell him your momma's secrets. Not yet.*

Cassie gave a little nod, hoping no one else saw her. She knew the rules but she didn't like them. She was so scared the fairy was wrong and she and her momma would be caught before help came, before someone could make all the bad men go away.

And her momma was getting so tired and worried. She didn't laugh like she used to, and though she always smiled whenever Cassie looked at her, that look of fear was still in her momma's eyes.

Cassie, you must stop worrying, her fairy cautioned her softly, a stroke of warmth drifting over her cheek where the fairy's fingers moved over it. *I promise I'll watch over you and your momma. Now, be good, obey the rules and do as I told you and one day, your momma will laugh again. I promise you.*

And her fairy had never broken her promises to Cassie.

Since that first night when her own daddy had tried to give her to the bad man and the bad man had killed him, her fairy had been there.

Dash Sinclair is a wonderful daddy's name, Cassie. Just remember that. And he will save your momma. Just as soon as your letters save him . . .

IRAQ, TWO WEEKS LATER

He was dying.

That knowledge drifted through the darkness Dash Sinclair found himself within as he became aware of the fact that he was . . . aware.

He'd have been amused if the part of himself that had awakened had the ability to be amused. Sadly, the only ability it seemed to have was keeping him alive when all he wanted to do was give up and drift away.

He was thirty years old, no doubt lying in yet another hospital, buried beneath more drugs, the clock ticking off the seconds, the hours since he'd known there was no avoiding the missile he'd heard whining its way to the chopper he and his men were in.

The eleven men he'd commanded for the past years had been laughing, teasing each other, sharing their plans of how they'd spend their leave once they landed.

How they'd leave the harsh desert behind for six weeks and re-turn to the States. They'd return to family, girlfriends or simply friends. They'd be welcomed, hugged and pulled back into the lives they'd left behind to fight a war halfway around the world.

They wouldn't return to an empty tent and they wouldn't search for missions to take until the unit came together once again.

Now they wouldn't be returning home either.

The blurred, distant knowledge that the soldiers he'd commanded were dead weighed on him. That knowledge didn't affect the beast that pulled him from that place where he could just drift away, though. Snarling and clawing, the animal dragged him back, held him with each fierce heartbeat and refused to let go. That secret, hidden part of who and what he was snapped at the darkness, threatened to wreak havoc, to break free and reveal itself if Dash didn't pull himself from oblivion.

And all he wanted to do was let go . . .

Every day of his life had been survival. No friends, no family, no one to call his own. Claiming someone meant making explanations. It meant trusting someone with his secrets. Secrets that could reveal who he was, what he was.

It was a risk he couldn't take.

He was alone. And so tired of merely existing rather than living. And why was he living when the men he'd commanded, men with friends, families, wives and lovers, were dead?

"Well, Dash, it would seem you have a fan . . ." The voice of his commanding officer, Colonel Thomas, penetrated the darkness and the hidden primal rage. His words caused Dash to jerk alert despite the pain that assailed him as he did so.

He had no fans.

No friends or family.

And he had lost his unit.

He was damned tired of hiding and fighting, and he couldn't let himself just sleep. And now the animal he had always fought to deny was awake as it had never been before and forcing him to listen, to pay attention.

"A nice little girl named Cassie sent you a letter. Let me read this to you real fast. I'll answer her until you're well enough to do it yourself. But I have a feeling this little girl would get right pissed if you didn't eventually answer . . ." His commander cleared his throat. "Listen close now. You don't want to miss a word of this." And he began to read.

"*I liked your name best when the teacher gave us the list. Dash Sinclair. It has a very nice sound to it, I think. Momma said it's a very brave, very handsome name, and she bets you like it lots. I thought it sounded like a daddy's name. I bet you have lots of little girls. And I bet they are very proud of your name. I don't have a daddy, but if I had one, then I would like a name like that for my daddy.*"

He had created his own name. Long ago. Far away. Created a name he had prayed would hide his past. Then he had fought to change himself as well. But he didn't have lots of little girls and he wasn't a daddy. The words his commander read seeped into his brain as a sense of urgency began to fill him.

"*My momma, her name is Elizabeth. And she has black hair kind of like me. And pretty blue eyes. But my eyes are kind of blue too. I have a really pretty momma, Dash. She makes me cookies, and even tells me it's okay to talk to the fairy that lives in my room with me. My momma is really nice.*

"*My momma says you are a very brave man. That you are fighting to keep us safe. I wish you were here with us, Dash, cause sometimes my momma gets very tired.*"

Even though he was in pain, barely conscious, a sense of alarm surged through him. He could hear her fear in that simple sentence, read by the colonel, who didn't seem to recognize it. It was a plea for protection. And he knew in that moment he'd have to fight to live.

He had to live.

He had to save Cassie and her momma.

Dash saw Cassie, small and delicate, whimpering in fear. But in bright, vivid colors, he saw her mother, desperate, frightened, poised in front of her daughter like a protective she-wolf, snarling in fury.

Why did he see that? Why did the image taunt him?

It was little Cassie who wrote to him, but with each line about her mother, each description, each phrase concerning the momma who looked after her, Dash's worry and need grew.

His sense of possessiveness, his hunger, his inborn knowledge that somehow, some way, Elizabeth and Cassie belonged to him, began to strengthen inside him.

Yes. The name Dash was a good name for a daddy. For Cassie's daddy. But it was also a good name for a mate. Elizabeth's mate.

The primal instinct of the animal he'd always denied refused to rest now. His senses became sharper and he became stronger as he fought against the pain and weakness to heal himself.

Twisting shadows of violence and the dark bloody stains of death began to emerge and coalesce around Cassie and her momma as the letters came to him. The child and her momma were his, and they were in danger.

He had to live.

He had a reason to live now.

"My momma says you must be a very kind man. Kind men don't hit little girls. Do they?" As his commander read that line, it echoed in his head, over and over again, allowing more of the fury, the strength and abilities he'd always allowed to sleep, to awaken.

"Damn, Dash." Colonel Thomas sighed. "That didn't sound good at all, did it? Some men just aren't worth the air they breathe, now are they?"

So innocently phrased, yet with a wealth of meaning. He strained within the dark agony that filled him, fought through the layers of pain to find consciousness, to heal. To live.

His mate. His child. They needed him.

And his commander was right, some men simply deserved to die.

As he fought to heal, grew stronger and swam from the bleak, black pit he'd sunk into, he waited for more letters. For that fragile thread of awareness that had the animal snarling, clawing to be free.

"My momma says there might not really be fairies but it's okay if I think there are. 'Cause nothing don't exist if you don't believe in it. And if you believe in it, then it's real as sunshine. I believe in you, Dash . . ." Thomas paused before asking him, "You going to let her down now, son?"

But the question went unanswered.

Dash could hear a cry when his commander finished the letter. It was inside his head, a woman's tears and muffled sobs. But it was the child's words the colonel read to him as he fought his way back.

A battle he often feared he would lose.

"My momma says leprechauns should be real. That gold at the end of the rainbow sounds really nice. I promise, Dash. I know a real fairy. I told Momma and she smiled and said I could ask her in for cookies and milk if I liked. I had to tell her that fairies don't eat cookies and milk. They really like candy bars . . ."

The kid's letters became a lifeline through long, bitter months of recuperation. It gave him something to hold on to.

He had no one. He was a man alone in the world and he had thought this was the way he wanted it, until Cassie's letters. Until a little girl introduced herself and her mother to a man literally dying of the loneliness that filled his world.

The letters were often peppered with amusing, cute little displays of affection toward a mother who apparently loved her daughter very much. And the daughter showered him with a sprinkling of the love her mother gave.

"Sometimes my momma is sad," Colonel Thomas read. *"She sits*

alone in our room and stares out the window and I peek through my eyes and I think I see tears. I think she needs a daddy too, don't you?"

The soldiers who accompanied the colonel ribbed Dash over that one. But Thomas shushed them quickly and continued to read.

Dash was conscious now, and growing steadily stronger by the day as he fought to heal and to get to Cassie and her momma. He fought like the animal he was, because of the woman's tears and a little girl's fears.

I wanted to send you a sparkling present for Christmas, she wrote just after Thanksgiving. *But Momma said we just didn't have the money this year. Maybe for your birthday, she said, if you will tell me when it is. So, I emailed Santa instead. I told him exactly what he was to get you but I bet your other little girls already thought of it too. I wanted a bicycle, but Momma said Santa might not make it this year. I told her he would. This year, Santa would know I'm big enough for a bike. I'm seven years old. Seven years old is a good bike age, I think.*

He was reading the letters himself, devouring each word.

With each letter, she wrapped around his heart, with her youthful wit and humor and her belief in everything good in the world. He wanted her to have that damned bike. He wanted her to know Santa looked after good little girls who saved worthless hides like his. He wanted her to know he was coming for her.

"Send her the bike," he demanded the next day when the colonel came to check his progress. "And this." He pushed the list into the colonel's hand. "For Christmas."

Christmas was for kids. He'd always heard the men in his unit sigh whenever the holiday came around and they received the cards and presents and grinned like kids themselves. Dash had begun making himself scarce years ago during that time of the year. It always made his men uncomfortable, almost guilty, because cards and presents never came in his name.

He knew even adults longed for something, someone, to remember them on that day, no matter how small the present or how simple the card.

That Christmas, Dash received a card with a note inside, and his own present. The note read, *Major Sinclair, Cassie still believes in Santa and I'd like to keep that alive in her for as long as the world allows. She wrote Santa and asked him to send you the enclosed present. Please consider this gift from Cassie and Santa.*

For the first time in his long, weary life, Dash received a present and felt his heart swell in his chest. The sturdy silver chain and St. Michael medallion opened emotions inside him that he had no idea how to process.

Elizabeth and Cassie had sent him someone to watch over him, he thought. The patron saint of the U.S. Army, for a mangy damned soldier who had never known the warmth of a Christmas gift.

Two weeks later, Cassie herself wrote back.

I got my bike, Dash. Momma was really surprised. On Christmas Day I was sure Santa didn't trust me yet. My bike wasn't under the tree. Then the doorbell rang and when Momma answered the door there was my shining red bike. It had my name on it. It was just for me alone and it was brand new. And it had a helmet. And I have gloves. And I have elbow pads. And I have knee pads. And there was even a present for my momma from Santa. Can you believe it, Dash? It was the best Christmas ever. Santa even remembered my momma.

He nodded as he read the letter.

"Thank you for sending the presents," he told the colonel, glancing over at where the other man sat, his expression quiet as Dash worked the weights strapped to his leg.

The long robe would keep the mother warm until his arms could do the job. Cassie had said her momma was often cold . . .

"There's a problem there, isn't there, Dash?" The colonel nodded to the letter Dash carefully folded and tucked into the small bag next to his side.

"No problem, Colonel," he lied. "Just a little girl . . ."

◆   ◆   ◆

For over six months the letters came every other week like clockwork. Dash had begun to mark his progress with each one. His level of strength, the full mending of broken bones, internal injuries and torn muscle. With each letter, he pushed himself harder.

Then he learned there was something that could push him to strengthen himself faster and allowed the parts of him he'd never let free to surge through his body.

Cassie's letters stopped.

The first week, he excused it.

She and her mother moved a lot.

Too much.

A few days here. A month there, maybe a week at the next location. They stayed on the move, steadily working their way west.

She'd write again as soon as her mother paused long enough for Cassie to post her letter, Dash assured himself.

The next letter would arrive any day.

At three weeks late, he contacted a private investigator through the colonel to find the little girl and her mother. He turned over the previous addresses, all the information he had on the mother and child, and began to prepare himself to leave.

He could feel the imperative need building inside him, the instinct that the danger Cassie and her momma faced had increased.

Finally, three weeks later, the investigator's report came in.

Colonel Thomas, I regret to inform you that little Cassidy Colder and her mother, Elizabeth, died in a fire that overtook their apartment building several weeks ago. The bodies were unrecoverable, but there is no doubt that they, along with several others, were caught in the blaze. There was some trouble associated with the child and mother, rumors I've heard of a contract on their lives. Please let me know if you would like me to obtain more information . . .

According to the report that accompanied the letter, neighbors had heard the screams, had seen the apartment building explode, had watched the flames overtake it in a matter of minutes.

The explosion had originated in Elizabeth Colder's apartment while she and her daughter had been inside. What few remains could be found hadn't been identified yet, but according to official reports, there was little doubt it was the little girl and her mother. The remains had disappeared, possibly misplaced, according to the coroner, though the investigator believed they'd been stolen instead.

Dash felt his world crumble. The little girl who had saved him, who had given him his will to live, was gone.

For days he sat silent, staring broodingly at the ceiling, the weight of the medallion Elizabeth had sent him heavy on his chest.

For so long he had been alone. He had awakened each day knowing he had no one. Had gone to sleep each night feeling the loss. Yet while he lay near death, God had brought him angels. Only to take them away once again. It was a terrible blow to the soul he thought had withered away years ago.

He knew only blood and death. Had never known innocence until Cassie and her momma, Elizabeth.

Elizabeth.

His Elizabeth.

In thirty years of living, Dash had never claimed any one person as essential in his life. He had grown up knowing his survival depended on having no one, knowing he was different, knowing how imperative it was that he hide those differences. He had made his own way in life, had literally raised himself as best he could until he was old enough to join the Army.

He had made the service his home. The men he fought with, though not close to him, had given him a base to interact, to sharpen his intellect, to learn how to lead.

For twelve years, he had done just that. Led. He moved up the ranks, joining the Special Forces and proving his capabilities there. He had thought he hadn't needed anything more.

Dash realized now how wrong he had been.

Elizabeth's and Cassie's deaths tore a wound in his soul he couldn't explain. He had never touched the woman, had never held the daughter. She wasn't his mate and her daughter wasn't his child, yet his heart screamed something different.

His soul howled at the loss and some instinct, some inborn knowledge, refused to allow him to deny the bond that existed between him, mother and child.

"Dash, you have to snap out of this." Colonel Thomas sat beside his hospital bed a week after the report had come in, his green eyes somber, intent. "These things happen, son. You can't explain them or make sense of them. At least you have a part of her to remember."

Dash stilled the howl that wanted to rise to his lips. He had nothing. A pile of fragile letters wasn't enough.

Not nearly enough.

His fingers curled into the sheet as he stared up at the dull white ceiling silently. They thought he had sunk into depression. Lost his will to fight. Nothing could be further from the truth.

He had one last battle to fight before he could give in to the soul-deep need to rest.

Vengeance.

It kept the blood pumping in his veins, kept his heart beating in his chest.

He gave his commander a long, brooding look. "I want to know what happened. They were running from something. Someone. I want to know who."

He should have already known. He'd just been so certain he would get to them in time.

Colonel Thomas sighed wearily, his gaze compassionate. "What does it matter, Dash? They're gone."

Dash felt fury engulf him. It mattered. It mattered because he intended to exact his own form of justice. "I want to know. Contact the investigator. I want the information before my release."

He had his plans in place. The investigator could provide the background he needed, and then Dash would finish the job.

"So you can do what?" Colonel Thomas leaned back against his chair, watching him with a frown. "You'll be assigned a new unit . . ."

Like hell he would be. He was finished fighting other men's wars.

"I was given the option to return stateside on deactivation." It was all he could do to keep from snarling. "I won't be returning to duty, sir. I've had enough."

Surprise glittered in Thomas's eyes and Dash knew why.

He'd been in the service since he was eighteen. He hadn't once taken a deactivation. Twelve years he had given to first the Army and then to the Special Forces units. He was one of the best, a natural leader and a savage fighter.

But he'd had enough. The unit he had fought with was gone.

The little girl and the mother who had seen him through the need for death were gone.

He needed justice.

He needed a way to balance the scales, and he needed to find the part of himself he had hidden for most of his life so he could exact payment for their deaths.

His commander sighed again before nodding. "I'll call him tonight. You'll have what you need."

He rose to his feet, staring down at Dash for long, silent moments.

"Vigilantism is a crime. You know that, don't you, Dash?" he asked him cautiously.

Dash smiled. A slow baring of his teeth that he knew the commander would recognize. Dash was one of the best for a reason. He knew what he was doing. And he knew how to do it right.

"They have to catch you first," he said softly.

While Dash waited on the information, he worked on completing his recovery. He was rarely still. He exercised his body and his mind constantly, making certain each was in peak condition. When word came through that the information was being sent to the stateside location Dash had chosen, he packed his duffel bag and prepared to leave.

"Major Sinclair, you have a letter." The private met him as he stepped from the tent to head for the airfield. "Colonel Thomas said you were to get it asap."

Taking the letter, he saluted the soldier absently as he stared at it, predatory anticipation rising inside him.

He knew the handwriting, not the name, Paige Walker, but the carefully written words were all Cassie.

He opened the letter quickly and scanned it, a rare, enraged growl rumbling in his chest before he could stop it.

I know you must have lots of other little girls to love. Momma says you must be married with children and don't need us. But we need you, Dash. Please help me and my momma before the bad guys get us. I used to be Cassidy Colder, but Momma says now my name is Paige Walker. Paige Walker's okay, I guess. And here. This is Bo Bo's kerchief. So you know it's me. Momma says you will think the splosion got us. It hurt Momma, but we're okay. Please help us, Dash.

It had been hastily scrawled and the words sent terror chasing down his spine.

Inside the envelope was the locket he had sent her for her eighth birthday, a picture of herself and her mother inside. The mother looked haunted. Big blue eyes stared in startled awareness at the camera while the girl smiled charmingly.

The small red kerchief it was wrapped in had been around a little teddy bear's neck that he had asked Colonel Thomas to order for her. Bo Bo, she had named it. He could smell her on it. Baby powder and innocence. But there was another scent, Elizabeth's, and it sent his hormones howling. Pure female seductiveness. Dark, sweet, like a summer rainfall.

His eyes narrowed on the picture in the locket, rage shaking his body at the thought of anyone daring to hurt either of them.

They were his. And no one dared touch anything or anyone belonging to Dash Sinclair. A rumble of pure menace echoed in his chest, a growl of foreboding, a promise of retribution.

The hunt was on.

He would go after the enemy later, though.

First . . .

First, he had to find the family he had claimed in the darkness of pain. The mate who needed warmth, the child who needed protection. He would find them first. If along the way, a few of the enemy died, too bad. It would be a few less to kill later.

He was a Wolf Breed.

Dash Sinclair had known what he was even before the news of the Breeds exploded around the world.

Thankfully, in him, the genetics had recessed and were only identifiable on the genetic level, rather than the physical. It was the reason he had been marked for death at a young age. But it was also the reason he had survived after his escape from the labs.

He had joined the Army as soon as he was old enough, had fought and killed and done his best to hide right under the noses of several of the men who had funded his creation. He knew who they were. He had seen them at the labs when he was just a child, remembered their faces clearly.

Dash never forgot the face of an enemy.

Over the years he had become confident, strong, and aware of his strengths in a way that kept him from making mistakes. He never told anyone what he was. Never took the chance of confiding in friends. Hell, he had never made friends. He was surly on the best of days, and downright dangerous any other time. Most people knew to steer well clear of him.

The enemy wouldn't know that. The enemy wouldn't know who he was or what he was before he struck, before he killed.

As soon as his mate and his child were safe, they would learn, though. And it was a lesson they would learn hard.

◆ CHAPTER 1 ◆

Six Weeks Later

Not today. Not today.

Elizabeth Colder chanted the words with silent determination as she ran through the dirty, run-down halls of the apartment building, fighting to get to the basement and the only avenue of escape left to her.

If she was lucky—God, let her be lucky—the men ransacking her apartment hadn't seen her in the hall. They wouldn't know she was aware of their presence and escaping. They wouldn't catch her before she could get away.

In her arms, held tight to her, the too-small, terrified body of her eight-year-old daughter clung to her with arms and legs, her shudders noticeable even as Elizabeth raced down the stairwell.

She fought to breathe, to go faster, to get away.

As she hit the bottom step she heard the door above them crash open and knew they were out of time.

Out of time.

"There she goes!" Furious, filled with the excitement of the chase, one of the men called out an alert just as Elizabeth rounded the corner and found a burst of added speed as she saw the opened door of the laundry room.

She prayed it was empty. She didn't want another innocent life destroyed because of the hell she and her baby, Cassie, were forced to live. She couldn't bear knowing the cost someone else would have to pay in her fight to escape.

Reaching the door, she slammed it closed as she entered the laundry room and hurriedly pushed the bolt in place before shoving the chair next to the door beneath the knob and jumping for the washers.

"Up, Cassie. Out the window." She lifted her daughter to the washers and pushed her to the open window as she climbed onto the appliance behind her.

Urging Cassie through the window, she was right behind her when the sound of the door crashing inward sent rage and terror tearing through her. Clawing her way through the small opening, she felt a shard of broken glass cut across her waist a second before the sound of a weapon discharging.

Fire burned across her leg as Elizabeth pulled herself free of the window.

Jumping to her feet, she ignored the pain.

It was bad, bad enough that tears burned her eyes and she was forced to lean more on her left side, but not enough to halt her flight.

Thank God Cassie was already in the car, the driver's-side door open, just as she'd taught the little girl to do. She was lucky the car hadn't been stolen yet, not that it was worth stealing.

She jerked the keys from her back pocket and within seconds the motor was running and she was pulling from the alley and shooting across the main road into the next alley. She'd already planned an escape route, already had another car in place, just in case this happened.

In the past two years she'd learned the tricks to surviving, to escaping. Too many near misses—far too many, actually—had forced her to learn. She felt like a mouse and the enemy was a cat watching her in anticipation.

"You're bleeding, Momma," Cassie whispered, her voice trembling, shaking just as hard as her thin body.

Yes, she was, too much. Dammit, she didn't have time to stop either. Not yet.

"Just a little cut, baby. Nothing to worry about," Elizabeth promised, glancing in the rearview mirror, then at the little girl. "Buckle your seat belt."

She checked the mirror again.

The other car wasn't much better than the one she was in and the tires were just as worn. That wasn't going to help, she knew, as she saw the snow falling in the air and remembered the weather report.

A coming blizzard.

God help her. She wasn't going to go far in a blizzard and she knew it.

It wasn't the first time Elizabeth had prayed in the past two years, and she prayed she and Cassie would live to pray another day. She had a feeling this was the end of the line if a miracle didn't come soon, though.

Unfortunately, she'd learned that miracles were few and far between in real life.

"I'm sorry, Momma," Cassie whispered, staring straight ahead, her expression dazed, her face white. "I'm so sorry . . ."

Cassie said that too often, as though she could stop any of this.

"Cassie, this is not your fault," Elizabeth snapped, not for the first time. "None of this is your fault."

And there was no convincing her daughter, not that Elizabeth could blame her. She alone had witnessed her father's murder, had seen the man who had killed him. She believed it was her fault because the man who killed him told her to watch and she'd obeyed him.

Elizabeth wanted to scream, to rage at whatever forces had converged on the very night Dane had insisted on having Cassie with him. Why had he allowed his daughter there, knowing his life was in danger?

Rather than saying anything more, Cassie huddled into the seat, shivering as much from fear as the cold. There hadn't even been time to get her coat. All her daughter wore was the sweater, jeans and sneakers she'd worn down to the basement. In a blizzard she'd be more than defenseless against the cold. Both of them would be.

As soon as she switched cars Elizabeth knew she'd have to find some place, some way to hide them for just a few days. Just long enough to contact the only person who might have the power to help them.

It would be a risky move, she knew. She didn't even know the man who had made the offer of help should she ever need it. She didn't know him and she sure as hell didn't trust him, but she knew she wouldn't escape the next time they found her. The next time, they'd kill her and then there'd be no one to save her baby.

But she was out of options.

And she didn't see a miracle anywhere in sight . . .

◆　　◆　　◆

Dash stood still, drawing in the scents of the small ransacked room, and felt rage wash over him. He'd been so close. So damned close to catching up with Elizabeth and her child, only to have those chasing her manage to get ahead of him.

Over the past six weeks he had investigated Elizabeth and Cassidy Colder until he knew even the most minute detail concerning them.

He'd made contacts while in the Forces. Contacts that owed him, and he pulled in each favor he could draw on once he reached the States to learn everything he could to ensure their survival.

Cassidy Colder was a little girl living on borrowed time. A child with a price on her head and a mother fighting to save her. The lengths to which Elizabeth Colder had gone to save her little girl made his gut tighten in fear each time he thought of the information he'd collected. Such a small woman should be protected, cuddled, just as the child should be, not running in fear for that child's life.

Yet that was exactly what was happening.

Staring around the small living room of the apartment from where he stood in the doorway, he drew the scents that lingered there inside his nostrils and let the information filter through his senses.

He could smell the little girl's terror, her tears, just as he sensed her mother's rage. He snarled silently at the scents, allowing them to fuel his rage. The men chasing them would pay.

Eventually.

He picked up a child-sized jacket, brought it to his nose and drew in deep.

Innocence and the smell of baby powder clung to it. But the fact that it was here and not wrapped around Cassidy's small body sent chills snaking down his spine.

It was damned cold out there. A little one would freeze quickly in weather like this. Not that the jacket would do her much good, ripped in half as it was.

He picked up a woman's sweater next and did the same.

Ahh, there was a smell a man would die happy to know. Female, fresh and clean, a hint of baby powder but filled with the delicate scent of womanhood.

His.

Dash stared around the room again. He wasn't far behind them and it was obvious they were still several steps ahead of the men chasing them.

He smiled slowly.

He'd find the woman and child first. It was too cold, too brutal out there to go hunting for the enemy with no assurance that what was most important was safe first. And Elizabeth and Cassie were most important. Their safety was paramount; even above the hunger to feel the enemy's fear as death came for them was the need for the woman's warmth and the child's safety.

In the middle of the room a little girl's doll was ripped apart, stuffing littering the room. Clothes were shredded, books ripped in half. He knew the smell of the enemy now and he drew it in, memorizing it, making certain he never forgot it.

Cassidy and her mother must have come in after the destruction of their temporary home.

A small basket of clothes sat by the door, left forgotten but undamaged. Laundry. Doing the laundry had saved their lives.

He dropped the garments. They wouldn't be needed after he found them anyway. He had everything they would require packed in an SUV. He had made certain that once he found Elizabeth and Cassie, they would want for nothing. He took care of what he considered his, and everything inside him screamed out in possession of Elizabeth and her child.

He stepped into the apartment and moved silently through the room, aware of the hidden bugs placed within it. He had smelled them immediately upon stepping through the doorway.

His lips twisted into a cold smile. He was dealing with amateurs. There would be little challenge in taking them out when their time came.

The scent of Elizabeth's fury and fear went no farther than the door, so he knew she hadn't taken time to investigate the destruction.

She was smart.

He'd been chasing her for weeks and only in the past days had he gotten close enough that he knew the end was in sight.

She wouldn't be easy for the others to catch up to. After he found her, they would never have a hope of capturing her.

But first, he had to find her.

He backed away from the doorway, closing the door silently before turning and drawing in the scents along the hall. Moving past the basket of clothes, he headed for the far end of the hall.

Moving carefully along the dirty passageways, he followed the scent of the woman and child down the stairs and then to the basement and into the communal laundry room.

There, a small window had been pried open. Stepping to the line of washers, he reached up and removed a tattered piece of flannel from the broken window above the machines and brought it to his nose.

Once again, Elizabeth's scent filled his senses. She had cut herself escaping. Blood marred the soft, worn fabric. But she had been smart. Smart enough to know the enemy was watching the front entrance. Over the past two years since she'd been on the run with her daughter, Elizabeth had grown in strength and instinct. She was smart and intuitive. She was learning to hone the abilities she needed to stay on the run and proving herself to be adept at evading the enemy. He'd seen proof of the fact that she'd learned to use her wits where she lacked physical strength.

As Dash stood there staring at the fabric, his fingers running over the dark stains that marred it, he felt another presence begin to disturb the air that flowed in through the opened door.

Animal senses snapped into place, increasing his ability to draw in and separate each individual smell with lightning-fast instinct. Strength filled his muscles, hardened them. Calculating, predatory, confident, he let the animal out to play.

And the animal demanded blood.

Dash paused, his head turning slowly to the partially opened door as a new scent began to mix with that of fabric softener, detergent and stale water. A scent that had his lips curling in a silent snarl of predatory fury.

The scent of the enemy was insidious. The stink of corruption and furious intent. It wafted through the cool basement air, dug into his senses, filling him with the need for blood. The prey was moving closer, unaware of the predator waiting for him.

The enemy was on the prowl, stalking him now, foolishly moving from cover to investigate a stranger's interest.

Dash was looking forward to the confrontation.

He stilled the warning growl that rose instinctively in his chest. The smell of cold steel moved closer, the tread of cautious steps. There was only one. He was confident, but filled with arrogance, bloodlust, and weakness. It was that weakness, that overconfidence that would destroy him.

Dash smiled. He'd so rarely felt the well-honed strength that flooded him now, the mercilessness or icy logic that now infused him. He'd fought to be human, forgetting for far too long that he wasn't human. And men such as the one he faced now deserved no more mercy than a quick death.

The man moving toward him was no more than a flunky.

No true threat.

A hired gun and little more. Disposable. It was a good thing because he wouldn't leave the building alive.

Silently, Dash waited.

He didn't have to wait long. The door swung open slowly, revealing the lean, tense form of the fool who believed himself to be a true killer.

He was a man full grown. A gamma trying to play alpha with an animal he had no idea existed. Dash allowed his lips to curl into an anticipatory smile, knowing the other man wouldn't see it for the lethal threat it was.

"Can I help you?" he asked softly, the graveled sound of a growl at the back of his throat ignored by the other man.

"Getting nosy, stranger?" the enemy grunted as he carefully closed the door and aimed his weapon at Dash's chest. "Put your hands up where I can see them and don't move funny or you're dead."

Dash lifted his arms, hands behind his neck, the fingers of one hand curling around the hilt of the large knife concealed in its sheath between his shoulder blades.

The blade was eighteen inches long, the hilt eight. Secured in a leather sheath attached to a shoulder harness and deadly when Dash wielded it. It surpassed deadly when training merged with instincts and strength that went well beyond human.

Oh yeah. Now he could play.

"Just checking some things out." Dash narrowed his eyes, aware of the gun barrel's angle, straight to the heart.

A silencer had been attached to the barrel. The other man was a cautious bastard; Dash gave him credit for that. But only for that. Otherwise, he was less than smart. He should have realized the threat Dash was and killed him instantly. If possible.

That was what he would have done.

Instead, the little slug wanted to play. Dash liked to play. And he knew for a certainty that his opponent would fall. It was the way of the beast. He could sense the weakness facing him. Overconfidence glittered in the enemy's eyes as the need for pain scented the air around him.

"Who are you?" Beady brown eyes narrowed. Thick, oily sun-streaked brown hair fell forward, framing a less-than-intelligent forehead.

"Not your concern." Dash shrugged as he allowed his lips to curl with insulting mockery. He refused to give respect to a creature so lacking in morality that he would hunt a child. "Who are you?"

Dash watched the other man closely, the shift of the lanky body beneath the ill-fitting, though expensive, coat he wore, the confident way he held his weapon. The other man was used to killing and he was used to doing it the lazy way. He wouldn't expect to face a man of Dash's capabilities.

It was almost too easy. Dash sighed. It was a shame; he would have enjoyed a fight.

"You're too nosy, dude." The surfer boy accent grated on Dash's nerves. The casual disrespect of the attitude was reason enough to kill him. "Way too nosy."

"Not nosy enough, perhaps." Dash watched the other man's gaze carefully as he allowed his smug smile to deepen. "She got away from you again, didn't she?" he said, taunting the younger man. "Elizabeth's smarter than you are, *dude*. Back off now while I'm willing to be merciful."

The challenge was made. Dash made certain the insulting derision in his voice was clearly understood. There was no fight here, no conflict. The enemy's blood would be shed, period.

Angry color filled the other man's cheeks, his gaze glittering with the need for violence as he stepped closer.

He would want to be closer, to be certain the bullet killed rather than maimed. To watch the pain and fear he hoped to see spilling into Dash's eyes as the blood spilled from his chest.

He let the man fantasize for a moment.

"She'll be a tasty treat to the rest of us when we give that little girl to the boss," the surfer boy sneered. "You like her too, big boy? Too bad. You're dead."

The other man thought he was close enough. His finger was tightening on the trigger.

The knife slid from the leather sheath with a whisper as Dash swung his arm, wrist twisting at the last second, dragging the blade across the tender flesh of the enemy's neck. The other man's eyes widened in surprise even as his jugular split beneath the blade.

Blood formed along the narrow slice. A heartbeat later, thick rivulets began pouring from the wound.

"No, dude. *You're* dead." Dash allowed the animalistic rumble free, glorying in the smell of blood, the bite of triumph and predatory strength that filled him.

The animal flexed inside him. Powerful muscle shifted, filled with strength, and the leash on who and what he was slipped another notch.

Dash slid to the side with smooth precision as the reflexive clench of muscle tightened the man's finger on the trigger. The bullet whizzed harmlessly past him.

Blood pumped in a wide, vivid arc, splattering across the sleeve of Dash's custom-made leather jacket and draining the life from the cruel gaze of a man who would kill a woman and her child.

The body fell heavily, sightless eyes staring back in macabre astonishment as the crimson wash of blood spilling over the cement floor widened beneath his head.

There was no remorse in Dash's heart for the death. Some animals were just plain rabid in the soul, and this one was one of them. There could be no regret for putting the world out of the misery they brought.

Casually, he dragged the blade over the dead man's denim leg, cleaning it quickly before checking the body for any usable information.

There was a phone number on the back of a wrinkled blank business card. No name. Dash tucked the card into his inner jacket pocket. Money. He tossed it by the body. A message to his boss. Keys.

A picture of the little girl and her mother. This too, Dash tucked into his jacket's inner pocket.

Seconds later, confident that the man carried nothing that could be traced back to Elizabeth, Dash rose to his feet, replaced the knife in the sheath, and used a discarded towel on one of the machines to clean the sleeve of his jacket. He threw it over the face of the dead man before striding to the door.

He jimmied the lock before closing it behind him, making certain it couldn't be opened easily. The apartment building echoed with the laughter of families, of children. He didn't want to chance a child walking in on the bloody scene or an innocent bystander taking the blame for the death. Not that he thought there would be many who would feel the loss of the man he had killed.

Dash stalked back to the front entry, then into the frigidly cold winter evening. As though he had nothing better to do, he ambled around the building, heading for the alley in the back, hoping to pick up more information there.

Elizabeth and Cassie had gone out the window that led into this alley. He doubted he would find much but he had to check to be certain. Being cautious had gotten him this far; he wasn't going to slack now.

He didn't see the navy blue sedan she was driving, thankfully. At least they were in the warmth in the vehicle rather than the biting cold of the frigid winter air. He knelt in front of the open window of the basement, surveying the displaced snow beneath it. The footsteps were barely visible now as they led to a set of tire tracks a few feet over.

No, they weren't too far ahead of him if the tracks in the snow were any indication. And if he wasn't mistaken, the bastards chasing them, minus the one he had just killed, were still watching the building.

His hackles had risen the moment he stepped from the front door and felt malevolent eyes following him.

Dash looked around carefully as he rose to his full height and began checking out the tire marks along the wide alley. From the looks of it they had left in a hurry. Checking the tracks he was certain matched the sedan, he guessed Elizabeth had headed into the heart of town. She wouldn't stop there, though.

He sighed heavily as he stared into the twilight sky. Snow peppered his cheeks and forehead and the smell of the air indicated a blizzard was well on its way.

They wouldn't be able to run for much longer tonight. He should find them soon. Keeping his steps casual, he moved back to the front of the building and his own vehicle. The four-by-four SUV would be traded in farther down the road for the military Humvee waiting at a local reserve depot. It would make short work of the lousy road conditions and keep him moving when no other vehicle would dare try.

To catch the woman he had claimed before he ever saw her face, Dash knew he would need that advantage. It was also a vehicle the enemy was unfamiliar with. That edge would be important in the coming days.

He watched the rearview mirror carefully as he drove out of the parking lot and pulled his cell phone from the holder at his hip. Nine-one-one was a quick call. Brief and to the point. A dead body, nothing more.

All the while, he kept the white Taurus parked across from the apartment building in his peripheral vision. Yep, definite interest from the single occupant inside but no attempt to follow.

They were certain the kid and her mother would return. They had no idea that the woman was smarter than a whole unit of dumbasses. He shook his head and made the turn that would lead him in the direction instinct assured him Elizabeth had taken. His hunt was nearly at an end.

Then he could begin playing in earnest.

. . . when we give that little girl to the boss . . . The dead man's words slid through his mind again.

Every piece of information he had said that the price on Elizabeth's and her child's heads was for death, not capture. Yet the gloating words, the truth that rang in the other man's voice, was unavoidable.

There was more going on here than the report he'd been given.

Far more.

• CHAPTER 2 •

Elizabeth was cold and hungry and desperately fighting the rage and terror streaking through her veins, pumping hard and erratically through her heart. The snow was coming down so damned hard she had been forced to pull into the nearly deserted diner to wait it out. There she fed Cassie, watching her baby attempt to eat, her light blue eyes still dilated in shock.

Poor little Cassie. Her life had been a series of upheavals and it didn't look like it was going to end anytime soon.

She hadn't even cried out when they walked into the destruction of what had once been their home and seen the men sent to kill her. Cassie knew that to do so could mean their lives. Cassie's involuntary cries had alerted their enemies more than once and the child had known it. It was a terrible burden for a little girl to have to bear.

She was only eight. Bright, beautiful. Too beautiful to live the way she was being forced to live. She was too small. She was losing weight, losing sleep, just as Elizabeth herself was doing. At this rate, the stress of running would kill them before Dane's enemies could.

Dane. She stilled the curse that rage fed to her lips. He had been Cassie's father. Not a good man, but Elizabeth hadn't believed he was essentially a bad man either. Not until he had placed his daughter's life in danger in an attempt to save his own skin. The bastard hadn't even cared what he was doing to the little girl. All he cared about was saving himself.

It sickened her to think of the bargain he had made with the criminal he had been stealing from. How easily he had betrayed Cassie, hoping to escape his own punishment.

"Maybe Dash will come tonight," Cassie mumbled softly to herself, barely loud enough for Elizabeth to hear. "Do you think he will?"

She wasn't talking to her, Elizabeth knew. When the shock and stress was this great, Cassie turned inward. She was eight years old and so traumatized that all she had was her own imagination.

She talked to the fairy that she swore followed them. A bright, beautiful form that whispered comfort to her, that assured her Dash Sinclair was a good daddy name.

That Dash would save them.

God, she wanted to scream out in rage that her child had been reduced to such fairy tales to survive the mental and emotional cruelties being inflicted on her.

Cassie was so certain the soldier she had been writing to would rescue them and they would all live happily ever after. Elizabeth didn't know how to explain to her daughter that men, no matter how strong or how kind, wanted no part of the trouble they would bring.

Not that the soldier hadn't made her daughter's life brighter for a while; the bicycle she had been given only a few short months to enjoy, a small doll that Elizabeth had seen torn to shreds in that damned apartment. And she knew he had been behind the gifts of food that had come for such a short while.

She had appreciated the gesture, but it had been just another burden. Another person to worry about.

She wondered if he had even realized Cassie's letters had stopped coming to him. If he had even cared. He didn't know them, had nothing invested in them and he was half a world away. If he did bother to check, he would believe they had died in that apartment explosion several months before.

Damn. It had been close. They nearly had died. The bastards chasing them couldn't even set up a decent assassination properly.

And now, here her daughter sat, another broken dream shredding her soul apart because she had believed so deeply that Dash Sinclair would be there. That he was searching desperately for them. That they wouldn't have to run anymore.

Cassie had been watching for him for a week now, hope gleaming in her eyes each time she caught sight of a tall, dark-haired man. Daily, the little girl studied the fuzzy, out-of-focus picture he had sent her, terrified that if she didn't recognize the soldier herself, he might pass by them without knowing who they were.

The picture was taken in front of a helicopter with eleven other men. Dash stood in the rear, dusty, dressed in Army fatigues, his features blurred. She wouldn't recognize him if he walked up to her.

"Eat, Cassie," Elizabeth whispered, reaching across the booth to smooth back her daughter's tangled dark curls from her white face. "We'll get a room for the night and see if we can get some rest." If Cassie didn't sleep soon she would become ill. Elizabeth shuddered at the thought of trying to find medical help for her daughter.

The attached motel seemed reasonable. A few hours' sleep wouldn't hurt either of them. There was no way anything or anyone was moving in that blizzard outside.

No one except the moron pulling into the parking lot in the military Humvee, that is.

Elizabeth watched as a large dark figure exited the vehicle before striding quickly to the door of the diner. He stepped inside, larger than life, looking stronger than a mountain, his eyes going immediately to her and Cassie.

For a moment, fear shook her before she pushed it away.

No. The men chasing her weren't that dangerous, that hard. If they were, she would have been toast two years ago.

He was tall, one of the tallest men she had ever seen. Dressed in jeans, boots and a cotton shirt. Thick black hair grew rakishly long, falling over the collar of his shirt. Intense brown eyes, almost the color of amber, surveyed the diner slowly before coming back to her.

Electricity sizzled in the air, as though invisible currents connected them, forcing her to recognize him on a primitive level. Not that she wouldn't have taken notice anyway. He was power, strength, and so incredibly male that her breath caught at the sight of him.

She watched his eyes flare with . . .

No, that wasn't possession. She was losing her mind. Sleep deprivation and pain had brought her so low that she was seeing only what she knew she wanted to see. It wasn't possible that a stranger could see her, feel possession, hunger and determination to the extent that she thought she had glimpsed in his gaze before it became shuttered once again.

For the first time in years Elizabeth felt her hormones flare to life. That look was almost physical. A caress. A statement of intent.

She blinked and shook her head at the hallucination. No. He was just a big, good-looking man, and she was getting desperate. Desperate to find help. To know her daughter was protected. He was big enough to appear able to protect them both. But she knew by now that no one could protect them. It had been driven home forcibly time and time again.

Elizabeth lowered her head, watching Cassie once again as the little girl listlessly nibbled at one of the fries from her plate. She had only taken a few bites of the hamburger, mostly because Elizabeth had forced her to.

"You have to eat, baby," she whispered softly, fighting to hide her tears. "It's okay now. I promise."

The knowledge that it wasn't okay filled her daughter's eyes, though, and her expression.

"I'm tired, Momma." Cassie dragged a fry through the ketchup now, but didn't eat it. She was merely playing with it and only half-heartedly at best.

"Eat, Cassie. And drink your milk." She pushed the glass closer to the little girl, her heart breaking as Cassie raised her head, staring at her with bleak, horror-ridden eyes.

Elizabeth had to fight to still her scream of outrage. No child should ever stare out of such shattered eyes.

"Dash will come tonight, Momma." Those tear-filled eyes stared back at her, so heartbreakingly sad that Elizabeth wanted to die rather than continue to face them. "I know he will."

"Baby . . ." How could she tell her? How could she explain that there was no way Dash Sinclair could even know they were alive, let alone that once again, their killers were only hours behind them?

The last attack wasn't the worst event of their long months on the run, but it was one of the hardest. The men had been waiting on them. If Elizabeth hadn't locked the basement door behind them and found the window so quickly, they would be dead. As it was, a bullet had grazed her thigh and then she had sliced her waist on the jagged window.

She was weak and hungry herself. But she was afraid if she spent more money on food tonight, then there would be none to feed Cassie later.

She was at the end of her rope and she knew it.

The address on the card she kept in the back pocket of her jeans couldn't be forgotten. All she had to do was get there. She just had to get to the address and punch in the code when she entered the elevator and she and Cassie would be safe.

Or so she'd been promised.

From the frying pan into the fire . . . She couldn't help but remember the phrase her mother used to mutter whenever Elizabeth's father came up with one of his schemes to pay a bill he'd forgotten to pay.

From the frying pan into the fire. That was how she felt whenever she pulled that card free and stared at it. What she was running to could be far worse than what she was running from, she reminded herself.

A movement from the man still standing by the door had her head lifting, a feeling of panic suddenly overwhelming her as his cool brown eyes met hers again. His face was savagely honed. Perfectly angled for a warrior. Or maybe an assassin. Could Dane's enemies have gotten tired of trying to do the job themselves?

Then he turned and walked to the counter instead, and to the burly, middle-aged waiter/cook watching him with a thoughtful frown.

Maybe they knew each other. What other reason would a man have for pulling into the parking lot in a military vehicle? Though the older man's expression held just enough curiosity that she suspected that wasn't quite the case.

Stepping to the counter, he nodded to the man behind it and said something. The waiter shook his balding head before he grinned, reassuring Elizabeth that there was no danger.

At least, not to her.

On the heels of that thought, he began moving toward her and Cassie then.

He didn't just walk; he glided. Smooth powerful muscles rippled beneath the shirt and jeans, bringing him closer by the second. As he neared them, his arm moved, slowly reaching behind his back.

Elizabeth stiffened fearfully, ready to jump over the table to shield Cassie if a gun appeared. Dear God. What now? They were trapped. Unable to run. No place to hide.

A grin tugged at the stranger's lips, as though he could sense her thoughts. It wasn't a gun he pulled out, though, but a wrinkled piece of paper. She watched, her heart in her chest, fear burning in her belly even as a strange, displaced desire warmed her thighs.

He stopped at the booth, staring down at her, then at Cassie. Elizabeth looked over at her daughter, seeing the rounded eyes, her pale cheeks as she stared up at the man.

"Cassie," he murmured as he handed her the paper. "I got your letter."

Elizabeth felt the world tilt as Cassie whispered his name.

"Dash?"

It wasn't possible, she told herself. This couldn't be Dash Sinclair. He couldn't have really found them. Couldn't have even known they needed help.

He glanced at Elizabeth. "Have you eaten?"

She could only shake her head. Dear God. It couldn't be. It was a trick. She picked up the letter from the table and unfolded it.

I know you must have lots of other little girls to love. Momma says you must be married with children and don't need us. But we need you, Dash. Please help me and my momma before the bad guys get us.

How had Cassie managed to post this letter without her knowing it?

She stared at her daughter, barely able to process the fact that she was speaking to the stranger. A dangerous, cold-eyed stranger who claimed to be Cassie's military pen pal.

Cassie's cheeks were flushed now. Hope radiated from her big blue eyes as shock was slowly displaced by happiness.

And exhaustion.

"You came, Dash." Cassie threw herself into his big arms, her tiny body looking frail and helpless against the man's chest, though his expression tightened with some undefined emotion as his arms contracted around her.

Dash Sinclair.

She had loved that name herself but had pushed it from her mind except for the few times Cassie had written the letters to the wounded soldier. That and when he had invaded her dreams.

She hadn't shared Cassie's belief that one day Dash would come riding to their rescue, though. That one day he would protect them both.

She was an adult. She didn't believe in fairy tales, though she had fought to keep her daughter's belief alive as long as possible.

"Eat, Cassie." He sat Cassie back in her seat, pointing commandingly at the food.

Surprisingly enough, Cassie dropped back to her seat and a French fry disappeared into her mouth immediately. Then another. Despite Elizabeth's thankfulness that her daughter was eating, she couldn't halt a small streak of jealousy. Cassie had refused to eat for her mother. Yet she was eating for a stranger.

"Mac." He called out the name of the aging, rotund man behind the diner's bar. "I need two cheeseburger platters, two milks."

Elizabeth shook her head. "No . . ." She knew one of those platters was for her.

"Thank you, Dash." Cassie laid her head against his arm when he sat next to her, and she chewed tiredly at the hamburger. "Momma was hungry. She didn't eat yesterday either. But I knew not to worry. I knew you'd be here. I knew you would, Dash."

Dash barely stilled his rumbled growl as Cassie leaned against him. He lifted his arm, curving it around the frail shoulders, and stared back at the mother, at his mate, with a determination he prayed she was taking in.

His possessiveness toward these two had grown only stronger, only deeper over the weeks he had been searching for them. With each miss, each added awareness of the danger they faced, his resolve had only hardened. As though the extra DNA he possessed inside his body were howling out for a claiming in a way that threw him off guard. He didn't like being thrown off guard. But he found himself accepting the responsibility of these two so naturally that he didn't question it.

He could sense Elizabeth's strength. It was there in her squared shoulders, the glint of battle in her weary blue eyes. She didn't trust him and she sure as hell didn't believe he was who he said he was. But he had expected that. He expected her to give him a fight. He had known she wouldn't be easy to conquer.

He didn't want her to be easy, though, Dash realized. She was a strong woman, and his dominating instincts would run roughshod over any woman who wasn't. She would have to learn how to stand up to him, when to push back and when to allow him to shoulder her weight. She would have to learn how to share the burdens rather than carry them alone on her fragile shoulders, as she was used to.

Careful of the little head tucked against his chest now, Dash reached into his back pocket and pulled his wallet free. Opening it, he laid it between them. It had his driver's license in one clear pocket, his service ID in the other, both easy to see.

He watched her as she studied both and then lifted her eyes, a single brow arching with suspicious doubt. She had spunk; he'd give her that. She wasn't taking anything at face value. Not the letter, not his ID.

Her gaze went to her daughter once again. Cassie had slumped against his side, her fragile body slowly relaxing as Dash felt her soaking in the heat of his body through her thin sweater.

"Eat, Cassie, then you can sleep," she admonished her child gently.

"Yes, Momma." Cassie was worn down, exhausted, just as her mother was, and it infuriated him.

Mother and daughter looked like they had spent too many days without sleep or proper food. Their faces were pale, their eyes overly bright from nerves and fear.

"I came to help, Elizabeth," he promised her as he replaced his wallet, aware of the burly waiter as he moved from the bar with the plates of food. "Eat and then we can discuss it."

He tried to sound reassuring. Tried to appear nonthreatening, but he knew it was like trying to hide an elephant with a blanket. He was dangerous when crossed in the wrong way. Dangerous period if the situation warranted it, as this one did.

Staring into her eyes, he reached beneath the shirt he wore and drew free the silver chain and medallion Elizabeth had sent. St. Michael, sword raised, hair flowing behind him, was pressed into the nickel-sized circular pendant.

She blinked. Once. As she swallowed in a hard, tight movement her gaze flicked behind him to the burly waiter/cook approaching the table.

Mac, as his name tag proclaimed, set the platters heaping with food on the faded top of the booth's table. As he did, the sleeve of his white T-shirt slipped up, revealing a Special Forces tattoo.

Dash filed the information away for the moment. He would need someone to cover for them when they left. With any luck, he could gain help there. Special Forces, active or otherwise, tended to stick together when trouble trailed one of them. Hopefully, this man's loyalty to the brotherhood was deeper than the need for whatever cash Elizabeth's enemies were offering.

"You're very bossy," Elizabeth murmured as she stared down at the food.

Dash could damned near see her mouth watering. Just as he could see her pride warring with her need.

"Realistic." He shrugged. "You don't eat, you can't fight. What's more important? Your pride or your health?" *Or your daughter.* He left those words unsaid, though.

He knew exactly how important her child was to her. She had prevailed against odds that many men would have faltered beneath to save her little girl. He wouldn't begrudge her the pride he saw glittering in her eyes, but she would eat.

She finally relented and, after a final warning look in his direction, began to eat. He ate his own food, watching carefully as she consumed more than half the huge sandwich and managed to put a dent in the fries. The milk was consumed with pleasure, a flutter of her eyelashes that betrayed her joy in the drink. As though it had been a while since she'd tasted it.

He wondered if she would find as much pleasure in being touched, stroked, as he had fantasized about in the past months. The closer he had come to finding her, the more explicit his dreams had become and the more savage his desire for her had grown. He wanted her with a hunger he had never known before.

But first, he had to get mother and child settled, get them to a place of safety. He couldn't relax his guard until he had managed that. To do it, he would have to drive through one of the worst blizzards of the century.

· CHAPTER 3 ·

Dash kept a careful eye on the parking lot through the mirror behind Elizabeth, making certain no other vehicles pulled in. There was a line of eighteen-wheelers extending for miles down the interstate because of the blizzard conditions, and the fluffy white stuff didn't seem to have a mind to ease up anytime soon. News reports were promising a full-fledged whiteout, which meant he didn't have much longer to get them to a place of safety.

Thankfully, one of the men he had fought with in the Middle East owned a ranch not too far away. Dash had contacted him on the encrypted sat phone he'd procured from a CIA contact just after entering the States. Before beginning his search he'd explained his situation to Mike, who had extended an invitation to come to the ranch.

For years Dash had fought alongside his fellow soldiers, maintaining a careful distance, keeping a rein on his need to draw close to others. He had feared he would be turned down when he saw he would have to ask for help along the way. Surprisingly enough, he'd been welcomed.

They had quite a drive ahead of them, and he still wasn't certain if their final destination once they left Mike's would provide the sanctuary he hoped to give Elizabeth and Cassie. But at least he knew the way there would be easier.

First, he had to get her out of the diner. And she didn't look predisposed to trust him. He had a feeling she was more inclined to run at first chance instead.

As he ate, one-handed to allow little Cassie her resting spot against his side, he watched her mother. Her delicate face was elegant: a sharp, determined little nose that rounded ever so slightly at the tip, hinting at a playfulness she had been forced to bury within her; wide blue eyes; high cheekbones; and delicate rosy lips he could fully imagine kissing.

And often had.

It would take a smart man to see the steel core of determined strength she harbored inside her, and Dash was proud to admit he'd known it was there from the first letter read to him that her daughter had sent. She wasn't a woman a man could keep secrets with, or one who would be easily satisfied with less than the whole truth. She was a woman who would fight beside a man, though. One he could be proud to say he belonged to, heart and soul, just as she would belong to him.

"Thank you for the food." She finally pushed her plate away, her gaze settling on Cassie.

The little girl had fallen asleep against his side, her slight body completely relaxed against him.

He glanced at her plate. Like her mother, she had been unable to complete her meal but she had eaten enough to satisfy him. Enough to help her sleep through the long drive ahead and replenish the energy that shock and fear had drained from her small body.

"She's so tired." Elizabeth sighed as she raked her fingers wearily through her long, tangled, dark brown hair. It was colored. He knew the silken strands should hold the deep burnished color of dark chocolate, soft and shimmering with auburn highlights. It looked dull, not dirty, but as tired as he knew she was physically.

"You're both exhausted." He tried to keep his voice soft, to still the rough growl that kept building in his throat, roughening his voice, making him sound hard, but he was unable to fully hide it.

Unfortunately, Dash thought, he was who he was, what he had been made into. He was hard, demanding, and made little allowance for any foolishness. Elizabeth would have to see that her only safety lay in him. He wouldn't accept anything less.

Elizabeth's saddened gaze touched her daughter, and in a second he watched her go from a mother's regret to determined protectiveness. Her gaze returned to him, harder, uncompromising. "Thank you again for the food, Major Sinclair, but . . ."

He didn't give her time to finish the demand he could sense getting ready to spill from those pretty lips.

"Don't bother," he warned her. "You're coming with me, Elizabeth. You and Cassie." He stared back at her firmly, watching her eyes widen. "I know you're wounded, and you're too exhausted to keep running like this. Both of you are. I came to help you and that's exactly what I mean to do."

She eased back, pressing against the back of the booth as she watched him warily. He could see the battle raging within her. The need to trust. The fear. She had been betrayed too many times to just calmly accept his offer.

It wasn't an offer, though; it was simply the way it was going to be.

At the moment, she, like Cassie, was more shell-shocked than anything. The earlier escape had been a close one, and he knew the terror of it still pulsed through her veins. Fine tremors shook her body occasionally, though she fought to still them, to maintain her appearance of strength.

"I appreciate the gesture . . ."

Dash grunted as he frowned at her heavily. "Don't say anything you're going to have to swallow later," he warned her, keeping his voice commanding. "While I've been chasing you down the past six weeks, I learned exactly what you're up against." He hated the way her face whitened further and the hunted look that strengthened the shadows in her eyes. "You can't fight this alone. You know that. They've worn you down physically, and though you may be sharp as hell mentally, that's not going to help you when you have to run again."

Her gaze went to Cassie, and Dash watched her eyes moisten with tears. She pressed her lips tightly together as her fists clenched against the stained Formica of the tabletop.

They were small, delicate hands, with long, graceful fingers. Hands a man would kill to have stroking over his body. He was dying to have her touch him. To see if the woman could match the dreams that haunted him.

"I don't have a choice." Her voice was rough, hollow. "I can't take the chance, Mr. Sinclair. I don't know you. I won't trust you."

They weren't empty phrases. She had been betrayed one time too many. Had fought too long to give in now and just accept anyone else taking over. Which was okay, he told himself silently. He'd let her fight as much as her pride demanded, but in the end, he'd win.

Dash allowed a smile to tip his lips. "I didn't ask you for your trust or your permission. I was stating a fact. We have to get you and Cassie somewhere safe, and then we can see about eliminating the problem."

If her face could have whitened more, it would have. He knew she had tried more than once to go to the authorities, to find a way to do what was right. But men, even those sworn to uphold the rights of the innocent, were often much too human. Those who couldn't be bought had been killed. And he knew her conscience had been laid bare by the deaths of those few who had tried to help.

"I went to the police. Once," she said bitterly. "I won't make that mistake again."

Not all of the officers at that station had betrayed her there. The chief alone had been responsible for that one. Several of the investigators were still looking for her, unaware of what had caused her to flee. They only knew she was in trouble.

In trouble, and a friend. Elizabeth had grown up with several of the officers in the small town she had been raised in. Several of them were still looking for her, determined to learn what had happened to Elizabeth and her child. Men who would die to protect her, but he also knew it was a sacrifice they'd most likely make and one that would destroy Elizabeth.

The small Virginia town Elizabeth had been raised in was a secondary home to a powerful criminal as well. A drug kingpin and murderous bastard. One willing to pay for the protection he needed. Unfortunately, Dane Colder had made the mistake of crossing the man.

Dane was resting in hell now, courtesy of the dealer's bullet as Cassie watched. There was no doubt she wouldn't have survived long if her mother hadn't arrived when she had.

Thankfully, Elizabeth had somehow known to check on her baby and had heard the gunshots, watched in horror as her daughter was locked into one of the bedrooms as her father's body was being disposed of.

How she slipped in and took her from under their noses Dash had no idea. One thing was certain, though; she had, and now she and her daughter were in more danger than they knew.

Terrence Grange wasn't just powerful on his own. His connections to the mob and the power structure he had built around his silent little empire had tentacles running all across the United States and into several government agencies. Now Dash had to figure out a way to save them, because who to trust, just as Elizabeth had found out, wouldn't be easy to decide unless the request he'd sent out when he found her and the child was answered.

"I didn't say we'd have smooth sailing, I just said we could do it." He shrugged. "It's your choice. You can come with me and live or keep running until the bastards take you down."

She drew in a hard, deep breath. Dash knew she was aware that soon she would fail. She didn't have the connections or the power to protect herself and her child. She was a woman alone and learning exactly what that meant.

"And how do I know I can trust you?" she asked him mockingly. "I don't know you, Major, and I sure as hell don't believe you would chase us for six weeks out of the goodness of your heart."

Dash glanced down at Cassie. When he returned his gaze to Elizabeth, he knew his own anger was flaring in the depths of his eyes.

"Wrong, lady." He wanted to growl with the strength of his sense of ownership toward the two females. "She saved my worthless life when it didn't matter to anyone but her. And I'll be damned if I'll let her or the mother she loves die. Now it's your choice if you come with me or if you stay. But Cassie will be protected. She goes with me."

He watched Elizabeth's eyes widen as fear shadowed them further. Dammit, he hated seeing her eyes go dark with terror rather than the pleasure he wanted to bring her. He could see it snaking through her, knew it would be chilling her blood as she fought to find a way to fight back. She was a strong woman, and having control taken from her wouldn't be easy for her to accept. But he had to do it. Had to establish authority with her and Cassie if he was going to pull this off.

A frown snapped in place. Battle glittered in the fierce depths. His cock hardened, which was more than disconcerting for the situation and location they were in.

"That's my daughter you're talking about," she finally hissed as she leaned forward, anger shaking through her. Which sure as hell beat the lethargy he had seen in her moments before. "You don't do a damned thing without my permission."

Blood surged through his body, hot and exhilarating, as her scent flowed to him, wrapping around him. She was aroused. Not a lot, curiously aroused maybe, a bit shy. He liked that. Liked that shyness, that hesitancy.

But even stronger was her sudden anger.

Her child.

Her responsibility.

She wouldn't let it go easily. Even to him. Which meant he would have to fight her for it.

He was looking forward to that fight.

"Your permission?" He tried to keep his voice soft, but he was aware of the throbbing growl resonating just beneath the surface of his words. "If you haven't noticed, I'm not asking for anything here, Elizabeth. I'm telling you. I didn't travel halfway across the world and chase your pretty little butt across half the United States only to have you pat my head and send me on my way. You can accept this gracefully or we can just go ahead and fight it out. But I promise you, I know who's going to win in the end. And it's not going to be you."

Her eyes widened in incredulity. He doubted any man had ever stared her in the eye and not backed down until now. Most men wavered when faced with a strong woman. When faced with this one, Dash didn't waver; instead, his erection hardened further.

"Are you insane?" she finally asked him with a sneer. "Or do you just have a death wish, Major Sinclair? If you know what I'm facing, then you know the men he's already killed to get to me. Do you really want to end up being the next bloody body he leaves in his wake?"

She was smart. He had known that all along. The mocking condescension in her expression and her voice would have given any other man pause.

Dash wasn't just any other man, though, and it was time she figured that one out.

"Actually, I was thinking more along the lines of making him the next bloody body I leave in *my* wake." There was no doubt in Dash's mind that he'd win either. One way or the other, his mate and her child would be safe. "Make no mistake, Elizabeth. I'm not so easily brought down."

More than one terrorist had tried, men more diseased than Grange and with a larger network of evil to back them. Dash knew well how to play this game and how to succeed.

He watched her, sensed the battle playing out within her, her instinctive knowledge that if anyone was capable of saving them, it was him. But she also doubted that there was any hope for her and Cassie to survive, period.

Hope was slowly dimming within his mate.

His mate.

Facing her now, her scent in his head, her fire reaching out to him, the last piece of the puzzle of what she was to him clicked into place.

She was his mate.

She was born for him, born to complete him. And if she hadn't been born for it, then that was just too bad, because she belonged to him. Her and their child.

He stood casually, laying little Cassie gently in the seat as he did so. Then he leaned in close, his hand flat on the table, his nose merely inches from hers as she stared back at him in surprise.

"We leave in five minutes," he warned her softly. "Me and Cassie, or you, me, and Cassie. As I said, it's your choice."

Her eyes narrowed, her delicate little nostrils flaring as heat swept into her cheeks. He could smell her excitement now, but he also smelled blood.

"I won't let you . . ."

He leaned closer. "You're hurt," he said, accusing her as she jerked back from his fury.

She shook her head quickly. "It's nothing and I've taken care of it. That's beside the point . . ."

There was no point. There was simply what would be.

"Fight me now and I promise you'll regret it. Now get ready to pull out of here. We're leaving." The blood didn't smell fresh, so she might well have fixed the wound for the time being. He'd check it out soon, though.

He didn't give her time to comment. He straightened, giving her one last hard look before turning and stalking to the counter. The husky ex-soldier waited, watching him with a narrowed, appraising gaze as he neared.

He'd already determined the mettle of the man who had stared at him with assessing, suspicious eyes when he had first entered the restaurant. Several times since, the other man had turned his attention back to Elizabeth's table, watching, waiting, though he'd made no attempt to contact anyone. He was a man who tried to live by a certain code, the same code Dash tried to live by himself.

"She's in trouble," Mac murmured, his balding head nodding to Elizabeth as Dash stopped in front of him. It wasn't a question. The man had an extra sense for trouble. It was something learned in combat, something never forgotten.

Pulling his wallet free for the second time, Dash opened it and laid it on the counter, letting the other man survey it, his eyes narrowing on not just Dash's rank but also the Special Forces insignia his ID carried.

If he was betrayed and Mac gave the information to Elizabeth's enemies, it wouldn't help them. Dash had made certain over the years that he had no friends, no associates that anyone would believe could be used against him. And tracking him through anyone would be impossible. He was a man without roots or ties.

A ghost.

"And I'm here to get her out of that trouble," Dash growled, refolding his wallet and sliding it once again into the back pocket of his jeans. "But I need a favor."

Mac stared back at Elizabeth and Cassie for long moments.

"Lot of money on their heads," he said quietly when his gaze returned to Dash's. "And the men flashing their pictures around here yesterday looked serious about finding her."

A piece of information the burly former waiter/cook hadn't given him earlier.

Dash's brow lifted. "I'm serious about ensuring they don't."

Mac nodded slowly at the statement, his gaze intent as he stared back at Dash.

"I haven't made the call. Had no intentions of making it," Mac stated, glancing at the two again, compassion softening his fierce expression. His attention turned back to Dash. The hazel depths were hard and cold. "Tell me what you need, boy."

◆　◆　◆

What was she supposed to do?

Elizabeth watched as Dash paid for their meals, then bought several bottles of water and snack chips as he talked to the waiter. Their voices were low, almost imperative. They were discussing more than the price for a few snacks.

She bit her lip hard, breathing in deep as she fought to clear her head of the exhaustion and pain. It had been harder in the past few months. As though Grange had grown tired of playing with her.

She rarely had more than a few days to rest, to work some under-the-table job for less than minimum wage before she was on the run again.

And Cassie. God, it was killing Cassie and she knew it. They couldn't keep running like this. She had to find someplace to hide her baby.

Her hand fell from the countertop, pressing against the wide bandage covering the deep gash in her thigh where the bullet had torn through the flesh. It wasn't too deep. It could have probably used a few stitches, but she considered herself lucky. It could have been a hell of a lot worse. The one in her side from the basement window paled in comparison, though it too was fairly deep.

She'd cleaned them earlier in the diner's bathroom, pouring alcohol straight into the wounds while Cassie stood trembling, watching her. It had been agonizing. More painful than receiving the wounds. But she knew she couldn't afford the infection. If she got sick, then there was no way she could protect her baby.

Her hand trembled, her stomach roiling with remembered panic as she thought of the agonizing flight down the apartment stairwell as she fought to get to the basement.

The past two years had been horrifying. Terrence Grange never gave up. He was like a pit bull, his jaws clamped on tight, refusing to let go or to give her any peace.

At first, she had prayed that if she merely ran, forgot about going to the police, stayed quiet and hid, he would leave them alone.

But he wanted Cassie.

His men had made that clear just after the explosion of their last apartment. Give Terrence her baby, and then she could go free, do whatever the hell she wanted. He didn't give a damn about Elizabeth. He just wanted her daughter.

The perverted bastard. She knew exactly why he wanted Cassie, and she would die before she'd allow it.

But what if she did die and he still managed to get Cassie?

Icy terror lodged in her chest at the thought.

She wasn't strong enough to fight much longer. And she was learning just how adept Grange was at cutting off every avenue of escape she found. He killed the people who tried to help her. Killed them or paid them off, leaving her with nowhere to turn.

Had he paid off Dash Sinclair? If he hadn't yet, then Elizabeth knew the offer would be made as soon as Terrence learned who he was. And the offers Terrence Grange made men were hard for them to turn down. As much as she wanted to trust this man, as much as she knew leaving him behind would break Cassie's heart, she knew his betrayal would destroy both of them.

She didn't have a choice but to run from him as well.

As Dash talked to the waiter, Elizabeth began to move slowly from her seat. He turned his back on her, surveying a small row of teddy bears behind the counter, obviously intent on picking one out. Would he buy a teddy bear for a child he was going to betray?

She took a deep breath.

God, she wanted to trust him. Wanted to believe he could help her, but she had learned better over the past two years. Had learned she could trust no one but herself.

She eased Cassie from the seat, her breath hitching in despair at the painful thinness of her little girl's body. Then she glanced out at the parking lot, fear streaking through her. They could die out there. What the hell was she supposed to do?

"I'll get her." She jerked around, her eyes wide, arms tightening protectively around her daughter.

He watched her somberly. For once, his gaze wasn't demanding, wasn't glittering with heat and anger. It was still, understanding as he gripped Cassie beneath her thin arms and lifted her easily.

"Don't hurt her." She couldn't stop the plea. For the moment, she had no choice but to trust him. She knew it, and it was like a blade digging into her heart. "Please don't hurt her."

Gentle arms cradled Cassie's body against his broad chest as savage eyes stared down at her with a hint of compassion.

"Get the stuff from Mac that I bought, Elizabeth. I got Cassie a stuffed bear to make up for the one that was destroyed. And some chips, in case she gets hungry before we get to our destination. We need to leave now." His voice wasn't gentle. It was cool, dark, deep. It stroked over her shattered nerves, surprisingly enough, stilling them.

She moved carefully for the counter, watching him, terrified he would simply leave her and take Cassie to the monster searching for her. Her body was tense, every muscle poised to jump and fight when she reached the bar.

"Trust him, little girl." The waiter handed her the sack, his hazel eyes kind as she glanced at him. "He's a good man."

Elizabeth flinched in surprise. How could he know? How did he know anything? But there was nothing else forthcoming. She took the bag and moved quickly back to the man intent on taking over her life.

Her life and her child.

Stepping into the swirling snow was like entering an isolated vacuum of icy beauty. It was nearly whiteout conditions, with at least six inches of the thick, slick crystals built up on the ground.

"We can't travel in this storm." Elizabeth shivered as Dash quickly unlocked the rear passenger door. He deposited a sleeping Cassie into the backseat before jerking a blanket over her. He then unlocked the front and urged Elizabeth in.

Neither of them had been wearing a coat, let alone clothing warm enough for such weather.

"Get in." His order was less than polite. "I figure those boys you have chasing you aren't too damned stupid. They'll guess the best time to catch you is during a snowstorm with a four-by-four. We have just enough time to pull out of here and get ahead of them."

She jumped into the seat, staring at the unfamiliar interior in confusion.

It was the most advanced vehicle she had ever laid eyes on. She had seen military vehicles before, of course, but had never been inside one. She doubted she could even reach across the console between the passenger seat and the driver's seat to hit at her new captor. She glanced back at her sleeping daughter then. Cassie had been strapped into the single, wide bucket seat in the back, her head resting on a pillow that lay on the padded console beside her.

"Buckle up." He stepped into the driver's seat and started the ignition.

"This is a blizzard, you know?" She did as he ordered, though, and buckled the seat belt securely.

He stared out the window, considering, then he shrugged. "I've seen worse."

He had seen worse?

Well, she hadn't. Still, the fear, worry and concern weren't exploding inside her and making her determined to get away. She would brave anything to save Cassie, even the worst snowstorm of the century. Yet here she sat, scared, yes, nervous. And so very tired. But that furious, savage certainty of danger wasn't there with Dash as it had been with others.

But it was a feeling she didn't dare trust. There was no escape right now and she knew it, and no matter how good his intentions, she knew how evil Grange's were, and she knew that escaping her would-be rescuer would become imperative.

Dash reversed the vehicle, a pensive look on his face as he exited the diner's parking lot.

"Mac, the owner of the diner, is retired Special Forces," he told her quietly as they hit the deserted interstate. "Most of us stick together. I'm pretty certain he'll cover for us, give Grange's men a bogus vehicle and directions to follow, but just in case, we won't be on the interstate long."

"We won't?" She couldn't imagine the back roads were passable at all.

"Not nearly long enough to allow them a chance to figure out where we're heading," he assured her.

Elizabeth gripped the edge of her seat as he picked up speed, making better time than she could have ever imagined on the snow-packed road. The windshield, amazingly, had night vision, giving the driver a clear view of the world outside without the betraying beacon of the headlights.

It was much more technological than she would have liked. She suddenly felt as though she had been thrown into a twilight zone. It made her off-balance, made everything around her seem a bit surreal.

This wasn't an ordinary vehicle, even by military standards, she didn't imagine. Just as she rather doubted the military gave its soldiers such free use of their vehicles.

"Who did you steal the Hummer from?" She rubbed her arms nervously as she fought the weariness dragging at her mind and the exhaustion dragging at her body.

He flashed her a surprised look. "I didn't steal it. I borrowed it. There was an Army depot close by. The commander in charge allowed me use of it to get where I needed to go. We won't be keeping it long."

Allowed him the use of it? Well now, wasn't he just special?

"Isn't that rather unusual?" She turned, bracing her back against the edge of the seat so she could watch him closely, or rather suspiciously.

The dashboard lights reflected on a hard, primal expression. He didn't glance over at her, though she had no doubt he could tell every move she was making.

He shrugged lazily as he pushed the vehicle faster through the thickening snow.

"Not normal, but not unusual exactly. I'm inactive for the moment but still part of the services. My record speaks for itself and the commander knew of me. There was no risk to loaning it." He shrugged as though the explanation should be enough.

"And it was just that easy?" Too bad it wasn't that easy to believe.

He was silent for long moments, his brow furrowed as though whatever thoughts held him were less than comfortable.

"My team and I pulled his boy out of a firefight overseas. He and his unit were pinned down by rebel fighters and they were losing fast. When I put in the request to deliver the vehicle to the depot close to our destination, he saw no reason to refuse it." There was something about that explanation that made her wonder exactly what he was leaving out.

"So you're just delivering it elsewhere?" The military worked a hell of a lot different than she'd imagined.

"Just delivering it," he agreed. "Nothing more."

· CHAPTER 4 ·

Silence stretched between them as Dash drove the heavy vehicle confidently through the snow. Outside, the world was a blanket of white, piling against the large eighteen-wheelers parked here and there. Thankfully, it seemed most people had heeded the warnings about the coming blizzard and weren't out on the roads. So far, they'd passed no stranded motorists or weather-related accidents.

As the otherworldly appearance of the night surrounded them, Elizabeth found herself studying the man more than the weather conditions. He acted as though his decision to protect her and Cassie shouldn't be a surprise to her, that she should just accept it as his right.

"Why are you here? And what the hell do you want with my daughter?" Elizabeth couldn't stand it any longer. The earlier explanation just wasn't working for her.

She was trapped in a blizzard with a man she didn't know and had no idea if she could trust. A hard, dangerous man. And he thought she should just accept it.

His hands tightened on the steering wheel.

"I didn't lie to you. I came to help. I got Cassie's last letter the day I was returning stateside. When the letters stopped coming I had my commander check into it." He paused for a moment, breathing deeply. "I thought something died inside me when he told me what everyone thought happened to you and Cassie. I lost something I didn't know I had. When her last letter came, nothing could have kept me away."

She couldn't stop the disbelief that filled her. "Look, I'm sure your family . . ."

"I don't have family. I've never had family." He shot her a brief, quiet look. There was no anger, only acceptance.

"Wife, lover . . ."

"I was in foster care until I turned eighteen and joined the Army. I didn't make friends easy and there was never a guarantee I'd return once deployed, so a wife was out of the question and my job didn't exactly leave a lot of time for steady lovers." A rueful curve of his lips came and went. "Cassie's first letter came while I was in a coma after the chopper my team and I were in was shot out of the sky. Everyone died but me. I would have died if something in those letters hadn't pulled me back."

The explanation, as brief as it was, silenced the pure disbelief she'd felt that a stranger, no matter how strong, would want to ride to her and Cassie's rescue. Not that she wasn't highly suspicious, because she was. It didn't mean she wouldn't run with her daughter at the first chance, because she would. But she gave him the benefit of a doubt. Not trust, just the benefit of a doubt.

Elizabeth heard the throb of pain in his voice, a fury that confused her. She didn't know what her daughter had written in her letters. Cassie had sworn she wouldn't tell the soldier the danger she was in, and Elizabeth didn't have the heart to refuse to allow her to write him.

Cassie had always believed in him, though. From that first letter until now. She was certain Dash would save them, and Elizabeth had no idea why.

It was during one of the rare times she had managed to get Cassie into school that the pen pal program had begun. She had bought illegal records, had nearly gotten herself arrested and spent countless nights pacing the floor in fear so Cassie could attend classes once again. So her child could have some sort of normalcy while her mother fought to make sense of the danger they were in.

The teacher had given the children a list of service members who didn't receive mail and a permission slip to allow the kids to write. Cassie had been excited over the name she chose.

The fairy said this one, Momma. She had giggled as she waved the piece of paper with the name and address on it. *He's got a nice name, Momma. I bet he's a good daddy.*

She was fascinated with the idea of good daddies. Daddies who didn't hit their little girls, who didn't bargain with their children's bodies and then get killed in front of their eyes.

The fairy, Elizabeth wasn't sure about. Cassie had been talking about the fairy since her father's murder. Elizabeth never pushed her about it. She never questioned her. Just like the elves and the unicorns and the other fantasies that played a part in Cassie's vivid imagination. Elizabeth didn't have the heart to take it away from her.

"You don't owe us your life, Mr. Sinclair." She shook her head at that thought. "I don't think I can bear being the cause of any more deaths."

He was a strong man. A determined man. She sensed that. But even he had his weaknesses and a bullet didn't make allowances for any man.

"I owe her more than my life." He finally shrugged. "Might as well give in, Elizabeth. You aren't going to win this one."

Elizabeth shook her head. She was tired, dazed. How could she be expected to fight him when she knew how desperately they needed him? She was living on nerves alone now rather than a clear mind and well-rested body. It wouldn't be much longer before she made a mistake and when she did, she knew Grange would be there waiting.

For the moment, she wasn't in danger of facing him alone, though. That quiet thought had her chest clenching painfully.

How had her daughter managed to find someone like Dash Sinclair to exchange letters with? What instinct had guided the child to choose his name above all others? Cassie claimed it was her fairy. Elizabeth was terribly afraid it was just another joke that fate was playing on them both.

"She cried for a week after I refused to let her write to you again," she finally said tiredly. "I didn't know she had posted that last letter. I don't know how she found the chance."

Cassie had been surprising her since day one, but still, Elizabeth truly couldn't have expected this one. That Cassie had found a way to send him a plea for help, or that the pen pal would actually show up, determined to protect them.

"Good thing for both of you that she did," he grunted, though he still hadn't looked over at her. "If she hadn't, you'd be in a hell of a mess right now."

She was already in a hell of a mess, though she refrained from pointing that out. The snow was getting thicker and she didn't want to distract him, didn't want him to become angry and possibly lose control of the vehicle. They were still running much faster than she thought safe.

"Relax." He was sitting comfortably in his own seat, gripping the steering wheel confidently, his big, lean body relaxed. "It's just a little snowstorm."

Just a little snowstorm? She restrained an unladylike snort. It was almost a complete whiteout. But as dangerous as she knew it was, she couldn't help but admire the sheer power and beauty of the storm. It enclosed them within the Humvee, insulated them from the rest of the world in an intimacy that left her mouth dry.

"You should try to nap." His voice was quiet, deep. There was nothing dangerous or threatening in his tone now. It lulled her mind at a time that she knew she should be even further on guard.

The dark velvet roughness of his voice had her longing to reach out to him, to be enfolded in the strength of his arms, to lean on his strength.

She was tired.

Elizabeth had known for weeks that she was approaching a point where her body would soon begin crashing. The thought of that had terrified her. The fact that this big, dangerous man was suddenly encouraging her to do so made her nervous as a woman, even as it stilled the fears that often swept through her mind.

"I will. Later." She wasn't about to go to sleep yet. Not until she was certain of what was going on. "Where are we going, anyway?"

"An Army contact owns a ranch across the state line," he said. "We'll stay there a few days until I can get further with another contact I have. I'm hoping to have you and Cassie in a secured area within a week. We'll decide our best course of action then."

The final statement had her staring at him doubtfully.

"We will?" she asked him archly. She had a feeling she wouldn't have a lot of say in whatever decision he made if he had his way. Dash Sinclair didn't look like a man who shared anything well, least of all responsibility.

His lips quirked. It was sexy.

That thought slammed into her head like a thunderbolt. Dear God, how long had it been since she had noticed anything about a man other than whether he was the enemy?

That little smile was incredibly sensual. A firm, decisive shift of his lips that looked erotic, making her wonder how they would feel against her own.

And that was something she definitely shouldn't be thinking about right now. Not while her daughter's life was hanging in the balance. Not while the man she was lusting after could be either friend or foe. Until she knew which, she had no business allowing her body to heat for him.

"We will," he finally allowed with an edge of amusement. "As long as the two of you are safe, then you can help decide."

Elizabeth rolled her eyes at the conditions. As if she was going to accept that one. But she couldn't stop the grin that tugged at her own lips. "Now that's not nice."

It was far too arrogant and domineering.

"I wasn't trying to be nice." But he was restraining a grin. She could see it. It made her wonder what he would look like if he smiled. Or even laughed.

"Well, you weren't succeeding either." Her eyelids drooped as she relaxed against the seat, but they didn't close.

"I'm a commander in the Army Special Forces, Green Berets," he said quietly, his tone holding an edge of something that resembled grief. "I'm used to making decisions, giving orders. I know how to protect you and Cassie. But you have to trust me."

Trust him? She was impressed with the title, she admitted, but he was still just one man, and she'd learned the risks of trusting anyone.

"That won't happen," she said sadly. "I can't afford to trust you."

But she could afford to gather her strength for the moment he would be in her and Cassie's lives. Just a few moments out of time to rest before they ran again.

She was so tired. How long had it been since she had slept? Since she had felt safe enough to close her eyes and allow just a few hours of deep escape? Not since the night she had arrived at her ex-husband's to check on Cassie and heard the sounds of gunshots.

She flinched, staring desperately out the windshield. Would she always see it? The view from the window of her husband's lakefront house. Cassie struggling in Terrence Grange's hold as he aimed a gun and delivered yet another round into Dane's body.

He had laughed when Cassie screamed out for her daddy. His evil, scarred face had held lustful intent as he stared at her baby. A baby. She shuddered, holding back the rage, bottling it inside her to keep from screaming out in fury.

She was silent, though she was aware of Dash glancing at her several times.

Elizabeth jumped when he moved, then breathed out a strangled sigh when he turned the radio on. Soothing, soft music filled the interior of the military vehicle, wrapping around her, lulling her back into that near-sleep existence she always feared.

The back of her seat lowered by several inches as he pressed a control at the front of the console. When he was satisfied with it, he reached between the seats and pulled a folded throw blanket from the top of a tote stored next to Cassie's head and placed it in her lap.

"Sleep, Elizabeth," he whispered soothingly. "Just rest for a moment. The storm, if nothing else, will hold Grange back. I'll wake you when we arrive. I promise you. You and Cassie are both safe."

Safe. Cassie was safe. For now. That was all that mattered.

"We have to hide her," she sighed, breathing out deeply as her head rested against the back of the seat, her eyes finally closing. "He can't touch her. I can't let him touch her . . ."

She was aware of him shaking the blanket out with one hand and easing it over her as she reclined against the seat. The interior of the Humvee was comfortably warm, the music soothing, the movement of the vehicle smooth and secure on the road despite the snow piling around them.

She could take this moment to sleep, to let the warmth surround her and the feeling of safety lull her away for just a little while.

"You're safe, baby." The words were quiet, almost a whisper as she felt herself slipping into the sleep her body so needed.

The endearment didn't threaten her, it didn't warn her of betrayal or weakness. It sounded natural, she thought. It sounded like what she needed to hear. That she and Cassie were important to someone besides a lunatic drug cartel leader.

In the end, it wouldn't matter, she knew. She would run. She and Cassie would fight alone until she managed to reach the one place she might have a chance of finding true help. The only place she might actually have a chance of keeping Cassie safe and the only man with enough power to ensure that her daughter disappeared forever out of Grange's sight.

If she ever needed help, she'd once been told, she had only to get to the address he'd given her. He'd told her where the key to the apartment was hidden, and that he'd know when she arrived.

It was all she had. The only hope she had. And she didn't dare tell anyone about it. Even the man beside her who had come so far and risked so much.

Not even him.

As she drifted off to sleep, she asked herself why she hadn't rushed to that apartment to begin with, though. Why hadn't she trusted him any more than she'd trusted anyone else in the past two years?

And why was a part of her demanding that she trust Dash?

◆　　◆　　◆

It was daybreak before Dash pulled into the back of a small motel just across the Kansas-Missouri border. He was dead tired and the snow had gotten hazardous hours before as the thick stuff increased to nearly zero visibility. There was no way he was about to make the trek to Mike's ranch until the snow lessened and he had a chance to rest. Until he had a chance to get a break from the intriguing scent of woman and shy arousal.

She was slouched in the seat beside him, her head often resting on the wide console between the seats. Once, he had dared to touch the silk of those curls, sliding his fingers through them and feeling the deep waves cupping his fingers.

She had the softest hair he had ever known, with surprisingly thick curls lying down her back. Hair that made a man think of sex, wild and sweet. But overshadowing the lust was the need to protect. To comfort his mate.

He wanted to pull her into his arms, hold her close to his chest and assure her she was safe. Promise her they would protect Cassie. Together. Swear on the Earth and moon if it would ease the haunting shadows he had seen in her eyes.

But he knew he couldn't do that. Couldn't make the promises even if she would accept them. Not until he knew for certain that the plans he had were actually doable. The chances of failure were too high at the moment. All he could do was fight with every weapon he possessed to ensure their safety. He was confident he had enough fight to do it. But first, they all needed to sleep. To rest, at least for today.

Thankfully, there had been a drive-thru open in the heart of town serving hot food. A quick stop and he had enough to feed himself, the woman, and the child.

They had both slept as he ordered and collected the food. Next, he stopped and gassed up the Humvee, careful to take the keys out of the ignition as he stood at the gas pump. He wouldn't put it past her to take off and run again. Hell, it was what he would have done in her place.

When he got back in the vehicle, Cassie was still sleeping, but her mother was awake. Not exactly aware—she hadn't managed more than two hours of restless sleep—but at least she'd managed that much.

He kept the coffee he had purchased hidden in the sacks from the drive-thru in the back until he pulled into the motel, checked in and then drove to their assigned room. It was far enough from the main road that it hid the vehicle and gave Dash enough confidence that he would hear anyone who pulled in. Not that many others would be able to navigate the slight incline that led to the back rooms.

He didn't waste time with words. He wanted the comfort of the room, the news and a secure landline to make the calls he needed. Neither the satellite phone nor his cell was exactly dependable in this weather.

After getting out of the Humvee, he moved around the vehicle to the passenger side, opened the door and lifted Cassie from the seat as Elizabeth moved stiffly into the frigid air. The snow went halfway up her legs and it was still piling up, but she never showed obvious discomfort.

She trudged behind him, just as silent as he was as he made a path to the door. He swiped the card, opened the door carefully and then stepped inside. Turning, he watched as Elizabeth moved quickly past him. It was still dark out and forecasters were expecting the storm to go on through the day and into the next morning. Hell, they all needed time to rest anyway before heading to Mike's.

Elizabeth was flipping lights on as he closed the door and walked to the farthest bed. He laid Cassie down on it slowly, pulling the blanket over her as her mother moved to her. Elizabeth had a damp cloth in her hand. She used it to quickly clean Cassie's sleep-flushed cheeks, her small hands.

A smile tugged at his lips at the motherly response.

She slipped Cassie's shoes off, then pulled the blankets over her once again. It was all done very efficiently, very economically. Dash shook his head, turning away from the sight.

He didn't understand mothers. But hell, he'd never had one. He'd turned out fine, hadn't he?

But had he?

He stopped at the end of the bed and turned back to gaze at the sleeping child broodingly. He'd survived because he was tough. Hard. Because he'd known how to fight, how to protect himself before he'd ever been placed in the first foster home.

Damn, he didn't want her to have to live that way. He wanted to see the sweet, charming little girl who had saved his life with her letters. He wanted to see her smile, see her secure. Mothered.

He shook his head as he turned and stalked back to the door and into the storm. He had clothes and supplies for the mother and child. Things they'd need, and he wanted to get them inside. He wanted his mate to know he could provide for her in all ways.

He had been hauling the damned things around for weeks once he realized that each time they were found they were forced to leave almost everything they owned except the clothes on their backs.

Minutes later he reentered the room, instantly finding Elizabeth in a defensive position in front of Cassie as the door opened. He set the large container he carried on the floor, then went back out. When he returned with his own bag and the food and coffee, she was sitting at the end of Cassie's bed, watching the door.

"There are nightgowns, clothes, and stuff in here." He set the fast-food bags on the small table. "I've bought things here and there as I realized everything was being destroyed from place to place. You should have everything you need."

He saw her startled look as she glanced at the hard plastic container.

"Why?" she whispered, turning back to him, confusion on her face. "Because of a little girl's letters, you've done all this? Do you realize how much sense that makes?"

It didn't have to make sense. Dash had never once considered whether any of it was logical. He'd awakened knowing how important it was to heal, to strengthen and to find her and the child who had reached out to him.

"More sense than the place I was in when the letters began arriving." She might not understand, but he knew that sometimes a man just had to believe in fate. "I was dying. Aware, but not awake." He shook his head, a rueful tug of his lips not quite a smile. "I'd never received a letter in my life until Cassie. And never had I received a Christmas card or gift until your 'Santa' visited. She forced me to fight to live; now I'll fight to keep her alive. It's that simple."

And yet it was far more complicated and Dash knew it.

Elizabeth stared back at him silently, obviously fighting to understand, to believe in something she simply had no experience in. A man capable of doing more than just helping her for the moment. A man determined to protect her and her daughter throughout their lives.

"Pajamas would be more practical," she stated, and he could sense her feeling of helplessness in the face of her inability to make sense of his reasons.

"Maybe." He grinned back at her, a bit abashed at that realization. "Should have thought of that."

He'd wanted to see Elizabeth in something feminine though, something soft. According to Mike, females liked female stuff, so that was what he bought.

She just stared back at him, all big eyes and confusion.

"I need a shower." He pulled his handgun from the personal bag he carried on his shoulder when she didn't say anything more. "If anyone comes to the door, let me know. Otherwise, there's food and coffee in the bag. Plenty enough for everyone."

He didn't expect a response. He didn't get one. She just stared up at him with those big sad eyes, so much like Cassie's, as though she couldn't decide if she was still dreaming or awake.

Dash ached to hold her. He couldn't stop the need, so he didn't fight it building in his body, but he kept his arms, his thoughts and his needs to himself. He had a lot of practice at that. Knew just how it was done.

Control.

That was all it took. And he had a lifetime in learning how to control every part of his body, every response. And he'd never failed until he'd attempted to control his response to Elizabeth.

Those shell-shocked eyes staring back at him did something to him that made his guts tremble with an ache so unfamiliar, so imperative, it was damned hard to fight.

Her eyes went to the gun as he stood there. An uncontrollable flare of fear flashed in her gaze. He couldn't blame her for it. But he hated it.

"I'll be out in a bit." He had to get away from her. If he didn't, he was going to touch her. If he touched her, stopping would be hell. And he would have to stop. Now was not the time or the place.

He turned the television on as he passed it—the steady noise would keep her nerves calm, he hoped—then moved into the bathroom. If he didn't get a shower and settle his own libido down, he was going to go stark raving mad. His cock was waging a constant war with his head.

It was hard, aching, needing her. Just a taste of her.

Damn, the woman's scent had been like a call to arms to his dick. It hadn't relaxed in the miserable hours of being confined in the military Humvee with her. It was steel-hard and insistent. Not exactly a condition he found any comfort in.

It wasn't as though Elizabeth was even in any shape to realize it. And if she did, it was the wrong place and the wrong time. First came Cassie's safety. Then he could claim the mother.

He shook his head as he entered the small bathroom, closing the door behind him, leaving it unsecured. He stared down at the lock and sighed wearily.

Building trust was a bitch.

CHAPTER 5

As the bathroom door closed behind Dash, Elizabeth moved to the tote of clothes and opened the lid slowly. Sinking to her knees, she stared down at the contents in surprise. The clothes were all new. Some designer labels, some not. All were functional and would be easily cleaned, a must for an eight-year-old child.

Stacked within the tote were clothes for her as well. She flushed as she pulled a pair of lacy thongs from the neatly folded contents. They were her size, but so delicate and sexy she would blush to wear them.

There were nightgowns and robes for her and Cassie, socks and dependable shoes still in their boxes as well as a pair of winter boots for each of them. He'd thought of everything.

She pulled a dark blue little-girl's nightgown free. It was long, cotton, with long sleeves and a lacy collar. There was a robe to match it. Several packages of little-girl's panties and socks, unopened.

Next, she pulled out one of the nightgowns and robes he had bought for her. A smile tugged at her lips. It was flannel and long, with a robe to match as well. Something to keep her warm. With it was a pair of thick, padded socks. Had the man forgotten anything?

She shook her head in confusion, wondering when reality had ceased to exist. From one minute to the next she had gone from pure terror to a sense of tentative hope. Surely if he was going to turn her and Cassie over to Grange, he would have done so by now.

But could she really trust her own instincts?

She rose to her feet, hearing the water cascading in the other room. Elizabeth swallowed tightly. God, she wanted to trust him, but fear was like a demon riding her mercilessly. The gun and the Hummer would get her closer to her own destination.

She looked at the clothes again, touched the soft gowns, and wanted to scream out in fury. She couldn't trust, no matter how desperately she wanted to. No matter how her soul screamed out in protest, she had to get Cassie away from this new, possibly unknown threat.

The sound of the shower was loud, the pipes groaning. She hadn't heard the lock click in place and she was desperate. She stood and moved for the door.

Stilling the tremors of exhaustion and nerves that wanted to shudder through her body wasn't easy. She hated the thought of betraying the only person left to stand between her and her enemies, but she couldn't bear the thought that she was wrong once again either.

As she neared the bathroom door, she thought of the others she had trusted. Admittedly, there hadn't been many. There was the police investigator in Arizona. She hoped he was living well on the little payoff he must have taken to reveal her location. On the other hand, she remembered too well the news report of the death of the auto mechanic who had helped her escape after repairing her car.

He was dead. Because of her.

Her hand gripped the doorknob, turning it slowly, quietly. He couldn't take the gun into the shower with him; it would have to be lying within reach. She inched the door open, slowly, carefully . . .

◆   ◆   ◆

Dash leaned his head against the wall of the shower stall, grimacing almost painfully.

Don't, baby. Please don't. The words whispered through his mind as Elizabeth's scent stirred the air around him. Even his balls tightened at the smell.

Female, sensually warm, determined, frightened. Her fear made his heart ache. Her warmth made his cock jerk demandingly. There was nothing about her that didn't make him hot and hungry.

Steam collected in misty tendrils, wrapping the smell of her around his senses, driving a bolt of hunger through the pit of his stomach straight to his throbbing erection. He could see her in his mind's eye, focused, steeling herself against her fear as she moved into the small room.

Trust was essential, he reminded himself firmly. She had to know he could protect them, that he would protect them. She had to know he was strong enough, confident enough, to even stop her if he had to. But once he confronted her, would he have the strength not to touch her?

Don't do it, Elizabeth, he groaned silently.

He clenched his teeth as the whisper of her slight body moving past the door frame had him tensing expectantly. *Leave! Don't let me touch you!*

If he touched her, he'd never stop. One taste could never be enough. She would be a banquet to his senses, a feast of erotic delicacies. But only if she trusted him. Only if she knew, beyond a shadow of a doubt, he was there for her and Cassie. Not for their enemies.

He was building trust, he reminded himself. Better to get it started and get it over with now. He couldn't help her if he had to guard against her as well as the men hunting her. If he could get past this initial surge of defiance, then they had a chance.

The defiance was tempting the animal he fought to keep contained. The one that knew this was his mate. Knew this woman was everything he had searched for in his life. Keeping it leashed was a battle he knew would slip quickly. Already, within hours of finding her, there was little he could think about except sinking into the warmth and heat between her thighs. Drowning in the hot depths of her body as she tightened around him.

Never, at any time in his life, had a woman affected him quite this way.

He let her move into the room. He felt the hot water pelting his skin, smelled her scent growing closer, tracked her with every sense he possessed as she moved steadily to the gun and the keys that lay on the shelf above the toilet.

Her steps were light. Silent and stealthy.

Damn, she was the perfect mate.

The thought shocked him, but he realized the truth of it instantly. She was light and steady, resolved in her course of action and making almost no sound as she went for the weapon. She would fight beside him, no matter the battle, physical or emotional. If her heart was committed, then it would be as fierce as any she-wolf's.

She was a bundle of dynamite; destructive to the enemy, life-giving to those she loved. But right now, until she knew if he was friend or foe, she would always suspect enemy first. She would always defy him. He couldn't allow that.

He gave her just enough time to feel victory. Just enough time to allow her fingers to whisper a caress over the weapon's handgrip before he moved. The shower curtain flew back and he was out of the tub, water spraying as he gripped her shoulders, pushed the door closed, then anchored her against it. The move was made within a second, with barely a whisper of a sound, though he had expected her to fight him.

She didn't scream.

Damn her to hell and back, she didn't even cry out. No more than a breath of air disturbed the silence as her gasp, quickly reined in, whispered past her lips and she stared up at him in startled fear and surprise a second before her knee cocked and let loose.

Dash barely had a second's warning before he could block the groin shot. One part of him admired the speed and effectiveness of her move while the other part was amazed at her daring.

One thigh pressed hard and tight between hers, lifting her to her tiptoes, grinding against the soft, hot pad of her sex.

Her response was instantaneous, though less than welcome by her, he could tell. She strained against him, jerking at the manacled hold he took of her wrists as he locked them behind her head with one hand, arching her breasts into his chest, his knee rubbing against her heat.

Lust was pounding through his system with every hard beat of his heart, stripping away the veneer of civilization that he kept pulled around him, tempting the hunger gnawing at his loins.

"Stay still, dammit. I'm not going to hurt you," he growled as she twisted against him, despite the fact that she wasn't gaining any headway in her struggles.

She was frightened. He could hear it in her harsh breathing, the struggle to hold back her sobs. She had taken a chance, and now she would fear the punishment he would exact. But he was careful not to hurt her. He restrained her, controlled her struggles, but he knew he wasn't leaving so much as the slightest mark against her skin. Skin already bruised, already wounded by too many hard knocks.

He pressed against her, holding her to the door as he stared down at her silently, feeling her soft tummy cushion his raging cock. And she hadn't missed the impact of the steel-hard flesh pressing against her either. That or the imperative need he allowed to glitter in his eyes.

One hand threaded through her hair, tilting her head back. His head lowered slowly as he stared down at her, watching her eyes dilate, her skin flush then pale alarmingly.

"When I let you go"—he allowed the growl building in his chest to echo in his words—"if I were you, I would turn that sweet ass around and hightail it back into the bedroom with Cassie. If you hesitate, even for a second, if you so much as breathe a hesitation, then I'm going to fuck you so hard and so deep against this door that you'll never hide your screams of pleasure from that child sleeping in the other room. Do you understand me, Elizabeth?"

His control was a fragile thing right now. The only thing stilling the hunger to taste her parted lips was the knowledge that Cassie slept only feet away from them. The fact that if he tasted her, he would need more.

Always more.

Her eyes widened further, the blue darkening in shock, in amazement. Strangely enough, also with a flare of arousal. Thankfully, she nodded quickly, but nothing could still the fact that her full breasts were rising and falling sharply against his chest. And her nipples were hard. Damn her to hell, they were hard as little pebbles, raking across his damp chest like pinpoints of searing flames beneath the covering of her shirt.

He moved his hand from her hair, gripping her wrists individually. Before she could resist, he wrapped the fingers of one of her small hands around the girth of his cock. They had no hope of circling it fully. She had small, delicate—God—soft hands. His groan was throttled, a sound of agonizing pleasure.

Her grip was like warm silk, her skin enflaming the already-burning need tightening his balls. He'd give his last breath if she would move them of her own volition, stroke the iron-hard flesh, pump it until he spilled his release to her touch.

Fuck.

"Don't . . ." Her breath caught as Dash realized he was moving her hand himself with his own as he held her grip around the throbbing shaft.

Small, slow little movements, vicious pleasure twisting his guts until he knew he was within seconds of losing control.

"Don't?" he asked, seeing the flush on her face, the heaviness of her lashes as he continued to hold her fingers in place. "What did you think would happen? That you could slip past me so easily and run into a storm you have no hope of surviving alone?"

Her lips parted and he saw the truth on her face. Mixing with the curious desire and fear was the acknowledgment that she would have done just that. Despite the danger and the fact that she wasn't going to be able to run much longer, still, she would have tried.

And that knowledge infuriated him.

"Never," he snarled desperately. "Never try this on me again unless you're prepared to accept the consequences. Because next time, I promise you, I won't let you go. The next time, I'll fuck you until you barely have the energy to breathe, let alone run from me."

He stepped back from her quickly, his heart nearly exploding in his chest at the brief hesitation of her fingers on his erection as he released her. Then she snatched her hand back, holding it to her chest, staring up at him, her lips parted, startled awareness darkening her eyes further.

"Go. Now." He clenched his fists. Fought his hunger.

She gasped. In a second she turned, fumbled with the doorknob and fled the small room as Dash threw his head back and grimaced against the building fury in his loins. Damn her to hell. He was starving for the taste of her.

He stepped back into the shower, slammed the curtain closed and flipped on the cold water. Son of a bitch. This hard-on would kill him.

✦ ✦ ✦

She should be running. Elizabeth paced the motel room, her body shuddering with wicked, pulsing tremors that teased at the emptiness between her thighs. She should bundle Cassie up and just run. Storm or no storm. She was in over her head here in a way she feared was certain to drown her.

She didn't even know him.

That thought seared her senses as she collapsed into one of the two chairs by the table. She knew nothing except the short, cryptic notes he had sent her daughter for a year. Sometimes humorous, but always with a dry, wry humor that had Elizabeth shaking her head. Cassie had liked them, though. She would giggle and say Dash just had trouble telling tales, to give him time and she would teach him. And perhaps in a way, she had.

The last few months Dash had written to Cassie, he told her the oddest things. How the scents of the desert were different from home. The sound of a helicopter. The quiet, cold nights in the mountains of a land Cassie would likely never see herself. Little things. But not exactly phrased the way other men would say it.

At least, no men Elizabeth had ever known before or since.

Dash was unlike any man she had ever known in her life. He didn't advertise his strength, but then, he didn't have to advertise it. It was there, like a sleeping volcano, just waiting for anyone stupid enough to present a threat.

Or the right threat.

She stared at her hand, heart racing faster at the remembered feel of her fingers curling around his erection. Hot, thick, iron hard. And far too tempting.

God, what was wrong with her? What was it about this man that had her so divided, so conflicted in her determination to run from him? Because it was obvious she didn't want to run.

Was she really that tired, that certain that Grange was growing impatient with whatever game he was playing and getting ready to move in and snatch Cassie from her?

Her suspicion that he was merely playing with her had only grown over the past months. She felt like a mouse to his cat, and he was just waiting to see what it took to eventually break her will.

He couldn't have anticipated Dash, though.

Hell, she hadn't anticipated Dash, and his offer of help seemed far too good to be true. He was too strong, too confident, too easy to depend on. And Cassie had been certain he'd save them.

Elizabeth was far too scared he'd destroy them.

Wiping her hands over her face, she fought to focus her attention somewhere besides on the man in the shower and the arousal she knew would torment her long after the man himself disappeared from her life.

She stared over at the television. The newscasters were once again covering the story of the amazing discovery of the feline Breeds. The men and women who had come forward were the wonders of the world at the moment. News reports had covered several rescues of other Breeds, a few Wolf Breeds but mostly feline. They were totaling in the hundreds now, six months after the first newsbreak.

The host of a popular news program was questioning several so-called experts about the chances of the Breeds having been raised as orphans or adopted children. Those experts were denying that any such possibility existed. The "creatures," as he called them, couldn't have been raised in the general public because all the children created were grown now or well accounted for.

Elizabeth snorted at the claim, just as a psychologist did at the same time.

"There were far too many safeguards in place," one of the scientists who had worked in a lab assured them arrogantly. "And attempts to escape were dealt with harshly. It couldn't have happened."

And he seemed to have no remorse. Which explained why he was speaking from inside a maximum-security facility rather than a lab.

Amazing. Elizabeth shook her head. The cruelty of humans never failed to amaze her. The Breeds had been created, trained and then hunted as though their DNA made them no more than the animals they were genetically related to. Like a modern-day safari, uncaring of the brutality or the horror they perpetrated, the Genetics Council had done everything to destroy their creations when they couldn't control them.

Yet somehow, rather than reverting to the savagery that was obviously a part of their DNA, the Breeds had instead maintained an honor, a strength, that had helped them survive the cruelties.

Elizabeth envied them in many ways. Even the females were strong, tough, trained to fight and capable of protecting themselves. It made her feel insignificant, very lacking, and she hated that feeling. Hated knowing her own faults, her own weaknesses. She hated the fact that she wanted nothing more than to feel Dash's arms around her again, for just a few wild moments, to forget the dangers and the pain and to be a woman once again.

She sighed wearily and pulled a cup of lukewarm black coffee from one of the sacks. There was a cola there as well. The other bags were packed with food. Two larger ones held five takeout breakfast platters. The smaller ones held a variety of biscuits. But she imagined a man that large could eat a lot of food.

Her stomach rumbled imperatively and she shook her head at the timing. She needed to think. To run. Not realize the smell of food was so enticing that she had centered on it more than she had on escape.

But it wasn't as enticing as what she had held in her hand when she'd dared to attempt to steal his weapon and the keys to the vehicle.

Elizabeth felt her entire body heat, flush in what she assured herself was embarrassment. Liquid warmth gathered in her vagina, spilling silkily along the swollen flesh between her thighs. Her response to him had been as hard, as shocking, as a lightning bolt.

She sipped at the coffee, her eyes fluttering in pleasure at the taste, then dug out one of the platters and a plastic fork.

Okay. She couldn't think while she was starving. And she had to think. Dash Sinclair was going to be more of a problem than she had ever anticipated. He could possibly be more man than she had ever encountered.

God. He was definitely more man than she had ever known before. Thick and hard, his erection had shocked her with its size. But his body in general had shocked her as well. Darkly tanned flesh stretched and rippled over hard-packed muscle.

It wasn't the awkward, graceless look of obscenely bulging muscle; rather it was corded, hard, filling out each inch of his body and shimmering beneath the skin with an aura of intense power.

Like an animal, well honed and conditioned and used to hard, intense battle.

A warrior.

That hard body defined the word, just as the man did.

There was nothing grandiose or egotistical about the power he possessed or his obvious strength. He knew who and what he was and needed no one to reaffirm it or pay homage to him.

And he wore the medallion she'd sent him . . .

She stilled at the realization that the silver chain and medallion she'd sent him from "Santa" hung around his neck, untarnished, gleaming against his hard chest. For some reason, the knowledge that he wore it had her blinking back tears.

She'd never imagined he would actually put it around his neck. It wasn't expensive, though it hadn't exactly been cheap either and the money could have been better spent elsewhere at the time. But Cassie had so wanted Dash to have the present that Elizabeth had been unable to deny the letter her daughter sent to "Santa."

The St. Michael emblem rested on that hard chest, though, on tough, sun-bronzed flesh that begged a woman to touch, to taste . . .

Trying to push aside the fascination and unwanted desire she could feel simmering inside her body, she turned her attention to the food again instead of the man and a passion that had no business tormenting her at the moment.

She swallowed the fluffy eggs and quickly polished off the rest of the food before turning back to the television.

It was a good thing she had eaten before watching the news, because what she saw would have easily put her off the meal.

They showed the victim's face, if you wanted to call him a victim. Elizabeth sat up straight, staring in shock at the image on the screen. She knew him. It was the same bastard who had tried to ambush her and Cassie in their apartment the day before.

He wouldn't be ambushing anyone else.

He was found in the basement of the apartment building, his throat cut. The newscaster called it a professional, highly skilled hit. He still carried his money. The diamond ring on his hand. His credit cards.

His identity was given, as was the police record and information on the current warrants for his arrest. She trembled, barely aware that the shower had shut off and the bathroom door had opened.

A sudden flashing memory had her gaze swinging to Dash. Beside the gun had been a long, sheathed knife. The wide hilt had looked imposing. Now she knew why.

He stopped, gazing back at her somberly as she stared at him in shock. For the first time, she realized that Dash's confidence wasn't as misplaced as she had feared it was. He appeared to be a well-oiled fighting machine because that was exactly what he was.

"You killed him," she whispered, watching him in amazement. No one who had gone against Grange's men had succeeded. They were either bought off or killed, according to how disposable his hit men considered them to be. Dash had been neither bought off nor harmed. He had killed instead.

Broad shoulders, still gleaming with moisture, shrugged carelessly. He wore soft sweatpants and white socks, but nothing more. In one hand he carried the clothes he had worn into the bathroom; in the other he carried the holstered gun and the knife.

His eyes went to the television, narrowing on the news as the reporter spoke into the camera.

"Took them long enough to report it," he grunted as he walked over to the bed he had laid his leather case on.

He pulled out a black plastic bag, stored his dirty clothes, then repacked it. The weapons along with the keys to the Humvee were tucked beneath his pillow.

"You killed him," she repeated, careful to keep her voice low in case Cassie woke up.

Dash turned back to her. There was no regret in his gaze, no sense of remorse or apology. His gaze was steady, though slightly quizzical, as though he didn't understand her shock.

"He was a diseased animal, Elizabeth," he said with a distinct air of unconcern. "He was waiting on you, certain you would come back, and intended to make you and Cassie pay for getting away. Anyone else who tries for you will die just as quickly."

Silence filled the room. Elizabeth could only stare at him as he moved away from the bed, taking the other chair and pulling two of the platters free as well as the last cup of coffee.

"You need to take a shower and sleep the rest of the day. From now on, we travel at night. If this blizzard has blown over by evening, then we'll head to a ranch just out of town. I fought with Mike overseas. He's dependable, and he can put me in touch with some people who can help us."

Elizabeth shook her head, wondering at the dreamlike fog that seemed to fill her mind. He was talking as though he hadn't been forced to kill a man because of her and Cassie. As though his life had never been in danger and he had done nothing out of the ordinary.

She could feel her heart racing at the knowledge, her mind scrambling to accept what he'd done. No one had been able to stand against Grange's goons before. They always fell, one way or the other. And yet here Dash sat, remarkably unconcerned about the danger involved.

Of course, he wasn't concerned. She blinked warily. He was stronger than they were, tougher and smarter and evidently a hell of a lot more determined. For the first time, she realized just how intent he was on protecting her and Cassie.

He glanced over at Cassie, a light frown creasing his brow as her little snuffles of sleep filled the room. Following his gaze, Elizabeth watched as the little girl moved beneath the blanket, a little smile tilting her lips, her legs stretching out as though in play.

"She sounds like a little pup when she sleeps." Elizabeth shook her head, trying to accept the changes occurring so quickly. "She's always done that. At least I know she's sleeping, not dreaming, when she does."

She watched her daughter sorrowfully, knowing the nightmares she suffered were based in fact, and it broke her heart. Sometimes, Cassie didn't sleep well for several nights straight when the nightmares began.

Right now, she was stretched under the blankets, her slight body relaxed and comfortable. Her dark hair framed her sleep-flushed features as she breathed softly, evenly.

No. There were no nightmares now.

"I want you to wake her. She needs to eat and shower, and then she can sleep until we head out tonight. I want her alert and focused." He was completely serious.

Elizabeth swung around, anger erupting through her system. Protector or not, she wasn't about to allow him to ruin the only true sleep Cassie had known in weeks.

"Do you have any idea how long it's been since she's slept so well?" she hissed, ensuring she didn't wake Cassie herself. "I'm not about to wake her up."

Dash sighed deeply. There was no returning anger, just determination.

"If you don't wake her up and keep her up for a while, then she'll sleep while we're awake and be asleep when we all need to be at our best. Or even worse, too damned tired to hold on to us, or run if she has to. We have only a few nights to get her ready for the trip we'll hopefully be making next. Now wake her up, or I will."

His gaze was level, commanding.

"You can't just make these decisions without talking to me first, Sinclair." She was shaking, fury nearly robbing her of any control. "That's my daughter. And I won't allow you to jerk her out of a perfectly sound sleep just because you say so. And you sure as hell aren't making any more surprise trips with her without telling me what's going on first."

Her fists clenched, anger building inside her as she stared up at him. He watched her with that cool, assessing gaze, as though she were an amusing little insect under inspection.

"As soon as the snow eases enough, we head to Mike Toler's ranch, just outside town," he repeated, then surprised her further. "Mike is former CIA and has some contacts and information I need about a possible safe house in Virginia. Until I find out if that house is available to me, I don't want to say more. Mike will shelter us as long as we need, but I only want to stay a day or so. Long enough to acclimate Cassie to me and to give you a chance to rest. Period. Then we leave. Satisfied?"

She pressed her lips tightly together. He wasn't being mocking or sarcastic. He seemed perfectly serious.

"Let Cassie sleep awhile longer," she stated firmly. "Another hour. She's just a baby, Dash. She needs this."

· CHAPTER 6 ·

He intended to take her and Cassie back to Virginia? She'd spent two years running from the state only to have him begin making plans to take them back. And what made him think there was a safe house there where Terrence Grange couldn't find them?

She moved to step around him, anger surging through her as she tried to make her way back to Cassie's bed. The pain in her thigh suddenly intensified, sending her stumbling as she forced herself not to cry out with the shocking strike of agony through the muscle.

She knew better, was her next thought, than to move without thinking first. The pain from the flesh wound had been growing steadily and she had a feeling it was going to bring her problems. Now it had thrown her back against Dash's body as he caught her against his chest, then swung her into his arms.

She gasped. His chest was just as hot, just as firm, as it had been in the bathroom. His arms flexed beneath her back and thighs, muscles rippling with strength as he stalked to the sink counter across the room.

"I forgot about your leg." Self-disgust filled his voice. "I should have taken care of that first thing."

He sat her on the counter before she even had a chance to get used to being in his arms.

"Stay put," he growled, giving her a hard, fierce look.

She stayed put. But she watched him closely as he went back to the bed, pulled out a small bag from his larger case, then lifted one of the chairs and carried both back to her.

"Let's check your side first," he announced. "I know you cut yourself shimmying out of that window."

She looked back at him in surprise. How the hell had he known that?

"A piece of your shirt was caught on the broken window," he said. "There was blood on it." He pointed out the rip as he lifted her shirt to see the jagged cut.

Elizabeth tried to breathe in deeply, naturally, as his fingers probed the tender area gently.

"It's not too bad," he murmured. "When you get out of the shower we'll put some salve on it and bandage it."

She nodded silently as he lowered her shirt again and then watched her expectantly.

"I'm going to put you back on the floor. Take off your jeans so I can check that leg." Elizabeth blinked. Out of her jeans?

"No," she snapped hoarsely.

The wound was high on her thigh, several inches above her knee and to the side. There wasn't a chance in hell . . .

"Don't make me cut them off you, Elizabeth." He sighed, staring down at her. "We're both tired and riding our tempers. If I don't take care of this it could become infected, and then you won't have a chance of helping Cassie. Is that what you want?"

Her eyes narrowed. "That's dirty," she hissed.

His expression grew harder. "That's the truth. Now take the jeans off, before I take them off for you."

His hands went for the snap. She slapped them back, almost laughing at the look of startled surprise that flashed across his face.

"I'm no child to have my hands smacked. Now take those jeans off or I promise you, I'll do it," he repeated, his tone harder this time, more determined.

Elizabeth's lips flattened in anger as she stared back at him.

His eyes narrowed, the dark golden-brown depths glittering in determination.

"Fine," she muttered, sliding off the counter, thankful her T-shirt was at least long enough to cover what was most important. "I'm starting to think you're too bossy, though."

He grunted. He didn't say a word, but the sound held a wealth of male superiority. She flashed him a resentful look as she eased the jeans down, biting her lip as the material scraped over the wound.

"Up." He gripped her hips and lifted her back to the counter; the jeans still hung at her knees. "You forgot your shoes."

Elizabeth forgot her sanity. He lifted her foot, propping it on his thigh and unlacing the cheap sneaker carefully. His long hair feathered forward, the roughened, damp strands caressing her upper knee as he removed the shoe. He shifted to the next, his hair stroking the skin over her other knee as he removed it as well. Her whole body flushed.

Had a man ever affected her this deeply? After less than twenty-four hours? Had one ever made her long to just touch him, to just stroke his flesh and revel in the feel of it?

As the second shoe fell to the floor, his hands—amazingly gentle hands—pulled the material from her legs, his head rising, his eyes meeting hers as he undressed her. The heat she saw there took her breath. It made his eyes lighter, appear almost amber rather than dark honey. His high cheekbones flushed, his lips becoming heavy with sensuality.

"It should be stitched, but I think we can get by without it now," he whispered hoarsely as he checked the line of raw flesh. "You were lucky, baby. It could have been a hell of a lot worse." The endearment sent a shaft of heat vibrating through her vagina and into her womb.

He opened the first-aid kit and took several items out, though she had no idea what they were.

"This will hurt," he whispered, and she saw his eyes blaze in fury at the thought. "I need to disinfect it, then cover it so you can shower."

She was entranced by his face, his expression. It was savage, so filled with hunger it took her breath and almost made her forget the pain in her leg.

"I cleaned it. At the diner," she said nervously, tucking her hair behind her ear before gripping the edge of the counter desperately. "It's not too bad. It stopped bleeding."

He shifted in his chair, his broad, callused hands probing at the wound as she gritted her teeth at the feel of his fingers against her skin. They were so warm, gentle.

"I killed that bastard for this alone," he whispered shockingly, causing her heart to race in her chest. "And I would do it again, Elizabeth." He raised his gaze, watching her closely. "It wouldn't matter who it was. I'll kill them before I allow them to ever hurt you or Cassie again."

He glanced back down at her leg before moving to his feet. She tried to ignore the tenting of the soft fleece of his pants. She really did. But he was huge. He ignored his own arousal, though. Removing a bottle of antiseptic from the kit, he dampened a large square of gauze before turning back to her.

His eyes were filled with pain. "I hate seeing you hurt," he whispered. "I can't bear it."

She would have reassured him. Would have told him again how she had doused it herself with alcohol in the diner if he hadn't shocked her beyond speech.

His lips covered hers as he laid the gauze on her leg. Fiery pain shot through her flesh as his lips swallowed her cry, then replaced it with such amazing sensation she wanted to whimper in return. He licked her lips. He didn't steal her kiss. He didn't take it. He cajoled it from her. His tongue swiped over the curves, pressed gently at the seam, licked at her heatedly until she opened her lips and allowed him entrance.

Did he growl? A short, rough sound echoed in his chest as his hand fell away from the gauze, both arms coming around her, pulling her against him, his lips slanting over hers as he began to feed from her mouth. There was no other way to describe it.

His cock was a length of hot steel pressing against her suddenly fiery pussy as he kissed her. It ground against her clit, made her body moisten, made slick heat slide free of her vagina and saturate her panties. He had to feel it, even through the fleece of his pants, had to know she was wet, her body wild from his touch.

He nibbled at her lips, his tongue raking forcibly past them to conquer her mouth with hot, ecstatic licks and smooth thrusts. He dared her to return each caress. Challenged her to give as good as he gave. And Elizabeth was helpless against the ravaging onslaught.

His kiss tasted like midnight, dark and deep, frighteningly savage and yet with a power so seductive, she became lost within it. Her breasts swelled, ached. Her nipples poked demandingly against the cloth of her shirt as he moved his bare chest against them.

He didn't take advantage of her arousal, though. Didn't try to force more, though Elizabeth wondered if she would have had the strength to pull away from him. He held her against him, his arms contracting around her, hands stroking over her back as his tongue learned every secret of her mouth and urged her to return the favor.

It was seductive. Tempestuous. Given and taken in silence, with only the hard rasp of their breathing disturbing the air around them as he kissed her with a hunger only surpassed, maybe, by her own.

His taste alone drove her to seek more, made her greedy for each stroke of his tongue along hers. Her hands stroked over his shoulders, his hair, on fire to feel as much of his body as this stolen moment in time allowed her.

How long had it been since a man had touched her? How many nights had she lain awake dreaming of this man? Envisioning him coming to her, whispering his need for her, his hunger, offering her his strength and his heat. She gloried in it now. She stretched in his arms, rubbing against him, feeling his warmth seeping into her skin, heating the chill that had filled her for so long.

They were both fighting for breath within minutes. Bodies strained to get closer, the air heating with a primitive lust that Elizabeth had no idea how to fight. She only knew how to arch closer to him, to feel the ache in her breasts for the touch of his broad hands, the pulse in her pussy for the thickness of his cock. To know she was alive. Finally, irrevocably alive and for one moment in time, a man had no other thought in his head than to touch her. To hold her. To—

"Momma. Momma, where are you?"

Cassie's frightened voice was like ice flowing over her as Dash jerked away from her, struggling for breath as he turned away, obviously fighting to hide his erection in case Cassie came running into the hidden alcove.

"Momma's here, Cassie." Elizabeth slid off the counter, limping quickly around the corner to allow Cassie to see her.

The little girl was sitting up in the bed, her eyes dark with fear as she clutched the teddy bear Dash had laid beside her. Long, black curls tumbled around her shoulders, surrounding her sleep-flushed face and fear-bright eyes.

"Was I dreaming?" she whispered, looking around the room, her eyes filling with tears and disillusionment. "Isn't Dash here, Momma? Did I just dream it again?"

"Cassie . . ." She felt as though she would choke with the painful realization of how desperately Cassie had been waiting for this.

"I'm here, Cassie." Soft as velvet, pitched low, Dash answered for himself.

Elizabeth turned back in time to see him coming from the sink area, his body obviously under control as he paced over to his own bed. He sent Cassie a reassuring look before he pulled a T-shirt from his bag and dragged it on. The soft gray cotton hugged his chest and hard abdomen, the sleeves stretching over his powerful arms. When he finished, he snagged the gown and robe from the top of the opened tote and passed them over to Elizabeth.

Flushing, Elizabeth held the long garments in front of her as she watched her daughter.

Cassie was staring back at Dash, her eyes wide, amazement reflecting in her expression.

"Wow, Dash, you're really tall," she giggled, her lips curving into a bright, pleased grin as he sat down on the side of his bed and looked at her curiously.

Elizabeth watched this first true meeting cautiously. Cassie had had such dreams of Dash coming to rescue them. And though she admitted that if anyone could save them, it was Dash, it was still hard to let go of the control she had maintained over the situation to this point.

"Do you think I'm too tall?" He frowned as though worried at the prospect. "It would be hard to shrink at this late date, Cassie."

A vivid smile broke across Cassie's face and before either Elizabeth or Dash could guess what she was about to do, she flew from her bed and jumped into Dash's arms.

Elizabeth gasped at Cassie's speed and daring. Her daughter had never been one to trust men; she hadn't even enjoyed her father's embraces, but here she was throwing herself at Dash.

He caught her to his chest in reflex, his gaze going to Elizabeth in shock, his eyes filling with an emotion she couldn't define as Cassie wrapped her arms around his neck and planted a loud kiss on his hard cheek.

Her daughter looked smaller, even more fragile as Dash held her, his gaze locking with hers as he swallowed tightly.

"I'm so glad you're here, Dash," Cassie cried against his neck. "I was so scared. So scared you wouldn't be able to find us. That I was wrong and that you wouldn't really come and help me and my momma. But you did. You came, Dash."

Elizabeth's heart clenched as Dash's eyes closed, his expression tightening with emotion.

"Yes, I did, Cassie," he whispered against her hair, holding her gently, holding her as her father never had. Comfortably. With warmth. With caring. "I'm here. Where I intend to stay."

Elizabeth gasped at the statement at the same time his eyes opened, the golden depths hardening with determination. She had a feeling she might have a chance of surviving the dangers surrounding her with Dash at her side, but she knew now, beyond a shadow of a doubt, that he had no intention of allowing them to escape him.

He had just made his claim. And it wasn't simply a claim to protect them.

"Come on, Cassie, we need to get a shower." She fought to keep her voice even, to still the tremor of nerves she could feel racing through her body.

He might think he had made his claim, she thought, and she might need him now more than she had ever needed anyone in her life, but he would learn she wasn't as easy to conquer as he thought she was.

"Oh, Momma, let me sit with Dash." Cassie turned back to her, her expression pleading, her eyes wide and distressed. "I'll be good. I promise."

"You're always good, sweetie," Elizabeth assured her, keeping her voice firm. "But you need a bath, and I need a shower. Now come on, so you can eat and maybe watch cartoons while you eat the breakfast Dash brought." She dangled the treat before her daughter, hating to take something away from her that she wanted. But she couldn't— wouldn't—trust Dash that far.

"But, Momma . . . ," Cassie whined.

"Now, Cassidy Paige." She used her full name, keeping her voice firm, aloof. She prayed Cassie didn't choose now to defy her. She didn't think she could handle the fight.

Cassie sighed deeply as she slid off Dash's lap. "You won't leave. Will you?" she asked in a small voice.

Cassie was obviously frightened to let him out of her sight now.

"I promise." He laid his hand against his chest, his expression somber. "I'll be right here, waiting on my cartoon partner."

Cassie giggled as Elizabeth moved to the tote and picked out the clothes Cassie would need. Toothbrushes, hairbrushes, little-girl's hair bows, a multitude of small, insignificant but prized items were all held within a large clear plastic carrier lying on top of the clothes. She drew it out, gripping her robe and gown before her as she backed to the bathroom. She kept her eyes on Dash, fought to keep her worries under control.

He watched her, his golden-brown eyes quiet and intense. Steady.

"Don't forget to put a decent bandage on your leg," he reminded her as she reached the alcove. "That soap will burn like he—" He cleared his throat. "Like heck." He glanced at Cassie.

Elizabeth flushed but nodded quickly before easing Cassie toward the bathroom door. Like Cassie, she wanted to ask him if he would be there when they were done. If he would promise not to leave.

Somehow, he must have read her fears. Keeping his gaze locked with hers, he returned his hand to his chest. *I promise*, he mouthed for her alone.

Drawing Cassie into the bathroom, she closed the door behind them and quickly got Cassie into the shower. As her daughter kept up a running dialogue, mostly with herself, Elizabeth undressed, wrapped a towel around herself and waited for her daughter to finish.

"I told you Dash would come for us, Momma," Cassie reminded her happily. "The fairy doesn't ever lie about things, you know. And he'll make sure we're safe too. I know he will . . . Do you think he has other little girls, Momma?" her daughter asked then, her voice suddenly lower, uncertain. "I forgot to ask him."

"I don't think Dash has any little girls, sweetie," she answered her daughter as Cassie peeped around the curtain.

He'd said he'd never received a letter or a present in his life. If he'd had a child with a woman, surely at some point he would have had at least one.

"Hurry now, Cassie, so Momma can shower." If she let her, Cassie would spend an hour beneath the shower's spray and even longer in a bathtub.

The child loved water.

Once the water shut off, Elizabeth helped her towel dry the long curls Cassie refused to allow her to cut, then got her dressed. Once the long gown fell around her tiny feet and Cassie pushed her feet into a pair of bunny slippers, she was practically walking on air.

They didn't sleep in pajamas or gowns. Elizabeth put her daughter to bed in clothes they could run in. Usually a pair of soft fleece pants and a T-shirt with socks. She kept Cassie's shoes by the bed, as well as her own, and she could be out the door in under a minute if she had to be.

The past two years had taught her to always be prepared, to always be ready, no matter what. And now her daughter was dressed in a little girly gown and robe, hair bows waiting for her hair, and another teddy bear to hug as she went to sleep.

Dash was going to spoil her, and once he did, what would they do when he walked out of their lives? Even if he stayed until the danger was over, that was no guarantee he would stick around once Grange was taken care of. Some men simply lived for danger, she knew; he could be one of those men.

The thought of trusting him for the moment wasn't nearly as problematic as attempting to get to California and trusting in the offer of safe haven there. It was an offer that had just seemed too good to be true once she and Cassie had been running. One a little too easy to reach out for. And even before Grange, Elizabeth had learned that nothing in life came so easily.

"Momma, do you think Dash likes puppies?" Cassie asked as Elizabeth wrapped her hair in a towel until she could get her own gown on.

Puppies. She almost smiled as she shook her head at the question.

"I don't know, Cassie," she answered. "But we've talked about puppies, haven't we?"

More than once they'd discussed puppies. A puppy was a responsibility, and one Elizabeth couldn't take on at the moment, no matter how protective the animal might become. If something happened to it . . .

She closed her eyes and pressed a hand to her stomach as she thought of the little terrier she'd nearly gotten Cassie while she was with her father that fateful weekend. If she had bought that puppy, Cassie's heart would have been broken to have to leave it behind or to give it away.

"Kitties are quiet, Momma." Cassie's voice was lower, the sadness in it breaking her heart.

"We'll discuss puppies and kitties some other time, okay?" she ventured rather than giving her standard rejection of the idea.

Pulling on her gown, Elizabeth pushed the curtain back to see Cassie sitting on the closed lid of the toilet, her head lowered as she played with the belt of her robe.

"Later, Cassie?" she queried again, knowing her daughter.

"Later, Momma," her daughter all but whispered.

⋆ C H A P T E R 7 ⋆

Dash watched Elizabeth sleep for hours. She was curled around Cassie's small body, protecting her, even while nearly unconscious from exhaustion. They had both fallen asleep during the first hour of cartoons, and he had let them be. Hell, he'd figure something out about the schedule. Elizabeth was right, Cassie needed to sleep, but so did her mother.

Dark circles ringed Elizabeth's eyes. They weren't as noticeable while she was awake; the vivid blue, so unlike the lighter tone of her daughter's, drew attention from her pale, tired features. But asleep, she looked wounded.

He sat on his bed staring at her. He couldn't help it. He had imagined her for over a year. Touched her in his dreams; loved her in his fantasies. What was it about her that it had only taken her daughter's smallest descriptions to fill his mind with her?

He wasn't a man who believed in soul mates. There were times he wondered if a creation of science could even have a soul. But Elizabeth made him want to believe. And as he watched her sleeping, he realized he did believe. He believed in it more than he had ever believed in anything. But it also made him realize the bleak, agonizing future awaiting him if he didn't do something about Terrence Grange. That, and convincing Elizabeth that she was his. That he was the daddy Cassie needed, the mate she longed for. Which meant he had work to do. He picked up the phone and called Mike.

Dash had fought for more than two years with Mike Toler in the mountains of Afghanistan, searching for the pockets of terrorists hidden within mountain caves and underground tunnels. He had saved Mike's ass more than once, and he knew the caliber of man he was.

Mike was ex-CIA, a rancher now, though Dash knew he still had enough contacts to get a line on any information he needed. There was something wrong with the situation as he knew it, Dash finally admitted to himself. Terrence Grange was a mean bastard, and a pervert, but he wouldn't risk his whole organization for one little girl. Even one who had witnessed a murder. Not to this extent.

No, he was after something more, Dash just wasn't certain what. Something that had him playing a very careful game with the child's mother as he pushed her, toyed with her.

Otherwise, Grange would have just waited. Waited until Elizabeth went to the authorities, waited until Cassie was in protective custody and in a place certain to allow him the opportunity to get to her. He wouldn't be running her and her mother down like animals. The situation had been growing more complicated by the day and it was making Dash more suspicious by the moment.

He had suspected, after no more than a month into the chase for Elizabeth and her child, that the complications were likely to build. He hadn't expected what he was facing at the time.

He had tried to accept that Grange was just an obsessed freak, an animal that needed killing. Which was true to a large extent. But still, there was more. He could feel it in the deepest reaches of his gut.

He called Mike as daylight turned to night and the worst of the blizzard had passed, at least enough to allow visibility in the Hummer. As he expected, Mike was waiting on him.

"As soon as the snow lets up, get on out here," Mike ordered him briskly. "I have my team at the house and we'll make sure those two are protected while I follow up on some other information coming in. Your instincts were right, though. As usual."

"What have you found out?" He kept his voice low. He didn't want to wake Elizabeth or Cassie.

"Grange is a dirty bastard. And a pervert. But little girls Cassidy's age aren't his preference. Nor is spending this amount of money on tracking down one little girl who was likely too shocked to even remember who killed her father. The rumor I managed to pick up is that the bastard has been letting them run but the mother has actually bested his men more than once. To add to that, it seems we have some nosy-assed South African businessman poking his head in. Someone named Vanderale. Dane Vanderale. You know him?"

Dash frowned at the information.

"Emerging Breed supporter from what I've heard," he said thoughtfully. "And you're right he's damned nosy. I just don't understand why this situation would draw his interest."

"No clue there," Mike agreed. "Word is he has a team heading out of Johannesburg to search for Elizabeth and her daughter, though. Right now, the details I have are sketchy but I'll have more coming in soon," Mike assured him.

He had a hell of a lot more than he'd expected, Dash admitted. "What about our contact in Virginia?" he asked the other man, aware of Elizabeth awakening, her lashes lifting to stare back at him.

"I talked to him an hour or so ago," Mike answered. "He's waiting on you to get to the ranch for a secure transmission. Get your ass out here as soon as possible."

He glanced toward the window. He wouldn't leave until dark. It was much easier to hide the fact that he carried a woman and child in the Hummer with him after nightfall.

"Tonight," he told him. "Expect us sometime after eight. I imagine getting this little pup Elizabeth calls a child ready to go will take a while. She has more energy than any kid I think I've ever seen." She had bounced around for nearly an hour before collapsing on the bed to watch the cartoons.

Mike laughed. "Yeah, they're like wild monkeys at that age. Take care, old buddy. I'll see you tonight."

Dash ended the call, wiping his hand over his face as he tried to pull together the fragments of information he had as Elizabeth rose from the bed and padded to the bathroom.

There wasn't much.

Dane Colder had been a prominent doctor in the small California town. He had married Elizabeth when she was fresh out of high school. Ten years older than she, he had wooed her within months before giving her an elaborate wedding. A year later Cassie had been conceived. Two years later, Elizabeth had divorced the bastard on grounds of incompatibility. Dash suspected other reasons.

She had fought visitation, but Colder had been determined. He was awarded one week a month with the child. From that time forward, charge after charge of abuse had been leveled against him by Elizabeth, only to be thrown out of court for lack of evidence by the judge. Colder had carried a lot of influence and had some powerful friends. A year before his death, he had hooked up with Grange for some unknown reason. Six months later Colder had sued for custody of Cassie. It was rumored he would have received it if his body hadn't been found in a dirty alley pumped full of bullets.

Something was missing, though. Some piece of information that Dash knew would allow everything to finally fall into place. Until he had it, he was working blind, at least until he got his hands on Grange. Until then, he had to make certain no one could touch Elizabeth or her child ever again. Which meant they would have to head out soon and get to the ranch tonight.

Moving to his feet, Dash laid out clothing and shoes for the mother and child before quickly loading the Hummer while Elizabeth was in the bathroom.

She was waiting for him when he returned, at the side of the bed, her expression weary as she sat silently, the warm, white robe he'd gotten her drawn tight around her.

"Should I wake Cassie?" she asked him quietly as he closed the door and met her gaze.

He shook his head and moved to sit on the side of his bed, facing her, their knees almost touching.

"We need to talk first," he told her, keeping his voice low. "How do you know Dane Vanderale?"

He hadn't believed she actually knew Vanderale until he saw the surprise in her gaze.

"Friend of a friend." She shrugged, watching him with a small frown. "Why?"

There was more, he could see it in her eyes.

"Don't lie to me, Elizabeth." He swore he could taste the scent of deception in the air. "Tell me what Vanderale is to you."

"A friend of a friend," she repeated, the snap in her tone unmistakable. "I met him several years ago, just after I left Dane. A mutual friend told him the trouble I was having with my ex-husband. Mr. Vanderale gave me his card with the address of his California apartment and told me if I ever needed anything all I had to do was go there and use the code for the elevators. He'd know when I arrived and he'd come help us."

Why?

What the hell did Vanderale have to do with any of this?

He continued to watch her, seeing the confusion in her eyes.

"Why didn't you contact him?" he asked her when she said nothing more.

"Because all I had was an address, not a phone number. Once Cassie's father and I began fighting over his visitation to her, my friend stopped talking to me, so I couldn't ask her." Frustration filled her face. "And every step I've taken toward California, Grange finds a way to knock me back two. I'm terrified to book a flight, because somehow he knew the one time I actually did so. For two years I've fought to just survive, Dash. Too terrified to actually reach out to anyone, let alone someone I just met once."

She didn't trust Vanderale. As he stared at her, he sensed the underlying answer beneath her words. If she had made it to California, she might have taken the chance on contacting Vanderale—might have—though Dash doubted she would have done so unless she had no other choice.

No, Elizabeth didn't trust easily. Except for him. She trusted him, she just didn't want to admit it.

"Do you know him?" she finally asked, watching him suspiciously.

Dash shook his head. "I only know *of* him, but evidently he's sent a team of men from South Africa to look for you and Cassie." Something predatory and dangerous reared its head inside him at the thought.

Fear flashed in her eyes then. "Do you think he's helping Grange?"

He didn't have to give that one even a moment's thought.

"Vanderale wouldn't bother himself with Grange unless it was to kill him. Then he'd just have his bodyguard, Rhys, take care of it," he snorted. "He's more a playboy than a criminal."

But even a playboy wouldn't trouble himself to this extent, Dash reminded himself.

There were too many questions. Too much he simply couldn't tie together just yet.

"We need to get ready to get on the road," he decided. "The snow is beginning to lessen, so it should be safe to travel soon. I'd like to be out of here in the next hour or so."

"Because of Vanderale," she stated, her expression tightening as she saw yet another threat to her daughter.

"Because too much doesn't make sense and I want you and Cassie safe before I begin hunting for answers." Vanderale was an unexpected development, and the man's reputation assured Dash he could potentially be more of a threat than Grange ever thought of being.

She rose from the bed then, and he waited patiently as Elizabeth woke Cassie, then helped her wash up, brush her teeth and comb out the mass of curls falling over her face.

Elizabeth didn't take nearly as long getting herself ready as she took taking care of her child. She gave the racy black thong and matching bra a long look before picking them up expressionlessly and adding them to the jeans, socks and thick long-sleeved blouse he had laid out for her.

Dash hid his grin. She was getting mad now. He could see it in her face, feel it in the air around her. She didn't confront him with Cassie watching them, though. She was careful to give the child every assurance that she was willing to work with Dash. Willing to do whatever it took to keep her safe.

His respect only grew for her. She was a damned strong woman. Not many people, male or female, could hold their tempers around him for long. He watched her disappear into the bathroom, wondering how long she would wait before she blew up and confronted him over the decisions he was making. Decisions that hadn't been passed by her first.

Cassie watched her too. Dash caught the little girl's expression as her mother went into the other room. It was equal parts deliberation and playful manipulation. Oh, she was going to be a handful for sure.

"Momma's clothes are pretty." Cassie bounced up on the bed beside him as he packed the small plastic bag Elizabeth had put their dirty clothes into, in the bag he used to carry his own. "Mine are too."

She ran her fingers down the soft gray velour sleeve of her shirt, then looked down at her new boots. It was obvious she was genuinely enjoying the feel of the outfit.

Dash watched her admiring the clothes and couldn't help but allow a smile to tilt his lips. She didn't hold much back, and she had something on her mind she was ready to say. Dash just wondered if he wanted to hear it right now. He had a feeling Cassie would keep him off balance every chance she had.

"Can you keep secrets, Dash?" she finally asked him carefully as she watched him zip the bag up.

Dash looked over at her quietly for long moments. "It depends," he finally told her gently. "If they're secrets your momma should know, then I might have to try to convince you to tell her."

She blinked, long thick lashes covering her eyes for half a second. "Would you tell her if I said don't?" she finally asked.

Dash sighed deeply. "I don't know, Cassie," he told her seriously. "Secrets are big things. Little girls should always trust their mommas with their secrets. Even if they think it could get them in trouble."

Cassie watched him silently. He could see her expression clearing, her eyes brightening a bit more than before.

"It's a good secret," she finally said. "A secret 'bout Momma."

Now how could he resist?

He grimaced. "Uhhh, Cassie, don't tell tales on your momma," he finally sighed. He was desperate to know anything she would tell.

She giggled lightly, knowingly.

"Momma might be angry with you, Dash," she finally whispered, staring up at him with big, blue eyes. "Be careful or she might yell at you. Momma doesn't yell really loud, but boy, she can be scary when she does yell."

Dash restrained his chuckle as relief poured through him. He wanted to know every soft inch of Elizabeth inside and out, but he didn't want Cassie telling tales either. This tale, he figured he could handle.

"What does she sound like when she yells?" he asked her, his voice just as soft as though it were actually secret. Hell, he knew she was pissed and getting madder by the second.

Cassie looked at the bathroom door. "Like she might take away the candy bars for a week." Cassie nodded solemnly, but Dash could have sworn he saw laughter lurking in the little girl's eyes. "You better be nice to her or she might not let you have any treats."

Dash almost winced. Yep, he agreed with Cassie, that might be a bad thing. Unfortunately, he had yet to know what it was like to be really treated by Elizabeth.

"I'll get my own candy bars," he confided with a grin. "What would she do then?"

Cassie evidently hadn't considered that angle.

"Oh." Cassie pursed her lips, thinking. "Would you get me one too?" Her curls seemed to bounce around her face as she smiled up at him sweetly.

Pure innocence. Or so she wanted him to think.

Dash snorted. Oh, she was a charmer all right.

"I don't know. Messing with your momma over your candy bars

might really get me in trouble." He frowned as though thinking the matter over. "I might not want to chance that, Cassie."

The little girl obviously liked her candy bars. But she was also enjoying the game of learning how great an ally Dash would be.

He watched as she pulled at one of her curls thoughtfully. Her head tilted and he swore he could see her quick little mind working in those wide blue eyes.

"I could tell you how to get her unmad at you," she finally confided sweetly. "I know the secret. Momma can't resist."

Now this might be interesting. Dash glanced over her. "You tell first. Then we'll talk candy bars."

Cassie rolled her eyes. "This information is worth a lot of candy bars, Dash."

She shook her head at him as though he disappointed her. She was obviously expecting so much more from him.

Dash wanted to laugh. He was surprised to realize how easily it was building in his chest. She was a tough little thing, for sure. He would have expected her to be huddled in fear, flinching at each sudden sound. Instead, she appeared to have completely forgotten about the day before.

"Hm," he finally grunted, as though he might be reluctant to bargain. "What amount are we talking here?"

He hadn't had much experience with kids, but Cassie made it real easy to find common ground with her.

"Well." She scrunched her face up as she glanced back at the bathroom door before turning back to him with an innocent smile. "At least three chocolate bars. I really like chocolate, you know."

Dash wiped his hand over his face, fighting his amusement. Damn. She was good. Her momma would kill him over three candy bars.

"Three, huh?" He sighed as though it could be a possibility. "How mad will your momma get over these three chocolate bars?"

She straightened the sleeve of her shirt. Ran her hand over the soft material again and then looked up at him with those angel's eyes as though she had nothing more on her mind than making his life easier.

"Well, it would be controllable if you knew the secret to make her unmad." She shrugged her pitifully thin shoulders negligently. "So, do we have a bargain here?"

Oh, she was good.

"I don't know." He cocked his head sideways. "I don't have any chocolate bars right now."

She pressed her lips together as she placed two small fingers at the bridge of her nose and shook her head as though she had lost all hope for him. Finally, she sighed as if more than put out. Her eyes were twinkling, though, the shadows of fear easing.

"I'll take you on your word, then," she sighed. "But you really should stock up on chocolate bars. They're more precious than gold when dealing with kids, ya know."

He nodded solemnly. "I'll keep that in mind. So what's the secret?"

"Kisses." She leaned back as though she had just pulled off the coup of the century. And to beat all, she was laughing at him.

"Kisses?" he asked her carefully.

She nodded confidently. "Lots of kisses, Dash. And Momma's already upset. You better pucker up."

She was giggling. She clapped her hand over her mouth, though, when her momma walked quickly from the bathroom, dragging a wide-toothed comb quickly through her unruly locks.

"You forgot hair bands for me, Mr. Prepared-For-Everything," she muttered in irritation as she swept the waist-length curls behind her shoulder and lifted her head.

Her eyes narrowed instantly. Her hands went to her slender hips, emphasized by the snug fit of denim and the black blouse tucked into the waistband.

"What are you two up to?"

Cassie's eyes rounded instantly as she jumped from the bed and flew to her momma's arms.

Elizabeth caught her easily, a smile crossing her lips, even if it was highly suspicious. She accepted the little girl's exuberant kiss to her cheek, though, and returned it warmly.

"Don't we have pretty clothes, Momma?" She leaned back to allow her mother to admire the soft gray velour outfit. "Dash has good taste, huh?"

The little girl was almost as tall as her mother. Dash watched them covertly as he rose to his feet, lifting the bag from the bed as he flexed his shoulder muscles, checking the fit of the leather bands that held the knife sheath between his shoulder blades.

"Yes. Dash has good taste." She allowed her daughter to slide to the floor, laying her arm across her shoulders. "Get your coat on now, Cassie. It looks like Dash is ready to leave." Her voice cooled measurably. "Maybe you better hurry and use the bathroom first, though. We might have a lengthy drive ahead of us."

Cassie bounced away while her mother looked after her. When the door closed, Elizabeth turned back to Dash.

"No chocolate bars," she said as she sat down at the edge of the bed to lace the boots Dash had provided for her. "It makes her too hyper and she won't eat her meals. Right now, vitamins are more important."

He knew there was no way she had heard their conversation. She lifted her head after finishing, glancing at his questioning expression.

"She bargains for chocolate, Dash. What did she promise in return?" He watched her lips press together as though she were trying to control her own grin. "Don't believe that child. She really doesn't know the secret to the universe, or ancient druid curses. She just thinks she does."

Hell, she hadn't offered those to him, he thought with a spurt of amusement. But then again, he knew the little girl was after a hell of a lot more than chocolate. The little conniver was after a bit of match-making.

He shook his head as Elizabeth rose to her feet, her eyes narrowing on him. "Well?" she asked him curiously. "What was it?"

He shrugged. "Can't tell. Chocolate secrets are sacred."

She snorted at that. Thankfully, Cassie chose that moment to come bounding out of the bathroom. Elizabeth turned quickly to take care of washing and drying her hands, then a quick pat to thick childish curls and getting her into her coat. The whole time, Cassie talked.

"Are we really going to a ranch, Dash?" She stared up at him in amazement. "I've never been to a ranch before."

"Definitely a ranch, Cassie." He opened the door.

Two feet of snow greeted him and more was still falling.

"Come on, chatterbox." He swung her up in his arms and began pushing through the snow to the Hummer, making certain to clear a path for Elizabeth as she moved behind him.

"I'm hungry, Dash," Cassie informed him as he strapped her into the backseat, looking up at him with wide eyes. "Can we get something to eat? I want some pizza."

He glanced back at Elizabeth, catching the surprise in her expression.

"Let's get rolling first, squirt," he chuckled. "Then we'll see what your momma thinks is best."

He closed Cassie's door, then opened the front passenger door, gripping Elizabeth's waist and lifting her into the high seat. He realized he had left her to make her own way into the vehicle the night before. She tensed in his arms but allowed him to help her in, casting him a surprised glance as he pulled her seat belt forward.

"I remember my manners sometimes." He cleared his throat as she snapped the strap in place. He made a mental note to remember them more often, though they were self-taught. He might have to polish them a bit. Maybe Mike would have some ideas. Hell, he was married now, he should know.

The outside lights cast a dim, ethereal glow around her. Her dark hair glistened; her blue eyes appeared darker, more mysterious. Her lips shone with the delicate coating of moisture from the nervous tongue she stroked over them.

She drew in a deep hard breath, lifting her breasts against her shirt. He remembered the bra. Lacy, flimsy. It was a tempting piece of confection that drove him crazy when he thought about it.

He cleared his throat. "Pizza?" he asked her softly. He was starved, but not for food.

She swallowed tightly. "That's fine."

They both jumped at Cassie's squeal of pleasure from the backseat. Dash nodded abruptly before he closed Elizabeth's door and strode quickly to the driver's side.

The pizza would be easy enough. Loosening up Elizabeth might be a bit harder.

CHAPTER 8

"This guy is a friend of yours?"

Elizabeth was nervous about their arrival at the Toler ranch. She had gone from having no one to help her, having no options, to having Dash take over and find options she could have never found for herself.

For two years she had depended on no one but herself. She had kept herself and Cassie alive, often only by the skin of her teeth, but they were still alive. She had made her own decisions. Had protected Cassie alone and accepted the responsibility that each move, each decision, was the best she could make at the time.

Now Dash was making the decisions and he was doing it without informing her of the consequences, should any of them fail. She felt as though she was in the dark, floundering for solid footing amid a situation she was unfamiliar with. She didn't know Mike Toler. Didn't know his family, his strengths or his weaknesses and she didn't feel safe.

Now, with the knowledge that Dane Vanderale had sent men to search for her and Cassie, she felt even more off balance.

Vanderale was crazy rich, according to Melissa at the time, though she hadn't mentioned the playboy part. Especially during the time he'd spent playing board games with Cassie while she and Melissa visited that day. According to her former friend, Vanderale had been there to pick up papers she'd brought from her boss for him. He hadn't left for several hours, though. And when he had, he'd found a moment to catch her alone and give her the card and the offer of help if she should ever need it.

Why?

How had he known or suspected she might need his help?

That question was the reason she hadn't used every resource she could think of to contact him in the past two years. She didn't know why he'd made the offer.

He didn't know her, and she hadn't known he existed until that day. Yet he'd made an offer she had found herself in need of less than two years later. She'd never been able to explain it, so she hadn't been able to trust in it. Or in the man.

Yet she hadn't had that problem with Dash.

She watched Dash now, noticing his relaxed posture, his air of confidence and control. How she longed to feel so in control of any situation. The lights from the dashboard reflected off his hard face, the dull gleam of the night vision windshield giving him an almost otherworldly appearance. The unfamiliar lights cast his expression in stark relief and made his eyes almost glow as he glanced over at her.

"He's a fellow soldier," he said simply as he shrugged those broad shoulders.

Hard, muscular shoulders. She had gripped the smooth, tight flesh earlier that morning, allowed her nails to clench on the supple skin as he ate from her mouth. Her fingertips tingled at the memory. Her mouth watered with sudden hunger to know his taste again.

"'A fellow soldier' doesn't tell me much, Dash." She pulled her mind back from the erotic possibilities that shimmered within her mind. She couldn't let herself lose focus. Cassie's life was too important. "Even friends aren't always dependable."

"Likely why I haven't made any." He didn't appear regretful or bitter. It was a statement, nothing more. "We fought in Afghanistan together. In conditions like we knew, you learn the mettle of the men you fight with. Mike wouldn't betray a kid. He put his life on the line too many times to save one. And he wouldn't betray me. He owes his own life to me."

It was information. That's all. There was little emotion in his voice other than respect. Elizabeth thought of the people she had believed were her friends once. People she cared for, had believed cared for her. She had loved them. Openly. Never questioning their honesty or their commitment to her. She had learned quickly that the least controversy had even those friends she had grown up with pulling back.

Yet here was Dash, going to a man he had fought with, confident of that man's loyalty, his honor. It made little sense to her.

"How can you be sure?" It was her greatest fear. A betrayal that would cost her the life of her child. "You're trusting this man with Cassie's life."

"I'd trust him with my own." He flashed her a dark look. "You don't fight with a man that long in hell and not know what he's made of, Elizabeth. Mike's a good man. He won't let us down."

"You expect me to just take your word." She kept her voice low, aware that Cassie was still awake in the back. She regretted the fact that her internal alarm clock had failed her today, allowing her to sleep so late. She had needed to talk this out with him.

"The fairy says it's okay, Momma," the little girl piped in then, her voice soft, reassuring.

Elizabeth closed her eyes painfully, her chest tightening. How she wished Cassie's fairy, whoever the hell it was, would tell her. But then again, this fairy thing was already starting to concern her. As they had walked from the basement to their apartment two days before, Cassie had whispered that the fairy didn't want them going back to their room.

Please, Momma. The fairy says to stay here. To wait. I don't wanna go up there. Had Cassie somehow known their enemies were there?

Elizabeth knew children had an advanced sense of their surroundings. One adults lost as they matured. The ability to see and sense things that parents rarely made sense of. Was the fairy merely a way for her to explain this?

"Tell the fairy I said thank you, Cassie." She looked between the seats, smiling at her little girl. "But Momma needs to make sure. Adults don't have fairies to guide them."

Cassie looked over at her with amazing sobriety. "You can use my fairy, Momma. I'll tell you what she thinks."

And how did she answer that one? Cassie never failed to surprise her.

"Thank you, honey, but Momma needs more than just the fairy's word right now. Okay?" She kept her voice gentle. She didn't want to hurt Cassie's feelings. Didn't want her to sense that her mother had lost her belief in fairies long ago.

"I understand, Momma." Cassie settled back in her seat, her smile flashing in the darkness. "You can talk to Dash all you like about it, then. I know it's going to be okay."

Elizabeth's fists clenched as she turned back and faced forward. Snow still fell, though not as thick as before. The roads were deserted, the country lane blending into the surrounding landscape until only the faintest hint remained that it was actually a road.

She hated not knowing. Not being certain. She didn't know this rancher, this ex-CIA agent Dash was taking them to. She didn't know Dash. Yet she was being expected to trust merely because she had no other choice.

"Why are you trusting me, Elizabeth, even this far?" he finally asked her. "You could have left the motel while I showered. You could have made any attempt to escape me. And you would have if you felt the need. Why didn't you?"

Dash's voice was gentle. It was dark and demanding, but the underlying softness soothed the ragged edges of her nerves.

She pushed her fingers restlessly through her hair. He hadn't hurt her when he'd had the chance. He had killed a man for her. He had followed her through a blizzard and taken her farther away from the men searching for Cassie. He had haggled with Cassie over chocolate bars and carried a tote of clothes for months, picking up more here and there because he knew theirs were being destroyed.

He had bought her daughter a bicycle. Had sent her a robe. He had done so many things, even before he found them, to make Cassie's life, and hers, easier. How could she not take the chance?

"You made your point." She laced her fingers together tightly. "But I still don't know this man. I can't trust like this, Dash. Not after all this time."

"Then trust me," he suggested. "You can, Elizabeth. You know you can."

She stared out at the steadily falling snow, trying to maintain her control as he turned carefully from the road and drove beneath a sign announcing the Bar T Ranch. They were within only a few miles of this potentially dangerous situation. She braced herself for it, knowing she had no choice now but to trust Dash.

The dashboard clock read nearly nine o' clock. The normally hour-long drive had taken over three hours, counting the stop for Cassie's pizza. Pizza that now sat like a lump in her stomach.

"Put on your coat, Cassie." She kept her voice even. If they had to run, she didn't want her daughter without some protection.

She tensed as Dash reached down between his seat and door, his body shifting, moving carefully. When he pulled the holstered gun from the cavity and handed it to her, she stared back at him in shock.

"I wouldn't take a chance with your life," he told her quietly. "I need your trust, Elizabeth. Here's mine in return."

She stared down at the weapon before raising her eyes to his once again.

"Would you expect another soldier to follow you blindly?" she finally asked him somberly. "Would you ask him, with no explanations, without outlining whatever plan I pray you have, to just follow?"

He was silent for long moments as he laid the revolver on the console between their seats, then gripped the steering wheel with both hands as he maneuvered through more than a foot of snow.

"There's a chance that I can arrange a place of safety for you and Cassie. One that Grange can't infiltrate or access in any way. A place where Cassie will be as safe as the gold in Fort Knox."

Elizabeth took a deep breath. She had been praying for nothing more. Nothing less. But the tone of his voice warned her that she might not like the answer.

"Where is this place?"

He glanced at her. "I'd rather not say until I can be certain, Elizabeth. This requires a place without little ears and more time than we have in this Hummer. Another soldier would understand this. Just as he would understand that I have those I trust. That even if he doesn't know them, he understands that the contacts are important. Another soldier would understand that a commander knows what the hell he's doing, and he will explain the full plan and discuss it when he knows it's a plan."

Elizabeth gritted her teeth. Tight. Damn him.

She bit back the curse that wanted to sizzle to her lips as she turned away from him, staring outside the Hummer resentfully. He was right. But she damned well didn't have to like it.

"Ohhh, Momma. Dash is good . . ." Cassie's awed voice was filled with respect for how easily Dash had managed to turn the tables on a mother she had never managed to outwit. *And never will,* Elizabeth thought with affection, though she was still a little irked at Dash.

Elizabeth snorted. "Remember the phrase 'getting too big for your britches,' Cassie?" she asked her daughter, using a firm tone of voice. "Dash could be in danger here."

"Uh-oh," Cassie singsonged. "Better remember what I told you earlier." Elizabeth glanced over at him curiously.

"Too big for my britches, huh?" he muttered for her alone. "Elizabeth, darlin', you have no idea." Then he said to Cassie, "I'll remember your advice, honey, just as soon as I get the chance. You got your coat on now? We'll be there soon."

Scarlet heat flamed through Elizabeth's body, flushing her cheeks in aroused embarrassment as she turned quickly away from him, remembering just how big he could get. Definitely too big for his britches. She swallowed tightly, then breathed in with slow, even breaths to fight the sudden hard thump of her heart. Damn him. Did he have a countermove for everything?

The rest of the drive passed in silence. Elizabeth steeled herself for the coming arrival. Death or safety. With each move she had made over the past two years, it came down to this. And though she was beginning to trust Dash to a point, finding it in her to trust someone on his say-so alone was harder.

The Hummer pulled through the snow easily, though Dash didn't push for speed. Still, all too soon they rounded the last small hill and the two-story ranch house came into view. It was well lit. The front door opened as the wide entrance to a garage slowly began to rise.

A tall man moved easily from the porch along a shoveled walkway, timing his steps to coincide with Dash maneuvering the Hummer into the wide garage. As they cleared the door, it began to lower once again, enclosing them in the brightly lit area as Dash cut the ignition.

"Momma." Cassie's voice was faint. "The fairy says it's okay. She really does." But Elizabeth heard her daughter's fear as the strange male began to come alongside the vehicle.

"Come here, baby." Elizabeth unbuckled her seat belt as Dash did, grabbed the service revolver in one hand and motioned her daughter to her with the other.

In an instant Cassie was over the console. Her thin arms wrapped around Elizabeth's neck, her head burying against it as she trembled.

"Elizabeth?" Dash turned to her, watching Cassie in alarm.

Elizabeth shook her head. "She's frightened." She ran her hand down Cassie's back soothingly. "Big men scare her, Dash. Except you. She thinks she knows you . . ." She let it trail off.

She and Cassie didn't know the man now standing patiently next to the vehicle, his expression concerned as he waited on Dash.

Dash breathed out deeply as she watched him somberly. "She's just a baby . . ." She tried to explain, afraid Dash would now expect more from Cassie than she could give. Cassie had her moments of terror. Her moments of happiness. Elizabeth had learned to accept each as they came.

"I know that, Elizabeth." His voice was soft, though his eyes flashed dark fire at her response. "I was worried for Cassie. Not Mike. We can sit here as long as you need."

Elizabeth shook her head. Better to find out now what awaited them here in this new atmosphere.

"If she finds safety, she'll calm down." She left the rest unsaid.

Dash pushed his fingers wearily through his hair as he pulled the keys from the ignition and opened the door. Cassie tensed, a small, mewling whimper escaping her lips.

Dash stopped. His jaw tightened before he closed the door back once again.

"Cassie." His voice was so incredibly gentle as he turned that Elizabeth wanted to cry at the sound. Had she ever heard a man speak to her or her daughter with such warmth? "Cassie. The door's closed, honey. Won't you look at me?"

Elizabeth rocked her baby slowly, knowing the fear could lead to deep, shuddering tremors that came so close to convulsions they terrified her.

Surprisingly enough, Cassie peeked up at him, though her arms gripped Elizabeth's neck so tightly they felt like bands of quivering steel.

"I'll be okay." Cassie was fighting to be brave, but her voice trembled with her fear. "The fairy said it's okay. The fairy is always right. She's always right." Elizabeth could hear the tears filling Cassie's voice now.

"You know, Mike has a little girl too," Dash said softly. "Just a few years older than you are. Her name's Mica. And I bet, living out here without any little girls to play with, that she'll be very happy when you come in the house."

Cassie's head lifted farther. She glanced outside the Hummer. "Is she here now?" she asked him suspiciously.

"She's in the house, Cassie," Dash said. "I heard her playing when I talked to Mike on the phone earlier. Would you like to meet her?"

Cassie didn't loosen her grip on Elizabeth, but the shudders eased perceptively. "You're sure she's here, Dash?"

"Tell you what, I'll step out here and talk to Mike and have him get Mica to come to the inside garage door." He indicated the closed door at the side of the wide room. "How does that sound?"

Elizabeth lowered her head, kissing her daughter's curls as she fought to hide her tears. Dash was being gentle, understanding. His voice wasn't patronizing as Dane's would have been, but kept its usual inflection without being demanding.

"He's a good daddy?" Cassie's voice was still rough. "He doesn't hit his little girl, does he?"

Elizabeth glanced at Dash. She prayed that only she saw the spark of violence that shot through his eyes for a second.

"No, Cassie." He swallowed tightly. "Mike would never hit his little girl. You can even ask her if you want to. Mike loves his little girl very much. He would never hit her."

"She'll come to the door?" Cassie worried. "I can see her before I get out?"

"Yes, you can. And I'll close my door when I get out. That way, you won't get cold waiting." Or frightened that the big man standing outside had access to her, Elizabeth guessed.

Cassie nodded cautiously.

"Good girl." Dash smiled tenderly as he eased his door open once again and stepped out of the Hummer.

✦ CHAPTER 9 ✦

Dash wanted to kill. Again. He wanted Grange in his hands, struggling, blood flowing as he pleaded for mercy. A mercy Dash knew he would never be able to give. He was shocked to realize how terrified Cassie had become when she saw Mike. It had been driven home to him then, just how much that little girl trusted him. How much she depended on him to keep her safe and how hard that battle was being fought.

He cursed silently, breathing out roughly as emotion swamped him. The fear he had smelled in that vehicle had nearly strangled him, ripping through his defenses, if he had any against her, and searing his soul with fury. Grange would pay for the damage he had done to that child and Dash would make certain of it.

"Hey, buddy." Mike's voice was questioning, and Dash knew his friend could sense his fury.

They had fought together too many times, had covered each other's backs in too many ways. Men who fought together learned the basics of each other's personalities, strengths and weaknesses in a way that otherwise took a lifetime during peace. War was an alien ground of kill or be killed, and the men you fought with were as necessary to living as breathing. You had to know the mettle of the man whose back you covered, who covered your back.

"Please tell me Mica's still up," Dash said wearily as he rubbed his hand over his face. "Cassie's edging into hysteria seeing only you. She's terrified to come out of the Hummer."

Mike stiffened imperceptibly. The implications of the reasons for such terror washed through his gray eyes. His jaw tightened, teeth gritting for a long second as Dash watched him fight his anger.

Mike finally glanced at the darkened windows of the Hummer. "Hang on. I'll get her."

Moments later, Mike's wife, Serena, a tall willowy blonde, and his petite blond-haired daughter stepped out. Mica wrapped her arms around her daddy's waist and leaned against him as she smiled back over at Dash.

"You remember Dash, don't you, Mica?" Mike asked his daughter softly. "The little girl he brought to visit is scared to get out of the Hummer. Why don't you go with Mommy and introduce yourself? Make her feel more at home."

Dash watched as the family came down the landing. Mike separated from them and returned to where Dash stood, watching quietly as the Hummer's door slowly opened. Soft female voices murmured through the garage. Dash had met the little girl and Mike's wife several times over the years during brief furloughs stateside. Both were kind and soft-spoken, and just what Cassie and Elizabeth needed right now, he thought.

"How bad is it, Dash?" Mike asked him then, referring, Dash knew, to Cassie's mental state.

Dash sighed deeply. "She's held up well until now. Men frighten her, though she came to me easily enough. Big men especially, from what I gather. I haven't had time yet to talk to Elizabeth in depth about what happened. I was hoping to do that while we're here."

Now Dash wondered if he would be able to contain his own rage if his fears held out. Had Grange touched Cassie before locking her in that bedroom and giving Elizabeth the chance to rescue her? If he had, Dash swore silently that he would make certain the man suffered a hell few would know before he died.

Mike breathed out deeply, his body tense with a need for revenge. Mike was a damned good father, and his wife and child were his life. He knew Mike would understand the rage threatening to engulf him.

Mike was almost as tall as Dash himself, with short, light brown hair and gray eyes. He was less broad than Dash, not as strong in some areas, but definitely a man who could carry himself, and others, in battle. He was a hell of a fighter, and more than trustworthy. But the bottom line was, Mike was a decent man and he would kill for a stranger's child. For a friend's, he would inflict a damage few enemies would ever want to face. In that, he was a lot like Dash. Loyalty and the bonds that came with it weren't easily severed.

"I appreciate you taking us in," Dash said quietly as Elizabeth and Cassie finally moved slowly from the Hummer. "Cassie and Elizabeth desperately need this chance to rest. I hope we aren't inconveniencing you."

"Not at all." Mike shook his head as he watched the movement on the other side of the vehicle. "You'll be safe here until we can figure out exactly what's going on and how to deal with it. But from what I've learned so far, there's a whole lot of pieces missing, Dash. Nothing's adding up here."

Dash was aware of that.

"Come on, let's go inside," Mike said as they moved cautiously toward the women.

Cassie had a stranglehold on Elizabeth's hand, but she seemed to be acting more naturally now that Mica stood talking to her. Mike's daughter had just turned ten. She was a sweet-natured girl whose lively gray eyes sparkled with happiness.

"Hey, Dad. Cassie's heard about the cat people too," Mica suddenly piped up. "They had another interview on the news tonight," she told Dash. The little girl followed the stories of the Breeds almost religiously. "I think they are so cool. And Tanner is really good-looking."

"He's a Bengal Breed." Cassie looked up at Mike, then Dash. "He's only twenty-five but he's becoming known as one of their greatest spokesmen. I bet he's really nice . . ." She trailed off faintly.

"Tanner's quite nice, actually." Mike smiled down at the little girl. "I met him this past summer with Kane Tyler. Both men are very good spokesmen."

Cassie looked impressed now, staring up at Mike thoughtfully.

"Kane Tyler doesn't like speaking in public much," Cassie said, frowning as she watched Mike, gauging his response. "He acts like Dash. Tanner is sneakier about what he says. So he's better."

Four adults stared down at Cassie in surprise. Mike chuckled. "She's about right there." He slapped Dash on the shoulder. "I wonder how much Kane will like knowing an eight-year-old has him pegged so easily?"

Cassie moved closer to her mother, gripping her hips tightly as she stared up at Mike with a suddenly fierce expression. "Just 'cause I'm short doesn't mean I'm a baby."

"Cassie." Elizabeth's voice firmed as she glanced down at her daughter. "Mr. Toler is our host. And I'm sure he doesn't think you're a baby."

Elizabeth didn't make excuses for Cassie's behavior. None was needed. But she was gently letting Cassie know she was stepping beyond her bounds.

"I thought you seemed awful old for your age," Mike teased her then. "Come on, ladies, I'm older than eight and I need a comfortable chair for visiting. Serena, don't you and Mica have homemade cookies cooling?"

Serena moved to her husband, her arm wrapping around his waist as she reached up and kissed his cheek softly. "We do indeed," she said with a smile before turning back to Elizabeth and Cassie. "Come on in and we'll get you settled in and get some cookies. Cassie, do you like gingerbread?"

Serena ushered Cassie and Elizabeth into the house as Dash and Mike trailed behind. Dash couldn't help but admire Serena and how easily she helped Cassie and Elizabeth feel comfortable.

"Thanks, buddy," Dash breathed as they entered the house. "It's been a long haul for them."

"I can understand that." Mike shook his head slowly. "Damn, Dash, I've had nightmares since you called, thinking about those two and what could have happened before you caught up with them. I don't know how they survived."

Dash knew he hadn't slept much himself before finding Cassie and Elizabeth. And he was starting to feel it.

Dash grunted. "They don't come close to my nightmares."

"Come on into the study and we'll talk." Mike nodded down a long hallway off the garage entryway. "I've been getting some reports together for you."

Dash nodded. "Let me talk to Elizabeth first and I'll be right there."

He stepped into the living room. Cassie was sitting on her knees in front of the television by Mica, absorbed in the news report and interviews of the feline Breeds. Elizabeth stood by the kitchen doorway, watching as Serena made coffee.

"Elizabeth." He said her name softly, gaining her attention.

She turned to him, her long hair swaying at her waist, her eyes dark and haunted. God, he hated that look, hated knowing that even now her fears assailed her. In one hand she gripped his service revolver, though she was careful to keep it behind her back so the girls couldn't see it.

She moved to him slowly, her deep blue eyes watching him carefully. She hadn't relaxed her guard, hadn't given in to her need to just rest since he had found her other than the few hours she had slept in the motel. She was still running on nerves and fear and it was making him crazy. She needed her rest. Something inside him insisted that she was too weak, too frail, for the hungers rising inside him.

"I need to talk to Mike for a bit, but I'll be just down the hall." He drew her back to the entryway, glancing at the revolver. "You want to keep it or you want me to hold it for you?"

She glanced back at Cassie, then at the revolver. Dash watched as she licked her lips nervously before extending the weapon to him. When she raised her eyes, he wanted to howl in misery at the fear and insecurity he saw there.

"Elizabeth," he whispered gently as he took the weapon with one hand, lifting the other to her cheek to touch her pale skin. Soft skin. Skin he wanted to spend the rest of his days learning the feel of. "I promise you. No one can track us here. No one will find us."

She swallowed as she nodded faintly. But the shadows in her eyes didn't lessen.

Dash reached out beside him and extinguished the light in the entryway, dimming the area as she stared at him in shock.

"I want to kiss you," he whispered as he backed her against the wall, pleased by the sudden flare of interest in her eyes.

Oh yes, he thought, she remembered how hot that last kiss had been, how good it felt. It made her eyes glitter with something other than fear.

"Do you know how soft your lips are?" He was careful to keep his voice from rumbling as he lowered his head to her. "How warm and sweet you tasted?"

Before she could answer he allowed his tongue to lick over her lips softly. Dash heard her breath catch, watched warm color flush her cheeks. He was hard and hurting, his cock throbbing imperatively as he fought to keep the caress light. If he kissed her as he wanted to, he feared he would never stop.

"Dash." Her hands lifted to his chest as though to push him away. Her fingers curled against his shirt as her breasts began to rise and fall with her increased breathing.

"I could eat you up, Elizabeth," he told her, allowing a small measure of his hunger to reflect in his voice. "While I was in that damned drug-induced coma, my only link to the world was Cassie's letters. And she talked about you. How pretty you were. How kind and good. Slowly, you ceased to be Cassie's mother, though. I didn't see a maternal figure, I saw a woman. A woman I needed to hold. To touch. I want to touch you real bad, Elizabeth. So bad my hands almost shake with it."

He was taking a chance. It could be too soon to let her see just how hungry he was for her. But damn if he wasn't tired of waiting, tired of needing. He wanted her to think about it. To think about him. To know it was coming.

"No." She shook her head, her eyes flaring with a sense of female panic as he put his claim into words.

"Yes, Elizabeth." Dash kept his voice low, but let it rumble with his arousal. "I lived for you and Cassie. But while I fought to live I dreamed, and it was this I dreamed of."

His lips covered hers swiftly, his tongue taking advantage of her gasp and sweeping in commandingly. He had asked for the caress earlier that morning; now he demanded. He conquered, he licked and stroked her tongue and gloried in her instant, if hesitant, response.

She was shy. Wary. She wouldn't give in to the heat pulsing be-

tween them easily. But she was curious enough about it to allow the
kiss. She leaned into him slightly, her body tense. She was determined
to try to control it, to explain it before she would give in to it. For
Dash, it was enough that he could feel the hunger inside her for now.
The time would come later to explore it more fully.

He allowed his lips to sip from her, his tongue to stroke hers, allowing the heat to build slowly. One hand gripped her hip as he held
her to him, his chest cushioning her full breasts as they rose and fell
harshly. Her shy tongue tangled with his as her hands splayed flat
against the tight muscles of his abdomen.

He was rapidly losing his mind in her kiss. The building sensations were sweeping through him, buzzing through his mind, his
senses exploding with greedy lust until he heard Cassie. Her voice
rose as she asked Serena where her mother was.

Pulling away from her was one of the hardest things he had ever
done in his life. But he did, reluctantly, forcing his eyes open, staring
into the shocked depths of hers. Her breasts rose and fell swiftly, her
nipples hard little points beneath the cloth of her blouse. Her hands
gripped his shirt, her delicate nails piercing against his skin, as
though it were a lifeline, as she fought for breath.

His hand framed her cheek, his thumb running over the slightly
swollen curve of her lips. They were reddened, fuller now from his
caress. Her eyelids looked heavy, her cheeks flushed, and he could
smell the essence of her need beginning to build. The slick juices
would be preparing her, heating her sweet pussy, preparing the way
for him. His cock throbbed heavily at that thought.

"Think about that, Elizabeth," he growled. "And then ask yourself
if you taste passion there, or betrayal."

Before she could speak, Dash turned and stalked down the short
hallway beside them, leaving Elizabeth staring in shock, in reluctant
hunger. And, he hoped, some small measure of trust.

◆ ◆ ◆

Elizabeth watched Dash walk away. She kept her back pressed to the wall, stilled an instinctive need to call him back to her and watched his powerful body move into another room. Her hand rose slowly to her lips. They tingled, bursting with heat from the touch of his, her mouth filled with the taste of him.

She couldn't seem to shake the mood the kiss had put her in. She returned to the kitchen, talked to Serena Toler, watched the kids play, and all the while she remembered Dash's kiss. His touch.

She thought about the way he had come out of the shower, pinning her to the bathroom door. His cock had been fiery, rock hard, pressing between her legs insistently as he stared down at her, eyes glittering with hunger. Lust was too tame a word for what she saw in his gaze.

Finally, Serena showed her and Cassie to their room. Dash had already brought in their clothes and placed them in the large bedroom. The queen-sized bed was turned down invitingly; the Victorian flowered quilt and matching sheets brought a pain of longing to her chest.

For one brief second she was at home again. The home her parents had left her. The small two-story brick house she had lovingly decorated after her divorce from Dane, filled with sunshine and Cassie's laughter, and a sense of roots. And Victorian flowered sheets and quilts on the bed. Pillows plumped. A little girl's frilly bedroom with the canopied bed and white oak furniture.

Her home. And it was gone now.

Forever.

Taking a hard, shuddering breath, she opened and closed her eyes. The guest room had heavy, dark furniture, comfortable and elegant with a thick forest-green carpeting as in the rest of the house. There was a small French door leading to the wraparound balcony. A Queen Anne chair sat beside it.

"Come on, Cassie." Elizabeth moved to the large tote Dash had brought in from the Hummer. "Let's get ready for bed."

She gathered the little girl's gown and robe and knocked softly on the bathroom door that connected her room to Dash's. When there was no answer she opened the door and entered it.

Getting Cassie ready for bed wasn't hard. The little girl was exhausted. She curled under the warm quilts of the bed half an hour later and settled right into sleep. Within minutes she had made one of the soft, mewling little sounds that always brought a smile to Elizabeth's face. She shook her head at the sound.

This new situation was so out of sync with the past two years that Elizabeth couldn't settle down. The awareness of danger that had surrounded her for so long was no longer present. She sensed the change on every level of her being. As though with Dash's arrival, there was now hope. How, she didn't know. But she felt the sense of hope building around her even as she instinctively doubted it. How could anything change so quickly just from the presence of one man?

But why not? He had changed something in her as well. In the space of twenty-four hours he had made her realize she was more than just Cassie's mother. She was a woman too. And it had been a long time, a very long time, since she had felt that surge of feminine need and the thick, juicy arousal pooling between her thighs. Her pussy ached. It had never ached like this, even during Dane's courtship. She hadn't been on fire from a single kiss. She hadn't wanted him so quickly or so heatedly as she suddenly realized she wanted Dash Sinclair.

CHAPTER 10

Elizabeth watched Cassie the next afternoon with the Tolers' little girl, Mica, as they played in the backyard. They were throwing snow-balls and romping through the snow, laughter echoing into the brightly lit kitchen where she sat with a cup of coffee.

Dash and Mike had left earlier for the study after explaining to Elizabeth that they were looking into safe houses for her and Cassie, as well as information on Grange. There had been an air of secretive-ness between the two men, as though they were delving more deeply into both assignments than they were telling her. But it didn't matter what questions she asked, she had learned no more than that.

Not that the two men hadn't answered all her questions. They had. It was just a feeling, a sense, that there was more.

She watched now as Cassie and Mica rolled in the snow, laughter and mock screams exchanged with the ferocity of little animals. Cassie had her teeth locked in Mica's jacket as the other little girl laughed uncontrollably.

"Mica is so happy to have another little girl to play with. I'm glad you were able to make it so soon." Serena Toler sat down across from her, a steaming cup of coffee in her hand, careful not to block Elizabeth's view of the girls.

"Thank you for allowing us to stay," Elizabeth said softly. "Cassie needed the time to rest. I just hope we don't cause you any problems." She was terrified she would bring Grange's wrath down on the family.

Serena snorted. "Mike and Dash should be so lucky as to have that bastard try to attack here. Trust me, Elizabeth; this house is better secured than Fort Knox. Mike doesn't take chances and he's seen worse than Grange."

Elizabeth couldn't imagine anyone worse than Grange.

As they sat there watching the children play, Elizabeth smothered her yawn, realizing this was the first time in as long as she could remember that she wasn't running or preparing to run. She had slept several hours the night before, but out of habit she was awake often, checking the locks on the bedroom doors, listening closely to the sounds of the house.

"Go lie on the couch and rest," Serena suggested softly. "I'll sit here and watch the girls, and Mike has several men from his old unit working the ranch. They're on babysitting detail outside. You need to rest."

Elizabeth had been introduced to the three men. They were a bit older than Dash, but just as hard and capable looking. And if there was one thing she had learned, it was to rest when she could.

"Thank you." She carried her cup to the sink, rinsed it and set it in the basin before heading into the large, open living room.

She could still hear the children playing, though the sound was muted. She knew they wouldn't be able to stay out much longer and felt confident enough to lie down and close her eyes for a brief time.

She realized as she drifted off to sleep that never, in the past two years, would she have trusted anyone else, anywhere else, to watch

Cassie while she slept. She was too vulnerable if her mother wasn't awake and aware. But somehow, Dash had instilled a trust in her that had sneaked up on her in the past twenty-four hours.

He had killed to protect her and Cassie. He had followed them in a blizzard, risked his own life to bring them to a place where they could heal, where they could rest, at least for a time. She no longer suspected him of betrayal, and perhaps that surprised her more than anything.

As exhaustion wrapped around her, though, it wasn't trust or betrayal that fed the rich visions within her mind. It was Dash. Naked, fresh from the shower, his body pressed hard against her, her hand overfilled with the hard length of his cock. She didn't think she had ever known heat as intense as she had when he brought her hand down and wrapped it around the rigid flesh. His eyes had flared. A betraying warmth and wet heat had assailed her pussy, making her throb, ache. She was still aching.

His kiss—she shifted restlessly—his kiss was like rough velvet and summer lightning. His taste was dark, heady. She could well imagine him laying her on a bed, his body covering hers, pressing her into the mattress, heavy and demanding as he placed himself between her thighs.

She almost moaned at the image, needing him with her now. Needing him to cover her, take her, finish out his threat to fuck her so hard and deep she couldn't still her cries. She had never been taken like that. Dane hadn't exactly been a passionate lover. And his kisses had never made her burn. Right now, Elizabeth was burning.

◆   ◆   ◆

Dash stepped into the living room, then came to a complete abrupt stop. His eyes swung to where Elizabeth lay, apparently sleeping, her body shifting restlessly on the couch. What was she dreaming? He could smell her arousal, hot and sweet, wrapping around him, tempting every primitive instinct rising in his body. His cock came to full, surging attention beneath his jeans; his flesh suddenly felt overly sensitive, as though he could feel the very air whispering around him.

He heard Serena puttering in the kitchen getting lunch together. The kids' voices echoed from the heated garage where they now played. Mike was still in the study, waiting on the call from Kane Tyler with word on the request Dash had made. He hoped Kane wasn't foolish enough to refuse him. A trip to Virginia via more conventional mode wouldn't sit well with Dash.

All that faded, though. The hot surge of arousal and need that swept over his body in that moment was so intense, so demanding, it had him automatically stopping to still the response. Never had a woman made him this damned hungry. So hungry he wanted nothing more than to throw her to her knees and mount her like the animal that resided inside him. If he didn't take her soon, he was going to go mad.

He stalked slowly into the living room, head lowered, his eyes going over her slender body, her full breasts pressing against the soft cotton of her blouse. A button had come undone, displaying a small amount of cleavage. She was still decently dressed, but the soft upper mounds of her breasts made his mouth water.

She would be wearing one of the silk and lace bras he had bought her, he thought. The ones with the little front clip, easy to release and peel away. Her breasts were full; her nipples were hard, so damned hard and tight beneath her shirt that his tongue ached to curl around them.

He knelt to the floor beside her, his hand lifting, his fingers smoothing a stray strand of silken hair from her cheek. Her whispered sigh was almost a moan, her pouty lips parting as though for his kiss.

She needed her sleep, he told himself as he stared down at her. She didn't need him awakening her, molesting her in her sleep. Too many choices had been taken away from her; he didn't want to take that from her too.

He was aware of Serena slipping on a coat in the kitchen, the whisper of the sliding doors as she left the house. Privacy. For what? For the hunger to rage inside him until he devoured her? He didn't think so. Didn't think she was ready for that step just yet.

Her eyes opened then. They were drowsy, slumberous, staring up at him with a hunger that was impossible to miss.

"I felt you," she whispered, a smile tilting her moist lips. "Watching me. Should I feel you watching me?"

Was she asleep or awake?

"Of course." He found the growl building in his throat. "Every time I look at you, baby, I touch you."

Her cheeks flushed as her hand reached up to graze his face. Cool, silken fingertips brushed over his flesh before they touched his lips. They traced the curves, her eyes darkening with need, the scent of her arousal wrapping around him until he wanted to drown in it. Drown in her.

His lips opened, drawing one of the slender tips into his mouth, caressing it with his tongue as he wanted to caress one of the hard little nipples poking against her shirt. His hand settled just under one of the swollen curves, plumping it up as a spark of surprise lit her eyes.

"When I get you beneath me, I'm going to devour you," he told her harshly as her finger slid from his mouth. "Every inch of your body, Elizabeth, I'll make burn for me."

She was breathing roughly now, her breasts rising and falling with her quick breaths.

"I already burn," she admitted with a natural sensuality.

"I'll make you burn brighter," he promised as his lips lowered, but rather than moving to her lips, he allowed his own to whisper over the soft curve of her breast revealed by the slipped button.

Her breath caught. He could smell her wet heat building, knew her cunt was pulsing, spilling the soft liquid of her arousal. And he wanted to taste it. Wanted to bury his tongue so deep between her thighs that he would always be a part of her.

"Dash." Her sigh was thick with pleasure as his thumb reached up and rasped over her hard little nipple.

It was killing him to touch her like this. To maintain a façade of decency when all he wanted to do was strip her and pound so hard and fast inside her gripping cunt that denying the need was agony.

"I have to stop this," he groaned, allowing his tongue to rake over her fragrant flesh. "Now, Elizabeth, or I'll embarrass both of us."

He would do worse than that. He would be fucking her on his host's couch within minutes if he didn't get the hell away from her. Mike was a pretty understanding guy, but Dash didn't think he would appreciate coming in from the study to find his guests fucking their way to oblivion on his couch.

He raised his head, seeing the hard flush of desire on her cheeks, her knowledge of where they were and who could walk in at any moment. She cleared her throat and swallowed tightly as he settled back and watched her. She pushed herself up until she was sitting on the couch, her trembling fingers fumbling with the button of her shirt.

"Let me." He brushed her hands aside and committed the ultimate sin. He buttoned her shirt, once again covering the perfection of the delicate curves.

"Dash." He could hear it in her voice. Knew what was coming. A carefully constructed excuse. A denial of what he knew would happen.

"Don't." He laid his finger against her lips. "It's going to happen, Elizabeth. You know it and I know it. Don't make excuses and don't try to deny it. When the time is right, when I have the privacy and the time to make you burn so hot you're screaming, it's going to happen. Don't think it won't."

Her eyes widened. Her little pink tongue peeked out to moisten her rose-tinted lips. The low moan that rumbled from his throat had her cheeks flushing further.

"Hey, Dash." Mike forestalled anything she would have said as he walked in from the hallway.

He paused, staring back at them. His expression suddenly reflected a wry apology. "Sorry. I was going to get lunch as soon as I could drag Serena back into the house. Hungry?"

Oh, he was hungry all right, Dash thought. He glanced at Elizabeth, seeing her chagrin.

"Lunch?" he asked softly.

She cleared her throat. "Lunch."

The tension slowly building between them didn't ease. Dash stayed locked in the study with Mike for the better part of the day, but he came out often. And when he did, he came searching for Elizabeth.

He gave her soft touches. A hand on her shoulder, at her waist, as he eased her against him. He smiled down at her, stealing cookies when she and Serena weren't looking, his eyes glittering with heat. He wouldn't wait much longer. Elizabeth could feel it in his tense body, see it in the way he looked at her. He had claimed her before he ever met her, and soon he would make good on that claim.

Finally, that evening, she found a few minutes to pin him down on the progress being made. Sitting around the house and waiting was wearing on her nerves. She could only rest so much. Serena was a perfect hostess, the kids got along well and Elizabeth found herself filled with so much nervous energy now that it was hard to control it. She was used to running and worrying. She wasn't used to a place of safety or any amount of time on her hands that wasn't filled with the fight for survival.

After dinner, Mike and Serena took the girls to the living room, leaving her and Dash in the kitchen to talk. Dash watched her closely as they left, his eyes somber, reflective, though arousal lurked hot and impatiently in the very depths of his gaze.

"What have you found out?" she asked him after the children were resting in front of the large television in the Tolers' family room.

Elizabeth watched Cassie for long moments, seeing a shadow of the once-playful little girl she had been. Her heart clenched. Cassie had lost so much.

When Dash didn't speak, she turned back to him, seeing his narrowed gaze on the little girl.

He turned back to her, his golden eyes pensive.

"Only more questions," he said quietly. "Grange has a lot of money on her head, Elizabeth. More than reasonable, given the situation."

Elizabeth snorted. "She saw him kill her father, Dash. She could have him locked away for a long time."

Dash shook his head.

"Look at this logically, Elizabeth." He leaned forward as she felt nerves replace the quiet calm that had been settling inside her. "Your husband was in deep with Grange. So he sells Cassie to him. I can see Grange wanting to get rid of the bastard, I really can, but"—he paused as he watched her closely—"why kill him in front of Cassie? To scare her? I don't think so. He has enough sense to see how much easier it would be to achieve his ends if he takes her away and then kills her father. None of this adds up."

Elizabeth licked her lips nervously. There was no other explanation. It had to add up.

"Maybe he just didn't care," she hissed. "He's killed and killed, Dash, and not cared."

He shook his head again. Elizabeth clenched her fingers on the coffee cup as he began tearing down the only reasons she could find for the hell she and Cassie had been through.

"He's killed secretively," he told her softly. "Everyone but Dane Colder. They were obvious murders but there was no way to tie him to them, or to you and Cassie. He's been trying to throw a very carefully constructed shield around the two of you. Running you ragged when he could have caught you several times."

Elizabeth breathed in roughly. "We were lucky." At least, that was what she had been trying to tell herself.

"You were." He was watching her intently. "Too lucky, Elizabeth. Things aren't adding up here. Until I can find a way to make them add up, then I keep working. If I have to, I go hunting. But I would like to get the information I need before I take that route. What exactly does Cassie remember about that night?"

The threat of an intended hunt hung between them at the final question. The one Elizabeth had been dreading.

"She wasn't making sense when I got her out of that room. She was almost hyperventilating she was so terrified, trying so hard not to make a sound. I couldn't make sense of anything she was saying once we got to the car. I couldn't understand a word of it." She fought to hold back the pain, the horror of that night. "She was completely silent for hours after that and then tried to act as though nothing had happened. I dressed her, took her straight to the police, and while we were there, two of his goons slipped in. Right before they got to the office we were in, Cassie started going crazy on me. She was adamant they were coming. I was so terrified I rushed her from the room. His men were coming down the hall as we left the office. We barely got away."

Dash frowned. "How did Cassie know?"

A bitter smile twisted her lips. "Her fairy," she sighed roughly. "Whatever the hell the 'fairy' is, it's saved us more than once."

Dash pushed his fingers through his hair wearily, causing the soft strands to feather around his face. He was worried. Elizabeth could see the frustration building inside him. Just as it had built inside her over the past two years.

They went over and over her memories of that night. Dash questioned her until she was ready to explode, until her nerves were strung tight and fear twisted her gut. It didn't make sense. It never had. Facing that wasn't easy.

Finally, he returned to the study with Mike to make more calls, to search for more answers. Elizabeth watched him leave, then turned, searching for Cassie. She frowned, seeing the pinched, almost fearful expression in her daughter's face as she watched the two men leave the room.

Finally, the little girl's head lowered and she stared down at her hands as though they were someone else's before turning back to the television. Elizabeth frowned as a sudden fear struck her. Was there more to it? Something more that Cassie was aware of and hadn't told her?

Elizabeth raked her fingers through her hair at that thought. She had questioned Cassie relentlessly those first months, fighting for answers. "I don't know, Momma. I don't know," was her standard response to most of them.

She remembered her father stripping her clothes from her body and pushing her to Grange as the other man picked her up.

"If you can keep her mother off your back," Dane had challenged him. "A bit more time and I'll have custody."

"Who needs custody? No one will find her where she's going," Grange had responded before killing Dane in front of his daughter.

There was nothing else Cassie could tell her. Grange had come for her, and Dane had wanted to wait until he could hand her over without problems. Grange had been unwilling to wait.

Later that night, after bathing Cassie and tucking her into bed, Elizabeth stood and watched the sleeping little girl. Dash's questions had bothered her, made her look harder into the past two years now that she had a chance to take a breath and think. She didn't like the confusion filling her mind or the sudden need to question Cassie further. The only person here who had the answers they needed was Cassie, and she feared the day was rapidly approaching when she would have to be questioned.

She lowered her head, shaking it slowly, needing Dash. Needing just a few more minutes to cherish the calm they had found in the middle of this horrifying nightmare. He was like an oasis of calm, of strength that she suddenly found herself craving.

All too soon she knew their time of quiet and safety would end and they would once again be thrown into the harsh reality of their situation. But for now, she could be a woman. A woman suddenly faced with the first man who had ever made her burn, made her long to cast aside common sense and lie beneath him, whimpering in pleasure.

"Hey." He was there. His voice whispered from the connecting door as she stood at the end of the bed, staring at her daughter yet seeing only the changes within herself.

Elizabeth turned to him slowly.

God, he looked good. Tall and broad, his muscular body backlit by the bathroom light. Jeans hugged his lean hips, denim cupping the full bulge between his thighs. She wanted to cup it, she realized insanely, feel his thick cock, not against her abdomen, but burrowing deep and hard inside the tight muscles of her cunt. Her breasts swelled beneath her nightgown. Her nipples peaked and her pussy began to moisten further. Just as guilt threaded its way through her soul.

Her daughter's life was in danger and the moment she found a chance to rest, she was thinking of fucking instead, of riding him, straddling his hard body, feeling him surge inside her.

Elizabeth cleared her throat. "She finally went to sleep." She gestured to Cassie. "I was just watching her."

Liar, a voice inside her screamed. His expression hinted that he suspected the falsehood as well. The sensuous heated light in his eyes made her pussy burn, her breasts swell with longing.

"Come talk to me a minute while she's asleep." His gaze was hooded, demanding.

Elizabeth stared at him uncomprehendingly for a long moment. Talk to him? Alone? She stilled the weakness in her knees at the thought of it. She didn't want to talk. Not yet.

"I'm tired . . ."

"Elizabeth." His voice was faintly chiding now. "Do you think I'm going to hurt you? Even now?"

She shook her head. No. She knew he wasn't going to hurt her. At least, not deliberately. It wasn't the pain she feared now, it was the closeness developing between them. It had become a bond she didn't understand and one she feared she would never escape.

"Come on." He held his hand out to her. "We'll hear Cassie if she wakes up."

She took a deep, steady breath. She had known the time would come when they would have to talk. Had known there would be so many things to decide. But why did she regret it? Why did she suddenly wish the world would just go away and leave her and Dash alone, surrounded by darkness, flaming with heat? But it wouldn't. And now was the time to deal with it.

✦ CHAPTER 12 ✦

Elizabeth followed him into his bedroom, suddenly nervous, too aware of Dash as a man and too aware of the needs flaming to life in her body. It had been so long since she had felt any need to be touched, any interest in a man. But the year Cassie had written to Dash, Elizabeth had been interested, as greedy for the letters as her daughter had been. The loss of that fragile connection had been missed not just by Cassie, but by her mother as well.

She knew when he drew her into the bedroom what was coming. Knew when he closed his door and went to the intercom installed between the two rooms what he intended. He turned on the receiver only. Elizabeth licked her lips nervously.

"This might be a bad idea," she whispered as he turned back to her.

She could easily read the intent in his gaze, the sexual hunger radiating in his large body. If a man could devour a woman with his eyes alone, then Elizabeth considered herself devoured.

"Might be." He walked to her purposely, never taking his eyes off her as her breathing began to increase.

"Dash, it might be a very bad idea." She was breathing roughly as she glanced down, seeing how the denim hugged a more-than-impressive bulge.

He was aroused and ready, a man who had put aside his need for as long as he could, and Elizabeth feared she would never find the strength to deny him once he touched her.

Her gaze flew back to his face as he stopped in front of her. His lips were tilted in a wry little smile.

"I only had to look at you and you knew I needed to touch you," he whispered darkly. "I came in to say good night, Elizabeth, that was all. I looked at you and I saw the need to touch. Nothing more, baby. A few kisses, a little petting. Because that's all you need right now. All you can handle, I think."

She drew in a hard breath, bitterness filling her, then smiled mockingly. "I don't need your pity, Dash."

She couldn't handle that from him. She had fought the need to feel sorry for herself and to sink into the pits of her own self-sorrow for too many years. She wouldn't let him drag her into it now. She didn't want his sympathy. She turned and headed for the door, only to have him grip her arm, pulling her against his hard body as he stared down at her with dark eyes.

"Was that pity you held in your hand the other morning, Elizabeth?" he asked her softly as she flushed in embarrassment. "If I'm not mistaken, it was my cock. Full and hard and ready to fuck the hell out of you. That's not pity, baby. And neither is this."

His lips didn't ask for anything. His tongue didn't seek permission. He covered her lips, plunged his tongue into her mouth and took without asking. It couldn't be called a kiss. It was a devouring, a feast of the senses, and Elizabeth was helpless against it. He bent her over his arm, arching her hips against his as he lifted her to her toes, pressing his thick, jeans-covered erection into the vee of her thighs as he gave her a taste of the hunger to come with his kiss.

She couldn't breathe. She didn't want to breathe. Her hands gripped his shoulders as small mewling sounds of hunger rose in her chest. Elizabeth could feel her body catching fire, her nipples, her clit, her vagina throbbing, aching for his touch, for the sensual devouring he was practicing on her lips.

His tongue plunged in and out of her mouth, mimicking a much more sexual act as his hands moved over her back, her hips. They were never still. Stroking her, caressing her body until one moved purposely up her side, cupping the swollen mound of her breast.

Elizabeth jerked at the sensation of his fingers suddenly gripping her nipple, milking it, rasping over it. Electric darts of almost agonizing pleasure ripped through her stomach and shot to her womb with a punch of sensation.

She cried out into his kiss, her hands clawing his shoulders, adrift now in a pleasure that threatened to consume her. In her sexual lifetime she had never known anything like it. Had never tasted such a dark kiss, one that warned her he had no intention of making allowances for sensual inexperience. He was hungry. Needy. And she was the meal he craved.

She had never felt her cunt clench, spasm, with such desperate need. All thoughts of danger receded. The situation, so fraught with desperation until Dash arrived, was swept from her mind. There was only Dash. Only his arms holding her, his fingers tugging at her nipple, his tongue sweeping through her mouth like a sexual marauder intent on conquest.

Elizabeth moaned into the kiss, her tongue twining with his, helpless against the sweeping sensations working through her body. She was only barely aware of him bending, lifting her into his arms and moving her to the bed. He didn't release her mouth. And every now and then she swore he growled against her lips. The sound was hot, blistering with hunger, and sent juices flooding her pussy.

She was going up in flames. She swore she was going to climax from his kiss alone.

As he laid her back on the bed, he released her slowly, his lips sipping from hers hesitantly as he finally broke the connection. Elizabeth lifted her eyelids drowsily, staring up at him, her breath catching as she saw him quickly unbutton his shirt, then strip it from his broad shoulders. His hands were strong and wide, lightly callused and so warm. Elizabeth realized she was almost shaking now with the need to have him caress her, to peel the robe and gown from her body. She wanted him to touch her, stroke her with those demanding hands.

And he did. As he stared down at her, his hands went to the belt of her robe. His lips covered hers again, his tongue pushing into her mouth as she moaned in hunger. He made her hungry. Hungry for every kiss, every touch.

Elizabeth arched beneath him as she felt the robe part, felt his fingers at the tiny buttons that ran down the front of her gown.

"Good God," he groaned as he spread the edges of her gown apart, staring down at the full, hard thrust of her breasts and their tight nipples.

Elizabeth flushed heatedly as he stared down at her. She watched his face, seeing the heavy sensuality that shaped his lips, made his eyes appear drowsy, his expression filled with lust and emotion.

"Dash." She whispered his name beseechingly, her nipples aching for the moist warmth of his mouth.

"If I touch one of those hard little nipples I'll never hold on to my control," he sighed, watching her breasts as they rose and fell roughly. "Do you understand that, Elizabeth? I won't stop."

She licked her dry lips, staring into the piercing depths of his eyes when his gaze returned to her.

"Then don't stop."

Dash felt flames sear his loins at her words. Quickly he turned, sat on the edge of the bed and began to remove his boots. If he didn't undress before he touched her, then he'd have no more control than what it took to loosen his pants and pull his cock free before pushing it inside her.

Lust raged through him now, nearly out of control as he fought to get the boots off his feet. Behind him, Elizabeth shifted, coming to her knees, her fingers smoothing over his back before halting on his right shoulder.

"How cute." Elizabeth traced the little mark on the back of his shoulder. "Cassie has a mark just like that."

Dash stilled.

She was tracing the genetic marker that shadowed his skin just below the curve of his shoulder. A particular identifying mark impossible to miss if anyone knew what it was.

A paw print.

It was a standing joke among the scientists who had coded it. Like a small strawberry birthmark impossible to be rid of.

"It's the same shape too," her voice was a bit amused. "Don't let Cassie see it. She already claims Dane isn't her daddy and that she's certain her daddy has a mark just like hers."

The blood began to rush to his head, knowledge flooding his brain like a sudden icy drenching. Cassie had such a mark? There was only one way a child could carry a mark like his. Only one way that genetic marker could have been placed. If Dane was a Wolf Breed. But that couldn't be possible. Could it? A Breed in such a prominent position as the renowned surgeon had been? No. No Breed would ever allow his child to be harmed, let alone attempt to sell her. What the hell was going on?

He turned to face her.

"Are you sure?" He fought to clear his mind. "Absolutely certain?"

She was staring at him, her smile slowly faltering as she saw his expression. "Of course." She frowned in confusion. "I raised her, didn't I?"

Elizabeth didn't have the mark. Dash knew she didn't. Her shoulders were a soft creamy shade of perfection, without flaw.

"Did Dane have the mark?" he asked her slowly, somehow knowing that he didn't.

"No." Elizabeth shook her head. "No one in his family did. I teased Dane that the doctors must have gotten his sperm mixed up with someone else's . . ."

She was talking. He saw her lips moving, bitterness lining her face, but it seemed everything inside him had shut down. He was watching her speak, hearing her, his brain processing the information while he seemed to shrink inside himself in horror.

Artificial insemination. Elizabeth had been unable to conceive because of Dane's low sperm count. So they had contacted a friend of his, a fertility doctor. Marcus Martaine. He had performed the procedure secretively because of Dane's pride. Dane hadn't wanted anyone to know he couldn't father a child. So they had gone another route.

Dane still hadn't been happy, though. He had never cared for Cassie. Always saw her as his failure, Elizabeth said. Cassie was a girl but he had wanted a son. She wasn't conceived properly. Didn't look enough like him. Dane's list had gone on and on.

Cassie wasn't Dane's daughter, though. She was Elizabeth's. He could smell it. He would have known it if she wasn't. The differences in the scent would have been too vast if Elizabeth's egg hadn't been used. But Dane's sperm hadn't been.

"Dash?" She was watching him in concern now as he stared down at her, everything suddenly falling into place.

Dane had to have known Cassie wasn't his child. That she was a Breed child. He had to have known because he had tried to use her as a bargaining chip. The information of the marker wasn't public knowledge. It was a carefully kept secret for the time being. Dash had made it his business to study every piece of information being given on them. There was a specific marker in a specific location for each Breed. The Wolf Breeds carried theirs on their right shoulders.

"I have to see it."

Suddenly, he had to be certain. Had to make sure Elizabeth wasn't seeing a resemblance that was possibly not there.

"What?" She shook her head, bemused. "See what?"

"The mark, Elizabeth." He gripped her shoulders, stilling her as she moved to turn away. "Show me the damned mark."

"On Cassie?" She frowned, fear starting to shadow her eyes as she pulled her gown and robe closed. "Why? What does it mean? It's just a mark. We asked the doctor about it."

And of course, Martaine would have lied to the doting mother. It was an experiment. A secretly conducted experiment. One Martaine had obviously told no one about except the father. He would have needed Dane's help. Somehow, he had talked Dane into the dangerous experiment.

"Show it to me." He gripped her wrist, dragging her from the bed and into the other bedroom, stopping beside the sleeping child.

"Dash, stop, you'll wake her," she whispered.

He ignored her, gently lifting the small strap of Cassie's gown and baring her shoulder. It was there. A dark shadow just under the skin.

A genetic marking of the Wolf Breeds. Had she been raised in the labs, she would have been branded, or tattooed when she was older, depending on the lab in question, to hide the marker. But she hadn't been. She had been born to a loving mother and a bastard father.

Dash bent close, drawing in the scent of her skin and shaking with the knowledge his brain was finally accepting. It was faint, a bit darker than he remembered. The genetics were obviously recessed, much as his were, or he would have detected the scent of a Breed sooner. But it was there.

She was a Wolf Breed child.

But whose?

What had they done? Dash knew Martaine well. He remembered the doctor visiting the labs, checking results, deciding who lived and who died. Dash had been picked to die. He was the runt of the litter and still smaller, weaker than the other Breeds of that pack. Martaine had been young then, not even in his thirties. A cold, brutal bastard.

Dash was breathing harshly, perspiration dotting his forehead as he fought the rage building inside him. They weren't containing the experiments to the labs anymore? When had they brought the genetic mix into the general population?

He eased the strap back, glancing at Elizabeth's tight, furious expression as he stalked from the room.

"God damn them." He had no sooner cleared his bedroom than he turned, ramming his fist into the wall. Plaster cracked. A solid two-by-four split. Dash felt it as the sound echoed around him.

He was aware of Elizabeth jumping back as she entered the room, a small cry smothered behind her hand as she stood staring at him, her eyes wide. Dash leaned his head against the wall, rolling it on the cool plaster as he fought to think.

"Was she naked when you took her from Grange?" His voice was a hard, vicious growl.

"No." Her voice was faint. Thin. "She was wearing her panties. But her nightgown had been ripped off her. Dash, what's going on?"

Grange would have demanded proof. Dane would have given it to him. Files, of course. He had to have had files of the experiment in case they were needed. And the mark. A mark that could be validated.

"I should have known," he muttered. Hell, he thought, he had known but had just refused to admit to it. The idea of it had been too extreme, too far-fetched to consider. How the hell had it happened? Martaine must have lost his mind. "God damn. I should have known. No wonder he wanted her." A short, bitter laugh escaped him. "Hell, sure he wanted her. She was a fucking gold mine."

He pushed his fingers through his hair as he fought to beat down the fury pulsing through his body. Elizabeth and Cassie had been through hell. Hunted. A price on their heads. All because Dane Colder had allowed his wife to be impregnated by Breed sperm. How had they managed it? Why had Martaine not informed the Council that he had discovered the secret to breeding the species? He hadn't, Dash knew. The experiments into the breeding were well documented.

"Dash." Elizabeth's voice was filled with fear. "Dash, what's wrong with her?" He shook his head desperately. He couldn't tell her. Couldn't let her know. Her voice was faint. "What does that mark mean?"

He looked at her, seeing her white face, her terrified eyes. How he had wanted to protect her. God help him, protect himself. Thinking he could be something to her, build a future and still hide what he was. Still know only her sweet passion and woman's heart rather than her disgust.

"I have to talk to Mike."

He had to figure this out. Had to inform Kane Tyler of the changing situation. This would ensure Cassie's acceptance into the compound rather than only the consideration of it. Dash had understood the Pride's stand and had been praying for a positive response. He hadn't expected his prayers to be answered in quite this way.

"No. You have to talk to me." She gripped his arm, her voice echoing with anger, filled with demand. "You talk to me first, damn you. What does that fucking mark mean?"

"Not yet, Elizabeth. I have to talk to Mike." He couldn't tell her.

"Like hell you do." She shook his arm furiously, fear echoing in her voice. "You tell me what's going on first, damn you. That's my baby, Dash. Not Mike's. What the hell is going on?"

Dash closed his eyes, shaking his head roughly as he tore his arm from her grip. "Go to Cassie. Now," he snapped. "I have to talk to Mike first."

He stormed from the room, knowing the lateness of the hour, the fact that Mike was comfortably in bed with his loving wife, likely dreaming dreams of bliss. A short bitter grunt sounded from his chest. Must be fucking nice.

He found his friend's room and rapped on the door with hard knuckles. He heard a grunt, a curse, Serena's drowsy voice. Seconds later, Mike opened the door, his eyes blurry with sleep.

"What?" His eyes cleared when he saw Dash. Dash knew the fury raging inside him was clearly in evidence.

"She's a Breed." His voice was flat with pain.

"What?" Mike shook his head, clearly confused.

Dash couldn't blame him. He was having a hell of a time understanding himself.

"Cassie," he growled. "That's why Grange wants her. She's a Breed, Mike. A Wolf Breed. Just like me."

"No!" Elizabeth's shocked, disbelieving voice had him turning slowly.

She had followed him. Somehow, his mind consumed with rage and pain, he had been unaware of her behind him. He knew now. She was staring at him like the animal he was. Her eyes wide, disbelieving, as she watched him with heartbreaking horror, fighting to deny the truth of what she'd heard. The truth that the man she had nearly taken into her body, the man whose tongue had plunged into her mouth, was an animal. Bitter acceptance filled his mind as he watched her. She looked like she was going to be sick.

He growled, a low animalistic rumble that had Mike cursing and Elizabeth shaking in terror. He knew what his eyes looked like in the hall, the dim light overhead reflecting at just the right angle, turning them a demonic red without the sheltering protection of the contact lenses he wore when needed. An animal. An animal she had nearly fucked.

He could see it in her eyes as she backed away from him. Saw it in the glazed need to escape as she turned and ran for her room. And he was behind her. She would try to take Cassie and escape him now. Run from the animal. From the beast. Escape a truth she didn't want to accept. There wasn't a chance in hell he would let her get away from him.

He caught her at his bedroom door, his arm wrapping around her waist as she fought him, clawing at him as he dragged her against the wall, her fist nearly connecting with his jaw as she broke from his hold. Breathing hard, her eyes wild in her white face, she faced him.

✦ CHAPTER 13 ✦

Elizabeth knew she shouldn't have been so completely shocked. The past two years had been a series of betrayals and upheavals that she could have never imagined. But this. She didn't know if she could survive this.

"You're wrong." She pointed her finger at him, then lowered it as she realized how hard she was shaking. "It's not possible."

"You saw the mark, Elizabeth." His head was lowered. His eyes blazed back at her in fury, in determination.

This couldn't be happening. She wanted to slap herself, to tear herself out of this new, horrible nightmare suddenly exploding within her mind. She couldn't be awake. This couldn't be real. Her daughter wasn't created in a damned lab. She had been conceived within her womb, carried to full term and delivered in a hospital under the eyes of a caring obstetrician. Tests. Immunizations. Every care had been taken to make certain Cassie was healthy, free of defects. A perfect baby girl.

And now he was ripping what was left of her life apart. Telling her that Cassie was more than she had believed, that her baby now faced the danger of not just Grange, but a deranged Council that was even more powerful. If they found out. If they knew . . . The consequences slammed into her head, making her fight it instinctively. Not her child.

"It's a coincidence." Her hands pressed against her stomach as she swallowed deeply, fighting the bile rising in her throat. It couldn't be possible.

He laughed, a low, feral sound lacking in amusement. The sound ripped over her nerves, shredding them further. It was animalistic, dangerous. There was no amusement in his voice, only savage acceptance of what he was and what he faced. The man she had fallen in love with before she ever met him would be taken from her as well. Not just her baby, but Dash would be gone. How would she ever manage to hold either of them to her now?

"If there's one thing I know, Elizabeth," he informed her harshly, "it's about being a Breed and how to hide it. You can't hide the marker, though. Nothing can erase it. It's a genetic imprint created to keep just this from ever happening. To be certain that if conception occurred, then a Breed child could be identified. The Council was fanatical about not mixing the animals in the general population."

She swayed. God. This wasn't happening. *Please don't let it be happening*, she prayed. If she thought the past two years had been a nightmare, then this was hell and she was being plunged in headfirst. No chance to test the heat. No chance to accept the danger and the pain. No chance to plan a way out. She wouldn't accept it.

"My daughter is not an animal." She wanted to scream the words, needed to make certain he heard her, understood her. She didn't care what he thought he was, but her daughter wasn't an animal. And she sure as hell wasn't an experiment. "And neither is she a Breed. She's my baby." Her hands knotted at her abdomen. "I had her. I carried her. She looks like me."

Her baby. Elizabeth fought Dash. Fought the sudden, sickening realization that he could be right. She had always known how special her daughter was. So unique and so gifted in so many ways that she had convinced herself that it was only a mother's pride that made her see it.

"She's still your child, Elizabeth." He tried to step closer to her, then stopped as she retreated in panic. She couldn't let him touch her. If she did, she would break. Shatter into so many fragments she would never be able to find all the pieces again. "I smell your connection to her. It's unmistakable. But Dane Colder is not her father."

She was going to faint. Elizabeth could feel it and fought it. He could smell it? No. Motherhood wasn't a smell. Or was it? Cassie had come from her body. Her womb. She trembled violently. How could he smell it?

"He is." She shook her head desperately, suddenly remembering Dane's desperation to convince her to have a child that first year. "He was desperate for a child. We went to the doctor's office together. He did everything he was supposed to."

She was fighting to deny him, to deny what he was telling her. Fighting to try to find a way out of this sudden, horrifying situation. She stared at Dash, silently pleading, begging him to take it back, to show just a small moment of weakness, a doubt that he could be wrong. If he would, then she could find a way to convince herself that none of this could be true. Instead, he gave her proof.

"Martaine was a high-level Genetics Council scientist," he said with chilling knowledge. Of course, he knew, she thought. He was a Breed. He knew the monsters who worked within those labs. "He worked in the initial phases of breeding, trying to reverse the coding that kept the males from fertilizing their females." A low, painful whimper was her only protest. "When he failed to do what they wanted, he was quietly retired rather than killed, in case they needed him later," Dash continued. "He went into fertility practice and evidently his experiments continued. Somehow, he figured out how to use the unique Breed sperm to fertilize the ovum. Because I swear to you, Elizabeth, Cassie is a Wolf Breed child. That is why Grange won't let her go. That is why he killed her father. And that was why Dane refused to accept the child. Because he knew."

"No." She shook her head desperately. "He wouldn't have done that. He wouldn't have."

"He did, Elizabeth," he snarled, the sound ricocheting through her body like a bullet. "Listen to me, damn you, because Cassie's life is in more danger than you ever realized. She is the first. Do you hear me?" She flinched violently. "She is the first female Breed child conceived outside a lab. The first created, in vitro, without first altering the ovum to accept the unique DNA. Do you understand what I'm saying, Elizabeth? She's unique. A bridge between humans and Breeds, and a female in the bargain. Breedable, Elizabeth. Grange would know that. He knows it and he wants her for it. And if he doesn't get her, his next step will be to sell this information to the bastards who created us to begin with."

Breedable?

She was a baby. You didn't breed babies. You cuddled them and you loved them and you raised them to be happy and free and to love you in return. She couldn't make sense of this. Couldn't accept the information battering into her brain.

"She's just a baby. You can't do that with a baby."

"Elizabeth." He groaned her name with agonizing emotion. "Listen to me, honey. You have to listen to me now. You can't protect Cassie from this. You can't shelter her or run far enough away to hide her from this."

Elizabeth stared back at him in shock. Couldn't protect Cassie? She had to protect Cassie. She was her child. She couldn't accept anything else.

"I won't let my baby die," she raged. "You're wrong. You have to be wrong."

"You know I'm not wrong," he snapped. "The sounds she makes while she's sleeping. There wasn't a Wolf Breed in the labs I lived in that didn't make that sound as children. When she was playing with Mica and bit her. It's instinct to use the teeth rather than the hands to gain freedom. Her canines are longer. Her intelligence is far advanced for her age . . ."

"Stop!" She screamed out at the pain radiating through her body now. She couldn't bear to breathe; it hurt so badly. She had to escape him. Had to help Cassie survive this. "Get away from me. Just get the hell away from me."

She moved for the connecting bathroom. She had to get to Cassie. Had to make sure nothing or no one could ever hurt her child again. She tried to run, tried to rush past him and escape the pain he was bringing into her life.

He caught her just past the chairs, moving faster than she could. His arms, so hard and strong, wrapped around her, dragging her against his chest as she collapsed. One big hand held her head against him, his broad chest absorbing her sudden scream of agonizing denial.

"No," she wailed against his chest, her fists slamming into him as hard as the truth slammed into her soul. "Oh God, no. He didn't do this to my baby."

She was shaking so hard in his arms she frightened herself. On one level, she was aware of the breakdown. The past two years had culminated in this. The fragile hold she held on her control crumbled and memories assailed her mind.

She hadn't been comfortable with Martaine. Dane had had to fight, beg and plead with her to allow the doctor to perform the procedure. Elizabeth had wanted someone else. Had wanted a doctor she trusted, one who didn't make her skin crawl. But Dane had been insistent. It would be private this way. No one would ever know that their child hadn't been conceived naturally. No one would be aware that he wasn't man enough to get his own wife pregnant.

The list of excuses had been long and the fights had almost been violent. Finally, Elizabeth had given in. Dane had been ecstatic until they had been told the procedure had been effective. Elizabeth had conceived.

He had been quiet. His excitement had slowly faded from that moment on. And she had never known why. Now she knew. It had gone from his wife and child to an experiment. Dane had been almost obsessively jealous. The realization that she wasn't carrying his child must have eaten him alive. It had. It had destroyed their marriage, and eventually his greed had taken his life.

"Mike, see what you can find out about Colder and Martaine, privately, such as any money owed or paid. I need as much information as I can get. Put a call in to Tyler for me. We have to talk again."

She had been barely aware of Mike and his wife entering the room as she and Dash fought. Now she was in Dash's arms as he held her tightly to his chest, crying. She didn't know why she was crying. Tears weren't going to help. But she couldn't stop.

As Dash threw out hasty orders to Mike, his hands were stroking her hair, her back, holding her close to the heat and hardness of his body. Sheltering her the only way he knew how. She recognized it. Had done it often with Cassie.

Her baby had been betrayed again, just as Elizabeth had been. It all made sense now. So many things she hadn't been able to explain: the sudden influx of money after she conceived, Dane's distance from the child, Martaine's interest in her. He had visited the house often before her divorce and had called her personally several times.

And Cassie. Elizabeth felt her heart stop. Her daughter knew. She knew and hadn't told Elizabeth. She had to know. She was there when Dane was killed, had heard her father haggling over the price of selling her to Grange. She would have to be aware of her birthright.

The pieces started falling into place. How Cassie had known all the times someone had been in the apartments they had lived in. She had stopped, fear holding her body rigid as she breathed in deeply. *They're here, Momma. The fairy says they're here.* The fairy hadn't shown up before the night Dane had been killed.

The fairy told her when danger was coming. Instinct. Animal awareness, as had been explained in the interviews she had seen with the feline Breeds. It developed in the young and only grew stronger as they matured. The fairy told her when their enemies were close. Instinct. She could smell them, just as Dash could smell the proof of her parentage. The fairy always knew the things that Cassie was training herself to accept and strengthen.

She pushed against Dash's chest, wiping at the tears on her face, fighting for control. He wouldn't let her go. He held her to him, knowing she wanted to run, to hide not just from Grange and the truth, but from him as well.

He had claimed her. He had already informed her of that fact. He wouldn't let her go. She remembered Callan Lyons's interviews. His fierce protectiveness of his wife, Merinus. The determination to see her safe at all costs. His eyes had blazed when he spoke of her, and she had seen a man who would kill to save his woman. As Dash had done. He had killed to protect her and Cassie. How many more would he be forced to kill now? The thought of that, the danger to not just her child but to Dash as well, was destroying her.

CHAPTER 14

"Let me go." She pushed against his chest again as Mike and Serena left the room. "I have to check on Cassie. Please, Dash. I have to check on her."

He let her go slowly as she fought to dry her face, to stem the tears still rolling from her eyes. She couldn't go in there like this. Cassie would wake up. She always knew when her mother was upset, when she was crying . . .

God, let her be asleep. She rushed to the room, somehow knowing Cassie was awake.

She was. Sitting up in the bed, her own face wet with tears as she clutched the teddy bear Dash had bought her at the diner. Her frail shoulders were shaking with her tears as she rocked to and fro. Silent, heartbreaking sobs that destroyed Elizabeth. How much had her daughter heard?

"Cassie?" Elizabeth realized she was shaking, trembling from head to foot as her daughter raised her head, shame and fear contorting her little face.

"I'm not bad, Momma," she whispered desperately. "I swear, Momma. I swear, I'm not an animal. I'm not."

"Oh God." She felt faint, in shock, seeing the truth in her daughter's eyes as she huddled so miserably on the bed.

Elizabeth rushed to her, pulling her into her arms, feeling her daughter's thin little arms wrap around her as sobs shook her body.

She couldn't breathe. Elizabeth fought the dizziness wrapping around her as she rocked the little girl, fighting the hysteria edging into her mind as Cassie's panicked voice echoed around her.

"I'm sorry," she was screaming against her mother's breast. "Momma, please. I'm sorry."

"Cassie." She fought her own tears as she pulled her daughter back, staring into the little face, seeing so much pain, so much realization of the cruelties of the world. "Why are you sorry, baby? Cassie, you haven't done anything wrong."

"He said you won't love me." Cassie was shaking so hard her teeth rattled. "Said I was an animal. Said I needed to be penned. That you wouldn't want an animal. And you don't like puppies. Or even cats. And he said you wouldn't want me."

Cassie's hands were clawing at her neck as Elizabeth stared down at her in such overwhelming shock she feared she was losing her mind. Cassie was screaming, crying, so hysterical Elizabeth knew she would make herself sick soon.

"Enough." Elizabeth shook her firmly. "Cassidy Paige Colder. That is enough."

She used the voice Cassie called the "no chocolate" voice. Firm, chastising, guaranteed to grab her daughter's attention.

Cassie's eyes widened; the tears still flowed, sobs still tore from her chest but she wasn't screaming, wasn't terrifying Elizabeth with her complete hysteria.

"Cassie. Why are you crying?" She fought the need to cuddle her baby, to rock her, but she saw the complete shock filling her child's eyes and knew Cassie would never hear the gentle words.

Cassie blinked. "I'm an animal, Momma." The pain in her voice was hard to hear.

"Is Tanner Reynolds an animal, Cassidy Paige? Callan Lyons? Are they animals?" she demanded, furious that her child would see herself in that light.

Cassie's breath hitched.

"Is that little baby Callan's wife is having an animal, Cassie?" she asked her daughter fiercely. "Is this how you see them? Those men and women who fought for their lives and their hearts, so perfectly beautiful. Are they animals?"

Cassie stared up at her in surprise. "No, Momma." She shook her head emphatically.

"Have I said they are animals, Cassie?" she snapped. "Haven't I always cheered for them right along with you? What makes you think I would believe you are an animal? Young lady, you are very close to losing chocolate for a month."

Cassie's mouth gaped open, her eyes widening as Elizabeth stared down at her with a mother's righteous anger.

"Maybe two months," Elizabeth amended. "Because if you know anything in this world, you should have known how much I love you, Cassie." Her voice broke then, tears filling her eyes, clogging her throat as she stared down at the vulnerable, almost broken child. Dear God, she could kill Dane herself for what he had done to Cassie.

"He said I was an animal." She shook her head slowly, the tears finally easing.

"No, Cassie." She gripped the girl's face, staring down at her with an inner rage that seared her soul. "You are my baby. And whoever your natural father is, wherever he is, I can only thank him for giving me a child as precious, as smart and as loving as you are. Do you understand me, Cassie? Do you hear what I'm saying?"

Cassie blinked up at her. In a second the little girl was in her arms, clinging tightly to her neck, a hard, desperate kiss plastered to her cheek.

"I love you, Momma," she whispered at her ear. "I love you."

"I love you, Cassie." She could rock her baby now. Could hold her in her arms and cuddle her, comfort her.

Elizabeth closed her eyes, fighting her own screams, her own sobs, as she held her daughter tightly to her breast. She pressed her lips to Cassie's head, sheltered her in her arms and prayed to God that they could find a way, some way, to protect her now.

It didn't matter that the Tolers were standing in the doorway. That Dash was watching them with hungry eyes. All that mattered now was Cassie. Her protection. Her safety. And Elizabeth knew that only Dash could ensure it.

She raised her eyes to him, fighting her tears, knowing Cassie could never handle seeing her mother fall apart now. But Elizabeth knew she was damned close to doing just that. She was shaking on the inside, light-headed, weak.

Dear God, what were they going to do now?

Mike and his wife slowly left the room as Dash neared the bed, his eyes bleak and filled with pain as he stared down at Elizabeth.

"Cassie." He sat down beside her. "You were eavesdropping, weren't you?"

Cassie tensed in her mother's arms, then nodded hesitantly.

"You heard what I am then, didn't you?" he asked her softly. Once again, Cassie nodded.

"When I was very young, Cassie, not much older than you, I escaped the labs and I ran as far and as hard from that place as I could.

Because I knew I wasn't an animal. I knew I deserved to live and to be free. Just as you do. You are a perfect, beautiful little girl. As beautiful as your momma is. But you have to believe that. Remember? You told me that in a letter. If you believe, then it's as real as sunshine. Do you remember that, Cassie?"

"Momma told me that." She hiccupped against Elizabeth's chest.

"And does your momma lie to you, Cassie?" He touched her hair softly, at the same time Elizabeth felt his arm steal around her shoulders.

He was heat and strength. God, she needed that strength right now. "Momma never lies," Cassie finally sighed.

"No, she doesn't." He pulled them both into his arms, holding them, protecting them. "And neither will I, Cassie. Ever. Now I need you to tell me exactly what happened that night. Until I know what happened, I can't protect you and your momma fully. You have to tell me everything."

Elizabeth knew when he said the words that she wouldn't be able to handle Cassie's remembrances of that night. She was right. But she stayed silent, fighting to escape within herself, to pull that mantle of distance around her shoulders that would keep her strong for her daughter.

Dane had owed Grange a frightening amount of money. When Grange arrived at the house, Dane had been waiting. He had already informed Cassie of her parentage, had raged at her, telling her over and over what a little animal she was, how she needed to be caged, penned up like the other animals in the world. That her mother could never want her now. Never love her. Didn't Cassie know how her mother refused to let her have a pet? He had told her cruelly. How did she think her mother would feel when she learned Cassie was nothing more than all the animals she had denied over the years?

Cassie had been crying when Grange showed up for his money. It was then that Dane offered him something much more valuable. A

Breed child. Conceived naturally, and without the genetic faults that kept the other Breeds from conceiving children.

Trainable. Breedable. To convince Grange, he had ripped Cassie's gown from her, showing him the genetic marker. The same marker notated in the top secret files Martaine had given him years before.

Grange had been ecstatic. But he had been smart enough to know Dane could never get away with selling his daughter. He had told Cassie to watch. To see how very easy it was to kill a man. That it would be the first of many lessons she would soon learn. In front of her eyes he had killed her father.

Cassie cried as she told them what happened, and Elizabeth didn't stop her. The sobs were heartbreaking, cleansing. Finally, Cassie was being allowed to face the truth of that night, as was Elizabeth.

When she finished, Elizabeth rocked her, hummed a lullaby to her and didn't protest as Dash sat, holding them both. Finally, the little girl slipped into an exhausted sleep in her mother's arms.

Elizabeth laid her back in the bed and smoothed the dark curls away from her face with trembling fingers.

"I'll wake up soon," Elizabeth whispered hoarsely. "I'll wake up in my house, in my bed and realize it's all been a horrible nightmare."

Dash sighed behind her as he rose from the bed. "When you do, wake me up as well," he sighed. "Then find an explanation for me being in that bed beside you. Because I won't let you go, Elizabeth. Not now. Not ever."

She stared down at her daughter, unable to turn and look at him.

"What do I do?" she asked him, fighting the feeling of helplessness suddenly overtaking her. "Tell me what to do, Dash. How do I protect her now?"

"You can't, Elizabeth." His voice was hard, cold. "But I can. And I will. Now lie down and try to rest. We'll plan this out tomorrow. And I promise you, Cassie will be protected."

CHAPTER 15

Tomorrow came too soon. Elizabeth sat hollow-eyed and quiet in the study as Dash and Mike Toler faced her. The plans he had made, without her approval, were insane. Somehow, as night had turned to dawn, she had known this was coming. She had listened to Cassie's soft little puppy sounds as she slept, and had known Dash would take her baby away from her.

It didn't matter that she knew beyond a shadow of a doubt that he wanted only to protect her. It didn't matter that she knew protection would come with a price. All she knew was that the culmination of two years of fighting, fleeing and hiding had ended with this.

She sat on the worn couch and faced the two men, her hands tucked between her knees, feeling disjointed, disassociated from the world around her. Her baby, the child she had raised, had been no more than an experiment to others. Elizabeth had been used and her daughter had been used, horribly. A little girl had been forced to grow up too soon. To see the horror of a life she should have never known. And now, they wanted to separate her from her mother.

"No." She kept her voice quiet, reasonable.

Dash didn't look surprised.

He shouldn't be surprised, she thought. He should have known she would never agree. He should have come up with another plan.

"Elizabeth." He sighed deeply. The sound was filled with regret. "Listen to me, baby. If you go with her, then we'll never draw Grange back to his estate at the right time. We get Cassie safe, then we take care of the monster. It's the only way we can do this."

There had to be another way, because she wasn't accepting this one.

"Cassie stays with me." She rose to her feet, staring back at the men calmly, amazed at herself and the lack of fury, fear or rage inside her.

She should be screaming this morning. Her insides should be a shuddering wreck at the thought of what her daughter was facing. She shouldn't have been able to function considering the state of shock she knew she had entered.

"Elizabeth." Dash stepped in front of her as she moved to leave the room. "We don't have a choice."

She stopped before she could touch him. She couldn't touch him. Couldn't let his heat seep past the icy protection she had pulled around her heart. She stared at his chest for long moments, seeing how well the Army T-shirt hugged the broad muscles, stretching and conforming to a body she hungered for. A body she couldn't touch. Had no right to desire.

"Of course we do." She shrugged as she finally stared up at him. "We do the same thing the Felines do. We go to the media."

She could almost feel the air humming around her now, charged with anger and volatile protest. It was a simple solution. The Felines had done it and were now so securely protected and autonomous that no one dared mess with them for fear of public outrage. Her daughter could be protected in the same way. Couldn't she?

"The media," Dash said carefully. "Think about that, Elizabeth. Cassie isn't an adult and she doesn't have a Pride backing her. What's more, she wasn't lab-created. She was conceived naturally, which raises the stakes in ways you can never imagine. You're a woman alone and the scientists who will be eager to get their hands on Cassie for studies"—he sneered the word—"could contrive any manner of charges against you. You'll go from a mother fighting to save her child to a money-grubbing mercenary using her baby to make her own way. They could frame you for Dane's murder. Make it appear you were in league with Grange . . ."

She shook her head desperately, panic flaring in her chest. "No . . ."

"They will, Elizabeth." Dash kept his voice soft, almost sinister. "Listen to me. Hear what I'm saying because you know it's true. They can do it. And they will. Cassie is exceptional. She's also exploitable. Don't think you can win with them. If you go to the media now, before she's listed as a Breed and under their protection, then you've lost her forever."

Elizabeth swallowed tightly as she stared into his eyes, seeing the total conviction there, the strength of his beliefs. She hadn't considered it, that they would try to take her child away from her, to manipulate opinion in such a manner. She looked over at Mike. His face was somber, his gaze concerned as he nodded in agreement. *They could do it*, his expression seemed to shout. *They* would *do it*.

And where did that leave her except without her child?

"But she'll be without me," she whispered as she turned back to Dash, wrapping her arms protectively around her chest. "You have to make them let me go with her."

She couldn't imagine being separated from Cassie. Not being

there when her daughter had nightmares, when she was frightened. If something happened. How else could she be sure her daughter was protected?

"Grange knows your habits, baby," Dash continued. "He believes you would never let Cassie go anywhere alone. He won't expect this. Then, when we're ready, we'll let him think he's found you. If you disappear with Cassie, then he'll go to ground, hide, until he gets his chance to take her. A chance you won't be able to anticipate. We have to take him out, Elizabeth. It's the only way."

Take him out. For a moment the memory of the news report flashed in her mind. Grange's henchman found in a pool of blood, his throat slit open, an efficient killing, the reporter had concluded. Dash had taken him out, completely.

"Kill him?" she asked him weakly. She had never killed anyone. But she had never been given a chance at Grange's throat either.

"Only if we have to," he promised her, but she saw the naked fury in his eyes. She had a feeling he would make it a "have to" case. "First we get Cassie protected. Then we see what we can do about Grange. We might get lucky and he'll listen to reason." He shrugged.

Elizabeth blinked. His eyes glittered savagely and his tone of voice clearly reflected his hope that Grange wasn't inclined to listen to any kind of reason. In that moment, he looked like what he had been created to be. A savage, merciless hunter.

"So in essence, we go hunting?" she asked him slowly.

The smile that crossed Dash's face was nearly a snarl. "That's a good description." He nodded. He seemed to like the idea.

Elizabeth watched him. As she did, she felt the blistering-hot fury creeping around the edges of the shield she had fought to put in place all through the night. Terrence Grange had hunted her and Cassie for two years. Killing anyone who would have helped them, standing in the way of any chance Cassie would have had at a normal life.

He had done it out of greed and a lust for power. To possess some-one so unique, so special, and use her for his own twisted, depraved ends. He was a demon. A monster that wouldn't stop until he de-stroyed Cassie.

She took a hard, steadying breath. "Teach me to hunt." She gazed back at him, allowing the anger to strengthen, feeling the shield crumble. "I mean it, Dash. You teach me how."

She wouldn't sit on the sidelines. If she had to do this his way, then she would fight as well. And she knew he could teach her how to fight.

His eyes narrowed, and what glowed there should have terrified her. It was lust. Hot. Hungry. As though the thought of her fighting him had ignited a flame he had no intentions of dampening.

"Train you?" he asked her carefully. "Are you sure that's what you want, Elizabeth? You could do this the safe way. I don't mind carrying the brunt of the work. I know how."

Her lips thinned, nostrils flaring as her head rose and she met his look directly. She could tell he knew how. He was like that, willing to carry it all whether it was his fight or not.

"She's my baby," she said flatly. "It was our lives he destroyed. If I have to send my child away to protect her, then someone is going to have to pay for it. It's his fault."

So he should pay. She left it unsaid.

Dash stared down at her for long, silent moments. In that time, the heat seemed to build in his eyes, in the very air around him. She expected any minute to feel the flames licking over her body. He looked like a man ready to give in to all his baser needs whether he had an audience or not.

"Mike," Dash murmured. "Can I talk to Elizabeth alone?"

There went the audience. Elizabeth stilled the tremble of trepida-tion that shuddered over her body.

Mike rose slowly to his feet, clearing his throat. "I'll just be in the kitchen, breathing in clear air. It's getting too damned hot in here to suit me anyway."

He was grinning as he passed them.

As the door closed, Dash turned back to her slowly.

"I'll fuck you," he told her softly, without a doubt in his voice that it would happen. "If I train you, I'll do more than just teach you how to shoot or how to fight, Elizabeth. I won't be able to stop it."

She licked her lips nervously. "You would have anyway. We both know that." It was something she had accepted as she lay in his arms the night before. There was no hiding from it. He could have had her then. Could have taken her there in his bedroom and she wouldn't have stopped him.

He shook his head warningly. "It's different, Elizabeth. Protecting you and fighting beside you are two different things. If you're tough enough to go for blood, then you're tough enough for everything I am. Every part of me. Are you willing to accept that?"

She frowned then. "What? You fuck different from other men?" She finally snapped. "What more could you do?"

He moved around her. He stalked, actually, watching her closely.

"I bet Dane fucked you missionary. Lights out. A shuffle in the dark, a grunt or two and then it was over." His disgust for Dane, dead though he was, was clearly apparent.

Elizabeth flushed. It was much too close to the truth.

"So?" She shrugged. "What will you do? Leave the lights on?"

He was behind her, his head leaning close to hers, his lips at her ear.

"Have you ever been mounted?" he asked her roughly, heatedly. "Taken to your knees because the lust was so hot, so powerful, it couldn't be denied? Your clothes ripped from your body and taken so deeply, so hard, you couldn't do anything but scream out your orgasm?"

Elizabeth's eyes widened, her heart suddenly racing in her chest. She shook her head slowly as she tried to speak. "No," she finally gasped.

He wasn't touching her, but her breasts were swelling, her nipples hardening almost painfully as her pussy wept its thick juices in need.

His hand moved over the curve of her rear, ignoring her flinch of surprise. "What about here?" He actually growled.

The sound rasped down her spine, but rather than fear, it brought an edge of excitement she couldn't deny.

His hunger pulsed in the air around her. It was deep, consuming, making her womb clench in response.

"What?" She was confused now. Distracted by the image of him mounting her, taking her.

"Have you been fucked up that tight ass, Elizabeth?" he asked as her eyes widened in shocked surprise. "Do you know every time I watch you walk, watch that pretty rear flex, all I can think about is sinking my cock inside it?"

As if it were possible! He was trying to scare her. Trying to make her back down, she was certain. She wasn't about to.

"Stop." She jumped away from him, turning back to him furiously. "Why are you trying to scare me off like this? I have the right to do this, Dash."

The look in his eyes was almost frightening. Dash didn't have blood on his mind; he had hot, explicit sex filling his head instead.

"You don't understand." He shook his head slowly, a feral smile tipping his lips. "You keep forgetting. I'm not just a soldier, baby. I'm a Breed. And trust me when I tell you you'll never fuck another man like me. You'll never be taken again in the ways I'll take you. I can protect you, and in doing so, rein in some of the harder aspects of my lust, for a while. But if I have to train you, teach you to fight beside me, then you'll take me. Every way. You'll have all I am, Elizabeth, not just the man you want me to be. Now make your choice. And know that once you make it, there's no turning back. No whining, no pouting, no false denials. You will accept it."

Her mouth was dry, but other parts of her body were too damned wet for comfort.

"Will you rape me?" she asked him suspiciously. No man would take her except on her terms. Dane hadn't and Dash sure as hell wouldn't.

He tilted his head, cool confidence washing over his expression. "I won't have to."

"No means no," she told him tightly. "Will you abide by that?"

He nodded instantly. "Of course." Then he smiled that smile that made her more than nervous. "You can't say no after the fact, though. Agreed?"

She looked at him sardonically. "Agreed. But that confidence could find you on your ass, buddy."

"Or up yours," he murmured. "So we have an agreement?"

She was agreeing to allow her daughter to be taken from her. To place her under the protection of strangers. To trust men and women she didn't know. But she also knew the hell those men and women had lived. They had been hunted, betrayed. They would care for Cassie, protect her with their lives, just as they had each other. But her baby would be without her. For a while.

She drew in a deep breath and swallowed tightly. "Agreed."

Oh Lord. If his eyes could have gotten hotter, they just had. The golden-brown was nearly amber now, glittering with lust. His nostrils flared, his expression becoming heavy with sensuality.

"Do you know I can smell your arousal?" he asked her softly. "I know when your sweet heat is flowing for me, Elizabeth. When your pretty pussy is coated with that slick dew, preparing for me. Like it is now. It turns you on to think about fighting me, doesn't it? Makes you wet and hot to imagine pitting your mind against my strength. Just like it makes me hard. So hard that walking could become a problem."

Her face flamed with mortification, because she was wet now and only growing wetter by the second. She should be thinking about Cassie, thinking about the separation, but all she could think about was Dash and the hunger building between them both.

Her gaze flicked to his jeans, then quickly back to his face. That zipper was going to burst soon.

And he was right. It did turn her on. He intended to take her, to make her submit. She could see it in his expression, hear it in his voice. She had never submitted to anyone. She didn't intend to start with Dash.

Elizabeth licked her lips, relieving the painful dryness, then swallowing tightly as he followed the movement.

"Go to Cassie," he finally growled. "Get away from me before I take you now. Kane and his brothers, as well as several of the main Feline Pride, will be here tonight. Get ready, Elizabeth, because when they leave, you'll see what it means to be my woman."

She backed up slowly. She wasn't running, she assured herself, she was exercising extreme caution instead. He wasn't joking. He was ready to take her, here and now, and she didn't know if she could honestly deny him.

· CHAPTER 16 ·

The feline Breeds were just as intense and gorgeous in real life as they had been on the television screen. They arrived after midnight in a large stealth helicopter, landing in the back pasture of Mike Toler's ranch.

Kane Tyler and three of his brothers were there. Callan Lyons, Taber Williams, Tanner, Dawn and Sherra had accompanied them. Each was armed and looked just as dangerous as they had been trained to be.

Elizabeth sat in the living room with Cassie, holding her against her chest, rocking her. Despite her dream of actually meeting the Felines, Cassie hadn't taken the news of her separation from her mother very well.

She had cried for hours. It broke Elizabeth's heart listening to her daughter sob and wail, begging her not to send her away. Elizabeth had cried with her. Emotionally, they were both wrecks by the time the large force entered the house.

Elizabeth could only stare at them in shock. They were as big and muscular as Dash, but their eyes were harder, their expressions carved in stone, until they caught sight of Cassie.

Elizabeth watched, amazed, as the two women turned away, their eyes shining with moisture. The three male Felines' and single human's gazes darkened painfully.

"Callan?" Kane asked softly, as though for confirmation.

Callan stepped closer, his eyes so golden-brown they were amber, his long, tawny brown hair flowing around the harsh features of his face. As he stepped to the couch, Elizabeth was aware of Dash moving behind her protectively, possessively. The other Breed noticed the movement as well, if the amused quirk of his lips was any indication.

"Cassidy." He sat on his haunches, staring at the little girl gently. "What a lovely little girl you are. I hear you might need our help for a bit of time."

His voice was deep, sandpapery, but exquisitely gentle as he watched the little girl.

"I wanna stay with my momma," Cassie hiccupped tearfully as Elizabeth fought the need to demand that her daughter be given exactly what she wanted.

Pain flashed in Callan's eyes. They were amazingly expressive as they watched Cassie, showing his sympathy, his need to comfort her.

"You know Grange is a very bad man, Cassie," Callan said softly. "I've been checking into him. You know he'll hurt you and your momma if he can get hold of you." He held his hand up as Elizabeth began to protest. "I won't lie to you, Cassie. I won't tell you any of this is going to be easy, for you or your momma. Facts are facts. Dash and your momma can't deal with Grange if you aren't hidden first. If they try, something could happen, and Grange could end up hurting you all."

Cassie trembled. "But the fairy can't help Momma if I'm gone," she protested tearfully.

Callan never looked away from the little girl. "But Dash can, Cassie. He and your momma can move faster and trick Grange easier if they know you're hidden and protected. And you'll be hidden and protected at my home. I promise you this."

"I want my momma," Cassie whimpered, her arms tightening around Elizabeth's waist. "I'm staying with my momma."

"Callan." The woman who moved behind him was much smaller than the others. Her soft golden-brown hair and eyes were immeasurably gentle. Dawn was a Cougar Breed, and Elizabeth could clearly see the influence of the animal's DNA in her. Her high cheekbones, slanted golden eyes and finely arched brows gave her a very feline appearance.

Cassie seemed to jerk in surprise when the woman approached her. She leaned forward, then back, then stared up at Elizabeth with rounded eyes.

Cassie cupped her fingers over her mouth and whispered up to Elizabeth, "She has a fairy, Momma. Right beside her. Just like mine."

Elizabeth wasn't certain what to say at this point. She had thought Cassie's fairy was no more than an excuse for the knowledge she picked up through her more advanced senses.

"She does?" she whispered back.

Cassie nodded. "But she's sad." Then she turned to Dawn. "Why is your fairy sad?" Dawn blinked, then glanced at Elizabeth.

"Cassie has her own fairy," Elizabeth explained. "She . . . comforts her." She didn't know what else to say.

Dawn finally smiled in understanding. "Perhaps my fairy gets tired of being alone." She sighed. "There aren't many fairies left in the world, Cassie."

Cassie tilted her head, considering. "No. She's sad because you don't hear her," she finally said. "You should listen to your fairy."

"You're right." Dawn nodded. "But I don't know how. Maybe I need someone to teach me how to listen to her."

Cassie was silent for long moments. "I don't wanna leave my momma." Her voice trembled tearfully.

Callan moved back as Dawn sat down on the couch beside Elizabeth and Cassie and watched the little girl with tender, though wary, eyes.

"I don't blame you, Cassie," she finally said sadly. "If I had a momma like yours, I wouldn't want to leave her either. But you and your momma will be safer if you are protected. And isn't that what's important right now? That you and your momma are safe?"

Cassie's fingers plucked at Elizabeth's shirt-sleeve for long moments. Finally she raised her eyes, the blue depths glittering with tears.

"I'm scared without you, Momma," she finally whispered.

"I know, baby." Elizabeth swallowed tightly. "And I'm scared without you too. But I can't make Grange leave us alone if he knows where you are. It's very important that he can't find you so that Momma can make him go away." *Far away*, Elizabeth thought coldly.

Cassie's head lowered again. "Will you come back?" she finally asked faintly.

"Cassie." Elizabeth lifted her daughter's face until she could stare into her eyes. "You couldn't keep me away. You're my baby. You know I'll come back for you. Right?"

Cassie swallowed tightly. "Even though I'm a Breed?" she asked her roughly.

Fury engulfed Elizabeth, though she fought to contain it. "Cassidy, being a Breed doesn't make you any different to me. If you want the truth, I'm so damned happy Dane isn't your daddy that I could kiss that doctor who thought he tricked us. Because he gave me the most special baby in the world. Do you understand me?"

Cassie grinned faintly, though her eyes still swam with tears.

"Dash could be my daddy," she whispered. "Maybe I wouldn't be so scared while you're away if I knew he was my daddy."

"Cassie." Elizabeth wasn't shocked, but she hadn't expected Cassie to strike so soon.

"Cassie." Dash broke in on her protest. "Do you know any other Wolf Breeds, young lady?"

Cassie raised her eyes and shook her head no.

"Then it looks like you're stuck with me. But I can't convince your momma until Grange has been punished. To do that, you need to go with Dawn and Callan. We'll discuss the rest of it later."

Cassie's eyes narrowed. Elizabeth had never known her daughter could be such a little schemer.

"You gonna take his chocolate, Dash?" she asked him, suddenly more than interested.

"Oh yeah, all of it," Dash promised her. "And he doesn't know the secret to get it back. Remember that."

Cassie's grin was wider now. "Can I have his chocolate, Dash?" she asked innocently. "Chocolate should be for good girls."

"A whole boxful, Cassie. But you have to go with Callan so your momma and me can take care of this. Okay?"

Cassie sighed and glanced up at Elizabeth again.

"One day, I can buy my own chocolate," she finally sighed. "You better bring me chocolate back, Dash, or I might have to tell Momma how you bargain for ways to stay out of trouble."

Elizabeth was watching Dash, saw his eyes narrow, though his lips tipped into a grin.

"We might have to see about an allowance when we get back," he finally said as though she had won. "Little girls need their chocolate money."

Cassie turned back to her mother, her smile sweetly innocent. "He will make a good daddy, Momma. I told you he would."

Elizabeth snorted. "Why? Because you can twist him around your little finger?"

Cassie sighed. "That's where all good daddies live, Momma. The fairy said so. We need to talk when you come get me. I could tell you all about it."

She looked so serious. Elizabeth blinked down at her daughter, not for the first time, amazed at the little girl's insights.

"We definitely will," she promised. "Does this mean you'll go?"

"Fine." She pouted. "But they better hope they have chocolate. And they better remember, wolfs eat cats for dinner. They better not mess with me."

Before Elizabeth could get past her shock, her daughter was off her lap and stalking to the stairs. She turned back at the first step. "And I want to take my pretty clothes too. And my nightgowns. And my bear Dash bought me. And you better come back for me, Momma, or I'll hunt you like the big wolfs and when I catch you, I'll bite you."

She stomped off, in full temper, as Elizabeth sighed roughly. "Well, at least she isn't crying. But I really don't envy any of you. Cassie in a temper is not always a pretty sight to see."

"I love her," Kane suddenly remarked from the other side of the room. "God bless her heart. I love her." He was chuckling wickedly as he looked back at the Felines staring at him. "Wolves eat cats for dinner. By God, I wanna be a wolf." He looked at Sherra and growled.

Elizabeth looked at Dash. "Good God. This man is going to be watching my daughter?" A flash of pure motherly fear rushed through her. Cassie and Kane Tyler together would be a catastrophe.

"Don't worry, Mrs. Colder," Sherra finally said coolly. "For the most part, we keep him leashed and gagged. We only let him free when the cute little animal jokes are needed."

"Kane," Callan said warningly. "Leave Sherra alone."

Kane sighed. "I'm going to have to discuss this with Cassie. I bet she could help." He started for the stairs as he turned back to the others. "I'll just, uhhh . . . help her pack her chocolate."

"No." Elizabeth was on her feet in a flash. She turned back to Dash worriedly. "Are you sure he's"—she swallowed—"sane?"

"Oh, he's sane enough." Dash laughed as he shook his head. "And he's just trying to rile Sherra. I hear he does that a lot. Elizabeth will get Cassie packed, Kane. I need to talk to you and Callan in the study. If you don't mind."

His voice assured them he really didn't give a damn if they did mind.

"Sure." Kane sighed as though disappointed. "I bet she knows some good wolf tricks, though. Shame on you, Dash, not letting your old buddy know about those savage little genes running loose in your body. I could have used some pointers over the last few months." He turned and followed Dash as Elizabeth shook her head in amazement.

"He's really harmless," Sherra assured her drolly. "But we wouldn't want his humor to infect Cassie, so we promise to keep them separated."

"Yeah." Elizabeth breathed out slowly. "That might be a very, very good idea."

CHAPTER 17

Kane hadn't changed much, Dash thought as he led the way into Mike's study. He was still as sarcastic and hell-bent on causing trouble wherever possible. The little feline Breed, Sherra, seemed to be the night's main course for him. Strangely enough, though, Dash detected a strong undercurrent of dangerous anger where the woman was concerned. He had known Kane for a long time, had fought with him, covered his back and had his own covered by the man, but he had never seen Kane Tyler quite like this.

A mocking, sarcastic Kane was often a sure sign of just how dangerous he was at that moment. If the cute retorts were any indication, the little snow leopard had seriously been on his wrong side for quite a while now.

"She's a cute kid," Kane remarked as he closed the door behind him. "She looks like you, Dash. Sure they didn't use your little soldiers for the experiment?"

Short and mocking, Kane had little regard for formalities or pleasantries when he was pissed.

Dash snorted. "They didn't have time to sample my little soldiers, Kane," he grunted. "I haven't been in the labs since I was ten years old."

Both men stared at him in surprise. Explanation time. Damn, he had thought this day would never happen. Briefly, he explained his escape at ten. Being as small as he was, slipping into one of the supply vans and hiding hadn't been hard. He had managed to work his way from the small lab in the Colorado mountains to Missouri in less than six months and after that, life got easy.

Foster care had seen him through school, then after graduation he had enlisted in the Army. The recessed genetics had never shown up in blood tests or in physicals, and from there, it had just been a matter of keeping his secrets and doing his job.

Both had been fairly easy. Dash had known what awaited him if the Council ever learned he had escaped and lived. They had been known to get possessive where their creations were concerned.

"You haven't mated yet?" Callan asked him softly as he and Kane faced Dash from the couch.

"Had sex?" Dash asked, surprised. "Getting a little personal there, aren't you, Lyons?" That was definitely none of the Breed's business.

"No." Callan grinned, shaking his head.

"You haven't yet marked the woman, Elizabeth, or I would have smelled it. Which means you haven't taken her sexually yet. Correct?"

Once again, none of his business, Dash thought. Damn. He was unaware that finding Cassie protection meant questions regarding his sex life. Especially the lack thereof with Elizabeth.

Dash frowned warningly. "What does that have to do with Cassie?"

"With Cassie, not much." Callan shrugged. "With you and the mother, perhaps much. Your recessed genetics may allow you a merciful escape from what Taber and I have learned. As for the Wolf Breeds, we can only assume it's the same, since we have yet to find any who have mated."

Which didn't explain the reasons for the questions, as far as he was concerned. His relationship with Elizabeth had nothing to do with Cassie or her protection.

Dash shook his head. "What the hell are you getting at?"

Callan leaned forward slowly. "The feline Breed males tend to show their relationship to our animal cousins in a unique way."

"That's a nice way of saying it," Kane snorted mockingly. "Didn't know you could beat around the bush so well, Callan."

Callan flashed him an irate glance before turning back to Dash. "Have you noticed anything unusual during sex with any other female?"

Dash flushed as he looked between the two men. Hell. Since when did a personal interrogation come with the agreement to help?

He finally shook his head as he watched Callan in bemusement. "Like what?"

Kane stared up at the ceiling as though the conversation were now beyond his control or his interest.

Callan sighed roughly. "When Taber and I found our mates, we learned that our bodies have a unique reaction to them during sex."

Kane grunted but kept quiet.

"Such as?" Dash asked in confusion.

Callan cleared his throat as a slight grin edged his lips. "Our cocks produced a phenomenon resembling the barb that actual felines have. It's blunt rather than sharp, but it locks us into our women for long minutes after ejaculation. It's possible a similar phenomenon occurs in the Wolf Breeds."

Dash stared at the man in shock. Felines had barbs, canines

had . . . He grinned and looked at Kane. "He's joking. Right?" He had to be joking. Elizabeth was an amazingly steady woman, but he wasn't certain how she would take such an animalistic reaction. Hell, he didn't know how he would handle it.

Kane shrugged, frowning. "Hell if I know. And I have no intention of finding out."

"He mated your sister," Dash pointed out.

Kane frowned heavily. "I do not discuss sex with my baby sister," he gritted out. "And I don't want to hear about the particulars either." He gave Callan a warning look.

"Then leave." Callan shrugged before turning back to Dash. "Whatever reactions each Breed has during mating is an issue we must be honest about. The frenzy isn't a comfortable matter, Kane, and could affect their ability to triumph over Grange."

"Frenzy?" Dash was lost.

Callan explained in clear, concise terms the "frenzy" he was talking about as Dash sat and watched him in shock.

"Damn," he finally breathed out roughly, checking his tongue for any swelling. "Okay. No gland issue there."

Now this he didn't need. Not that he wouldn't mind having Elizabeth pinned under his body until she conceived the child he had only dreamed of as his own, but he was sure she wouldn't appreciate the experience. Enjoy it, yes. Thank him for it? She might well kill him for it.

"Perhaps she is not your mate," Callan suggested. "We've found the changes to only occur with one person. Women, in Taber's case and mine, who complemented us in every way. It's a mating. There is no other word for it. She could be the wrong woman."

Dash growled in protest. "Or perhaps the Wolf Breeds don't have this reaction," he pointed out. "And we also have to consider the recession of the genetics in my case. The scientists were going to kill me because I was human rather than animal. This discussion could be a waste of time."

He really hoped this discussion was a waste of time. He couldn't see himself explaining this to Elizabeth as such a change occurred in his own body. But the thought of it was so incredibly erotic that it caused his cock to twitch in reaction. Her slender body beneath him, locked to him, unable to escape, unable to do anything but tremble in pleasure as her body soaked up his seed.

"And your genetics can change overnight," Callan assured him, shrugging. "It's something you should be aware of. Something that other Wolf Breeds will need to know about, should it occur. We have a few at the Feline compound, but not many as of yet. We're still uncertain if the original pack in Mexico survived."

Dash's pack.

He shook his head wearily as he remembered the small group of children he had left behind in Colorado, just before the prepared move. At the time, he had no idea where they would go, and had been unable to find them later.

"If anyone could save them, it would be Wolfe. He was a born leader, even as a child. I won't believe he's dead until I hear they found the body. As far as I've heard, they can't be certain either way at this point, which tells me they escaped."

He had suspected all along that they had escaped but hadn't made attempts to try to track them down since learning of the location of the lab. His life had been too consumed with finding Elizabeth and Cassie.

Finding his pack could come later.

"We have lines of communication open," Kane said firmly. "I have several men checking on some leads. If we hear anything, we'll let you know when you get back."

Dash nodded. "I expect at least a month before we can return. I need a week, perhaps two, to run Elizabeth through some basic training before we go after Grange. I want her ready to fight in case it's needed."

Callan frowned. "You should allow her to come to the compound as well. Take some of my men, Dash, and take care of Grange. There's no reason to endanger the woman."

"She's my woman, Callan." Dash shook his head. "If she stays, life won't always be easy. I won't be hemmed up in a compound unless I have to be. Elizabeth and Cassie will both have to learn how to protect themselves. You get government acceptance for Cassie and I'll take care of Grange. The rest we'll take care of as we have to."

"Grange won't be easy," Kane warned him. "I checked him out before heading in. He has several high-level government friends, which is why he's running around without a leash. He knows of Cassie's genetics; he'll know the minute we put in for government acceptance of her."

"I thought of that." Dash shook his head. "All a child needs is the father's name," he reminded them. "List my name alone and leave mother and child's names blank, as well as the ages. After the papers come back, you have six months to return them with the names of the mother and child." It was a safety measure the Felines had demanded for any minor Breeds found. "I'll claim parentage. That's all we need."

Callan nodded and turned to Kane. "Can you get the papers together before we leave?"

"I brought the laptop." Kane nodded. "I'll contact Merinus and have her send the file immediately. All he has to do is sign the government copy. Elizabeth has to sign our copy and I'll notarize them. We can have it done within the hour."

Dash nodded. "Let's do it, then. I want to get Cassie out of here as fast as possible and get on the road. We're safe enough here, but I don't like taking chances."

"Very well," Callan said as they all rose to their feet. He extended his hand to Dash. "Welcome to my Pride, Dash Sinclair. It's good to include you."

Dash accepted the handshake, feeling more than just a binding of an agreement. For the first time in his life, it was almost like having a family.

◆ ◆ ◆

Elizabeth signed her name slowly to the papers. In them, she agreed that Dash Sinclair was the paternal parent of her daughter, Cassidy Paige Colder, and as such, she had agreed to legally accept the change of name for her daughter from her birth name to that of Cassandra Angelica Sinclair. The name was picked by Cassie, of course.

"Cassandra Angelica is what my fairy thinks." She had nodded firmly when Elizabeth informed her of what they were doing and why. "And I like having Dash for my daddy. I think I deserve chocolate. This matchmaking stuff is hard work."

She didn't get chocolate, but she did get a daddy. Dash signed his own name firmly beside Elizabeth's and handed the papers over to Kane to notarize.

The decision to change Cassie's name had come after Dawn had brought up the fear that any female child would be immediately suspect if Grange did indeed have contacts within that branch of the government. Cassie's age would be left off, but a slightly altered description would be included. Once she was at the Breed compound, her dark locks would receive a temporary color and her change of identity would be established.

Elizabeth felt as though she were losing her daughter. The decisions she was being forced to make didn't sit well with her. She had always cared for Cassie, had always made certain she was protected and safe and loved. Allowing others to do that, as well as changing her name and appearance, twisted her heart.

They had her packed and dressed in her new coat all too soon. Elizabeth carried her to the waiting shadow of the helicopter, fighting her tears with every breath. She was letting her baby go. How was she supposed to let her baby go?

"The fairy says you'll come back for me, Momma," Cassie whispered in her ear as she clutched the chocolate bar Elizabeth had given her. Dash had slipped it to her minutes before they left the house.

"I'll definitely be back, Cassie." She prayed she would be.

"The fairy says Grange is bad, and that Dash will make sure he never hurts us again if I go with the feline Breeds," the little girl said softly as she lay against Elizabeth's shoulder. "He'll be my daddy and everything will be okay."

"It will be, baby." Elizabeth paused at the dark opening of the helicopter. Everyone had already entered the large aircraft except Callan Lyons.

"I love you, Momma." Cassie was near tears again, and Elizabeth knew she wouldn't be able to contain her own much longer.

"I love you, baby." She kissed her forehead softly, lingeringly. "You be good for Momma, and I'll come get you soon."

She handed her baby to Callan. Cassie looked so small, so defenseless in the other man's arms as he lifted her up to Dawn.

He jumped into the helicopter as Dash wrapped his arms around Elizabeth and pulled her back. The door closed, blocking out the sight of Cassie's pale face. As she and Dash drew back the required distance, the motor was engaged, the huge blades whipping up the snow on the ground, and then it slowly lifted away.

"Cassie," she whispered painfully, allowing her tears to fall now that her daughter was out of sight. Hot, scalding streams of moisture poured from her eyes as her chest tightened violently. "Oh God, Cassie. Momma already misses you."

Dash's arms were around her, holding her tightly to his chest, his head lowered over hers as the helicopter sped swiftly away from them, carrying away her reason for living.

"It's okay, baby," Dash whispered at her ear, his voice husky, dark. "It's okay. We'll make him pay for it. I promise you, he will pay for it."

CHAPTER 18

The Tolers returned to the ranch early that morning as Dash was packing the Hummer. Elizabeth was sleeping. Finally. She had cried herself into exhaustion as he held her. She was grieving, he knew, hating the separation from her daughter and the fear that filled her. But he knew it had been a cleansing thing, a preparation for what she was aware was coming. So he had let her cry, holding her, stroking her long hair back from her pale face and murmuring gently to her.

He had never been comfortable with a woman's tears before. Had never known exactly how to handle the feeling of manipulation he had always known during them. It was absent in this case. It was the first time he had seen Elizabeth cry, had seen the control she kept so firmly in place slip. Or had it? It was hard to tell with her. She was equal parts warrior and woman. As she cried in his arms he could almost feel her resolve strengthening, her rage and pain forming into the core of steel she would need to see her through the coming days.

He could have accomplished this much faster, much more easily and with no threat to her if he had taken Callan up on his offer. But Dash had known even before then that Elizabeth would have to see this through before she would have the courage to face the life ahead of them. He had chosen her as his mate, and she knew it, even if she never spoke of it. He was now, legally, Cassie's father. The little girl was unique in so many ways that protecting her would be a full-time job until she was old enough to protect herself.

She would need parents who knew how to defend her, knew how to fight together. Dash would make certain Elizabeth was in the least amount of actual danger possible. But to be assured she could face the dangers that could come in their lives, he had to allow her this. There was always the chance he could be killed. A chance that once again she would be alone, facing dangers she had never imagined from the Council. He had to make certain she was able to protect herself, Cassie, and any other children they might have along the way.

When she had fallen asleep, curled up in the bed Cassie had slept in, Dash had slipped away and began preparing for their departure. A plane would come for them later that night and fly them to a deserted airfield not far from the cabin he had rented for a month's stay several hours from Grange's estate. There, he would train her, see how tough she was and make plans to get to Grange.

Mike was insistent that Dash allow the bastard to live. All they needed were the files Grange possessed, detailing the experiment done in vitro on Elizabeth. That alone would secure Cassie's safety, as much as anything else would. Once she was under Pride protection, the news of her existence would be revealed and would pull the teeth from the threat Grange posed. But Dash knew men like that. Knew that Grange would never be satisfied, never be content, until he destroyed Cassie. He wouldn't allow that threat to continue. Grange was a drug runner, a slaver, a child molester. A man whose soul was so dark and diseased that he caused misery wherever he went. Dash knew he would likely have to kill him. He wouldn't feel guilt over that fact, or remorse. Such monsters didn't deserve to draw breath.

He loaded all the equipment necessary into the Hummer before packing the backseat area with weapons and ammunition. Getting to Grange wouldn't be that hard, but he wanted Elizabeth familiar with the weapons he would be carrying.

"This is too risky, Dash," Mike warned him again. "If you won't accept the offer Callan made, let me send a few of my men in with you. Make short work of the mission and get out. You're placing Elizabeth in too much danger."

"I did that when I came for her." Dash ran a mental checklist as he stared at the store of weapons. "What she'll face later will be even more dangerous. She needs this to continue, Mike. Life may not be easy from here on out."

"She's not a soldier, Dash. She's a woman. Cassie's safe now; her concentration will be fractured. I don't think she's strong enough for this."

Dash braced his arm on the top of the vehicle's frame as he leaned in to check the store of ammo stacked in the floorboards.

"She's strong enough." He had no doubt about that. It was the strength and experience needed to work under this new stress that bothered him. "I'll protect her. I know what I'm doing, Mike."

He had pulled too many civilians out of situations more exacting than what he was leading Elizabeth into. Grange was a wart on society's ass. Burning him off wouldn't be the problem. Knowing that Elizabeth would survive with her honor and strength intact was the problem. He didn't want to break her. Didn't want to ask more of her than she could give. But he had to know she could follow him. Follow him, fight beside him and protect herself if she had to.

"I know you think you know what you're doing," Mike finally sighed. "For your own good, I hope you do. Just in case, I'm sending

Matt and Joey out there. They'll be in town if you need them. Don't hesitate to use them."

"Why?" Dash turned back to him, confused now.

Mike was watching him with a frown. "Because you might need help," he snapped. "You might think you're Superman, Dash, but you're not. I don't want to have to bury you, if it's all the same to you."

Dash shook his head. "If I die, then I reckon they'll dispose of the body somehow, Mike. What does that have to do with anything?"

Mike was silent for long moments. "If someone massacred me and my family, Dash, what would you do?" he finally asked curiously.

Dash shrugged. "Go hunting. They wouldn't live long."

A grin tugged at Mike's mouth. "Why would you do that? I'm sure my and Serena's parents would bury us."

Dash was suddenly uncomfortable. "It would piss me off," he growled. "I might need your ass one of these days to help put out a fire."

Mike shook his head. "Why not admit we're friends, Dash? I've noticed you do that a lot. Forget you have friends. Steady, dependable friends. Why is that?"

Dash sighed wearily. "I'm a Breed, Mike. You let your friends know you. Knowing who and what I am puts you at risk."

Mike shook his head again. "We were already friends, buddy. You need to loosen up some and accept that. Friends share the burden. If my wife or daughter were in danger, you would have been the first person I contacted because I know you would be the one most likely to never flinch in protecting them. Our friendship would ensure that you would never betray them. Not just because you're the best damned warrior I know, but because you're a friend, one I know and respect. It's that simple."

Dash pushed his fingers through his hair, sighing roughly. "I don't know how to be a friend, Mike."

"Like hell." Mike frowned. "You've never been anything but the best friend I ever had. You think I don't know who was looking after Serena and Mica on that last mission I took? You requested leave, flew over here, and spent a damned month in the hills watching the house to protect my family. What was that if it wasn't friendship?"

Dash was more than surprised. "How did you know?"

Mike shot him a sardonic look. "Come on, Dash. You were damned good, I admit. But there's no way those two 'hunters' that turned up dead on the other side of the mountain were anything but Gorley's men. And you forget, that nice clean little swipe across the throat is one of your trademarks. I knew the minute I got the information what was going on."

Dash cleared his throat uncomfortably. "The knife doesn't make as much noise as a gun." He shrugged. "Besides, I liked Serena. She's too good for your sorry ass, though. I told you that already."

But Dash was realizing something more. He was realizing that, despite the fact that he had fought to keep himself distant, a loner, the people he depended on were more than military contacts. He had told himself that was all they were, and yet, at the same time, he had formed bonds he now realized were stronger than he could have imagined.

"Everything packed, then?" Mike asked as he closed the door to the Hummer.

Dash nodded. "I'm going to head up and get some sleep before leaving tonight. I appreciate you returning the Hummer for me."

The supplies would be transferred to the plane when it arrived, then to the truck Dash had arranged to be waiting at the airfield. The plans he had worked out with Mike after receiving confirmation that Cassie would be accepted into the Breed compound were coming together quickly.

"You need any other help, you be sure to let me know, Dash."

Mike sighed. "You have a lot of people who would help you in a heartbeat."

Dash took a deep breath. He had never considered how close he was to some of the men he had fought with until his near-death. And even then he had shied away from the knowledge, always feeling that he would bring friends more danger than comfort if his secret was ever revealed.

"Serena, Mica and I are heading into town for the day," Mike told him as they entered the house. "We'll be back in time to catch you before you leave. Rest while you can. I'll talk to you soon."

Dash didn't go to his room, though. He went to Elizabeth's. She was still curled up in the middle of the bed, a slender mound beneath the blankets, her hair flowing in wild abandon around her.

He listened as Mike and his family left the house, shaking his head at the knowledge his friend—and he admitted it now, Mike was a friend—had forced him to realize.

He had more than he ever dreamed he could have. A child, his woman and a network of men and women working to make certain he could protect them both. Not because they were fellow soldiers, but because they were friends.

And those friends were now gone. The house was silent. There was no one there but him and Elizabeth, and the raw, aching throb of his cock. As he stood there, she rolled over, her eyes opening drowsily, watching him with a silent question. He could smell her heat, smell the soft cream building between her thighs, the need racing through her system.

"Undress, Elizabeth." He almost winced at the growl that rumbled in his throat. "I can't wait much longer."

Amazingly, she moved from the bed. Her hands were shaking, the vein at her throat pulsing almost violently as she began to undress.

Her shirt fell to the floor. She loosened her jeans, drawing them slowly down her hips. Elizabeth watched him closely as she revealed the black silk-and-lace thong he had bought her. The scraps of sensual material matched the bra hiding the full mounds of her breasts from his view.

He undressed slowly, watching her, knowing this first time could be more than either of them could handle. If what Callan suggested was the truth, it would be better to learn now rather than later. Better to let her go before this went any further. He also knew there was no way he could wait any longer.

"Take off the rest." His gaze never left hers as she unclipped the bra, drawing the cups back from the swollen mounds and shrugging it from her shoulders. Her hands went to her panties, slender fingers hooking beneath the elastic and easing them down her hips. He wanted to moan in hunger as she stepped out of them, revealing the smooth, shaven mound beneath. It glistened with her juices, the sweet earthy scent making his mouth water.

He laid his clothes over the chair as he stroked the tormented length of his erection. He was thick and large and would fill her until she screamed with the pressure. It wasn't abnormal, but it was striking. Her eyes widened as she finally glanced lower than his face. He knew the one time she had held the hard flesh in her hand hadn't been long enough for her to realize the full effect of this erection. He would more than fill her. He would take her as no other man ever had. Perhaps in ways neither of them could imagine.

He had never been with a woman like Elizabeth either. One so small, so sexually uncertain and inexperienced. His women had always been raw-boned and lusty, well able to take the formidable flesh he pushed between their thighs. Elizabeth was delicate, slender. The thought of the amazing tightness he knew he would find when he entered her was enough to make his breath catch in need.

"I don't want to hurt you," he whispered as he approached her, feeling the hunger for her rising so sharp and fast it nearly overwhelmed him.

Her scent wrapped around him, made him drunk on the need to touch her, taste her. He stopped in front of her, his cock throbbing and heavy between his thighs, pressing against her tummy as he leaned his forehead against hers. Her hands were trembling as he linked his with them, pulling her arms gently behind her body, arching her breasts against his chest.

She was breathing roughly, staring up at him with those dark, hungry eyes.

"Maybe I need it to hurt a little." Her whispered moan had his jaw tightening with the effort to control himself. "I never asked you to be easy, Dash."

He growled then. "You have no idea what I've imagined doing to you, Elizabeth," he told her roughly. "The many ways I've taken you in my dreams. How many times you've screamed for me in my fantasies. Screamed because you needed what I was giving you. Begging for more."

She swallowed tightly as his head lowered, his tongue licking at her shoulder as her hands flexed within his.

"Have you ever been tied?" he asked her. "Completely restrained? Helpless? At the mercy of the man taking you?"

"No." She shook her head roughly.

"I want you helpless beneath me, Elizabeth." He wanted it, needed it until it was a hunger in his soul. "I want you begging, so wet and hot that when I start stretching you open you can only beg for more."

He heard her whimper, a sound of naked longing. His sweet little Elizabeth, always so in control, always so proper and levelheaded, was shaking in arousal at the thought of being tied down for him.

"I won't lie to you." He secured her hands in one of his while the other ran over the soft curve of her rear. "I won't be easy on you. I can't be. You won't let me protect you from everything else, I'll be damned if I'll protect you from who or what I am. Do you understand that?"

"I don't need another warning, Dash." Her eyes flashed in the dim light of the room, her body straining closer to him. "I don't need protection from anything. Least of all you."

Her lips moved over his shoulder, and then her teeth scraped before nipping at him gently. Dash closed his eyes as he fought the need to take her fast and hard.

"Shall I show you," she asked, "just how much I do want you, Dash Sinclair?"

Her lips moved farther down his chest as she tugged roughly at the grip he had on her hands. Her tongue, liquid fire, lashed over a hard male nipple as he groaned roughly and released her.

Dash stood there, damned near helpless in ways he had never been, and watched one of his greatest fantasies come to life.

CHAPTER 19

Elizabeth had never known a need in her life as powerful as the need to taste Dash. To lick his skin, feel the muscles rippling under his tight flesh. His hands released her wrists, caressed over her arms as she moved lower and sampled his rapidly moving chest. His skin was free of hair except for a very faint, very soft covering of tiny fine hairs that tickled her tongue. But even that was erotic. Sensual.

Everything about the man was sexy as sin.

She sank her teeth into the thick muscle below a hard male nipple, her womb clenching at the growl that tore from his throat. His hands clenched at her shoulders, his fingers rubbing against her bare flesh as her head moved lower. Down, past his heavy chest until she was exploring the tight muscles of his abdomen. Her tongue licked over the hard, tanned flesh, her teeth nipping, moving steadily closer to the hard, thick erection awaiting her below.

"Elizabeth." His voice was a dark, sexy rumble that had her pussy creaming with hungry abandon.

Her vagina ached, her womb clenched convulsively as her hands moved to his thighs. She licked closer, excited, frightened, wondering if she could possibly contain the bulging head of his cock in her mouth comfortably. Who said science didn't know what the hell it was doing? When they created Dash they gave him everything a man would need: a tall, strong body, an honorable heart, and a cock that would fill her in every way imaginable.

She went to her knees, her fingers gripping the smooth, heated flesh as she slid her tongue delicately over the throbbing head. It was the size of a large plum, dark and velvety soft, tempting her as her hunger demanded she consume him.

"Sweet heaven," he groaned as she slid her lips over the hard flesh. Surprisingly, a soft pulse of pre-cum shot from the tip into her mouth. She hummed her approval of the taste. A mix of salty sweetness that made her long for more but had Dash whispering a heated curse and trying to pull free of her.

"No," she whispered as his cock slid free of her mouth. "Not yet." Her mouth covered him again as a strangled growl echoed around her.

"Wait," Dash protested, but his cock slid deeper as his hips thrust against her.

Her fingers enclosed the length, her mouth taking him as deep as possible. Another hard pulse of fluid shot into her mouth as she tightened on him, hearing his gasping breaths above her, feeling the tense, desperate arousal that tightened his body.

"Elizabeth, we need to talk first." Another small spurt of pre-cum pulsed in her mouth, making her hungrier for more.

She licked the underside of the shaft slowly, suckling at the hard flesh hesitantly as she fought to accustom herself to the thickness. She had rarely gone down on Dane. He hadn't liked it. Hadn't wanted her mouth there. Dash hadn't been far from the truth when he said missionary only and lights out. She wasn't terribly experienced, but she was greedy now. She wanted to experience with Dash every sexual act a man and woman could experience. She wanted it all.

His fingers threaded through her hair, tightening in the long strands as he pulled at them gently, as though to dislodge her. As though he would pull her from the treat she was giving herself. She rarely allowed herself any type of treats, especially one like this. She hadn't been touched sexually in more years than she cared to count. Now here she was, on her knees, this powerful cock filling her mouth, this strong man breathing harshly, desperately, as she suckled at his flesh and decided now was the time to make up for her lack of treats.

"God help me, Elizabeth, please . . ." Another strong pulse of fluid filled her mouth now. The pre-cum was liquid silk and slid easily down her throat as she drew on his cock slowly, gaining confidence as he fought and failed to pull away from her.

Surely she was doing it right, she thought. Something he enjoyed as much as she enjoyed his touch. He couldn't stop, even though she knew he seemed unwilling to spill himself into her mouth. Still, he thrust against her, moaning with a pleasure that made her skin prickle with awareness.

Her tongue flickered over the pulsing head with greedy licks. Her hands pumped the shaft, slick now with her saliva and the slick essence of his pre-cum. His thighs were corded and tight, his hands kneading her hair, sharp growls rumbling from his throat as she pleasured him.

Elizabeth felt her own arousal surging at the knowledge that she was pleasing him, that he was unable to pull from her, that the sensations she delivered to his throbbing erection kept him from forcing his will on her. For now. She knew it wouldn't last long, that each second was a miracle as he allowed her to push him closer to the climax she knew was building in his scrotum. She could feel the tight sac beneath his shaft, drawn close to the base of his cock, flexing periodically as she drew on the pulsing head.

She wanted to taste him, wanted him filling her mouth with his cum, hearing his cry as he released his semen, his release shuddering through his body. She wanted it all as she had never wanted anything in her life.

"Damn. Baby." His voice was guttural now, harsh and exciting as he fucked against the strong pull of her mouth.

Shallow, strong strokes powered past her lips, sinking the head of his cock deep in her mouth as she tongued it hungrily. Another pulse, a hard throb of his cock and then he stilled, his hands tightening in her hair, holding her steady as he pulled slowly from her mouth.

"No. Dash, please." She tried to follow, to take him again, to force him back.

He pried her hands from his cock, then pulled her to her feet, jerking her against his chest as she stared up at him, needing him. Her cunt wept with the need; her body vibrated with it.

"Look at me," he growled with feral savagery. "We might have a serious problem here, Elizabeth."

She stilled in his arms. "Is someone else in the house?" She listened closely but could hear nothing above her own heartbeat.

"No." His hands clenched on her hips as she moved against his cock, cushioning it firmly against her belly.

"Then I don't care." She shook her head desperately. "I need you, Dash. I don't care about anything else right now."

"Wait, Elizabeth," he groaned as she moved against him, her hand reaching up, threading through his hair and bringing his lips to hers. "I could hurt you."

Her tongue moved over his lips as she stared up at him, dazed with the arousal pulsing through her body. "I won't break," she whispered against his lips. "But if you don't fuck me soon, Dash, I just might have to hurt you."

Her explicit words seemed to tip in her favor. Flames erupted in his eyes, his face flushing with arousal, his cock jerking against her stomach as she stared up at him. Before she realized his intent he lifted her from the floor and tossed her to the bed. She rolled, coming up on the far side on her hands and knees, staring at him as he moved onto the mattress, his knees sinking into the soft pad.

"That's the way I want you eventually," he told her, his voice rough. "On your knees, bent over for me, screaming as I push my way up your tight pussy. Turn around, baby. Let me show you what I can do."

She smiled slowly. His voice sent shivers up her spine. It was part threat, part pure seduction as he stared at her, one hand gripping his cock, his fingers stroking over the shaft slowly.

"You think it's going to be that easy?" she asked him, fighting to breathe now. "You want it, you can take it."

His smile was intent, confident. "I can do that, Elizabeth," he whispered. "I really could. But if I start wrestling you down, I'm not going to have the control to take time to eat that sweet cunt. And I really want to taste that hot cream I smell flowing from your body, baby."

Elizabeth trembled. His voice was so rough, so dark, it was almost a physical caress as it stroked over her senses. Her pussy clenched at his dark offer, an ache like nothing she had ever known before pulsing in the very depths of it. She wanted him there. Wanted to feel his tongue stroking over the flesh she kept free of hair, waiting, anticipating a time when she could feel his touch against it.

"Lie down." He moved to the bottom of the bed, watching her intently. "Come on, baby. Let me show you how a Breed male makes a meal out of his mate."

She trembled, licking her dry lips as hunger throbbed in her womb. A Breed male. The words sent shivers racing over her spine. Nothing was known about their sexuality. Nothing documented that they were different from any other man. But it was hinted that their savage natures could slip over the edge of humanity and enter into that unknown sphere of the mixed DNA. Some scientists had hinted that it could go further, that the men could show actual characteristics of their animal cousins. That the Felines could exhibit a barblike growth. That the Wolf Breeds could exhibit much more.

It was rumor rather than fact. But Elizabeth was now more than eager to know the truth. Dash had stoked an arousal inside her that nearly consumed her dreams before she ever met him. Now that he had touched her, it didn't matter if he was man or animal. She had to know his touch, had to know his possession.

His mate? She moved to the center of the bed, watching him carefully. "Who says I'm your mate?"

His smile was so certain it sent pulsing shivers washing over her flesh.

"Oh honey, we both know you are. Now come on, let me love you for a while before I lose my sanity and start fucking you until we both scream."

Yes. That was what she wanted. She wanted to scream. To be so insane with the pleasure and the need that nothing could hold back her cries. To know and experience pleasures she had only heard about but had never known herself.

"I could handle that." She was panting as she lay down slowly, watching as he came over her.

He didn't answer her. His lips moved over hers roughly, slanting against them as he claimed her with a kiss that rocked her to her toes. His tongue pushed past her lips, pumping into her mouth with slow, deliberate strokes, teasing hers, making her groan in hungry need as her arms came around his shoulders.

His hands smoothed up her waist, cupped her breasts. His thumbs traced slow, intricate designs around her pebble-hard nipples as he possessed her mouth, moaning against her as she pushed up, her soft abdomen raking the heavy length of his cock.

"God, you make me crazy," he muttered as his lips slid from hers, tracking down her neck as she arched it just for him and shivered in pleasure as his teeth raked her skin.

"I need you," she panted as his lips feathered over one nipple. "Now, Dash."

"Not yet," he groaned, his hand plumping the mound of her breast a second before his lips covered it.

He suckled her deeply, moaning against her flesh, his tongue lashing the little bud before he moved and treated its twin similarly. Then his lips were moving lower, his hands pulling her thighs apart, lifting them, spreading them as his mouth covered the swollen, desperate flesh of her clit.

Rockets of sensation burst through Elizabeth's skull as his rough, heated tongue moved slowly against the little pearl. She was so close. So sensitive that she could easily find her release with just the right stroke. Evidently, though, he was determined to torment her.

His mouth slid lower, his tongue stroking through the narrow slit of her swollen folds. He parted them easily, drawing the thick juices into his mouth, lapping at her heatedly as he stared up at her from between her thighs.

"I've dreamed of this," he whispered against her sensitive flesh. "Dreamed of drowning in your pussy, lapping all your sweet juices into my mouth, fucking my tongue hard and deep inside you."

His tongue plunged into the clenching depths of her vagina as she arched violently against him. A thin wail of need echoed around them as she fought to close her thighs, to hold him inside her. But his hands were there, spreading her farther apart, his eyes staring up at her over the mound of her pussy.

It was the most incredibly erotic thing she had ever known in her life, feeling his tongue lapping deep inside her cunt as his golden eyes mesmerized her. Then watching him move, licking delicately through the slit once again and circling her clit with tormenting strokes before returning to the pulsing well of her pussy.

Over and over again he tormented her, licking at her teasingly, pushing deep and hard inside her clenching vagina as she screamed out at his tormenting touch. Her fingers were locked in the blankets beneath her, her head twisting against the pillow in desperation as she gave up watching him. Her eyes were closed, her mind rioting with the sensations spearing through her womb.

"Dash, please." She was nearly sobbing now as he sucked at her clit again, his tongue stroking softly around it. "Please. Please. You're killing me."

He moaned thickly. His thumbs spread the folds of her pussy apart, his mouth moving deeper against her, his tongue increasing its strokes as she held her breath in anticipation. Yes. Like that. She could feel the heat coiling in the little bud, the wracking sensitivity increasing as his lips and tongue drove her closer to the edge.

Elizabeth trembled in anticipation, her thighs tightening against his shoulders, her hips writhing beneath him. Closer. Closer. Her eyes flew open as it struck her. Like a blast of heat, an explosion of pure, intense sensation swept through her body, arching her back, dragging a strangled cry from her chest as she came apart beneath him.

The pleasure beat at her brain, ripping past the fabric of reality and flinging her into a world of bombarding colors and light. She shuddered, convulsing beneath the whiplash of his tongue as the world dissolved around her.

"Now." He moved before the last violent pulses stilled.

He came over her body, catching his weight on his elbows, staring down at her with savage intensity as the bulbous head of his cock nudged against the sensitive opening of her pussy.

"Now," he whispered again. "I make you my woman, Elizabeth. Now."

CHAPTER 20

Dear God. He was so big. Elizabeth felt the bulging head of Dash's cock pressed against her sensitive opening and caught her breath at the tight stretching sensation that began to burn her tender flesh. He watched her carefully, kneeling between her thighs, her legs raised, knees bent over his arms as he lifted her to him.

She whimpered in distress as he paused, then shuddered as she felt a hard pulse of the silky pre-cum throb from his cock. Dane had never done that. Had never spilled that slick fluid inside her as he entered her.

A second later, another followed. As it did, she noticed a slow loosening of her flesh around the thick head and he slid forward marginally. Oh, that was so good. She was stretched tightly around his cock, gripping the small amount of it he had worked inside her, and she was greedy for more.

He groaned as yet more of the pre-cum spilled within her. With each short spurt of the fluid, her muscles eased more. Distantly, she realized this couldn't be natural. That there was no way pre-cum could relax her tight, unused pussy, but it was doing just that.

"Dash," she whimpered, suddenly nervous despite the incredible pleasure filling her.

He slid forward another inch. The head of his cock was now buried inside her, and every few seconds the short, sharp ejaculations were released inside her.

"You're so tight, Elizabeth," he groaned as his gaze moved to the point where he was penetrating her. "So hot and sweet, it's almost impossible to wait to sink inside you."

He retreated marginally before working the erect tip back inside her, loosening her further, easing her open for him. His muscles were taut, his body corded with his fight for control as he watched his cock sink inside her. Elizabeth twisted beneath him, breathing roughly as she felt him stretching her, feeling a fire raging inside her that threatened to destroy her sanity.

The pulsing liquid he spilled inside her sensitized the tissue, making each inch he worked within her caress nerve endings that screamed out for relief. She was stretched so tight around the broad shaft now that she could feel every vein, every detail of the velvety shaft working inside her.

"Dash." Her hands were ripping at the sheets, her head tossing as he began to pump gently inside her, stroking deeper, filling her further as her cunt slowly relaxed enough to allow it to slide in.

It was exquisite, a building, blistering sensitivity and heat that had her gasping, her womb convulsing as her pussy spasmed around his cock. Dash was the most erotic sight she had ever seen in her life. His muscles bulged as he fought for control, his golden-brown eyes blazing down at her, his black hair falling forward around his face, creating the impression of a savage, lusty male animal.

Elizabeth arched to him, taking him deeper, working in time to his strokes as he muttered a prayer, then whispered a curse as she stretched around him.

A hard jet of fluid suddenly filled her as Dash stilled, shaking his head, gasping for breath.

"Elizabeth, ah God. Baby. I'm sorry." He was breathing hard, rough. A little more than half of the straining flesh filled her now, throbbing hard and hot up the once-narrow channel of her pussy.

"Dash?" Her own voice was strained as she felt her cunt milking his flesh, drawing at it, urging it deeper.

"I can't wait." He was fighting for breath now, for control. "I can't wait, baby. You're so tight, so sweet . . ."

His eyes closed as he drew back marginally, caressing the sensitive nerve endings of her cunt before he stilled again. Elizabeth barely had time to draw in a deep breath before he slammed hard and deep inside her.

She wailed his name as he pushed past the clenching tissue, separating it, stretching it as his cock jerked with several more hard ejaculations inside her.

Elizabeth writhed beneath him, fighting to accept the ample width of male flesh impaling her.

Dash's eyes blazed down at her, his hands gripping her thighs as he breathed out roughly. "I'm an animal, Elizabeth," he growled, his voice rough as his cock pulsed again. "Feel it. Feel what I'm shooting inside you." He sounded agonized, but that didn't keep him from moving deeply inside her, or from spilling yet more of the fluid within her.

"Dash." She shook her head desperately. The blend of pleasure and pressure inside her pussy was making her crazy now.

"Feel it, Elizabeth," he demanded roughly. "Feel what I'm doing to you, dammit. Only an animal would do this."

He was tortured, tormented. He growled when she felt him pulse inside her again. Distantly, Elizabeth was aware now of what the fluid was, a natural side effect of his DNA. A lubrication that eased and prepared the female entrance for his penetration. She was thankful for it. She needed him. Needed him inside her, filling her as she had never thought possible. Without it, there wasn't a chance she could have taken him comfortably.

"Dash." She reached for him, her hands sliding up his damp chest, nails scraping lightly as he shivered beneath the caress. "I don't care."

And she didn't. She moved her hips against him, her breath hitching in desperation as she felt his cock moving snugly within her. He was so hard, so hot, so firmly embedded within her cunt that she knew she would never forget the feel of him now.

"You don't care?" he groaned as he moved convulsively inside her, spreading her thighs farther as he released them and leaned over her.

His bigger body blanketed hers, his elbows catching his weight as her hands slid over his shoulders, relishing the feel of his skin against her. It also changed the level of penetration, causing him to sink deeper inside the giving flesh of her pussy.

Sensations piled atop each other, lightning-hot flares of pleasure and pressure building in her womb, streaking through her cunt. Her clit was swollen, throbbing, rising eagerly as his pelvis ground against it. Her nipples were cushioned against his hard chest, the smooth muscle rasping over them, the tiny, fine hairs caressing them heatedly.

"No," she gasped as she arched beneath him, pressing the aching buds tighter against him. "I don't care."

One hand cupped her hip as he drew back. He slid smoothly within the tight entrance, retreating then forcing his way back until he was once again buried to the hilt.

"I could knot you, Elizabeth. Like an animal." Her eyes widened at the harsh words, staring up at him in shock.

She couldn't make sense of the words, couldn't imagine his DNA affecting his sexuality to that point. But she realized she didn't care if he did. Didn't care how he took her, how much he filled her, as long as she knew that for now, she belonged to him.

"I've never done this with a woman in my life. But that could happen as well." He was breathing roughly, fucking her with almost involuntary strokes, lifting her hips to him, sinking deep inside her.

She knew she needed to retain her grasp on this conversation. Knew she needed to make sense of it. But Dash was moving now, his cock retreating then burying inside her, over and over again, stroking sensitive tissue and firing nerve endings to screaming life. She couldn't concentrate. Couldn't make sense of anything he had to say. And he wasn't talking anymore anyway. He was breathing roughly, his head lowering so his lips could caress her shoulder as he thrust inside her with steadily increasing strokes.

Elizabeth could hear herself mewling in pleasure. Her legs wrapped around his hips, lifting her closer to him, thrusting back against him, the searing impalement sending sparks of fire zipping through her entire body.

"Harder," she gasped, protesting his almost gentle thrusts now.

He was growling at her shoulder, his teeth scraping the flesh as she bucked beneath him. Sweat soaked their bodies as she felt Dash clinging to his control with desperate fingers.

"Wait. Elizabeth," he groaned desperately as she moved beneath him.

She couldn't wait. Didn't want to wait. She was on fire. Her pussy spasmed around his thick cock, needing more, starved for the driving, fierce thrusts she had never known during her marriage to Dane. She had never known anything like this. Wild and hot, shredding any sense of decorum, any modesty she once possessed. She needed him deep, hard, plunging into her as they set fire to the world around them.

"Please." She tightened on his throbbing erection. "Please, Dash. Fuck me now. Fuck me harder. Please."

Her explicitly hot demand exploded through his head, shredding his control. Her soft voice, so sweet and husky, almost innocent, begging to be taken, to be fucked, was more than he could stand.

Dash groaned desperately, fighting the urge to lock his teeth on her delicate shoulder and give her exactly what she wanted. He had fought the instincts, the driving hunger, as long as he could. When her words whispered over his senses, he was lost.

He snarled at her shoulder, gripping it with his teeth as his hands tightened on her hips and he gave her what she was begging for. Sinking into the slick, ultra tight tissue, he set a hard, fast rhythm that drove his erection to the very depths of her, burying his cock to the end and fucking her with a hunger he had never known in his life.

She was his. His woman. His mate.

Elizabeth was screaming out beneath him, her nails piercing his back as his teeth pierced her shoulder, his dick piercing her tight pussy. He could feel his release looming, as he could feel her flesh rippling over his cock. So close. He held her still as he pumped inside her harder, the sounds of wet sex filling his ears, sucking cunt wrapping around him as he felt her explode around his cock. Her pussy tightened, milking his flesh, fighting to hold it deep inside her as her juices spilled around it. It was too much. Too hot. Too damned tight. He felt the last of his control snap as his own release broke free of his restraint.

"No. Fuck, no." He tried to pull back as he felt the first hard jet of his semen spew inside her, then felt something more.

A desperate swelling in the middle of his cock, a pulsing erection blooming that terrified him.

"Oh God! Dash!" Elizabeth screamed his name as he felt her body shudder spasmodically beneath him, her orgasm rising in power, ripping violently beneath her flesh.

She was so tight around him. Her flesh stretched, hugging him, giving way to the knot blooming in his cock and locking him deep inside her. He couldn't move without hurting her, couldn't jerk his swelling flesh free of her tight pussy. He could only groan in defeat, hold her to him and allow his release to surge through his body.

Each hard pulse of his seed throbbed in the hard knot, triggered contractions in her cunt that had her screaming hoarsely. She writhed beneath him, struggling to accept the additional girth as another orgasm peaked inside her, causing her to shudder harshly as she was forced to accept every hard pulse of his semen inside her already overfilled depths.

Dash tasted blood and realized the sharp tips of his canines had pierced her shoulder. His tongue licked over it, his mouth suckling the small wound as she whimpered beneath him. The wracking shudders that had slammed through her body were weaker now. She trembled beneath him, her pussy clenching on the hard knot locked inside her as she moaned at the intermittent bursts of orgasmic echoes.

Her hands had fallen to the bed, her legs sliding weakly from his hips before he finally felt the easing of his flesh inside her. It was slow. It was destructive. Hard, hot blasts of his semen spewed inside her with each flexing throb of the knot, though they lessened in intensity as the swelling began to diminish.

Dash held her close to his chest, breathing roughly, fighting his own shock and horror until he could finally pull free of her, exiting her pussy as it gave a soft, resounding farewell kiss to his flesh.

✦ CHAPTER 21 ✦

He had meant to move away from her, to leave the bed, the room, to find someplace away from the sweet scent of her heat where he could think. Where he could consider this new, shocking development clearly. But as he moved from her, she whispered his name, drowsy with repletion, her body exhausted from the demands he had made on her. It had sighed over his flesh like a whisper of silk as she moved against him.

She tugged at him, pulling him down beside her, moving into his arms and laying her head against his chest. He stared down at the tangle of dark hair that spilled to the bed. One slender leg was crossed over his; her arm lay over his stomach. He was tied as securely to the bed now as he would have been if it had been chains instead of one delicate woman.

What was he supposed to do?

Tentatively, he turned to her and wrapped his arms around her, expecting the position to be uncomfortable. It wasn't. She fit against him as though she had been made for him.

He had never allowed himself to hold a woman after sex. Had never felt comfortable enough or relaxed enough to sleep with one. And he had sure as hell never been able to keep from pulling away from one. But Elizabeth was different. In more ways than one.

God. What had he done to her? He closed his eyes, swallowing tightly at the remembrance of the thick swelling into her already snug pussy. Like an animal. But nothing could eliminate the fact that the pleasure had been so intense, so much deeper than anything he had known, that he wanted nothing more than to repeat it.

Instead, he held her against him and let her rest. He hoped she was sleeping. Prayed she was sleeping. Because if she wasn't, there wasn't a chance in hell he could keep from taking her again.

Dash let his fingers sink into the soft waves of hair that flowed over his chest and down her back. She was such a creature of sensuality, hot and erotic once the restraints had come off. She had burned him alive.

He rested his chin against her head, wondering at this strange change within him. He knew she was his woman. His mate. He had accepted it over a year ago when his commander had first begun reading him Cassie's letters. There was no other way to explain the soul-deep possessiveness that had filled him, the inborn knowledge and rage that had gripped him while buried beneath the drugs as his body healed. He had known her. Known her laughter, her touch, her heat. By the time he awoke, he had been filled with a determination to hurry and heal and strengthen that he had never known before.

He had amazed the doctors who had fought to save his life. He had exhausted his therapists as he worked to get stronger. Every minute of that long, painful battle, all he thought of was Elizabeth and Cassie. His woman and his child. They needed him. He needed them.

The response of his body to her had been shocking, though. Never had he done anything like that with another woman. Never had he produced an ejaculation like the small, slick spurts of fluid that had eased her vagina around him. And never had he conceived that anything could have occurred like the thick swelling that locked him deep inside her already tight vagina.

It had been like nothing he could have imagined. Filling her with his seed, knowing there wasn't a chance in hell that so much as a drop of it could spill before being given the chance . . .

Oh hell. The chance to impregnate her. He swallowed tightly. She wasn't on the pill. He knew she wasn't on the pill. And for the first time in his life he had taken a woman without even thinking about protection.

His cock jerked and seemed to harden further at the thought of making a child with Elizabeth, one as sparkling and filled with life as Cassie. Perhaps a little boy. One who was tall and strong and filled with the same sense of determination and strength as his mother. His arms tightened around her, his heart racing as he imagined the family he could have. The family he had never dared dream of until now.

◆　◆　◆

Elizabeth lay silent, still. Dash wasn't restless but he wasn't sleeping either. She could feel his chest beneath her cheek, his heart racing, feel the tense readiness of his body. She would have moved from him, but when she glanced from the shield of her lashes, down the length of his tall body, she had seen his erection, thick and strong, still glistening from their combined releases as it lay against his lower belly.

The flesh was at least as thick as her wrist. Long, steel-hard. The mushroom-shaped head was a dark color, almost violet, indicating the level of Dash's arousal. Not more than her own, she thought. Even now, mere minutes after she had managed to pull him down beside her, she still ached to feel him buried within her once again, locking tight and hard inside her.

She barely controlled a weak hitch of her breath at the memory of the swelling. She knew what it was. Just as she now knew what the silky ejaculations had been. A lubricating fluid, somehow enhanced to relax the desperate tightness of the female channel. She had felt it when the fluid mixed with her own juices, heating inside her, easing the resistance in her vagina as he pushed past the snug muscles of her pussy.

It had done the same to her mouth, her tongue. Before he had pulled free she had wondered if she could take that bulging head clear to her throat. It was amazing. Unlike anything she could have imagined. Yet not completely unexpected.

Elizabeth wasn't fooling herself in any way. She had wondered if it would happen. Wondered if he possessed not just the sense of the wolf, but in some part, the sexuality as well.

The feline Breeds called their women their mates. In one interview, Callan Lyons and his wife had been amazingly reticent about the sexuality Callan displayed. But Elizabeth had known that something had bonded them closer than just love. She could see it in their faces, in their eyes as they gazed at each other. That little glimmer of a secret. And she had been envious.

She knew Dash would have warned her beforehand if he knew this would happen. Knew he wouldn't have hidden it from her. And he had been even more surprised than she had.

It filled her with a sense of pride, of feminine possessiveness, to know that he had not given that experience to any other woman. It was hers alone. As shocking, as amazing as it had been, it was still hers alone. Just as that magnificent hard-on was hers. Period.

She watched as it flexed, throbbed. Tempted her. Her hand smoothed over Dash's chest as he suddenly tensed further, down his abdomen, across the top of his thigh.

"Elizabeth." His voice was dark, thick, his fingers tightening in her hair.

"Hmm?" She caressed her way between his powerful legs, her fingers moving slowly until she was cupping the smooth, silken sac of his scrotum. "Why don't you have any hair here?"

"Ah God." His hips arched as she caressed his testicles softly, running her fingers over the ultra smooth, obviously ultra sensitive flesh. "Because I'm a Breed." He seemed to have pushed the words between clenched teeth.

"Am I hurting you?" She stilled, watching the soft pearl of liquid forming at the opened eye of his cock.

"No," he breathed out roughly. "But are you sure you want to keep this up?"

"Mmm." She pressed a kiss to his chest, watching his hard flesh jerk as she cupped the sac more fully within her palm. "I'm sure."

"Elizabeth," he groaned as she moved lower, her lips stroking over his flexing abdomen. "Baby. Wait."

"For what?" Her hand stroked up from his testicles to the hard shaft of his cock.

Her fingers couldn't circle it, but she could stroke it. She watched as her hand slid up the thick pole, her finger rubbing over the slick essence that seeped from his cock.

"We need to talk." His voice was strained. "About earlier. Elizabeth, we have to figure this out."

"What's there to figure out?" She laid her head on his lower stomach, the bulging head of his erection just below her. Before he could speak, her tongue peeked from her lips and swiped along the glistening head of his cock.

"Oh hell. Elizabeth," he muttered, his fingers tangling in her hair as the muscles of his abdomen clenched harshly.

She went lower, despite the pressure he exerted on the strands he gripped. Her mouth capped the hard crest, her tongue flickering over the little eyelet at the tip before stroking around the bulging crest. She was rewarded with a small spurt of the salty sweet fluid that had released into her mouth before.

"Enough." Before she could tempt him further, tease him further, he gripped her shoulders and flipped her to the bed as he rose over her. "Are you insane?"

She licked her lips slowly as she watched him from beneath lowered lids, hungry for the taste of him. There was something wickedly exciting in drawing his cock into her mouth. Something that fired all her baser instincts and made her completely wanton.

"Not insane," she whispered as she lifted her head and licked her tongue over his lips, pressing against them, slipping it between them.

She shared the taste of his essence with him then. Her gaze locked with his, seeing shock flare in his eyes a second before he groaned roughly; the hand that had tightened in her hair pulled her head back until he could take control of the kiss.

His tongue tangled with hers, then followed it as it retreated behind her lips. He swept into her mouth demandingly, licking at her lips, her tongue, kissing her with a heat and hunger that had her moaning and arching into his touch.

"Damn you." He tore his lips from hers, breathing roughly as he stared down at her. "You felt what happened last time, Elizabeth. You know what I did to you."

"Yeah," she sighed, smiling in anticipation. "Now do it again. Let's see if it will work again the second time."

Shock filled his gaze, then heat. Incredible, incendiary heat as he stared down at her intently. Slowly, a smile that could only be called wolfish curled his mouth.

"I'll make you scream harder this time," he warned her softly. "I'll make you . . ." He stopped, his head suddenly rising, eyes narrowing as he stared at the door. "Dash?" Elizabeth felt his body tense dangerously, rather than in arousal.

He was moving from her as she heard feet pounding up the stairs, then a hard knock at the door. "Get ready, Dash. Grange has men in town and they could be heading out here. We have to get you moving. I've called the pilot; fifteen minutes to landing."

Dash snarled as his head turned, but Elizabeth was already out of the bed and pulling on the clothes he had left lying out for her.

"So much for a damned shower," she muttered as she pulled her panties over her long legs, covering the glistening, soaked mound of her pussy. "Dammit, I hate wearing wet panties."

Dash turned for his own clothes, snarling in silent fury. Her panties were wet, his cock was steel-hard and they were heading to a cold plane.

He reminded himself to make sure he hurt Grange—really bad—before he finally got around to killing him.

· CHAPTER 22 ·

"You were loud enough to wake the dead," Dash snapped as Elizabeth slipped around the corner of the cabin nearly nine days later. Sweat poured from her braided hair and down her face; her clothes were damp with it.

She had worked her way down the point in twice the time it should have taken her, and she had ignored half of what he had told her along the way. He had caught her scent first thing simply because she hadn't tested the direction the wind was blowing. He had heard her skirting the small clearing five minutes before, going in the complete opposite direction than she should have gone.

She stopped, frowning, her blue eyes flashing with anger.

Her breasts were heaving with exertion and nerves and he doubted she could have heard anyone sneaking up on her for the pounding of her own heart.

"I was quiet, dammit. I didn't make a sound."

"Do you think I would lie to you?" he growled. "I heard you coming five minutes ago. If this were Grange's property the guards would have already had you down, stripped and fucked. I told you, Elizabeth. Quietly. I showed you how."

He was being hard on her. But if he could hear her that far away, then those damned dogs patrolling Grange's estate could too.

"How much quieter do I have to be?" She was tired, irritated and ready to tear into him now.

"A hell of a lot quieter," he snarled. "Turn around, get your ass back up to that point and try it again. Grange returns to his estate in two weeks. That's it. End of training and kill time. You won't be ready."

"The hell I won't," she snarled. "Son of a bitch. You're a Breed. Of course you heard me. Grange doesn't have Breeds for soldiers, does he?"

"No, he doesn't," he said softly, smiling tightly, controlling the instinctive rush to protect her. "He has dogs. Big mean dogs trained to fuck nosy little girls who come creeping around his estate. You've had a taste of it, baby. Wanna try for the real animals now?"

Her face flushed in fury, her lips thinning as she stared at him coldly.

"Aren't you just a barrel of laughs this morning," she sneered. "Too bad you're not as well trained as Grange's dogs are."

She turned on her heel and slipped back around the cabin as he felt offended anger flow through his body. He stomped after her, determined to teach her that soldiers never sassed their trainers. Not and get away with it.

As he rounded the side of the cabin he had no more than a second's warning before his feet flew out from under him, leaving him on his back with a furious Elizabeth straddling his chest, the sharp end of a stick pressing to his throat.

"I get breakfast now, big boy," she snarled, curling her lip in sneering triumph as he narrowed his eyes at her. "Who says I can't be quiet?"

She had him. Damn her, she had tricked him so quickly he hadn't even considered she would turn so sneaky.

He lifted his hand and pulled the stick away from her, tossing it aside as he stared up at her.

"Next time you come over me like that you better be naked," he growled.

"Next time, I'm going to stomp your balls for being so insulting," she snapped back.

He had no doubt she would. If she got the chance.

He lifted her off him, then rose to his feet as she stood, watching him in triumph. "You did good. Not good enough, but good."

She breathed out roughly.

"Not good enough?" She placed her hands on her hips as she watched with a frown. "I got you. Fair and square. How is that not good enough?"

"Because I trust you and I have the added handicap of being so damned hot to fuck you I can't consider you a threat just yet. Bad move on my part. I won't make that mistake again." Damned if his pride could handle it.

They had been working for most of the morning. He had dragged her out of bed before dawn, marched her to the top of the rise above the cabin and told her to wait before heading back down. On the way up, he had taught her how to move through the brush, keeping her steps light, her breathing slow and easy. How to pace herself, time her steps and move without causing a ripple of sound.

Not that he had expected her to pick it up as well as she had. She had actually surprised him. But she could be better. If his instincts were right, she had the potential to move as silently as any hunter ever born. And she was willing to work for what she needed to know. That was imperative. Elizabeth understood that she needed what Dash was teaching her, just as Dash himself was aware of it.

"That's a poor excuse," she finally grunted before turning and heading back to the front of the cabin. "I need a shower and breakfast. I'll try it again after I've thought about it."

She was rolling her shoulders, her voice was thoughtful, as though something had come to her that she wasn't quite certain of, and her ass was filling those jeans out like a dream.

Dash grimaced as his dick throbbed and his lust seemed to hit peak level. He hadn't touched her since the night at Mike's ranch. The rushed departure, exhausting flight and journey to the cabin had been made in less than twenty-four hours. They had both collapsed into the bed and slept like the dead as soon as they had eaten a hastily prepared meal.

Training had begun yesterday as soon as they left the cabin, and by the time he nearly carried her back into the cabin last night, he had known sex wouldn't be at the top of her list of priorities. But it was rising quickly to his.

He watched her disappear into the bedroom of the small cabin, and minutes later he heard the shower turn on full force. He put together a quick breakfast: two large filled omelets, fried potatoes and orange juice. Fresh coffee brewed on the counter, and by the time she walked out of the bedroom nearly thirty minutes later, he was setting breakfast on the table.

"Eat. We'll practice self-defense after breakfast, then give it a break until evening."

He sat across from her, digging into his own food. It was fuel, pure and simple, high on carbs and protein with plenty of running power. She would need the energy to get through the next two weeks. She was already run-down, tired. She wasn't living on shattered nerves and fear now. That adrenaline heightened the senses and gave an

added edge, even if it was a false one. Now she was going to have to
teach her senses to work in the proper direction. Without the nerves.
Without the adrenaline kick that the life-or-death situation she had
faced before had given her.

She drew in a deep breath, but rather than arguing, only nodded.
The action drew his attention to her breasts. Unconfined, without the
bra, they were still ripe and full, plump little mounds that his hands
itched to cup and caress. He was dying to take her again. To see if the
sensations were as intense a second time around or if it had all been
a dream.

Training first, he reminded himself as he finished his meal, then
sat back to enjoy his coffee. It was his first cup in days and damned if
he hadn't missed it. The caffeine jolt to his system was almost immediate, making him contain a hum of pleasure.

Elizabeth wasn't nearly as reticent. A long, low sound of appre-
ciation vibrated in her throat as she closed her eyes, relishing the taste
as well as the jolt. Her expression was pure sensual delight and as she
swallowed the hot brew, her tongue peeked out to catch an escaping
drop on her lower lip.

Dash's cock jerked in awareness. He remembered her licking her
lips in just that manner once before. When she had licked the last
taste of his cock from them after he pulled her from him right before
Mike's interruption.

"I almost forgot how good it was." She sighed as she opened her
eyes, her gaze meeting his.

A flush instantly filled her cheeks as his gaze dropped to her damp
lips.

"Finish your coffee." Dash rose to his feet, clearing their plates
from the table. "I want to start teaching you how to fight with more
than nerves and fear. You have to keep your head clear to be efficient.

To deliver a blow that will disable instead of merely stun. If you just stun your enemy, you risk him coming up behind you later. If you disable him, you can put him out indefinitely. Short of killing him, that's your best bet."

"If he's the enemy, why not just kill him?" She rose to her feet as well, moving to the coffeepot to refill her cup. "I didn't notice you caring much for disabling that guy you killed at the apartment."

"There was no other choice." He shrugged. "He had a gun in my face and he was depressing the trigger. It was kill or be killed. I chose to live. You go around leaving dead bodies and you're drawing more attention than necessary."

"Beats having a bunch of pissed-off enemies following after you," she commented dryly as she lifted the cup to her lips.

"The key is, you keep the enemy from knowing who you are or why you're striking," he told her, fighting to keep a measure of pride from his voice. Damn her, she was bloodthirsty as hell. He loved it. She wouldn't balk if blood had to be shed, but she had to learn that there were different levels of enemies. Only the upper notch really deserved death. "Dead bodies leave a trail for the simple fact that everyone has a preferred way of killing. Mine's the knife. If I left a string of bodies behind me, the media would start yelling 'vigilante.' Someone I've worked with would hear it, and instantly, the facts of the killing would make him suspicious. There's your first domino falling and toppling the rest."

"So, learn another way to kill." She was damned sure enjoying that coffee as well as whatever bloodthirsty little fantasies she must be having about now.

Dash sighed. "You're not as hard as you're pretending to be, baby. Taking a life isn't that easy."

"Killing Grange won't cause me to lose even a moment's sleep. It will help me sleep better," she assured him, her voice hardening. "Don't fool yourself, Dash. If I could have killed those bastards without my baby seeing it over the past two years, I would have. Easily."

Dash nodded. "And I wouldn't have blamed you, Elizabeth. But the heat of battle and killing in cold blood are two different things. Right now, you think it's not. You're filled with rage and a need for vengeance, and that's good. It will keep you strong. Make you learn. But when the killing time comes, it won't be so easy. It's damned hard to pull that trigger and to know, *know* in your soul, the man you're taking out deserves no more chances to live."

"I thought you were harder than that, Dash." She surprised him with her harsh words. Or maybe she didn't, Dash thought. This rage had been brewing in her for a long time, hardening with each strike against her and her daughter.

He sighed wearily. "My first kill, Elizabeth, was against a monster. I knew he was a monster. He had brutalized men taken hostage. Had turned good, strong women into broken shells of humanity. He had nothing to redeem him. Except one thing. The man was a born fool over a tiny little scrap of humanity he had sired. He had nearly destroyed his little wife, but after that child was born, he treated her like gold because that kid loved her. I had to take him out to secure the release of two of my men he had imprisoned in a cellar room near the house. Didn't have a choice. Even though I knew that kid and his mother would suffer. And I did what I had to do. It was him or my men. I made the choice. But I'll regret having to make it to my dying day. Nearly everyone has a weakness. Somewhere, somehow. He didn't deserve to live because nothing in this world was safe but that child and her mother. But if she ever learns the identity of the man who pulled the trigger, she will come hunting. I knew it then. I know it now."

Elizabeth finished her coffee, turned back and poured another cup. When she finished she watched him curiously. "Am I supposed to feel sorry for Grange now?" she asked him coldly.

Dash shook his head. "No, baby, I don't expect that from you. I'd be surprised if you felt it. He doesn't deserve your pity. The choice of life or death is yours to make. You're the one who has to live with it, has to lie down and sleep at night with it. Just remember what I said. When it's your life or theirs, it's different. When it's cold blood, you're no more than the animal you've come to despise. And then, it gets damned hard to sleep at night. And damned hard to remember what makes you human. Now finish that coffee so I can teach you how to fight."

Elizabeth watched as Dash cleared the living room, pushing furniture against the wall before folding out a large exercise mat he had hauled from Mike's. He moved efficiently, gracefully for a man. There were no wasted actions, was no puttering around. Within minutes the mat was unfolded and he turned back to her with a lift of his brow.

She lifted her coffee cup silently. She wasn't finished. And she couldn't attempt to focus on letting him teach her how to fight with her mind in the state of turmoil it was in now.

Could she kill Grange? That question haunted her now. She had been so certain before. Had convinced herself she could easily put a bullet between his eyes and never think twice. Anywhere. Anytime. Cassie wasn't with her now. Her innocence wouldn't be a casualty to the blood her mother shed.

She turned from Dash and stared out the window over the sink as he moved to the mat and began a series of warm-up exercises. The forest was thick, sheltering, hiding the little cabin perfectly.

A secure place, he had called it. A fellow soldier lent it out. No big deal.

A friend. She noticed everyone was an acquaintance, a fellow soldier, part of the Forces. He had contacts to hell and back, and his voice reflected his respect and often affection for each man he had talked about. But he never called them friends. Never gave voice to the bond she could hear that tied them together. They were a part of a network of honor, of dedication to each other.

He had killed to save her and Cassie. He had killed to save his men. He had killed in the heat of battle and didn't question the lives he had taken. It was kill or be killed. But he wouldn't kill in cold blood. And she was terribly afraid she could.

Grange was a monster. As long as he was alive he would pose a threat to Cassie. He would never stop in his desire to take her. Men like that didn't stop.

She sipped at the coffee, remembering the two years she had spent running. The lives Grange's men had taken. The times they had hunted her without mercy, without emotion. As she finished the coffee and rinsed her cup slowly, she realized that the haze of anger and pain that had filled her over the months had been slowly hardening inside her.

"Elizabeth?" She glanced at the reflection in the window, seeing Dash behind her, staring down at her gently.

She swallowed tightly. "Does it make me a monster too, Dash?" she asked him. "Am I unredeemable?"

His hands settled on her shoulders as he drew her to his chest, meeting her gaze in the window before them.

"There's nothing more dangerous than a window, Elizabeth," he told her rather than answering her question. "You feel safe in the house. Everyone does. They don't think about windows. But hunters do. They watch the windows, hidden, safe, their sights trained on that small square as they wait for the target to pass by, to stop and admire the view. Then they have you."

She stared back at him in shock. "So we're standing here why?"

"You're always vulnerable. Everyone is. And you're smart enough to know that what goes around comes around. Grange is a monster. If he makes getting Cassie's file a danger to you or me, then he's dead. Period. If not by your hand, then by mine. Nature takes care of the diseased, baby. Eventually Grange will fall, if not sooner, then later. When he does, there will be a dozen more monsters to take his place. It's the way of evil. Always there." He drew her away from the window, leading her to the mat. "Now get ready, because I'm going to put you on your ass."

· CHAPTER 23 ·

He did put her on her ass. More than once. Over and over. Snapping orders at her like a damned drill sergeant when she didn't move as fast as she should have or how he thought he had explained to her.

He was cheating. She knew he was. He was aware of every move he had taught her and he knew exactly how to counter it. And he was doing it with amazing efficiency, then daring to laugh at her as her frustration mounted.

She tried to pull his hair, but the pressure he exerted on her wrists had her releasing him immediately. She went for his eyes, but he was taller than she was and always waiting on her. Cool and determined, those golden-brown eyes never missed even the slightest flinch.

She came to her feet slowly, facing him, breathing roughly. She was too aware of her swollen breasts and the peaks of her nipples rasping against her T-shirt. Between her thighs, the seam of her jeans exerted just enough pressure against her sensitive clit to make her yearn for more.

She was hot and sweaty and getting more pissed off by the minute. Damn, he wouldn't even pretend that she might not be ready for him.

"Turn around," he ordered her coldly. "You're on point. You're watching for me. You're covering my back, Elizabeth. Now turn around."

"This isn't working," she complained heatedly. "I can't do anything like this but take the beating you want to dish out."

"Better me than Grange or his men." He wasn't the least sympathetic. "Now turn that tight ass around. Wiggle it or something. Maybe you'll distract me with thoughts of fucking it."

She rolled her eyes, still catching her breath. He insisted on threatening her with it.

"Like any of Grange's men have a cock like that," she pointed out breathlessly. "If it were normal-sized, Dash, I might let you try."

His eyes narrowed. "Oh darlin', I'll do more than try when the time comes. Now flip it around and let me see it."

"Let me catch my breath." He was a demon.

"Tell it to Grange," he snarled. "See if he lets you rest before he kills you. You might catch him in a good mood."

Her teeth ground together as she fought a vicious reply. But every time she snapped at him he came back with something that only pissed her off further.

"Fine." She flipped around. "Get a good look, assho—"

She was on her ass. Before she could prepare herself he was on her. Hard hands flipped her around, a foot sweeping hers from beneath her as his big body followed her down, immobilizing her.

"Who do you think you're wrestling here, baby?" He taunted her as she struggled weakly against him. She was on her back, staring up at him, breathing heavily as he smiled with lazy humor. "I'm amazed you've managed to escape Grange for two years. I thought you were better than that."

She was exhausted. He had outmaneuvered every lowdown dirty trick she had ever learned, as well as the ones he had taught her. "Not fair," she panted. "You were expecting me."

She closed her eyes, feeling him hovering over her, his heat wrapping around her and driving her crazy. What the hell was wrong with her? They had been at this for hours and her cunt was only getting progressively wetter. Her panties were wet, and that was something she just didn't like at all. They clung to the bare lips of her sex and rasped her swelling clitoris erotically.

"You think they aren't expecting you now?" His hard thigh was pressed against her mound, one hand smoothing up her leg as he stared down at her. "They were waiting on you at the apartment. Nearly had you that time, Elizabeth. They're getting wise to you."

She had realized that then. Her teeth clenched in frustration. Her arousal was making her insane. She could barely think for the pulse in her pussy. It was a steady, driving throb that kept her off-balance as much as he did.

"Okay. Okay. I'll try again." She was trying. She was, she assured herself. But every time he touched her she went weak with lust.

Dash moved quickly to her, reaching down and giving her a hand up as she moved into position. She turned her back on him, flexed her shoulders and waited. Sometimes he made her wait forever. Other times it was a quick attack. She could never be certain when it was coming.

She tensed, preparing herself.

"Loosen up." She flinched at his hard, merciless voice. "You're tiring yourself out waiting on me to attack. Listen, Elizabeth. Close your eyes. You're in the middle of Grange's estate, not a safe little cabin. The attack could come from any quarter. You're ready, but relaxed. You're listening. Smelling the air . . ."

"Dammit, Dash, I'm not a Breed . . ." He came at her then. His arm went around her throat as hers flew up. One hand latched onto his arm at her neck as the other flew behind her, going for his eyes. At the same time her ankle wrapped behind his as she moved, jerked, went for a blinding stroke.

He went down hard, rolled to his feet and narrowed his eyes on her as he faced her now. A smile lingered on his lips.

"Oh, good, baby," he crooned in approval as she stared at him in shock. "Now do it again. Turn around."

She backed up instead. How the hell had she done that?

"You'll be expecting me," she argued, shaking her head, more than amazed herself.

"I'll pretend I'm not," he snapped. "Turn around and do it again."

"I can't do it on command." She shook her head, breathing roughly. "I don't know how I did it the first time."

"Then you're dead," he said cruelly. "A bloody dead mess, Elizabeth. Let's call Cassie now so she can start grieving for her mother. Now turn around."

"I can't do it again." She backed away from him nervously. "Let me think about it. Figure out how I did it the first time."

"No. Turn around." His eyes were snapping in anger, but that was okay, because his domineering attitude was really pissing her off too.

"I'm not ready."

He came for her anyway. Before she had time to consider it, she saw the anger, the determination to force something from her, and she moved quickly aside, barely evading his grasp. He turned back to her.

"You want to kill Grange?" he grunted. "You can't kill anyone, Elizabeth. You don't have what it takes. You don't have the courage to learn your own strengths, let alone your weaknesses. Grange will take Cassie, just like he plans to, because we'll never get those papers and you'll be dead. He can move right in then, kidnap her at first chance, and he has her. No one will be able to save her, Elizabeth. No one. Because you'll fail."

"The papers alone won't save her," she argued desperately. "A bullet to his head would be more effective and I know how to shoot a gun."

"Those papers pull his teeth," he informed her coldly. "We steal the papers, the proof of the experiments, and we expose his plan along with your and Cassie's testimonies on Dane's death, and he's gone. Legally. Broken, Elizabeth. You pull the teeth of the monster. Killing isn't easy. Neither is it always beneficial."

Fury was mounting inside her. She wanted Grange dead. Wanted him to bleed, to suffer, and Dash was taking it all away from her.

He came for her again. Rushing her, moving in fast and hard as she dropped to the floor and rolled for his feet. He had taught it to her. He leapt over her quickly, then turned for her again, but she had stayed down, moved to the side and gone for his feet again. He went down this time and she was instantly on his back, her hands tangling in his damp hair, jerking his head back.

"Next time," she snarled, "I'll have my own damned knife."

Before she could gasp he had a hold of her wrist, pulling her off him and straddling her body as he slammed her wrists to the mat.

"You hesitated." His lips pulled back from his teeth in fury. "You gave a warning rather than a killing stroke. Your enemy has you down now, Elizabeth. You're dead."

"Am I?" she panted, enraged.

Blood rushed through her veins, adrenaline surging through her system and throbbing in her pussy. She stilled, tamping it back, relaxing beneath him so suddenly he automatically tensed.

"You're hurting me," she fought to breathe. "We can talk about this, Dash. Really. I'll do better next time."

His eyes narrowed.

"I'm tired." She gazed up at him innocently before her gaze flicked to the hard bulge in his pants. She allowed a smile to tip her lips. "We could play for a while now instead."

Elizabeth wiggled her wrists beneath his, watching him with lowered lids as she licked her lips slowly, dampening the dry curves. "I'll make you a very happy man, mate."

He leaned back slightly, loosening her wrists. Just a little more, she thought as she took a deep breath, lifting her breasts as his gaze went to them. At the same time she moved her legs, a powerful upswing that sent them around his arms and torso as she jerked back, surged up, put her hands together in a fist and delivered a blow to his lower abdomen.

He grunted. Yes! He fell backward as she scrambled away from him and faced him triumphantly.

But now he was more than just determined. Lust filled his eyes as the thought of her making a surprise move, tricking him, and gaining freedom had fired a hunger he could no longer sustain. The same hunger that had been boiling in the depths of her wet pussy.

"You're fucked." His voice was a hot, sexual growl. "So fucked, Elizabeth."

She raised her hand, flicking her fingers back toward herself. "Come on. Knot me, baby. I dare you."

Dash ignored the lurch of his cock beneath his jeans; ignored the heady demand to rush her. He could see her readiness now. Not her tense nervousness, but her readiness. She was confident. She thought she was in control. Thought she had gained the upper hand. She was getting good; he would give her that. In a few hours he had done no more than begin polishing the weapons she had developed herself.

Now, with her defiance, her willingness to fight him back, he was suddenly so damned horny that all thoughts of training her in anything but fucking had fled his mind. He was going to take her down, rip those jeans off that tempting ass and give her every hard, tormented inch of his cock.

He moved around her, watching as her eyes narrowed and her nipples tightened further. He could smell her arousal. Had smelled it from the minute she joined him on the mat. It was sweet and hot, like an intoxicating elixir that he had to have more of.

She licked her lips, running her tongue over that full lower curve and dampening it temptingly. Sooty lashes were lowered deceptively, casting intriguing shadows on her creamy cheeks.

Knot me, baby. The words had been like a fiery sword slashing through his groin, drawing his testicles tight against the base of his cock. He was dying to see if it would happen again. To feel the hot flex and ripple of her pussy as he filled it further than any other man ever could.

"Scared?" She taunted him, watching as he moved carefully around the mat.

"Debating."

"Hm." She lifted a brow mockingly. "And what are you debating, big boy?"

"Just how fast it would take to work my cock up that tight ass." He bared his teeth warningly. "Or if I have the patience."

Her laughter was low, amused. "That threat is getting old, Dash."

He just smiled. It wasn't a threat. There was a particular heady pleasure in taking a woman anally. Having her bending before him, submissive, accepting him easily, willingly. The need to do so had never been as driving as it was now, though. He wanted her bent before him and screaming out in pleasure as he stretched that little nether hole. Stretching wide for him, submitting to his pleasure and taking her own at the same time.

"Turn around," he said, daring her.

She smirked. "Do I look stupid to you?"

"You look eatable." He allowed his voice to deepen, the instinctive growl that gathered in his chest to echo within it. "Deliciously eatable. Now turn around."

She shivered. He loved it when she did that. And her pussy was getting hotter. He could smell it. The sweet temptation of it was nearly more than his dick could bear. If he didn't fuck her soon he was going to be howling in misery.

"I don't think so." She shifted to the side as he stepped forward. "I have a feeling I should really keep an eye on you right now."

She was smart. He had always said she was smart, he thought with growing pride. She would never be tamed, but damned if he wouldn't have fun convincing himself he could do it.

Dash moved slowly, carefully, watching her as he gripped his T-shirt at the neck and tore it from his body. Her eyes widened. He loved it when her expression went from wildfire or fury to innocent and sensually aware all at once. He was barefoot, so there were no boots or socks to worry about. His hands went to the metal buttons of his jeans.

Her nostrils flared, her lips parting as she began to breathe raggedly. He loosened the first two buttons only.

"Turn around," he whispered.

She shook her head.

Dash smiled in anticipation. She wanted the battle. She wanted to be taken as much as he wanted to take her.

"You will go down," he warned her gently.

"Maybe you will instead." He watched her brace her body, arms loose and relaxed at her sides as she narrowed her eyes on him.

He shook his head slowly. "You will go down, Elizabeth. And when you do, you're fucked."

Amusement flickered in the heat of her gaze. "You gonna talk me to death first, or go for it?"

He went for it.

• C H A P T E R   2 4 •

Elizabeth was determined she wasn't going to make it easy. The adrenaline pumping through her body, the rush to pit herself against him was throbbing too hard, too fast. Her pussy was wet and hot, her breasts swollen and nipples aching, she wanted to be taken. But not easily.

When he came at her, she slid quickly away from him, trying to trip him and grimacing at the low laugh he directed at her. He was playing with her, damn him.

Dash rushed her again, giving her just enough time to slide away before his hand hooked in the neckband of her T-shirt, ripping it away from her body. She struggled with the scraps as she turned to face him, tearing them from her and tossing them to the floor.

She wore only a white, fragile lace bra now. Her breasts were heaving, nipples rasping against the fabric as he stared at them. His chest was glistening with sweat, the crotch of his jeans so tight it looked ready to burst.

When he came for her again she gave him a second to think he had her before she sidestepped, ducking low and throwing herself at his legs. He flipped. Son of a bitch did a perfect flip before turning and watching her with heated warning.

"Jeans go next," he snarled as he came at her again.

She went down. His hands went to the snap and zipper of her jeans as he allowed her to fight. He wrestled them down her hips, then gripped the legs and tugged as she abandoned the jeans in exchange for freedom.

A thong and bra were all she had left on her body. She flipped around, coming to her feet, staring back at him as he tossed the jeans over his shoulder.

"I'm going to knot you, baby," he told her, his voice hot and rasping. "Next time, you stay down."

Her cunt was so wet she could literally feel her panties soaking from it. He rushed her again. As she moved to slide under his arm, he dipped, caught her and rolled with her until he had her on her stomach, his bigger body pinning her to the mat. His hand hooked in her panties as he gave a jerk.

Elizabeth screamed out in frustration as the panties snapped and a second later they were tossed aside. Her arms were stretched behind her as Dash locked her wrists in one hand. Then he pulled her up to her knees as she felt him working at his jeans.

"Mounted," he growled. "Submitted."

She struggled against him, almost throwing him off balance as he released his cock from his pants. It was destructive being held this way, unable to fight him, unable to get away from him. The heat of it wrapped around her senses, making her body so sensitive that when his fingers smoothed over the slick folds of her pussy she nearly climaxed then.

"Like it, baby?" he growled as he positioned his cock at the entrance of her cunt. "God, I love having you like this. Restrained. Submissive. It makes my dick harder than it's ever been."

The steel-hard flesh nudged against her, a silky spurt of the precum jetting inside her. They both groaned. It was so warm, making her hotter, slicker, as he began to work his cock into the tight entrance, pushing her shoulders to the mat as he forced her legs to stay bent, her rump raised to his burrowing impalement.

"Damn you." She panted deeply as she struggled against his hold, still fighting to get free, bucking against him then groaning roughly as it only lodged the thick head deeper inside her.

Oh, that was too good. The painful pleasure of the abrupt impalement had her nerves screaming, her clit throbbing in desperation.

She tugged at the hold on her wrists, wiggled her hips, dislodging him once, then groaning fiercely as his hand connected sharply with the cheek of her ass. Okay. She liked that too much.

He nestled his cock against the entrance again. She felt another spurt of fluid as he slid in. Pulling back, he began to work his erection inside her once more. She dislodged him again.

Dash chuckled. "Do you like being spanked, Elizabeth?" His hand connected to the curve of her ass again, causing her to jerk and moan heatedly. "I think you do, baby. I think you like having that pretty ass spanked. I bet you'll like having it fucked even better."

"Don't you dare," she cried out as his fingers slid against her anus. Thankfully, his cock tucked against the folds of her pussy once again.

"Do it again, Elizabeth, and I'll take you hard," he warned her. "Don't play with me right now."

And she was playing with him, tempting his control and she knew it. She wanted him hard and deep, wanted to shake that tightly held power he had over his own actions.

He spurted inside her again and she felt her vagina relax. She struggled harder, laughing when he cursed, turning her hips to the side and dislodging him again as she bucked back, surprising him into releasing his hold on her wrists to keep from hurting her. She scrambled away from him, glorying in the hard growl that erupted from his throat a second before he gripped her hips and jerked her back.

His cock pressed hard inside her again as a hard jet of fluid filled her a second before he pushed half the hard erection inside her with a swift thrust.

"Dash." She arched, screaming out at the pleasure/pain as he pulled back, then thrust deeper, then again, until on the third stroke he impaled her with every hard, thick inch of hungry, throbbing cock.

"Oh God!" she cried out, fighting to relax around the engorged intruder as it moved back and thrust home again.

He thrust hard and deep. He was breathing roughly, his hands gripping her hips, working his cock in and out of her with surging thrusts that had her crying out in greedy lust. He was stoking a fire inside her that threatened to steal her mind, stretching her wide, filling her before retreating, only to open her again.

Fire streaked up her spine; pleasure tore through her womb before arching along her body. Each time he filled her, groaning harshly as her pussy gripped him heatedly, her orgasm tightened in her belly.

He was making few allowances for her now. The strokes were increasing in thrust and depth, powering inside her as she screamed out beneath him, twisting and thrusting back to drive him harder into the convulsing muscles of her cunt. They fought for the dominance of the act then, to see who could push the other further. To see if Elizabeth would explode or if Dash would lose that last hold on his teetering control. She was determined to win.

As he plunged inside her she tightened her cunt, milking his flesh as he growled in resistance and pulled back, fighting her hold on him.

She fought her own release, knowing if she came before he lost his own control then she would have lost that dominance in this act alone. The ability to make him need her above all things, to take her as he needed her, to accept her as his woman, his mate, able to accept every facet of his needs, was imperative.

"Harder," she cried out as he kept the thrusts timed, groaning with each forward stroke as though it were killing him. "Damn you, Dash. Fuck me harder. Now."

She pushed back, not allowing him to draw from her, stroking his cock with the flexing of her muscles as his hands tightened at her hips.

"Elizabeth," he moaned almost brokenly. "God, baby. I don't want to hurt you."

She fought his hold, bucking back and driving him deeper, flexing around him as tight as she could bear as she felt him shudder behind her, felt his hands tighten convulsively on her hips as a tremor shook his hard body.

Elizabeth moved back harder, driving him deeper as she reached beneath her body, her hands finding and caressing the hard, tight sac beneath the base of his cock as a strangled groan filled the air and he lost all semblance of control.

He was taking her in hard, deep, fast strokes that powered into her as the jets of fluid fought to relax the desperately tight muscles of her pussy while she clenched further around him. She was going to climax. It was building in her womb, surging through her body as she lay beneath him, crying out, screaming his name as the pleasure overwhelmed her.

"God. Elizabeth . . ." He slammed hard and deep and moved to pull free again when she felt it happen.

The tight stretching, the knot swelling midway up the length of his cock, filling her, locking into the rippling muscles of her pussy as she exploded beneath him. Her scream was torn from her throat as she felt his harsh explosions at the mouth of her womb, filling her, searching for fertile ground as she pulsed and exploded in her own release.

It seemed never-ending. She collapsed to the mat as Dash followed her down, buried inside her, locked in the depths of her convulsing cunt as their bodies shuddered with each hard spurt of his semen.

Sweat coated their bodies as they fought for breath. Dash's head lay beside hers, his teeth locked on her shoulder from the moment his release began, his groans sounding more like feral growls each time his seed jetted inside her.

Finally, long minutes later, she felt the fierce swelling begin to ease, felt him shudder and then pull free of her tight grip with a deep, harsh moan. He fell beside her, breathing harshly, his hard body trembling.

"I should spank you." He gasped for breath as he looked over at her with rueful amusement. "I could have hurt you, Elizabeth."

She laughed weakly. "Yeah, well, you didn't. 'Could have' doesn't count."

Her eyes closed. Damn, she was tired. So tired she could fall asleep where she lay. She let herself drift, darkness closing over her, feeling Dash beside her, comforting her, protecting her. Her body was replete, her mind, for the moment, at ease. It all combined to lull her into the deep, dark comfort of rest.

CHAPTER 25

Dash made her wake up for a quick shower. He placed her in the bathtub, turned on the spray and washed her efficiently from head to toe as she watched him in bemusement. As though no one had ever bathed her. Her body was sweetly curved, lean and compact with firm muscle. To him, she was perfection.

Between her legs she had shaven her little pussy free of soft hair that was beginning to regrow. It hadn't bothered him, but he knew the stubble must be uncomfortable for her.

"Soap or baby oil?" He knelt at her feet as he spread her legs, cleaning her with the soapy rag, careful of her tender flesh and sensitive clitoris.

"What?" She shook her head.

"Do you shave your pussy with soap or baby oil?"

She flushed lightly as she cleared her throat. "Oil. Lots of oil. But I can do it."

Something akin to panic flared in her eyes as he reached toward the recessed shelf in the shower wall and drew down the bottle of oil he had brought for her.

"Shush," he commanded roughly. "I do have to shave my face often, so I think I can care for one little pussy."

Rinsing her quickly, he flipped off the shower and dried them both before laying a thick towel over the closed toilet seat. "Sit." He pushed her down on the seat and knelt before her once again.

Dash knew he didn't dare linger on the job. Already his cock was engorged, ready to take her again.

He spread the oil thickly over the folds of her pussy and proceeded to shave the silken skin, marveling once again at how delicate she appeared there to him. When it was free of any stubble and as soft as anything he had ever known, he reapplied a coat of oil to soothe the freshly shaved folds.

Not a word was said. As she accepted that his mind was set on the job, she merely watched him, blushing faintly, but staying in the sprawled position he needed to access her pussy.

She was going to be the death of him. Dash carried her to bed, tucking her in before moving tiredly beside her and drawing her into his arms. The woman had a power over him that shook him every time he realized how deep she was digging her way into his soul.

There was nothing like loving her, being so deep inside her he could feel himself sinking into her cells. The very mouth of her cervix had cupped his cock as he locked in her, shooting his semen into the dark, rich depths of her womb. He had never known anything like it. No matter how hard he tried to still the swelling, it overruled his control and left him gasping in painful pleasure as it locked him inside her.

And now, it left him wondering what the hell he would do if anything ever happened to her. He was getting ready to lead her into a war zone. Into a hell that could destroy her if he couldn't still the fury raging inside her. If he managed to keep her alive and she killed Grange in cold blood, he worried for her. Elizabeth wasn't a killer. She could defend herself, just as he would expect her to. She could kill if she had to and survive it. But from what he knew about Grange, if she ever faced him, he wouldn't push her to kill him. Grange would depend on her being weak. Honorable. If she killed him under those circumstances Dash wouldn't think worse of her for it, but he feared what it would do to her. As he had told her, she would have to be the one to live with it.

Dash sighed deeply at that thought. In another day or two, they would leave the cabin and get ready. He had a house set up not far from Grange's estate, and he would begin the nightly forays around it. Mike's men were watching for Grange, tracking the security and getting information on the men he used as guards. Some might be vulnerable to bribes; it seemed Grange wasn't well liked, even by his own men.

Mike was working on information about Dane's death, getting the case ready to go to a special prosecutor for Breed Affairs when they returned with the files Grange had taken from Dane. Cassie had clearly remembered the thick manila envelope splattered with the dead man's blood. Grange had been ecstatic as he read it.

My own little bitch, he had told the little girl as he looked over at her.

What Elizabeth had been unaware of, another piece of information Cassie had held back from her mother, was that Grange wanted Elizabeth too. The best Dash could figure, the man had been testing her and Cassie. Pushing them to their limits to see how strong each was. He wanted more Breed children, and Elizabeth was a proven breeder.

That thought caused his chest to clench almost painfully. He turned to her, his hand moving softly to her belly, his eyes closing. Could she be carrying his child now? He knew from the information

Callan had given him that no birth control had stopped his or Taber's mates from conceiving. Did he somehow carry the hormone that would counteract those precautions as well? That thought had tormented him since the night he had first taken her. There was little chance that his semen wasn't reaching her womb. Each time his release swelled in his cock, it locked him tight, forcing the opening of his cock against her flexing cervix. He could feel the little entrance there cupping over the spurting tip, soaking in his seed, greedily consuming the hard ejaculations.

Was he risking not just his mate but also his child in this mission? He was getting ready to take her from the protection of the cabin, allowing Grange's spies to catch sight of her in town and draw him back to her. He was getting ready to place her in the worst sort of danger, all in the name of a prayer that she could survive.

He wasn't a fool. He prided himself on facing reality at every opportunity. There was no way to keep the information of Cassie's birth a secret, no way now for him to stay hidden from the Council's knowledge. The public might not know the truth of him as they did the Breeds, but their enemies would.

Elizabeth could be forced to fight, to defend herself and Cassie, and possibly another child, if worse came to worst. He couldn't protect her. She wouldn't allow it if he tried, and he knew that. But realistically, no measures he took would safeguard her.

"I can hear you worrying." She shifted against him, her hand smoothing over his abdomen, her lips whispering against his chest.

He glanced down at where her head lay against him, certain that the fierce throb in his chest at her softened voice couldn't be a good thing. She was his weakness. He was only just realizing that, but it was one he couldn't let go.

"We have to leave here soon." He sighed regretfully. "I wish we had longer. There's a lot I have to teach you."

"We'll have time later." He could hear the reflection in her voice now.

But would they? There were so many possibilities, so many things that could go wrong. He found himself hesitating now, wishing he had forced her to go with Cassie to the Breed compound, to be safe while he took care of Grange. He could have trained her later. Could have seen how strong she was at another time. No matter how safe he thought he could make her on this mission, there would have been another, something else safer that he could have tested her on.

"You could be carrying my child, Elizabeth." He stared at the ceiling as he spoke, feeling her stiffen against him.

His chest tightened further at the thought of that. God, what was he doing with her? Risking her in the same ways he risked his own life? There had to be a way to keep her safe.

"It's the wrong time. We could be safe."

He hoped she was. At least for now. But he couldn't discount the information the feline Breed leader had given him.

"It didn't help the Felines. No birth control worked with them. Their scientists suspect it would be the same with the Wolves. The hormone that produces the swelling also works to ensure conception. We could be risking another child."

He couldn't hold the truth back from her. He wouldn't lie to her or hide any part of the dangers they faced.

"Then it's better to rid ourselves of Grange now," she said quietly, though he could hear the trepidation in her voice.

His hands smoothed over her back, relishing the feel of warm, silken flesh and well-toned muscle. She was like a young she-wolf. Lean and fit.

"I'm going to send you to the Breed compound before I go after Grange," he finally decided. "You were right; separating you from

Cassie wasn't a good idea. We'll let his men get a good look at you in town, then I'll send you back . . ."

"The hell you will." She sat up, her eyes sparkling in fury as she faced him, her nakedness all but forgotten as her gaze cut into him with lethal intent. "I won't be pushed aside and protected, Dash. I deserve the chance to do this."

"And if you are carrying our child?" he asked her softly. "Do you deserve the chance to risk that life?"

"If I conceive, then any child would be placed at risk by the very fact that it will be a naturally conceived Breed," she reminded him angrily. "I'm not stupid, Dash. There are a lot of things I've taken into consideration. I haven't made these decisions lightly."

He stared up at her, frowning. "You don't discuss anything you've considered with me, Elizabeth. How would I know what you anticipate?"

She rolled her eyes. He had never seen that particular expression of female exasperation from her before. It was endearing.

"You're one to talk," she snapped. "You weren't even going to tell me you were a Breed, Dash. Wouldn't I have been in for a hell of a surprise when you locked inside me if I hadn't known?"

"Yeah, would have been nice to have had someone else as shocked as I was," he growled.

He watched her, seeing the anger, but seeing something more. A cool, quiet calm that was as much a part of her as the heat of her sensuality, the depth of her acceptance. As though the past two years had tempered a steel core of strength inside her soul. She was the most giving woman he had known, and the strongest. The years had been cruel, harder on her than he could have imagined, but her very survival had molded her into a warrior.

"I do have a mind, you know," she finally told him with an air of amusement. "You've seen me as this soft little woman who needs to be protected and coddled. I don't want to be protected. I don't want to be coddled. I want to share the responsibilities, Dash."

She should have been born a Breed. She was as tough as either of the two Feline females he had met.

"I know you have a mind," he told her quietly. "I have nothing but the greatest respect, Elizabeth, for the very fact that you still live. Most women would have failed to even rescue Cassie, let alone run with her for two years."

She shook her head, a sharp sigh escaping from between her lips as she moved from the bed.

"You sound very patronizing, Dash," she told him softly as she pulled on her robe. "Any mother would have given her life to protect her baby. I got lucky."

"You were smart." He sat up in the bed, watching her curiously. "I'm not patronizing you, Elizabeth. If I didn't think you had what it takes, you would be in Virginia with Cassie rather than here, training to go after those files and Grange. Never doubt I don't have the highest respect for you. As a woman, a mother, and a mate."

"A mate," she murmured, shaking her head. "You found me less than two weeks ago, and you've already claimed me for life." She pushed her fingers through her hair as she skirted the window and curled up in the large chair that sat against the far wall.

Distance. He saw the need to escape the intimacy that the bed afforded, and he allowed her that. For now. The days they had spent together had been so rushed, so filled with the need to protect Cassie and then to complete the minimum amount of training he required. There had been little time to talk. What he knew in his soul had never been expressed to Elizabeth. Not that he had the words to do that now, but he saw in her a need to know more than she had learned so far.

"I found you over a year ago, Elizabeth," he reminded her. "Through Cassie's letters."

"The letters." She sighed deeply. "God, it was so dangerous putting her in school then. I don't know how I let her talk me into that. I was completely against letting her go and allowing the pen pal thing, Dash. I worried myself to exhaustion that year."

"I know you did." And he did know. Somehow, some way, he connected to both Elizabeth and her child. Seeing their pain. Their fear. "When the letters began, I had just been in an accident, Elizabeth. I lost men I had fought with for years. Good men. Friends. No one was expecting me to live. I was in a drug-induced coma the first three months of those letters. If it hadn't been for my commanding officer's belief that Cassie's letters would penetrate it, I would be dead now."

Her eyes widened slowly, flickering with pain, fear. "I didn't know."

"I know you didn't," he said gently. "My CO wrote her back at first, until I could. But while I was in that haze . . ." He shook his head. "I wanted to die then. I was tired of hiding, of having no one. I had let myself get close to the men in that unit, and then they were gone as well. I was tired of fighting. Then he read that letter. And I saw you, Elizabeth. I saw you just as you are now. Your hair tangled around you, your eyes dark and haunted, and I knew I had to live. I knew that you and Cassie needed me. Each letter only strengthened that impression."

He watched her breathe out roughly, saw the shock, the bemusement in her eyes as he moved from the bed and walked to her.

Her gaze flicked to his straining erection, but at this moment, it wasn't sex he needed. He knelt in front of her, staring back at her, his arms lying along the sides of the chair.

"I saw you crying, Elizabeth. I heard you whisper my name and ask God on a prayer to bring you a miracle. And in just that instant I woke up. I made myself wake up, because I knew to my soul you were my mate. My woman. And I knew I had to find you."

Her eyes were filled with tears, brilliant sapphire gems that pierced his heart with beauty and her pain.

"I was," she whispered before swallowing tightly, her voice hoarse. "I was standing there, and it was raining. Cassie had gone to bed whispering that you would save us. How did she know, Dash? How could she have known?"

"It doesn't matter how she knew," he told her firmly. "All that matters was that she did and it was right. You're right, Elizabeth. I don't know a lot of very important things about you, but I know your strength, and I know your heart. And nothing or no one short of death will take that from me. So never, ever doubt that I do know and respect the abilities you've shown to protect yourself and that child. I respect them, and I thank God for them daily. For them and for you."

✦ CHAPTER 26 ✦

She was crying when he leaned forward, his lips touching hers, rubbing against them gently. As the small rivulets of moisture reached his mouth, his lips moved to her cheek. With infinite tenderness he kissed them away, drawing the moisture into his mouth as his hands cupped her head.

Warmth rushed through her, piercing the shell she had fought so desperately to keep between her heart and this man's total acceptance of her. From the first moment in the diner, he had taken over, clearing her way, sheltering her and Cassie as she rested. He had paved the way for her daughter's safety, given her a chance to once again regain control of her own life, and in the bargain, he had given her the very core of who and what he was.

Gentle words. Soft kisses. Like now, his lips moving over her face as he crooned gently to her.

"Don't cry, baby. Your tears rip at my soul. Don't you know that?

I would move heaven and earth to wipe away any pain you would know, if I could."

And he would. She saw it in the somber lines of his face, the golden glow of his eyes. The man couldn't be real. It wasn't possible. How had she ever deserved for God to answer her prayer in this manner, with this man? He was strong, too arrogant, and too sure of himself for her to be comfortable with, but a man whose voice rang with quiet honor, with acceptance of all he was.

He never made excuses. He didn't pretend to have all the answers. But he was like a boulder of strength beside her, clearly willing to shelter her however she needed. And he had come to her without expectations, knowing the danger she and Cassie faced. Knowing the risk to his own life.

When he drew back, staring down at her with a flare of heat and a gaze filled with adoration, she didn't know what to say. No one had ever accepted her so completely.

"You don't know me," she said, suddenly afraid that the faults she knew she possessed would weaken what she saw in his eyes. "You don't know what I'm like."

"And you don't know what I'm like," he agreed softly. "You don't know how I have to fight my possessiveness and my need to hold back to keep you safe. How dominant I get and how kinky I can get sexually. I have the same fears you do, Elizabeth. We'll work through them."

"How can you be so certain?" She was frightened now, terrified one day he would see her as she knew she was. Grumpy in the mornings, irrational during PMS, and most of all, willing to kill a man in cold blood.

His fingers slid over her cheeks, his thumb smoothing against her lips.

"I don't know how, Elizabeth," he said. "All I know is that the bond with you was stronger than with any other woman, before I ever found you in that diner. That I knew you in my dreams, in the darkest depths of unconsciousness. That I know I would kill anyone, without first considering his right to live, who attempted to harm so much as a hair on your head. You complete something that has been missing inside me. That's all I know. I don't ask for more. The rest will come in time."

She breathed in raggedly as she stared back at him, feeling the heat of his body enfolding her, the warmth wrapping around her like a cloud of comfort. It sent shivers chasing up her spine to realize she had never known anything like it. At the same time, she realized how swollen her breasts were, the nipples throbbing in longing. Between her thighs, her cunt pulsed, spilled its precious moisture and further slickened the plump lips there.

"I can smell your heat," he whispered as his lips lowered to hers, barely brushing against them as he stared back at her with drowsy sensuality. "Hot and sweet. Do you know what that does to me, Elizabeth?"

He urged her to unfold her legs, pulling them down until they lay along the outside of his. His fingers worked at the knot of her robe then, loosening it slowly.

"What?" Her breathing was rough now, heavy, as she fought to drag in air to combat the extreme excitement his touch always caused to rise within her.

"It makes me very hungry," he revealed. "It makes me want to eat you slow and easy, drawing every drop of cream into my mouth and making more flow as I lick into your tight pussy. It makes me want to hear you scream, feel you shudder and pulse and spill your sweet juices against my tongue."

"God! Dash!" He made her weak, made her shiver in anticipation as he drew the edges of the robe back from her body.

"Oh, look how pretty." His gaze went to her straining breasts. "So full and sweet, with the prettiest little berries resting atop them. I want to taste your pretty breasts as well, Elizabeth."

Her head fell back against the chair as she watched his head lower. His hands cupped the full mounds and lifted them to his mouth, his gaze never leaving hers as his tongue licked over a nipple slowly.

"Dash. Are you going to torture me?" She gripped the sides of the chair in desperation.

"No, baby. I'm going to love you." He laved the hard tip with wicked flicks of his tongue, watching her closely as he did so. "Do you like it, Elizabeth?" he asked her softly seconds later as his lips rubbed over its twin mound and began to caress that as well.

"Too much," she panted.

She had to touch him. Had to touch that smooth, hard flesh. Her hands moved to his shoulders, palms sliding over the flexing muscles there and watched as his lips opened and he drew one desperate nipple into the suctioning heat of his mouth.

His teeth rasped the little bud, his tongue licked, his mouth suckled. Sensation after sensation slammed into her womb, convulsing her stomach as she fought for control. She could feel her cunt growing wetter, her clit swelling hard and tight.

"Damn, you taste so good," he growled as he moved to the other breast. He repeated the procedure there, growling his pleasure in her, the sound vibrating on the sensitive peak as her nails bit into his skin.

She wanted to close her eyes, wanted to revel in the sensations, in the darkness of the sensuality he called within her, but she found him holding her gaze. His eyes were demanding, glowing with his lust and hunger, the lids lowered to half-mast, his lips swollen from the meal he was making of her nipples.

Each sip, each rasp of his tongue, each draw of his strong mouth was a whiplash of pleasure nearly too devastating to bear. She was whimpering from the hunger rising in her own body. Dash could do things to her that no man had ever accomplished. Never had she been poised on such a sharp precipice of arousal and need, knowing that when her orgasm came, it would rip her out of herself and throw her into a place of such ecstasy she feared one day she might not return.

"Delicious," he groaned as his lips lifted from her nipple, then began to sprinkle light, delicate kisses over the full mounds.

Even the smallest amount of flesh was not left unattended.

"You're going to kill me." Her head tossed against the back of the chair as he gripped her hips and pulled her forward.

"No, baby. I'm going to love you," he crooned, his voice velvety and dark, sending ripples of pleasure over her flesh. "And how I do enjoy loving you."

He lifted her legs, spreading them wide, pulling her buttocks to the edge of the chair and staring between her thighs with hungry intent. His hand smoothed up the inside of her thigh seconds before he allowed it to cup her pussy, his finger moving up the narrow slit and coating his finger with her juices. Then his eyes rose to hers.

"Taste," he whispered. "See why I can barely keep my lips from your juicy cunt, no matter how dangerous things get."

Elizabeth gasped in shock as he smeared the thick moisture over her lower lip, his gaze flaring with such fiery lust it nearly stole her breath.

"Taste," he urged her again.

Her tongue flickered out. He grimaced in almost violent pleasure, which did no more than urge her on. She loved that look on his hard face, the intensity of arousal, the nearly painful desire.

Her tongue ran slow and easy over the curve then, drawing in the thick moisture, pleased to realize it was a pure, earthy taste.

"Damn. Elizabeth." That hard, primal growl was back a second before he pressed his finger between her lips, allowing her to suck the rest of her juices from his fingers. It wasn't unpleasant; it was arousing to taste herself, to see his eyes darken, to see the hunger grow to an almost mad desperation as he watched her.

He licked his own lips, as though envious that she had tasted of the sweet moisture and he hadn't. His shoulders lowered, his long body sitting on the floor now as he placed his hands on each thigh and bent his head to partake of her smooth flesh.

The first slow lick between the full, swollen lips of her pussy had Elizabeth stiffening in violent pleasure. Arcing flares of pulsing sensation ripped and ricocheted through her body at the speed of light as her hips jerked involuntarily.

"Dash." She moaned his name as her fingers speared through his hair, eager for a firmer touch, to have him eating her with all the hunger she could feel vibrating in his body.

"Mmm," he mumbled against her clit as his tongue made a slow, delicious trek around the straining nub.

His tongue licked and probed at the throbbing bundle of nerves, flickering against it with light, wet caresses that had her straining to him, her fingers clenching in his hair, her body set afire with the needs rocketing through her flesh.

"I can't stand it," she cried out, overwhelmed by the tenderness he displayed in his greedy feast of her body.

"You have to," he groaned heatedly, his breath searing her soaked cunt as he tried to lick every drop of the flowing syrup from the shallow slit. "God, Elizabeth. You intoxicate me. I could lie between your thighs for days and survive merely on the soft cream that flows from you."

She would have protested his declaration. Would have begged for him to take her if he hadn't chosen that second to sink one broad finger into the clutching depths of her pussy.

She arched her hips, a strangled scream tearing from her lips at the penetration. He worked the digit in slowly, smoothing past the convulsing tissue and coating his finger once again with her juices.

A protesting cry broke free of her as he retreated and shock coursed through her body as the finger slid against her lips. His lips slid lower. As Elizabeth accepted her own taste into her mouth, his tongue plunged hard into her quaking vagina and his groan echoed through the room.

She sucked his finger into her mouth. Her tongue licked at it desperately as his tongue flickered inside the tight depths of her pussy. He was eating her like a man starved, dragging the flowing moisture into his mouth and returning for more. His tongue fucking her with hard, heated strokes until it whipped a firestorm inside the rippling channel.

She would have screamed, but that would have meant releasing the hard finger lodged in her mouth. She was terrified the plunging thrusts up her pussy would stop if she did, so she hung on, her lips clamped around it as she exploded violently.

Strangled screams tore from her throat as his finger slid free of her mouth, his tongue sinking over and over into her spasming tissue. He was groaning intently, obviously determined to suck every drop of juice from the tunnel before he finished.

· C H A P T E R   2 7 ·

Elizabeth was so aware of every sensitized nerve ending in her pussy that it was nearly torture as Dash withdrew his tongue and came quickly back to his knees.

"God, I should move you to the bed," he whispered as he stared down at her. "But you're so damned hot, splayed out in that chair, ready for me, that I want to see you just like this as I fuck you past sanity."

Elizabeth was breathing hard, her gaze flicking to his straining erection, the purpled head violently aroused and gleaming with his pre-cum. He lifted her knees, holding her as he spread her further.

"Elizabeth," he groaned. "Touch your breasts."

"What?" She shook her head.

"Play with your nipples," he told her roughly. "I want to watch you, see you pleasure yourself as I fuck you. Let me see you play with your pretty breasts. Please."

She was shocked. Even more than she had been when he needed

her to taste herself. She could feel the flush moving up her neck, her face, as she watched him. There was no denying him. No protesting his needs or her own need to please him.

Elizabeth cupped the full mounds, her thumbs and forefingers gripping her nipples, pulling at them slowly.

"Sweet God!" he groaned, his hips jerking, raking the tip of his cock against the swollen folds of her pussy. "Yeah. Just like that. Let me see you do that as I fuck you, Elizabeth. Let me watch."

She watched him too. Her gaze lowered, her eyes widening at the sight of his bulging cock nestling inside the bare, pink folds of her flesh. She felt the soft spurt of his pre-cum then, the lubrication that would relax her tense tissue and make her pussy burn that much brighter. She groaned at the warmth of it flowing into her, mixing with her own wetness and making her slicker, hotter.

Dash flinched, as though the sensation were too pleasurable to endure. His eyes flicked to her face, then back to her hands at her breasts.

"Yeah, pull at them," he groaned as his cock pulsed again and she pinched her own nipples erotically. "They're so pretty and red. Such hard little berries, Elizabeth. Do you have any idea how good they taste to me?"

She moaned. His words alone had her on the edge of orgasm. She could feel her muscles relaxing around the hard, silk-covered steel wedge working inside her pussy, stretching her, throbbing with hot demand as he pressed into her. The intermittent spurts of his fluid were so sexually arousing she was gasping, the fire igniting in her cunt driving her to the edge of madness.

"Are you ready for me yet, baby?" He eased the tense flesh from her cunt as she cried out in protest before easing back into her hungry vagina, spreading her tightly, heating her lusciously. "Are you ready to take me?"

"Yes. Yes. Dash, please. Fuck me." Elizabeth could feel her juices flowing from her cunt, coating his flesh as he began to sink farther inside her.

A strangled moan echoed from her as she watched the plump lower lips spread around the hard flesh impaling her. It was erotic, lascivious, watching him enter her, working his cock back and forth, the flesh dripping from her flow of juice as he spread her deliciously. Another, harder pulse of pre-cum had her arching, groaning in need.

Inch by slow inch he invaded the tight channel, working his engorged cock back and forth, hard growls of hunger issuing from his throat as his cock continued to sporadically pulse its hot warmth into her pussy.

Never in her life had she known anything so explicit, so erotic. She had never dreamed of being taken in such a manner. Of being possessed, impaled, as she watched the penetration into her hot pussy. It was killing her. Making her mad with the pleasure. She was certain she would never survive it, but knew she would surely die happy.

"You like that, don't you, baby?" he whispered as she convulsed, on the edge of orgasm, shuddering with the growing heat coiling in her belly. "Watching me take you. Watching your pussy flatten out around my cock."

No. She loved it. She was shaking with the pleasure, shuddering with her need to orgasm.

"Yes," she panted, never taking her eyes from the sight.

He was flattening the curves, drawing her flesh tight around him, making her clit stand out in swollen demand.

"Touch your clit." His voice was hoarse, rough with hunger. "Play with your nipples with one hand and touch your clit with the other. Hurry, baby. Play with it while I push every hard inch of my cock up your tight pussy."

Elizabeth whimpered. One hand fell to her straining clit, her eyes never leaving the sight of roughly a third of his cock gleaming outside her vagina.

"Beautiful." He was straining to hold back. She could feel it in every hard throb of his cock inside her. "Now keep stroking your pretty clit. There you go, baby. Show me how you like it. Let me watch."

Her fingers were rubbing around the pulsing nubbin, her gaze mesmerized as he watched his cock draw back slightly. Then he was pushing back, spearing into her, filling the clenching depths of her pussy with every hard, blistering inch of his engorged cock.

She was filled with him. She could feel her muscles straining around the thick flesh, at first protesting, then greedily milking at his erection. Inside, she felt another fierce blast of fluid and fought for the strength to scream at the pleasure. Her fingers paused on her clit until he groaned in protest, then began to stroke it faster, sliding in the thick moisture that dripped all along her pussy.

"Elizabeth. Baby. Yes. Hell, you're so fucking tight you're killing me." Perspiration gleamed along his body, small rivulets sliding from his shoulders.

The pressure was building in her clit now. The stimulation of that little bunch of nerves, her fingers at her nipple, Dash's hot gaze and his cock nudging at her cervix almost sent her over the edge. She would have exploded then. Could feel her body igniting, beginning to ripple. But he chose that moment to move, to slide back, to tempt her and tease her as he built the sensations inside her body.

Slow, agonizing strokes had her mewling in protest as he seemed to relish each stroke of her pussy over his cock.

"Dash. Please," she moaned desperately.

"Not yet." He grimaced. "I want to watch you, baby. Watch you stretch so tight around me while you pleasure yourself. I want to make you come so hard you'll never forget the feel of my cock inside you. Never forget how hot the hunger gets."

She would die. She knew she would. His erection was hot, throbbing. She could feel the threat of the knot pulsing in the center of his flesh, the deep, flexing ripple of need that echoed along her body.

"Now," she whispered, her fingers moving in firm, even strokes against her clit as she watched him fucking her.

He was drawing out, the engorged flesh dripping with their combined juices before pushing back in a surging thrust of desperate hunger. He was watching her fingers on her moist flesh. She was watching him fuck her. It was so damned explicitly sexual she knew she would never forget the sight of it.

"I'm going to come, Dash." She was arching closer to him, driving him deeper inside her with each hard stroke he gave her. "I have to come. Please. Please, I need you. I need to feel you stretching me more. Locking inside me . . ." Her voice rose, roughened, as she remembered the feel of his seed blasting hard and deep inside her womb.

She worked her pussy on the thick pole penetrating it. Deep, desperate lunges as he groaned, growled and picked up the pace of his fierce thrusts. He was fast and hard now, the sound of sucking flesh and desperate moans filling the room as Elizabeth felt her orgasm tightening in her body. Her clit was straining beneath her fingers, her cunt tightening on the flesh driving inside it.

Elizabeth writhed against him in desperation. She thrust into the powerful strokes, her cries rising, becoming hard and hungry, ripping involuntarily from her throat as she felt the fragile threads of her control snap.

"Fuck me," she screamed, feeling her clit swell further, harden, the lightning-fast arcs of pleasure and searing heat ripping through it as he lunged inside her. "Oh God, Dash. Now. Now . . ."

She lost her breath, lost her sanity. Her clit exploded as her pussy began to ripple, spasming around the hard, immediate swelling in his cock. She felt the thick head nudging against her cervix, the knot inside her aligning the hard flesh until the opened eye was lodged against the entrance to her womb and the hard jets of his semen began to pulse inside her.

Gurgled screams escaped her as she began to twist, to convulse, her hips jerking against him, driving him harder against her as another explosion tore through her body. She couldn't stand it. She wouldn't survive it.

"Dash . . ." She screamed his name, crying, pleading as the pleasure consumed her. "Oh God. Dash. I can't stand it, I can't . . ." She arched in his arms as her body tightened to a near breaking point, hearing his agonized groan, the flexing of his muscles, his hard hands gripping her hips to hold her to him as his release tore through him.

"Elizabeth. Baby. Baby." His voice washed over her as his body collapsed against her, holding her still as he spilled every rich drop of semen into her convulsing womb.

She had heard of it. Had heard Dane once discussing the phenomenon of the cervix capping over the spurting head of a cock, opening enough to suck the fertile seed inside it, but she hadn't thought it possible. Hadn't believed it could actually happen. Until she felt it. And not for the first time. Distantly, hazily, she knew it had happened each time Dash had taken her. Each time he had swelled inside her.

The hard, surging explosions repeated each time she felt the swelling throb, each time she felt his seed erupt from his cock. As though her mind had opened as deeply to him as her body had, she was aware of each contracting orgasm that shuddered through her body, and his moan of pleasure as it caused her pussy to milk the knot locking him inside her.

His body was tense, tight, as he covered her. His lips were at her shoulder as she realized he was once again biting her, his teeth sinking into the same area of flesh he had marked before, his mouth drawing at it as the dull pain of the bite blended in with the agonizing pleasure echoing through her.

It seemed to last forever, draining her, sapping any strength, any energy she could have possessed, just as it had before. All too soon, she felt his flesh begin to relax inside her, his teeth releasing her shoulder as he moaned with low, desperate satiation.

"I love you, Elizabeth," he whispered in her ear, faint, almost too low to hear. "I love you."

CHAPTER 28

He was in love with her. Elizabeth watched Dash the next morning as he moved through the brush ahead of her, showing her by his actions how to pass through the forest without a sound. It amazed her. As he moved by, he disturbed nothing. Not a leaf or a breath of air. Birds chirped in a steady symphony, squirrels continued to play and the sounds of the mountain remained steady, uninterrupted.

When she moved to follow him, no matter how hard she tried, the forest around them stilled by several degrees and she felt as though the wildlife were laughing at her attempt to mimic Dash's grace and ease of movement within the forest.

He watched her with narrowed eyes for long minutes. "Stop. Watch."

He wasn't big on words during the training phases he had set up. Since the night before and his whispered declaration, he had been even quieter than normal. She knew she had hurt him. Knew her silence had pricked at him.

She watched him now as he had ordered. Watched each shift of his body, each ripple of muscle. He had discarded his shirt earlier and was now dressed only in the camouflage pants he wore in the wilderness. The dull, forested colors seemed to suit him, blending in with the raven's black of his hair, the dark, tanned tint of his flesh. He moved through the trees and underbrush with a confidence born of his savage DNA. He was natural, a part of the land and the battle for life that flowed through the mountain.

"Your objective is to blend with the area around you as much as possible." His voice was smooth, flowing, caressing over her like the soft breeze that rustled the trees. "If you know you can't achieve the silence needed, then wait for the breeze. It ripples through the land, and any slight noise made then can be attributed to it. Your enemy is listening for the unusual, the out of place. He's not searching for the sounds that are commonplace in his territory."

He waited for another breeze before slipping through a thick growth of fern and tall, blossoming bushes. She saw the leaves rub together, saw his legs as they parted the brush, but the sound of the wind whispering through the leaves overhead covered it.

"There will be dogs on the estate," he told her as he paused at the other side of the greenery. "Highly trained animals. We'll go in downwind of them and time our penetration of the house with the guards' rounds to keep them from catching our scent. But it means we'll have to be fast. Fast and quiet aren't always good companions. So you have to get this right."

She did love him. She watched him move through the thickest parts of the underbrush, teaching her what she needed to know to survive, to go after an enemy that would kill them if they were caught. He trusted her to cover his back, to fight alongside him. And despite her refusal to give him that final commitment, he hadn't wavered in his determination to protect her and Cassie as best he could. And he knew she would have to fight, have to be a partner as well as a lover when knowledge of Cassie's birth was revealed.

"Remember, Elizabeth, the mission comes second to making certain we survive it. We do nothing that stacks the odds against us, because we can always fight another day. And there are other ways to protect Cassie if we have to. This is the most efficient and the most logical at the moment. If it fails, we pull out. Do you understand me?" His voice had hardened as he turned back to her.

She nodded slowly, watching him with careful intensity. His expression was somber, as he always was while training her.

"Good." He nodded, a bleak, dark look entering his eyes for just a second. "Any questions?"

"Why do you love me?" The question seemed to surprise them both.

He stared at her in amazement for all of five seconds before his brows snapped into a fierce frown.

He grimaced then, shaking his head. "Hell, Elizabeth, why do you do that?"

"What?"

"Wait until I'm fucking distracted to ask something so idiotic. For a smart female, that was one of your dumber questions."

Her lips thinned at the insult as she crossed her arms over her breasts and watched him angrily.

"I don't consider it a stupid question," she informed him heatedly. "Seriously, Dash. It's not as though I have a lot of experience with men telling me they love me. Maybe I need a little clarification."

"Clarification of what?" he snapped, his eyes glittering dangerously. "Figure it out. When you do, let me know, because right now I'm more inclined to turn you over my knee and paddle your ass for asking me that question. Now get your ass over here and don't make a sound doing it."

Her blood heated at the order. She more or less stomped over to him, stopping an inch from his body and staring up at him confrontationally.

"You're dead," he snarled. "If this were Grange's estate you would have just alerted every damned guard and dog on the place."

"Well, it's not Grange's estate, and I asked a perfectly logical question," she informed him furiously. Sometimes he reminded her that he was still a man, even if he was a Breed. And men were nothing if not harder than hell to get along with. "I deserve an answer."

"If you don't know, then you don't deserve jack shit," he snapped.

"Fine." She was ready to kick his shins for being so damned stubborn. "Keep it to yourself, big boy, and I'll keep just as quiet about why I love you. Better yet, I'll be quiet, period. I'm going back to the cabin."

She turned to do just that, but before she moved more than a step he had gripped her arm and jerked her around.

"What did you just say?" he growled.

"Not a damned thing." She jerked her arm out of his grip. "Now, if you'll excuse me, I'm hot, I'm hungry and I'm mad. So you can kiss my ass. I've had it for the day."

He snagged the back of her pants, pulling her to a stop as he loomed over her dangerously. "You're going to keep teasing me with that sweet ass, baby, I'm going to take it."

She tossed him an exasperated look. "You can stop with the threats. We both know there's no way. Now, I'm hungry. Go away and hunt or something. You're bothering me."

He released her, but she was more than aware he did so, not because she was able to jerk away from him, but simply because he had decided to do so.

"You go right ahead and convince yourself of that, baby." He smirked. "Go on to the cabin. If I don't find my self-control, I'll show you just how possible it really is. And we'll discuss your lack of common sense in daring me later."

An unladylike snort was her only response as she hurried away from him. It would teach her to tell that hulking, arrogant piece of male flesh that she loved him. But she realized she was smiling as she trekked back to the small cabin. She was smiling and filled with a warmth she hadn't believed possible. He had to really love her, she thought as she came off the mountain. Otherwise, he would have been pissed rather than just irritated.

Then she stopped. For a moment, she wasn't certain why, she came to an abrupt stop and slid behind the trunk of a centuries-old oak. Her heart was suddenly racing out of control, her skin prickling with a sense of danger, with a sudden change in the air.

There wasn't a sound. The birds weren't singing, and it felt as if the forest were held in a suspended state of waiting as the land watched whatever new game was playing out. She felt behind her, gripping the butt of the gun Dash insisted she carry. She pulled it free, checked the clip silently and flipped off the safety.

Where was Dash? She turned, staring back from the direction she had come, but seeing nothing. Could he sense the change from above her?

Don't do anything stupid. The refrain began to repeat through her mind. *Retreat if you have to. Fight another day.* But where was Dash?

She forced her heartbeat under control, breathing deeply as she calmed the heavy throb of her pulse in her ears and fought to listen closely to the sounds around her. A breeze, a rustle to her right.

She shifted again, moving along the trunk of the tree to ensure she stayed hidden. Weapon ready, she crouched along the base of the tree, peering around it carefully. There. A swiftly moving shadow, as though something or someone had slipped along the edge of that outcropping of boulders several feet from the tree she hid behind.

Oh God. Had Grange found them? Had he somehow learned what they were doing? She turned, putting her back to the tree, watching the area around her with narrowed eyes as she considered her options. Whoever it was, was more a danger to her than to Dash. But what if the irritation filling him had dulled his senses? He was upset with her. He might not be as careful as he should be.

How many were there? Where were they?

She breathed in deeply, nostrils flaring as she had watched Dash do, but nothing came to her. She couldn't sense where they were hiding, had no idea how to get into position for a better view.

"Hey, lady, where's Dash?" She flinched as the male voice echoed from the boulders she had spied seconds before.

She stayed silent.

"Come on. I know he's up here. I just have to talk to him. Just let me know where he's at and everything's cool."

She was trembling. She could feel the breeze whispering over her chilled flesh as a sense of dread filled her.

Stay silent when uncertain, Dash had told her the day before. *If you're hidden, you're hidden. No matter how much they think they know where you are, there's always a chance you managed to move. Your best defense is silence.*

She stayed silent. She didn't shift or move, merely watched the land before her. She could see nothing from her side, couldn't sense any movement behind her.

"Lady, I'm getting pretty tired of sitting back here. I know you're there. I can smell Dash all over your body. Now tell me where the hell he's at."

Fear flashed through her. Oh God. How could he smell her? He had to be a Breed. Or lying. Lying, she decided. Callan and the Felines were the only Breeds aware of their location, and they had Dash's cell number. They wouldn't be sneaking around the mountain.

"Killing you would be so easy," the voice snarled with controlled fury. "Stop being stupid and answer me."

"Killing you would be easier." Dash. His voice seemed to echo around her as dizzy relief flooded her body. "Drop your weapon and move out where she can see you. Don't fuck with me either. This is my territory. You can't win." Silence filled the mountain for long moments. "Elizabeth, move around to your right carefully, and keep that gun trained between his thighs until I get there. We don't want to kill him if he gets stupid, just hurt him real bad."

Giddy pleasure washed over her as she moved carefully to do as she was ordered. As she rounded the tree, she almost dropped the gun in shock before she managed to direct it as Dash had ordered her.

She blinked over at the stranger, watching as his pale eyes regarded her calmly, his hands held carefully away from his body.

"You're his woman." His eyes were narrowed on her intently.

She swallowed tightly, refusing to speak. His lips quirked in amusement. "He did good." He nodded. "Better than I expected."

"Simon, you stupid son of a bitch." Dash entered the small clearing, anger vibrating through every pore of his body. "Are you trying to get your ass killed?"

He was obviously a soldier of some sort. He held himself with careful readiness, his lean, muscular body poised for action. He had short dark hair, pale blue eyes and the face of a fallen angel.

"Trying to help you." Simon shrugged. "I waited forever at that cabin and decided to come looking for you. Your woman sensed me, though. She's good."

Dash glanced over at her and Elizabeth basked in the approval of his gaze.

"Elizabeth, meet one of the men I fought with overseas. What the hell he's doing here I have no clue." He flashed the man a hard look as he lifted his arm and indicated to Elizabeth that she should come to him.

"I told you what I was doing here," he said with a slow, soft southern drawl. "I'm not alone. I have a unit waiting back at that cabin. We didn't want to surprise you too bad."

Elizabeth felt Dash's body tighten in surprise. "A unit?" He frowned. "What the hell for?"

"Caught wind of what you were up to here." He shrugged as he leaned down carefully and retrieved the weapon he had dropped. He holstered it immediately. "Taking that bastard won't be easy, Dash. I've pulled my old team together and we're here to help."

Despite the soft, pleasant drawl, Elizabeth glimpsed a stubbornness in the man Dash called Simon that warned her he wouldn't back off easily.

Dash was watching him, not suspiciously, but in confusion.

"Why?" Dash shook his head. "This isn't your fight, Simon. Or your unit's. And I sure as hell can't afford your fee."

Simon's full, sensual lips quirked mockingly. "Consider it a freebie," he said softly. "Let's head back to your cabin. I have Stephanie making coffee. Hope you don't mind. And the others are waiting impatiently."

There was a long, tense silence then.

"Oh hell. You pulled the Ladies in," Dash groaned as though pained. "Simon, dammit, those women are vicious."

"Best kind." Simon nodded. "And they've been damned worried about your sorry ass since hearing about this fool's mission you're on. Don't you know better, Dash? Grange will have an army waiting on this pretty thing you've got. And if he gets her, you know damned good and well he'll have the kid eventually."

The lazy drawl, redneck attitude and sinfully good looks were a combination that could have been devastating if it weren't for the fact that her body and her heart belonged to Dash. Simon was the least likely looking soldier she could have imagined. He looked like a good ole boy playing at being a warrior.

"Is he for real?" Elizabeth asked Dash.

"Unfortunately, he is." Dash sighed. "Come on, you can meet Simon's Ladies."

"His Ladies?" she asked suspiciously.

Dash glanced down at her with something akin to resignation. "Yeah. His Ladies."

CHAPTER 29

Dash had some strange friends. Ex-CIA agents as ranchers, Special Forces types who baited feline Breeds, and a smooth-talking southern boy with a harem all his own. A very dangerous, lethal harem, if Elizabeth wasn't wrong.

The small cabin was filled with estrogen and female hormones and it was all directed one way. Toward the soft-spoken fallen angel who very obviously enjoyed them all.

"This is Stephanie, my little lady of passion." He drew the nearest woman into his arms as they entered the cabin. She was tall, slender and stacked. The woman showed an excessive amount of skin in the snug bra-type gray top and form-fitting black leggings. She had a gun strapped to her hips, a dagger sheathed on her thigh and a gleam of laughter in her dark, chocolate-brown eyes.

"Or so he likes to think." She looked up at the man with a mocking smile. "It's good to meet you."

"This is my little Danica. She takes care of all our . . . uhh, social engagements." Long black hair and wearing form-fitting clothes, weapons in place and loaded. Her blue eyes glowed with adoration as she stared up at Simon.

"Nice to see you again, Dash." Danica greeted him before nodding at Elizabeth. "I'm pleased to meet you."

"Glori, baby." He drew the smaller brunette into his arms. "This is my humble baby, Gloria." He dropped a kiss to her lips as she snuggled against his side after Stephanie moved away.

"Hi, Dash." She flashed Dash a wide smile. "You training her?" She nodded at Elizabeth. "You need to buy her some better clothes than jeans." She ran her hand over the hip of her snug spandex leggings. "This is freer."

Dash cleared his throat but didn't say anything.

"Janette, Oleta and Kimberly." Janette had a pair of handcuffs dangling from the wide belt that crossed her hips. She was a blond siren. Stacked. Oleta was a vibrant brunette with subtle hints of dark blond highlights, and Kimberly was a redhead with a definite gleam in her eyes when she looked at Dash.

Elizabeth frowned as she glanced up at her lover. Dash looked down at her with a wry glint of amusement, which only made her more suspicious. The women were just a little bit too familiar with Dash to suit her.

"We'll have dinner soon," Stephanie called from the open kitchen. "Coffee's on now. Good thing we brought supplies with us. You guys actually think that stuff you called food was healthy?"

Elizabeth frowned. She rather liked the stews and chili that Dash had been putting together.

"My Steph is a whiz in the kitchen." Simon beamed. "We'll have a meal you'll not soon forget."

Elizabeth kept silent. The women were moving around the kitchen and living room now; a few were cleaning weapons, two were cooking and the other two had taken watchful positions at each window.

Dash sighed. "Elizabeth and I are going to go shower. Make yourselves at home, Simon. We'll talk later."

"That we will." Simon leaned lazily against the wall, his arm going around the redhead who moved in against him. "You go on. I have some things to show you this evening and then we can plan."

Elizabeth followed Dash into the bedroom, waiting until he closed and then, strangely enough, locked the door behind him. He moved the straight-back chair from the side of the wall and propped it under the doorknob. She lifted her brow mockingly.

"Don't trust him?" she asked softly.

Dash stared up at her in surprise. "I trust him well enough, I just know him too damned well." He raked his fingers through his hair in a gesture of obvious irritation. "Damn, I wasn't expecting this." He seemed more than bemused by the turn of events.

"I thought you said you didn't have friends." She kept her voice low as she watched him curiously.

Dash was frowning. He glanced to the door, then back at her.

"Simon's an anomaly. Ignore him." He glanced back at the door, appearing more confused by the second.

"What?" Elizabeth asked him.

He shook his head. "Damned man. I have no idea what the hell he thinks he's doing here."

"Sounds to me like he's here to help you." She sat down on the bed and began unlacing her boots. "For a man who claims he doesn't have friends, you keep accumulating a bunch of them."

He didn't answer her, just stood watching her with a dark, wary expression.

"Dash, you're worrying me." She removed her boots before standing up and pulling her T-shirt over her head.

She hadn't bothered with a bra that morning. The damned things were too restricting and uncomfortable when trying to move about the forest. Then she unsnapped her jeans, pulled the zipper and drew them from her body. When she looked up at Dash, he didn't appear concerned anymore. He looked hungry.

"I don't think so," she snorted. "There's no way you're going to make me scream with all those women standing in there listening. They would attack you the minute you left the bedroom."

Unfortunately, he didn't deny it. Instead, he began to strip himself as she headed for the bathroom.

He caught up with her as she was adjusting the water, gloriously naked and more than a little aroused.

"Elizabeth." He caught her against him as she moved to step beneath the spray, staring down at her with those golden eyes that never failed to make her breath catch. "I love you because you hold my soul," he told her simply. "I've always loved you. I just haven't always known you."

Damn him. Just when she thought she had one or two defenses left against him he pulled something like this on her.

She laid her head on his chest, because she knew if she continued to watch him she would end up crying again. He broke her heart sometimes. She had never been loved, been accepted so deeply, as Dash loved and accepted her.

"I love you for the same reasons, Dash." She finally admitted what she had known when he was no more than a weekly letter, a ray of sunshine into her and Cassie's dark life. "For the same reasons."

◆　◆　◆

"Okay. Here's what we have." Simon accepted a thick sheaf of papers from one of his Ladies as they sat at the kitchen table after dinner. "There are Wolf Breeds that escaped that lab. We estimate at least half a dozen. Maybe more if the young survived." He spread out several official documents as he spoke. "Soon as I learned what you were and what you were up against, I put the Ladies to the computers and told them to hack to their hearts' content." He cast smiles to the women arranged around him. "They're good too."

Dash sighed. He had been doing that a lot lately. "What I want to know is how you found out," he finally said. "The information was supposed to be contained within a small circle."

Simon shrugged his broad shoulders. "I know a few of the Felines. Rumor has been circulating for months in the underground that Grange had him a Breed kid. When the little girl showed up at the compound last week while Dani was there, she let me know. She also overheard your name mentioned. Next day, your papers as a Breed were filed as well as your paternity statement with Breed Affairs in Washington. It was kind of a no-brainer from there, Dash." He shook his head as though Dash hadn't given him enough of a challenge.

"We've also met what we suspect to be Wolf Breeds." Dani spoke up then as Simon seemed to beam in pride. "A young woman named Faith, no last name, and her brother, Aiden, in Colorado. A few months later we met up with a big guy named Jacob. Once again, no last name, this one in Texas meeting with a well-known Breed sympathizer with mega cash out of South Africa. All three have the same lack of histories, and none of them can be traced via computer or records. All three have definite agendas where the Breeds are concerned."

"Aiden, Faith and Jacob were the names of three littermates I was raised with," Dash informed them. "The pack leader, Wolfe, named them himself. We were given numbers in the labs rather than names. It sounds like they escaped after all."

"They disappeared again, though," Danica said sadly. "We haven't been able to make further contact, though when the papers hit Washington and news started spreading of a naturally conceived Wolf Breed child, contact was made in high-level offices within Breed Affairs. Word is that the child is currently on the move and in hiding.

No definite place of residence was listed. You can bet Grange is tracking this one."

"Grange has also beefed up security at his estate," Stephanie said as she rifled through the papers. "Three new guards were hired and rumor says he's home next week. His young mistress has been reinstalled and everything is being prepared for his return."

Elizabeth listened as the information was relayed at an almost furious rate for over an hour. They had everything. Locations, destinations, names, addresses and family members of the guards, and they were even certain they had several that could be bribed to allow them into the estate. Two of these were brothers of the young woman who had been forced to take the position of mistress in Grange's bed. He liked his women young. This one was barely eighteen, and Simon's reports stated she had been treated for a suicide attempt within months of going to the monster's bed.

"I contacted Mike last night." Simon was talking again. "I know you have a few of his boys out here, and I found out Callan has dispatched several Felines, as well as a couple of the Tyler brothers to help you. We have a small army going here, Dash. Let's get this done fast and right and take the bastard out this time." There was suddenly a dangerous flare of anticipation glowing in Simon's eyes.

Elizabeth glanced at Dash again. He was fingering several of the papers, his gaze reflective as he pretended to read one.

"Look, Dash." Simon leaned forward. "I know how you feel, man, after losing your unit. The more people involved, the bigger the risk of losing more than just yourself. But you saved my ass and my girls too many times to count. I'm not letting you take your woman in there alone. I know she has to go. I understand that need, if nothing else, from her standpoint. But alone isn't the way to do it."

Dash stood up from the table and for the first time Elizabeth noticed the tense, wary set of his shoulders.

"I saved your ass and those girls because I didn't want you dead, Simon," he snapped. "This isn't a job you were hired for and it's not your fight. You have no business here."

Simon turned to Elizabeth then. She watched the somber glint in his eye for a second before he hid it with cool laughter. "He's a stubborn bastard," he drawled. "Has he told you yet he doesn't have friends?"

Elizabeth cleared her throat. "He mentioned that."

"He likes to lie to himself." Simon leaned back in his chair. "We've had more than a dozen calls regarding half that many units he's fought with that have made themselves available to join in. That boy has a load of friends chewing their fingernails to the quick worrying about his John Wayne do-it-myself attitude. Thinks everyone needs help but him."

"Shut up, Simon," Dash growled. He didn't sound amused. He sounded worried and pissed.

"'Nother thing about Dash I've always noted." Simon smiled a bit sadly. "He always thinks it's his fault when one of those nonfriends gets their ass in a sling or ends up resting eternally. Doesn't matter to him if he was there, involved or knew what the hell was going on or not. Always thinks it's his fault. Has he told you about Afghanistan yet? He lost his brothers there . . ."

"Goddammit, I said to shut the fuck up." Elizabeth flinched in surprise and fear as Dash's rough, desperate voice seemed to echo around the room.

Silence filled the small cabin as all eyes turned to Dash. He turned from them, raking his fingers through his hair, the muscles in his back rippling with tension.

"Yeah, sure, Dash." Simon's voice was curiously gentle as he stood to his feet. "We have the cabin at the base of the mountain. We'll head back now. Here's my cell number." He scribbled the numbers on one of the papers. "We'll be back in the morning first thing for breakfast. Steph thinks the two of you might be undernourished or something. Come on, ladies."

They gathered around the tall dark-haired man, all of them casting Dash quiet looks so filled with caring and pain, for his sake, that it broke Elizabeth's heart.

"Thank you, Simon." She moved to him, giving him a hard, brief hug as he opened his arms easily to her. He had grown on her in the space of a few short hours. Equal parts hard-edged warrior and playful immaturity that endeared him to her.

"Take care of the stubborn ass," he finally sighed. "Talk some sense into him, maybe. He listens when he has to."

Dash ignored them all until Simon and his Ladies left. No sooner had the door closed then he moved. Elizabeth gasped as she was pushed roughly against the wall, his eyes blazing down at her, his hands hard, almost hurting, as he held her pinned to the wall.

"Never," he snarled, his eyes blazing furiously. "Never fucking touch another man in my presence, Elizabeth. Never, do you hear me?" His lips were drawn back, his expression so explosively enraged her heart jumped in fear for one hard minute.

Then anger filled her. Furious, blinding anger that ripped through her stomach, her chest. Before she knew what she was doing her leg came up, her knee contacting hard and fast between his thighs as he suddenly paled and swayed.

Jerking away from him, shaking with her fury, she turned back to him.

"Don't you ever manhandle me like that, Dash. Never again. And don't you dare try to pretend to know anything about me when you can't face your own truths. Now I'm going to bed. I've had about all I can stand of your churlishness and your refusal to accept yourself, let alone those around you."

She stomped away from him, confident that he would recover from the blow that was, at best, light. She could have put him to the floor. She also knew he would follow her. Aware and waiting. By God, she'd put his balls in his throat the next time.

CHAPTER 30

The lights were out and Elizabeth was lying stiffly in the bed an hour later when Dash finally slipped into the room. He removed his clothes in the dark, then eased beneath the blankets.

"I'm sorry." His voice wrapped around her, filled with regret. "I had no right to act that way."

Elizabeth sighed wearily. "So why did you, Dash? Simon came to help you, and I appreciate that. Besides, he's harmless . . ."

Dash snorted. "Elizabeth, Simon is the least harmless man I know. But I know he would never touch you with anything other than respect. The hug was harmless, a part of who you are, and I know that. I don't have an excuse for what I did."

She stared up at the ceiling, letting the scene replay in her mind once again. Dash had been on the edge of his control. Something had triggered a ragged fury inside him that she thought confused even him.

"Why don't you admit to having friends, Dash?" She knew that had been the key to his anger. "Everyone has friends somewhere. Everyone accepts that. Why not you? Why does the thought of having them make you so angry?"

At first, she thought he wasn't going to answer her. When he did, the ragged sound of his voice alone broke her heart.

"I was the runt of the litter I was created with," he told her bleakly. "Half the size of the other Breeds, and scrawny as hell. One of the scientists seemed to have taken me under his wing, though. Devroe. A cold-eyed bastard, but he seemed to like me well enough that it kept me alive for ten years. I endured tests that I cringe to think of now, because they were so painful, because he asked me to. I saw him as a father. Until the day I heard him planning to put me down." He grunted mockingly. "'Just like an animal. Bastard's never going to grow into anything,' he told his supervisor. 'We'll put him down next week.'"

Elizabeth closed her eyes in horror.

"I saw him as a friend. A mentor. All the things kids look up to, but that day, I saw the monster he really was. Two days later I found my chance, hid in one of the supply trucks and shipped out with it. I knew I'd have to hide. I'd have to be smart and careful, and keep my guard up unless I wanted to return to my own death. Friends make you weak. You want to trust them. You want to depend on them, let them depend on you. I saw all the hazards of that after I found foster care and began growing."

He had been a child, she thought. Ten years old and alone. His voice washed over her as he told her about the life he found. Foster care hadn't been easy for him, but he had excelled in school, and finally started growing. And he made sure no one else had the chance to betray him. He didn't make friends. Stayed to himself. When he joined the Army and then the Special Forces, he had kept that determination.

But as he talked, Elizabeth realized that the honor and determination to save lives that filled Dash had run the course of his Army life. Men he had held at arm's length owed him their lives, just as he owed several of them. His voice became softer, a bit amused as he spoke of those years and those men. And she saw how he had protected himself, never admitting to the bonds that had formed.

Finally, he came to the year he was sent to Afghanistan to weed out a new contingent of terrorists that were hiding in the mountains there. His voice changed then, becoming cooler, though she heard the pain beneath it.

"There were twelve of us," he finally said softly. "We'd been fighting together for over a year. My longest unit assignment. I was usually moved around pretty regularly as I was needed. I'm a good tracker." His voice was hoarse. "You get close when you fight that long together." He sighed. "You learn each other's dreams. You know who carries secrets and who doesn't. You . . ." The silence surrounding them deepened for long minutes. "You become brothers," he finally finished. "We were the Deadly Dozen. And for the first time in my life I was thinking, you know, maybe it wasn't so hard having friends. I had hidden for so damned long, Elizabeth. Sometimes it was scary, how fucking alone I tried to make myself."

She moved closer to him. He wasn't alone. He never had been, but she couldn't tell him that yet. Couldn't say anything until he was ready to hear it. He had thought himself alone, and as she told Cassie, what you convinced your mind of was all that mattered.

"We had just cleared up a killer mission. Son of a bitch, we pulled it off without a casualty. Those men were bruisers and we covered each other's asses like underwear. We'd just been airlifted and were heading home. I was thinking of putting in to take command of the unit. I was unofficial commander for a year. I thought maybe it was time, that maybe I could find a place for myself. Kind of a family." He cleared his throat as his voice became thick, rough.

"Jack and Craig, they were damned good sharpshooters, were joking about going home to their girls for the weekend. There were a few nurses on base they had been seeing. J. B. and Tim, the explosives experts, were divorced and were talking about getting drunk and calling the exes. The others were ribbing each other, flying high on adrenaline and success. And I was sitting there watching them. I kept pushing back that little warning in the back of my mind. That something that kept telling me things weren't right. The world went to hell two minutes later."

She lay against him, desperate to hold him. Her arm went over his chest as she lay against his body, feeling his arms close convulsively around her.

"I was close to the door and was thrown clear as the helicopter went down. I don't even know how that happened. The others were dead before they hit the ground. The impact of the explosive was damned precise. They knew what the hell they were doing that time, Elizabeth. They knew we would be there and they knew who they were hitting. And they killed every damned one of those men because I wasn't on guard. Because I let their camaraderie and their friendship distract me. I got them all killed, Elizabeth, because I let them be friends."

She heard the ragged edge of guilt, the torment he felt because he had been unable to control the events that happened. But she saw something more as well. She saw his fears of losing those he cared for, the scars it left on his soul because he couldn't save everyone.

She rose up in the bed, turning so she could stare into his eyes. The dim light from the moon spearing into the window lent just enough of a glow to allow her to see the moist pain in his gaze.

"You can't run from this one, Dash," she told him gently. "You can deny the friendships until hell freezes over and it won't change anything. Just like all the guilt in the world won't change the fact that you couldn't save those men, that you had no way of controlling what happened that night. You have no way of controlling Simon, his women or me. But you can still accept us, and you can still love us. And you can know that if any of us dies at any time, we died loving you and knowing that somewhere along the way, you enriched our lives. There's no more you can do."

"You, I can control," he almost snarled. "Don't think for a minute, Elizabeth, that I won't have your ass covered. Simon . . ." He sighed. "That man is like a Texas whirlwind and refuses to listen to good sense. Those Ladies of his aren't always as careful as they should be either. They live for the adrenaline and for Simon. Just as Simon lives for them. It's damned scary to watch them together."

"Why?" She tilted her head as she watched him closely. "Because you know he loves them? Because you know if he lost just one of them, it would rip him to shreds? And he's your friend, so you worry about that. And you feel helpless, because you know if he lost one of them, you couldn't ease the pain."

He was silent now.

"But, Dash, I saw something you might have overlooked," she said softly. "I saw six women who found in one man something to hold on to, to balance the ice inside them. Those women are dangerous. I could see that and I would rather face Grange than piss one of those women off. They could kill you without blinking. But Simon tempers them. He gives them someone to love, something to hold on to without fear. And he loves them back. Without each other, they would already be dead. And I think, at one time or another, without you, they would have been dead as well. They care for you too, Dash."

He breathed in deeply. It was the sound of a man fighting to deny what he already knew was the truth.

"I would die without you," he finally said. "I'd be crazy with terror if there were six of you to defend. Not to mention crazy, period." There was a vein of amusement in the final sentence.

She took his hand and moved it to her abdomen. "Did I ever tell you, Dash, how much I dream of babies? Lots of babies. I wanted at least three, more if I could. And if what you say is true about your semen counteracting birth control, do you think you might not have plenty of little girls to protect and go crazy over? What will you do then? Stop having sex with me?"

She saw the pure terror that glittered in his eyes for just a second. Raw, blistering hot fear as his fingers flexed against her abdomen.

"God help me," he groaned. "You will make me crazy, Elizabeth." He moved, gripping her hand and drawing it down to his erection. "Just the thought of making babies with you drives me crazy."

"That's not crazy, Dash," she murmured as her fingers gripped the steel-hard weight of his bulging cock. "That's horny."

"Yeah, does that to me too." He lifted his hips for her, pushing his cock against her fingers. "I'm sorry, Elizabeth." He drew her to him, his lips brushing against hers. "I shouldn't have taken it out on you. I shouldn't have been an asshole. I don't ever want to hurt you."

"You didn't hurt me." She smirked, her fingers flexing on his cock. "I can see I didn't hurt you either."

He grimaced. "Well, took a while to pull my balls out of my throat, but after I got them back in place I figured I could count myself lucky."

Elizabeth pushed the blankets back from his body, revealing the erect flesh straining between his thighs. She was wet and eager for him. She was always eager for him. Her pussy stayed slick and ready, her body always humming for his touch.

"Are you sure?" he groaned as she began to straddle his body, her head lowering to his lips once again.

"Hmm. Sure about what?" She eased against the bursting head, feeling it nudge into the folds of flesh and tuck against the opening of her vagina.

"Damn. Nothing," he panted. "God, you're so hot and ready for me. No one has ever wanted me like you do, Elizabeth. Always so sweet and hot and slick."

He spurted inside her. She loved it when he did that. "Your fault." She could barely talk now.

Elizabeth began easing down on the hard shaft, working it into the snug depths of her swollen pussy, relishing the painful pleasure that streaked into her womb. A part of her realized there might be something just slightly depraved about her. She loved that flare of pain as he entered her, or when he locked inside her. The burning blend of agonizing pleasure that sent her rocketing to orgasm.

"Easy, baby." His hands gripped her hips as she lowered her head to his shoulder. "I'm afraid I'll hurt you."

"So hurt me," she groaned roughly as she raked her fingers over his shoulder, remembering how good it felt when he did that to her. "Take me, Dash, like you need to. Now. Don't hold back for me."

His muttered oath was thick with need. "I'll hurt you, baby."

"I'll love it." She was breathing roughly.

But still he hesitated. He worked inside her slow and easy instead, his body tight and corded with the need to hold back. She didn't need him to hold back. She let her teeth grip the flesh of his shoulder lightly, then gathered herself, forcing the muscles of her pussy to relax a second before she impaled herself hard and fast on his shaft.

She bit him. God, she knew why he did that now. It was agonizing. Savage. He howled beneath her, a primal sound of such pleasure that her body shuddered with it as her pussy convulsed in spasmodic ripples of sensation. Her orgasm was instantaneous. Too much sensation. Too much fiery pleasure inside the swollen depths of her already sensitized pussy.

His cock was spurting hard inside her now, as though the ultra tight grip had signaled something inside that hard muscle that regulated the flow of the pre-cum. He was moaning hard beneath her, his hands gripping her thighs, his hips bucking against her, stroking through the violence of her orgasm and building another as they cried out at the intensity of feeling.

She was biting him hard. She knew she was and couldn't help it. Her hips writhed, twisting against the hard throb of his cock lodged inside her as his thighs bunched and he began to thrust in and out in powerful lunges as he lubricated her further, intensified sensation and threw her headlong into her next release.

Dash was only seconds behind her. She felt him swell, lock inside her and then spill his semen deep inside her body.

"Elizabeth." Minutes, hours later he shifted beneath her as his cock began to slowly lose its desperate swelling inside her. "Honey, let go of my shoulder."

His voice was thick, replete, but edged with amusement.

Elizabeth tasted blood. Gasping, she drew back, her gaze flying to his in horror.

"Shh." He laid his fingers against her lips as regret began to spill from her. "I loved it, baby. Bloodthirsty little thing." He lifted her from him then, groaning as his cock slid free of her, her pussy kissing it loudly as it exited. "Sleep, woman. You're killing me."

"I love you, Dash." She snuggled against his chest as he turned to her, his body sheltering her.

"I love you, Elizabeth." He sighed roughly. "More than I've loved anything in my life."

But the fear was back. She could hear it in his voice, feel it in the tenseness of his body. They would go after Grange soon, and she knew that it would be not only her greatest test, but Dash's as well.

CHAPTER 31

There was indeed a small army. The next morning, before the sun had risen over the cabin, Simon was back with his Ladies. Before breakfast was ready, several feline Breeds arrived, three men claiming to be Callan Lyons's brothers-in-law, four of Mike Toler's men and a handful of soldiers packing their duffel bags, fresh off a plane from the Middle East. There were over two dozen men in all and Simon's six lusty Ladies. Dash was furious.

"Get your asses right back on that plane," he was yelling at the dozen soldiers watching him dispassionately. "I didn't ask you to come out here and I'll be damned if you'll risk your asses like this."

"Sorry, Major. It's not happening." The unofficial leader of the unit shook his head. "Took us weeks to arrange leave without giving a proper reason. We're not going back."

Dash was cursing. Elizabeth watched from the doorway of the cabin as he raged. She hadn't seen Dash so worked up over anything. He was usually calm, holding his control tightly in check. It was more than obvious he was ready to lose it, if he hadn't already. Some of the words spilling from his lips she hadn't even imagined existed.

"Jonsey, are you that eager to make that new wife of yours a widow?" he yelled heatedly at one of the younger men. "Son of a bitch, I thought you loved that girl."

Jonsey was a tall, lanky young man. Maybe twenty-five, with wide hazel eyes and thick red hair.

"I do love her, Dash." Jonsey nodded solemnly. "I've had a year with her. A year I wouldn't have had if you hadn't pulled her out of that hospital they bombed. Cindy agrees with me being here. I'm not going back."

Elizabeth could hear Dash growling in irritation.

He turned to the man beside Jonsey. He was nearly as tall as Dash, with short, spiked brown hair and deep brown eyes. His face was lined with exhaustion and he had obviously had enough of Dash's temper.

"Don't you even start on me, Major," the soldier snapped back. "I've not slept in a week to bring my ass out here and I'm not in the mood for your god complex either. So just tell me where I can sack out for a while and then we'll discuss your plan of action when I wake up."

He was snarly. Elizabeth perked up, as did several of Simon's Ladies. They sauntered from the house, immediately drawing attention. Eyes were bugging out of sockets as the men caught sight of them.

"Hell, Simon's here." One of them seemed to sigh in reverence. "Oh man. This is gonna be a good fight."

"Excuse me, Major. I might have found someone to keep me warm." The soldier looked damned near ecstatic as one of the Ladies sidled up to him, cooing gently about his weariness.

"Damn you, Chase." Dash was growling now.

"Give it up, Dash," the tall feline Breed growled back from the sidelines. "This isn't just about you anymore, or about your woman. Chill out and accept the help or ease back and we'll do it ourselves. You're mated now. Mated to a woman proven to be able to conceive easily with Breed young. We can't afford to lose you or her."

Fury ignited in Dash. Elizabeth watched as his head lowered, turning as he stared at the Feline in building fury.

"My woman is not a breeder for the fucking Breeds," he snarled, his voice low, dangerous.

"She will be if you get your ass killed. Whatever Breed the Council managed to make mount her. Her and that kid. You want to risk it?" Mercury Warrant was only a bit larger than Dash. If it came to a fight, either man could have come out the winner. "Get a handle on yourself, boy. You never were alone in this world." He nodded to the soldiers. "And you sure as hell aren't now. Let's all get some rest and we'll see what kind of plan you have in place. And stop growling at me. It's pissing me off."

As she watched, Elizabeth was aware of Simon moving up behind her, watching curiously.

"Could get interesting now," he said softly. "Dash thinks he has to do everything on his own. Thinks he has to save everyone he takes under his wing. Usually manages to too. But he doesn't accept help so well. It will be interesting to see how gracefully he accepts us poking our noses in his business." Simon sounded like he was looking forward to any fight that arose.

"Fuck," Dash finally snarled so violently, so furiously, that Elizabeth flinched.

He turned away from them and stalked away from the cabin, moving purposely into the woods surrounding it as she moved to follow him.

"Wait." Simon caught her arm. "Give him a few minutes to work through it first. Let's get these boys fed and bedded down for a while. They're a tired bunch. Then you can go after him."

◆　◆　◆

What the hell had happened? Dash couldn't understand it for the life of him. He had fought to stay distant from the men he fought with, to do his job, keep their asses alive and go his merry way. If knowledge of what he was had leaked out while he was fighting with them, he would have put every man in whatever unit he was in in danger. The Council didn't care who they killed. But evidently, he hadn't stayed distant enough. He had over two dozen fighters standing in the clearing of the cabin awaiting orders. Orders he didn't want to give. He didn't want to lead them into his personal battle and have one of them die because of it.

Damn. He sighed wearily. He was pissed as hell, but he knew those men wouldn't leave. Not unless he did. And they would follow. They were damned good men too. The best. As good as or better than the unit he had lost in Afghanistan.

He stopped his furious trek up the mountain, pausing at a sheltered bench of land that looked down on the cabin. Tents were being pitched and voices were raised as coordination among the men began to establish itself. He knew the minute he saw the first arrivals that this mission had turned into something more than just the fight to save Elizabeth and her child. It was now a fight to establish dominance, to show the Council and those who would strike out against the Breeds in general that there was a bigger battle than they wanted to face.

There was no way Grange could anticipate over two dozen men moving in on him. Men so adept, so well trained in every area of battle, that he didn't have a chance of fighting against them.

Finally, his lips quirked in amusement. Grange would fight and there was always the chance of losing one or more men in the group. Dash could do nothing but make certain they planned for everything and pray they all got through it alive. It was all he could do.

As he sat there, watching with narrowed eyes as the clearing turned into an armed camp, he watched Elizabeth leave the cabin slowly. Damn. She was like a ray of sunshine. Moving past the soldiers working around her, she headed up the mountain. She was graceful, a creature of such fluid movement and erotic design that it made his loins clench in sudden hunger. How had he ever deserved anything so beautiful to call his own? He couldn't make sense of it, but he had never wanted to fight it either. As though he had waited all his life for that moment in the diner, his body had instantly recognized her scent, her blue eyes, her quiet strength.

She was a mate who would fight beside him and protect her young and him, if needed, against all odds. She had proven that in her determination and quick thinking in saving Cassie. She wouldn't balk, no matter what was needed.

"Done pouting yet?" She moved to him, watching him in concern as he gripped her wrist and pulled her down between his thighs.

He nestled her back against his chest, wrapping his arms around her, and propped his head on her shoulder as he watched the action below them.

"They're damned good men," he said softly. "Good fighters too."

"Yeah," she agreed softly. "They seem to be."

"Jonsey, he has this pretty little nurse for a wife. She was hurt badly in that bombing. Lots of bleeding, in shock. I didn't think she would make it." He sighed. "I kept telling her how Jonsey was on his way. She loves that boy, Elizabeth. I guilted the hell out of her. She lived because she knew she had to. Knew if Jonsey saw her like that, all bloody and broken and dead too, that he wouldn't survive it. They were married a year later. Took her that long to recover."

"She sounds very strong." Dash nodded.

"Simon and those women." He shook his head. "They're like trouble waiting to happen. But they're damned good at cleaning it out and celebrating later. The man has his own personal harem devoted to his pleasure and his happiness above all things. They're dangerous as hell, and at any given time they're ready to reward any man lucky enough to become deserving of their attention. But all Simon has to do is lift his finger and they're back in his arms. They love that crazy cowboy more than he deserves sometimes."

And on it went. Each man. Another adventure, another tale. He knew every facet of their personalities, what made them strong, what made them weak. What made them love or hate.

Elizabeth sat against him and, not for the first time, marveled at the man who had walked so calmly into her life and taken it over. The man who had given her his love before he ever met her. Who had dreamed about her as he lay in a medicated stupor and woke up because he saw her crying.

For the first time in her life, Elizabeth knew what love was. Not just his love for her, but his love for those men working to set up a usable camp and determined to fight by his side again. His friends.

Finally, he was quiet, watching as she was, holding her close as he grunted or chuckled at some action below them. Simon's Ladies were, of course, helping. In ways that made Elizabeth blush a bright crimson. They were earthy, strong women. And Simon looked on like a proud parent as they tempted and teased the appetites of many of the men below. They steered well clear of Jonsey, though, and he made certain he steered clear of them.

"Time to get ready," he finally sighed quietly. "We leave here tomorrow night, Elizabeth. Grange returns in a week. You sure you want to do this?"

Oh, she was damned sure.

"I'm sure, Dash," she promised him quietly. "I miss Cassie. I want it done and my daughter safe. I want it over."

"Come on, then." He moved to his feet and pulled her up beside him. "Let's go whip these boys into shape. We'll let Simon's Ladies take care of their lusts and then we'll start planning. We'll get him, baby, and then we'll go home."

CHAPTER 32

A week later Elizabeth was being dragged roughly into the house that had been rented in the small town she had run from two years before. Dash had a manacled grip on her wrist, his body was vibrating with fury and she wasn't any less pissed.

Behind them, Simon and his Ladies trailed more slowly, as did several others of the group that amassed together. The rest were at logistical points around the Grange estate or working with the two guards who had been bribed from Grange's service. She and Dash had been slipping through town, testing the determination of the men Grange had in place to catch her.

His orders to her had been precise. She knew when she slipped from the shadowed alley to be certain Grange wasn't in the car they had been watching, that he would be pissed. That he would, in no uncertain terms, let her know how displeased he was. But she hadn't expected this.

She had been so close. She had nearly been in the right position to check the identity of the two men when Dash had grabbed her, dragging her back into the alley and then to the car awaiting them on the other end. He had been chillingly silent, angrier than she had ever seen him.

"Dammit, Dash, stop dragging me around." She tugged on his hold as he pulled her up the staircase.

She was fighting tooth and nail, but it was follow him or be dragged. She wasn't in the mood to incur any more bruises along the way.

Dash was madder than she had ever seen him. Stone-cold enraged rather than growling mad. His expression was savage, his lips pulled back in a silent snarl as he glanced back at her, his golden eyes glowing with liquid fire. She was almost trembling in fear.

When he reached their bedroom door, he opened it, jerked her inside and turned to close it with deadly silence. The *snick* of the lock turning caused her to flinch.

"I won't be manhandled this way by you," she charged him fiercely, trying to ignore the weakness in her knees as he faced her.

"Take your clothes off."

"Why?" she snapped. "So you can show me my place? Under your body? I was safe, Dash."

"You broke formation. You disobeyed orders. Do you know what I would have done to Jonsey, or Chase, or any of the others who so blatantly threatened not just the mission but also their own lives?"

His voice was deadly.

Elizabeth shook her head. "I was safe."

"You were a fool. You were being tricked, Elizabeth. There was another vehicle pulling in no more than ten feet from you. You were nearly seen," he told her quietly, the dark, harsh timbre of his voice making her tremble.

"They wouldn't have seen me," she argued furiously. "I was being careful."

"And if they had?" he asked her with deadly calm. "If they had managed to take you or, God forbid, just kill you and have it done with. What then?"

She blinked up at him, horror filling her. "They couldn't," she whispered. "I was hidden."

"If you had moved forward so much as another inch, you would have been seen," he said, his voice still throbbing with fury as he jerked his shirt over his head. "You risked my men, but even more, you risked my mate. Possibly my child, and everything we've planned for, Elizabeth. Now take off your clothes."

"Why?" She backed away from him, the horror of what she had nearly done still vibrating through her. "I'm sorry, Dash. I was being careful. I just thought . . ."

"I didn't tell you to think on this mission unless it went to shit real fast," he informed her coldly, his hand going to his pants. "Now take your fucking clothes off before I rip them off."

"Not like this." She shook her head desperately. "Not while you're so mad at me, Dash."

He stilled. "Mad at you?" Agony resonated in his voice now. "You think this is mad, Elizabeth? This isn't mad, baby. If I were mad I'd be stripping the hide off your bones with every insult I could come up with. I'm not mad. You scared me out of ten years of my life. Now take those fucking clothes off."

He didn't stop undressing after casting her that first, incredulous look. Before her eyes, he dropped his weapons, his boots, his clothes, standing before her gloriously naked and aroused. Adrenaline was still pumping through her body, fear and remnants of anger and a sudden excitement that shocked her. He was going to take her whether she wanted him to or not. Like a traitor her body heated, her pussy clenching in hunger. She backed away from him.

"I don't think so," she snapped, her gaze flicking to the straining length of his cock before going back to his face.

He smirked as he inhaled deeply. "I'm going to mount you and I'm going to show you who's boss in this little endeavor, baby. A lesson you won't soon forget. Now take your clothes off."

"Boss?" She lifted her brow with what she knew was haughty disdain as she watched him carefully. "I don't think so, Dash."

His hand had fallen to his cock, his fingers gripping the abundant flesh and stroking it lazily. The engorged head was glistening with moisture and throbbing wildly with arousal.

"You know, it was driven home relatively hard tonight that you think you can get away with anything in this relationship," he growled. "You continually tempt my possessiveness by hugging around on my soldiers and generally babying them. Simpering and so damned sweet it's enough to give me a toothache. But I handle it," he stated with a vast amount of male pride. "I handle it well, I think. But I'll be damned if you'll be allowed to disregard my orders on a mission. Not now, not ever."

"It won't happen again." But she knew it likely would. She wasn't stupid. She was used to being in control, not following someone else. "You can fuck me after you've calmed down."

He smiled slowly, rather coldly. "No."

He began to stalk her then. The bedroom was large, but it wasn't that damned large. She didn't have a hope of escaping him. The thought of that sent her pussy convulsing, spilling the thick cream along the plump curves and preparing her for his penetration.

She moved to the edge of the room, her eyes darting anxiously from side to side as she tried to find an escape route. There weren't any, and Dash was getting closer by the second.

As he neared her, she jumped to move. His hands hooked in her shirt, ripping it from her body. She turned on him furiously.

"I'm tired of you tearing my clothes off me."

"Then undress." He was calm, determined. "Do it now. Take your punishment like a good girl, baby."

Her eyes narrowed on him. "I don't think so."

He shrugged easily. "Then I'll tear every shred of cloth off your body and buy you more when you need them."

Elizabeth gritted her teeth in fury. She was closer to the door now, her only chance. She turned and ran for it. Unfortunately, Dash was faster. Before she could escape he was on her. Hooking his arm around her waist, he dragged her to the bed, threw her on it, then followed her.

Rolling to her stomach, she had every intention of escaping. Before she could do more than come to her knees, he had her again. Fighting, twisting, she fought him with every breath as he curled his fingers in the waistband of her leggings and tugged them over her hips.

Screaming out in frustration, she kicked back at him. He rewarded her with a chuckle as he pushed the material to her knees and left it there. She was twisting against him when his hand suddenly landed on the rounded curve of her bottom. Shocked, she stilled for a second. In the next she was reaching back, clawing at him, cursing him until he caught her hands in one of his and held them to the middle of her back.

Struggling was getting her nowhere. But worse, it was making her hotter, making her pussy cream furiously as his hand landed on her rump again. She jerked in amazement.

"Are you spanking me?" she screamed out at him. "Son of a bitch, I'll kill you when I get up."

"Then maybe I won't let you up." His hand landed again.

It wasn't a hard smack, but enough to warm her ass, to make her wiggle in protest. It was making her pussy blaze. Her breasts were swollen with arousal now, her nipples hard little points that brushed against the sheet, sensitizing further with each move against the material.

"Dash, I swear, you'll pay for this." She meant to sound tough, threatening; instead it came out more like a moan, a sound of hunger.

The small, hot smacks to her ass were making her crazy. Being pinned beneath him, helpless, on fire, was destroying her. Both half-moon curves were attended to, his hand striking her, burning her until she was writhing beneath him, but whether in pain or pleasure even she couldn't say for certain.

She gasped as his hand pushed between her thighs, his fingers smoothing over the syrupy slickness of her bald cunt. Every nerve in the swollen flesh pulsed to life. Her clit throbbed in impatient demand as she whimpered against the small caresses he stroked around it. Pulling his hand back, he gathered the slick essence, smoothing it back along her pussy to the cleft of her buttocks.

Elizabeth flinched as his fingers pressed against her anal opening, pushing the silken natural lubrication into the tiny hole.

"Dash." An incredible flare of aroused pleasure streaked through her as the tip of his finger pierced the little opening and muffled her small protest.

It felt too good. The tip of his finger moved gently inside her, stroking deeper and deeper until the full length of it was buried in her backside. Elizabeth was shocked. She had never been touched there, never caressed or penetrated in such a manner. She moved back tentatively, trying to hold back the groan of pleasure as his finger slid out, then back in, tunneling inside her with carnal intent.

"Elizabeth." She tensed; his voice was crooning, deliberately gentle. That was never a good sign.

"What?" She was gasping as another finger joined the first. She was raised perfectly for him now, her shoulders flat to the bed, her butt elevated for his decadent exploration as he held her hands secured at the small of her back.

"I'm going to fuck your ass, baby," he told her, shocking her, heating her blood with the sensual promise. "Hard and deep, Elizabeth. I'm going to show you what happens when you rouse the animal inside me. I'll show you, baby, not to ever put yourself in danger like that again."

Her eyes widened as she trembled.

"Don't hurt me, Dash." Was he going to punish her with pain now?

His fingers slid free of the tight channel. A second later a resounding crack to her ass had her jerking away from him angrily.

"Have I ever hurt you?" he snapped as he shifted behind her. "Have I, Elizabeth?"

"No." She moaned, feeling his cock slide along the cleft of her ass.

He was thick and full and she knew there wasn't a chance in hell he was going to manage to work it inside her. It wasn't possible. His fingers returned to their previous work, sliding through the juices easing from her vagina and spreading them back to her anal entrance as he worked his fingers slowly inside her.

"Damn. You're tight here," he whispered as she clenched on him. "I bet, Elizabeth, that when my cock shoots that lubrication up your sweet ass, I'll slide right in. You'll be all nice and hot and so tight around my dick I'll go crazy with it."

She trembled at the explicit words. She was fighting just to breathe. It was too sensual, too depraved, being held down as she was while Dash eased her ultra tight anal muscles.

Long minutes later, she whimpered. The bloated head of his cock pressed against the sensitive entrance as Dash tucked it tight into the small opening he had created. Immediately a hot, surging pulse of pre-cum shot inside her.

"Easy." Dash released her hands as his own smoothed down her back, gentling her. "It's okay, baby. Just relax for me."

Her anus heated, sensitized. Suddenly, it seemed as though a million little nerves were whipping to life and they were pleading for his cock to surge inside her. The muscles began to loosen marginally, and she felt the head of his shaft sink in a bit more. For each small penetration, the hot fluid jetted inside her, easing her, making a way for him to work the thick head past the tight little entrance.

She was on fire. She could feel her flesh stretching around his, cupping the throbbing head of his cock as the Breed fluid pulsed inside her, forcing her body to stretch, to accommodate the thick erection sliding into her untried anus.

"Dash." Her fingers gripped the blankets; her ass rose for him as she trembled beneath him. She was scared. The sheer domination of the act was overwhelming her as nothing he had ever done before had. She felt taken in ways she could have never imagined.

"Never again, Elizabeth," he said as the head of his cock finally slipped in fully, popping through the tight anal ring as she bucked, crying out beneath him. "Never disobey me in such a manner again."

"No." She would have promised him anything then. What was more, she knew he would make certain she stuck to it.

The head of his cock was embedded in her now, throbbing, spurting inside her, filling her rectum with a heat she didn't know if she could survive. His hands held her hips steady, his big body looming over her as he began to work the thick tip in and out of her. He was sinking deeper with each small thrust, stretching her further, creating a blooming fire in the depths of her ass that she could have never imagined possible.

With each ripple of movement inside her, the small channel accepted more and more of his erection until finally, she screamed out in pleasure/pain as the full length slid inside the tight depths.

Elizabeth could feel his pelvis pressing into the cheeks of her rear, his hands gripping her hips, holding her tight against him as several more silky pulses of fluid filled her rectum. His bigger body was covering her now, his thighs holding her in place.

"This is mine," he growled in her ear. "Mine to protect. To fuck. To love. You will never again endanger it in such a way. Do you understand me?"

"Yes." Elizabeth nearly shrieked.

She was impaled in a way she could have never imagined possible, her muscles easing around him just enough to send hard, fiery arcs of agonizing pleasure straight to her womb.

"I'm going to fuck you now," he told her softly, though his voice vibrated with a lust-driven hunger she had never heard from him before. "I'm going to fuck your sweet ass, Elizabeth. Because it's mine. Mine to fuck. Mine to shelter. You will never again forget to take care of what's mine." He was snarling as he began to move inside her, a deep, growling sound of carnal greed that sent shivers racing over her flesh.

Then she knew nothing but his cock driving up her ass. He pulled back until only the head remained before surging forward again, stretching her, burning her as she bucked beneath him, swept away by sensations she couldn't imagine fighting.

She could feel the channel stretching, straining around him as each thrust sent another burning pulse of fluid jetting inside her, making each stroke easier to take, each impalement driving her closer to the brink of a release she knew would terrify her. He was groaning at her ear, fucking her with a hard rhythm, throwing her closer to orgasm as the coil of pleasure/pain began to tighten in her womb.

Elizabeth couldn't move, could do nothing but tremble under his heavy weight, crying out at each penetration, feeling herself being sucked into her own destruction. Streaking arcs of sensations tore through her body with each thrust, driving her higher, hotter, until it reached its zenith. She tightened around him, hearing his desperate moan as his thrusts increased. The slap of flesh, the sucking echo of hard strokes into the well-lubricated tunnel of her anus and her own desperate, strangled screams heralded her orgasm.

Like a supernova, she exploded. White heat filled her as she felt Dash's teeth grip her shoulder, felt him suddenly swell, terrifying her with the building pressure as she climaxed beneath him. Suddenly, she was climbing again. She could feel the fierce swelling pressing into the thin wall of flesh between her anus and her cunt, filling her pussy, causing the muscles to ripple against one another, as an exacting pressure tightened around her clit and she rocketed into oblivion.

It was devastating. The hard, agonizing pleasure was consuming her, ripping through her, streaking with hard, powerful shudders through her body as she bucked and writhed beneath him, her body consumed by a release that shocked her so thoroughly, ripped through her mind so swiftly, that before Dash had finished filling her rectum with his hot seed, darkness overtook her.

Long minutes later, Dash felt his cock ease, felt the agonizing heat and tight grip around his flesh relax, and he pulled free wearily. He was more than aware that the final, violent orgasm that had ripped through Elizabeth had left her unconscious. Damn. He'd never fucked a woman into a faint in his life. He didn't like having his mate be the first.

He dragged his body wearily from the bed and padded into the bathroom. There he cleaned himself, then wet a clean washrag and returned to the bed. He cleaned Elizabeth carefully, wiping away the semen and lubricating fluid that dampened her buttocks and thighs before spreading the delicate cheeks and washing the cleft.

Traces of his semen still spilled from the reddened little entrance. His eyes closed, remembering the brief glance he had allowed himself of her flesh stretching around him, hugging his cock like a tight leather glove and making him crazy to fill her with his seed. But he had intended to pull free instead. He had never meant to allow the swelling knot to anchor him in the tender hole.

It had been her climax. When she tightened on him, holding him inside her as she climaxed, his brain had exploded. Before he could pull free, his cock had locked inside her, spilling his release into the blistering depth of her anus.

He was completely exhausted now. The emotional and physical demands had taken a toll on his body, and he couldn't wait to lie down beside her and sleep. Returning to the bathroom, he dumped the cloth into the basket there and returned to their bed. Pulling her into his arms, he grinned at the grumpy, less-than-pleased sound of her sleepy groan, but she snuggled into his chest, breathed out softly and continued to sleep.

"I love you, baby," he sighed, kissing her head.

He loved her, but he swore if she ever did anything so stupid again, he was going to blister her butt with the palm of his hand. On the other hand, another scare like that would give him a stroke. Grange hadn't been in the car Elizabeth had been checking. He had been in the one pulling in behind it. And he was watching for Elizabeth. He had been within a second of having her. The terror that had filled him when he realized that had been unlike anything he had ever known before.

His arms tightened around her. What the hell would he do if he lost her?

CHAPTER 33

"Remember the plan." Dash cast Elizabeth a hard look two nights later as the team prepared to invade Grange's estate. "We go in quietly. Grange will be in the study. Elizabeth, Merc and I will slip in, get the files, disable Grange and be on our merry way. Should be simple and easy. No problem. Let's not create any."

Three of Simon's Ladies had managed to catch Grange's attention earlier that evening and were now within the mansion, occupying the bastard until they could get in. Grange liked playing in his study, from what his young mistress had said. Her contact with them minutes before had confirmed he was now in the room with the women.

There were plenty of outside guards to keep Simon and the other three women satisfied hunting. The unit of soldiers that had come in to help was stationed outside the perimeters, ready to back them up along with the Tyler brothers and the other feline Breed, Tanner.

Nods accompanied Dash's orders, especially Elizabeth. She had no intentions of pissing Dash off again where a mission was concerned.

Not that she hadn't enjoyed the anal adventure he had given her, but the intensity of her orgasm wasn't anything she was ready to experience again any time soon.

"Merc, you're with me and Elizabeth. Let's keep this as clean as possible."

It was much cleaner than Elizabeth had anticipated. The two guards Dash's men had bribed made certain the path they were using into the estate's mansion was clear. The back door was unlocked. They moved into the darkened back hallway quietly and made their way to the foyer at the front of the house.

Checking the well-lit area, Elizabeth watched as Dash turned to Merc and motioned him up the curving staircase. When he had made it safely to the top, Elizabeth followed suit, joining Merc on the landing; they both stood ready as Dash moved silently up the steps as well. Timed perfectly. They stood tense, expectant, as the guard made his round then, shuffling drowsily through the foyer and into the kitchen.

As he disappeared, Dash gave the signal to move forward. The upstairs was a series of hallways and closed doors, with Grange's study occupying the middle suite. They paused at the door, listening carefully at the tinkling laughter and Grange's smooth, cultured voice from inside.

Weapons ready, Dash knocked quietly. A careful pattern of small thumps that first resulted in silence, then a furious curse from Grange as the three women obviously made their move. The panel was jerked open quickly by Stephanie. Her eyes were cold, her expression bloodthirsty as they stepped into the room.

"Elizabeth." Grange was sitting behind his big oak desk, hands lying carefully on top of the smooth, polished surface as Danica stood behind him, a knife at his throat. "How interesting. And I see you have friends with you."

Elizabeth stilled her shudder of revulsion as she stared at the monster who had hunted her and her daughter for over two years. He was carefully groomed, his thick brown hair sweeping back from a face that could have been passably handsome if it weren't for the jagged scar sweeping across one cheek and the glint of cold mockery in his hazel eyes.

"Yes, she does," Dash answered with an edge of amusement as Merc closed the door behind him.

"Mercury Warrant." Grange watched the big Breed with a glimmer of fascination. "How interesting." He turned back to Elizabeth. "I guess you finally figured out what a little gold mine you conceived, darling. Dane wasn't so pleased with the pup after all, was he?"

Her daughter wasn't a pup. Elizabeth stilled her fury as she aimed her gun at his head. "I want those files." She was amazed at the veil of ice that spread through her body. Her soul. "Now."

Grange's eyes narrowed as his gaze flicked to Dash. "She could bring you millions. But not without help. I have the Breed semen . . ."

Dash laughed. "What you have is a joke compared to what I have." He smirked.

He turned, jerking the sleeveless T-shirt he wore over his shoulder to reveal the shadow mark. When he turned back, Grange appeared suitably impressed.

"Amazing," he breathed. "Martaine swore the Wolves had been killed. I guess he was wrong."

"I guess." Dash sounded unconcerned, but Elizabeth had detected the shadow of pain that edged his words. "Give us the files you have, Grange."

The other man's thin lips quirked as Danica moved carefully away from him, content to let Dash now handle the control of their enemy.

Grange sighed. "I think not." He smirked as he looked between Dash and Elizabeth. "Is she breeding yet?"

Elizabeth smiled. "Let me kill him, Dash," she whispered. "We can find the papers later."

Grange's gaze flickered in concern.

"Not yet, baby." Dash sighed. "I told you, if he cooperates he can live. We need the papers more than we need his death."

Elizabeth shrugged. The look she gave Grange warned him, though, that she would relish the chance to kill him.

Grange cleared his throat. "Ah well. It was a good plan if I could have pulled it off." He shrugged carelessly as he nodded toward the safe Danica had found while checking behind portraits and prints that hung on the wall. "The file is in the safe."

"Combination." Dash moved to the metal door. "And don't fuck with me, Grange. Elizabeth will take your head off your shoulders with that gun. It was all I could do to convince her to do this my way."

She fingered the trigger of the gun as she begged Grange with her eyes to give her an excuse, any excuse, to pull the trigger. He gave them the combination instead.

Elizabeth kept her gaze on Grange, watching carefully as she listened to Merc communicating with the men outside and Dash punching in the numbers to the combination. She was expecting an alarm to sound. Was praying Grange would give her an excuse to kill him.

"Got it." Dash's voice had her grimacing.

"He has you leashed. Interesting." Grange smirked. "Tell me, Elizabeth, what's it like to fuck an animal?"

Elizabeth snorted. "I have no idea. Let's call your mistress in here and ask her." His expression tightened as anger flashed in his eyes.

"Elizabeth, that trigger isn't something to play with. It's damned touchy," Dash warned her as he moved carefully behind her. "Merc, watch our buddy there while we go over this file. I need to make certain everything we need is here."

Elizabeth turned to Dash, almost missing Grange's sneer of satisfaction.

She watched as he opened the file. The first page had him stiffening. Several more pages later and he turned haunted, shocked eyes back to her.

"Martaine did enjoy his little experiments," Grange sighed with smug amusement. "I thought it very ingenious, actually. The creatures have no soul, I'm told. Vicious killers who enjoy playing with their prey. I had high hopes Cassie would live up to her DNA. He made certain he gave it every chance, of course."

Elizabeth felt her heart explode in her chest as she moved over to Dash. "Elizabeth." She stopped as she saw the grief in his eyes.

"I want to see it," she whispered. "I want to know what they did to my baby." She moved until she could read the notes Martaine had made.

Genetic splicing of the Coyote and Wolf DNA was successful and not nearly as difficult as I first surmised. I have created enough of the unique sperm to ensure the chance of conception with the right female. Dane Colder seems more than interested in my little experiment. His sterility makes him a viable partner in this, as does his belief that a man should kill if necessary and train his children to take what they want. It will be interesting, watching the growth of the child. I can only hope it's male.

DATED THREE MONTHS LATER

The in-vitro process was more successful than I had hoped. I wonder if Mrs. Colder is aware of the little abomination growing in her womb. All initial test results from the amniocentesis shows the DNA has held. I'll have to be certain to be there at the birth to perform all tests on the infant myself.

Elizabeth made it through the first page before she stared up at Dash in horror. They couldn't let Cassie know. Couldn't allow this information to ever become public knowledge. Already the news was littered with rumors of the Coyote experiments. Human animals, experiments that had finally given the scientists the killers they had been working to create. So far, none had been found, but the lab reports, training notes and scientific files attested to the fact that they existed. Cold-blooded, as soulless as their animal cousins and glorying in the blood they could spill. It would destroy Cassie if she ever learned she was part of the creatures the Council had created.

"Stephanie, you and Gloria secure the exit out," Dash ordered the other woman. "Merc, contact the men outside and make certain the guards are disabled. Danica, tie that bastard up before we leave."

Grange sneered humorously. "I'll be certain to follow her maturity, Elizabeth," he told her coldly. "Once that information gets out, there's no way you can hide it from her. No way you can stop her DNA from shaping her. She has no soul. She's a corruptible little shell, nothing more. A bitch to breed the perfect son."

Elizabeth aimed the gun in her hand. She saw Cassie, so sweet and loving, her soul shining brightly in her eyes, in her laughter, in her love for everyone around her. She saw the strength it had taken the little girl to rise above what this monster had already done to her and she wanted to scream out at the cruelty, the monstrous lack of decency it had taken to do what he had tried.

"Elizabeth?" Dash stood behind her, not stopping her, no censure in his voice, only love and understanding. "He's not worth it, baby. We know better."

"He'll destroy her," she whispered hoarsely.

"Not if we don't let him. Cassie's stronger than he is."

Danica stood to the side, watching the scene carefully as she held the length of rope Merc had brought along to restrain Grange.

Elizabeth turned to Dash. As she did, from the corner of her eye, she saw Grange move. His hand whipped under the desk, a gun emerging, pointing toward her, fury lighting his face.

Elizabeth smiled as she lifted her arm just as quickly, in a split second, aiming her weapon as her finger tightened on the trigger. Grange would never hurt anyone else. She saw surprise flash in his eyes the second the bullet buried dead center between them, even as his own weapon discharged. Fire seared her chest, took her breath, causing her legs to buckle as Dash screamed out her name.

She collapsed in his arms, her gaze going to the rapidly spreading stain across her shirt. She raised her gaze to Dash, agony searing her soul at the horror in his eyes.

"Protect my baby," she whispered.

"God no. Elizabeth, don't you fucking die on me!" Dash screamed as he lowered her to the floor.

She could hear Merc yelling out orders in his comm link, felt Danica press a cloth hard to the wound, but she could feel ice spreading through her body. Her breath hitched as pain seared her heart.

"I love you." She fought to hold back her tears. "Forever, Dash."

"Merc, get that ambulance here now. Have Chase contact Mike and meet us at the hospital. Have the men pull back. All of them. Goddammit, get her some help."

He was holding her, rocking her. She felt his arms around her, felt the dark edges of cold peace shifting at the corner of her mind. Dash would have to ease Cassie's fears now. He could protect her. She had killed the monster. She had made certain Cassie would never know.

"Elizabeth. Stay with me." Dash's voice was fierce as he picked her up in his arms, rushing from the room. Sirens were echoing in the distance, shouted orders filling her head. "If you love me, if you love Cassie, then you stay with me, damn you. If you love that baby you're carrying in your womb now, then by God you'll live."

She blinked up at him. His gaze sliced down to her.

"My child, Elizabeth. You're carrying my child. Do you really want it to die as well?"

"No," she cried weakly. She could feel the cold spreading through her, the blood pumping from her chest. "No. Dash. Dash . . ."

"Stay with me, Elizabeth." He was running down the stairs, Danica at his side, somehow managing to hold the makeshift compress to her chest.

The foyer was chaos, a dizzying rush of color and pain and Dash's voice yelling at her, begging her. And she fought. She fought, but the crashing waves of dark ice were covering her, slipping through her mind, carrying her away. Her last thought was of Dash. His touch, his gentleness, and the price he had paid for letting her close. He had lost the protection he had kept around himself so long. His protection and now the child he had dreamed of. Like Elizabeth, he had lost it all . . .

✦ CHAPTER 34 ✦

⊖NE WEEK LATER

"Remember, you have to be quiet." The hospital door opened and Dash eased in, carrying the somber, frightened little girl who clutched her new teddy bear with desperate hands.

Elizabeth opened her eyes groggily, her heart swelling in her chest as she saw her baby for the first time in nearly a month. Dash held Cassie against his broad chest, his golden-brown gaze meeting hers with warmth and love as he carried her child to her.

"Momma." Her voice was whisper-thin as tears sparkled in her eyes.

Dash brought her to the chair that sat by the hospital bed, settled into it and let Cassie lay her head next to her mother's on the pillow.

Elizabeth couldn't contain her tears as she turned to the little girl, reaching up painfully so she could sink her fingers into Cassie's curls as a thin little arm curled around the top of her head.

It had been so long since she had felt Cassie's warmth, seen her innocent little face and known in her mother's heart that her baby was safe. The hellish events of the week past were a recurring nightmare: her struggle to breathe, disjointed memories of agonizing pain and bright operating lights as surgeons rushed around her.

Thankfully, the bullet hadn't caused any lasting damage, though it had been close. She had been lucky, she was told. Very lucky. As was the child resting safely in her womb. Despite the terror of those conscious moments, she had lived and would heal.

"How is my baby?" she whispered weakly. "Momma missed you, Cassie."

Cassie sniffed back her low sobs as she nodded faintly. "I missed you, Momma. I was so afraid you wouldn't come back. That I would be all alone and scared for forever. I'm so glad you're okay."

Elizabeth lifted her gaze as Dash smoothed his hand over Cassie's hair. Elizabeth knew he had been the one to tell Cassie of her mother's accident and that she would be confined to the hospital for a while. Exhaustion had sapped her body before she was wounded, making her healing take progressively longer. But she would be leaving the hospital soon. In a few days. Though the doctors warned her she would have to take it easy.

"Hey, beautiful." Dash touched her cheek as she gazed over at him. "I couldn't keep her away. She's as stubborn as her mother is."

His voice was rich and gentle, nothing like the hoarse, pain-filled tone he had used to scream at her as the darkness flowed over her the night she had been shot. She could still remember the horror that had echoed in his ragged howls as the darkness closed over her. She didn't want to ever hear such pain coming from him again.

"Hm." She smiled sleepily. She was sleeping a lot. The doctors had assured her it would help her heal. "I get to leave soon." She couldn't wait to sleep in his arms again, to feel him holding her, loving her through the night.

He stayed with her as much as he could at the hospital. When he wasn't there, Dawn or Sherra, who had come from the Breed compound with Cassie, stayed with her instead while guards waited outside the room. No chances were being taken with either her or Cassie's protection.

"Soon," he promised.

"Momma?" Cassie raised her head. "Dash said I'm going to have a brother or sister. Am I?"

Elizabeth smiled, fighting to hold her eyes open. She had missed Cassie so desperately, she hated to fall asleep on her.

"Yeah," she sighed sleepily. "You like that idea?"

"Yeah." Her head bobbed swiftly. "We should celebrate with chocolate, though. I told Dash we need a big ole chocolate cake, just like the one Simon brought me the other day. It was all kinds of chocolate."

Elizabeth winced, frowning over at Dash's chagrined expression. "Simon, huh?"

She felt sorry for Cassie's babysitters. There was nothing like chocolate to keep her running at full speed for hours on end.

"Oh yeah. He's really nice. And he doesn't mind tea parties either. Him and his Ladies had tea with me twice." Cassie stared down at her with all seriousness, as though the man she had been having tea with wasn't the same man who had hacked his way through six guards as he heard Dash's howls shatter the night.

Elizabeth fought the weak laughter building in her chest. Lord, she would have loved to see that one. Her eyes drifted closed a second before she fought to open them once again. And there was Dash, watching her, loving her. Her heart swelled with emotion at the thought.

"Come on, pumpkin. Kiss Momma asleep and head outside with Merc and Simon. I'll be right out," Dash finally told Cassie softly as Elizabeth's eyes fluttered sleepily.

Cassie smacked a loving kiss on Elizabeth's cheek before she jumped down from Dash's lap and headed to the door.

Dash turned back to her, his eyes dark with concern as he leaned close, touching her cheek gently. "Doing okay?"

"Great." She had to keep her eyes open. Had to stare into his wonderful gaze as long as she could. "You?"

"Damned cold at night," he sighed. She could see the effects of his sleeplessness. "But everything is arranged. When you're released we'll stay at the Breed compound until you're strong enough, then we'll head home. I have a place . . ." He watched her carefully. "It's a nice little house, Elizabeth. Big enough for a family, not too far from town, but we'll be safe there."

"As long as we're together, Dash," she whispered. Nothing else mattered to her.

"Yeah." He lowered his head then, his lips whispering over hers. "I love you, baby."

She smiled as her eyes drifted closed. "Love you . . . mate. Forever."

Dash left the hospital, catching Cassie up in his arms as she threw herself at him. She had barely let him out of her sight since the morning after Elizabeth's surgery. She cried if he left without her, and Dawn said the little girl would sit at the window, watching the road with a desperation that broke all their hearts until he returned to the hotel.

He hugged her close, feeling her tremble in his arms as he carried her out of the hospital. She was quieter since Grange's death. Almost as though she was expecting something more to happen now. Expecting a kick that would once again tumble her into the nightmare of the past two years.

"Do you still love me, Dash?" She whispered the surprising question in his ear as he stepped into the elevator.

He looked down at her head as the doors slid closed. "Of course,

Cassie, why wouldn't I? I told you, you're my little girl now. That won't change."

She sighed as though in relief. "Can I call you Daddy now, Dash?" she asked him as her head rose from his shoulder, her eyes staring back at him with such warmth, such love, he felt humbled by it.

"Yeah." He grinned, feeling as proud of himself as he had when he realized Elizabeth had conceived his child. "Yeah, Cassie, you can indeed call me Daddy now."

He hugged her to him, and knew that whatever the future brought, it wouldn't bring the killer Grange and Martaine had dreamed of. He would make damned certain of it.

◆　◆　◆

Everything is okay, Cassie, just like I told you.

Cassie sat alone in her bedroom weeks later, watching the soft misty form of the fairy as she sat on the side of her bed. The fairy had been there when the other man had killed her father. Not her daddy. Her daddy was Dash. Dane had been her father, but he hadn't been nice to her like Dash was. But it was then that the fairy had come. Urging Cassie to be quiet, to be calm, that her momma would come and that everything would be okay. She had stayed with her ever since, always promising her that everything would be okay. But Cassie was still scared.

"My momma is okay. That's the best thing," Cassie said, even though she could feel her chest aching that funny way when she wanted to cry but couldn't.

Cassie. Are you worried again? The fairy always knew when she was.

"Will I be bad?" Cassie whispered the words as the ever-present fear grew within her.

That's up to you, Cassie, the fairy whispered as she reached out, touching her cheek with a feather-soft caress. *You were blessed with light and given life for a reason. It's up to you how you live that life.*

The fairy didn't always make sense, but she understood enough to know that it appeared to be her choice. Her momma said she was a good little girl, and Cassie was determined to always be a good girl. She hugged her new teddy bear closer. It was bigger than the last one. Fluffy and warm and she didn't feel so alone when the fairy left her side more often these days. Besides, Dash said if she got scared, all she had to do was call to him and Momma. They always came to her, sat with her when she was frightened or when the nightmares were too bad.

But she couldn't tell Momma why the nightmares were bad. She couldn't even tell Dash. She hadn't been born to be a good girl; the man with the scar had laughed at her when he told her that. She had been born to be an animal. To be a killer. But all she wanted to be was a good girl.

Cassie, didn't I promise you that everything would be okay? the fairy asked her then. *Have I ever lied to you?*

"No," she whispered, wanting, needing to believe her.

Sleep, Cassie, the fairy whispered then, a gentle smile tilting her ghostly lips as a feeling of warmth accompanied the soft touch she made to Cassie's forehead. *Rest, little one, and know you were given a soul as bright and shining as your smile. Sleep.*

Cassie closed her eyes. As she felt the warmth slowly ease away, she peeked from between her lashes and watched as the fairy stood to her feet and began to dissolve.

Good night, Cassie. The soft glow eased away, leaving her alone as her lashes fluttered sleepily.

"I'm a good girl, Bo Bo," she whispered to the teddy bear as she hugged it tighter. "Momma says I am. And Momma doesn't lie to me. Maybe not all Coyotes are bad. I'll be a good one . . ."

Keep reading for a special preview of Cassie Sinclair's
story in the next Novel of the Breeds by Lora Leigh

CROSS BREED

Available from Berkley March 2018

This wasn't happening.

A rarely felt, overwhelming panic began to invade Cassie's senses, threatening to rip away the logic and careful thought she normally approached all problems with. It was rising by the second, tearing through her mind and beginning to shred the fear that the knowledge of a mating had brought.

This had just slipped past anything even remotely resembling fear. She realized in that moment that she could have handled a mate after all. A Wolf Breed mate, a Feline Breed, hell a Reptile Breed or human mate.

She could have handled a mate.

She couldn't handle this.

"Breathe, Cassie," he whispered, those strong arms she'd once longed to feel around her enclosing her like iron. Like a prison. A cell from which there was no escape. "It's okay, baby, just breathe."

Rage.

It clawed at her, mixed with the panic, with the overwhelming sense of helpless confusion. It burned inside her chest like a viciously hot poker, stabbing at her over and over again.

"You lied to me." The words escaped despite the tightness of her throat and the feeling that she was strangling on her emotions. "You lied to me."

Mates weren't supposed to ever lie to each other. She had never lied to him. She had always been completely honest with him. Always.

Those strong arms slid away from her, but that feeling of imprisonment didn't recede. It couldn't recede. There was no escaping.

"The blocker wore off," he muttered, the knowledge, the resignation in his voice an affront to her fury.

"You stink." Cassie forced herself to rise from the bed despite the agony she could feel tearing through her, spreading from her senses to her blood, to her muscles and bones.

She hurt now in every molecule of her body. The pain resonating with blistering intensity.

"Well, love, if I stink, then it's a stink you'll carry from this day on," he grunted as though the statement hadn't bothered him in the least. "And it's one I'll make damned sure you carry often."

Mocking amusement was the trademark she'd always sensed, yet, until now, he'd never turned it on her.

What was she going to do?

She couldn't deal with this!

She had to run, to leave . . .

Yet even now the despised reaction of her body to the Mating Heat was already building again, sensitizing her, forcing her to fight herself, to fight the steady increase of the hormones now racing through her.

She wanted him again. Wanted his flesh throbbing between her lips, wanted his tongue burrowing inside her sex again, spreading more of that sickening hormone.

Her hand clamped over her mouth as she felt her womb tightening, demanding his release, demanding he flood her body with his semen again.

She jerked to her feet, only distantly aware of him moving from the bed, but all too aware of the fact that he was aroused, erect and ready to give her body exactly what it was beginning to burn for.

For a moment, all she could do was ache for her mother, her father. Ache to beg them to fix this as they had so many other things in her life. To smooth it over, to make it better, to help her find a way out.

And there was no way out.

She knew there was no way out.

"Should I take you again, mate?" There was an edge to his voice that sliced at her, that dug into her chest and made the pain brighter, more intense. "Shall I just bend you over the bed and push inside you? Ride you hard and fast and give your body what it needs? Just stay behind you, so you don't have to see the breed you mated?"

Cassie jerked, barely holding back a cry rising unbidden to her lips as her sex spilled its liquid heat and her stomach rippled with the clenching of her womb, with the need, the hunger.

Yes, that was what she wanted, she screamed silently, agony tearing through her. Take her like the animal she now knew lurked inside her.

A low, male chuckle followed her as she shook her head and headed for the shower. She had to think. She had to figure out what to do.

"Cassandra . . ."

"Cassidy . . ." She corrected him almost automatically, feeling so dazed, so off-balance and filled with violence that keeping the explosion of pure murderous fury contained was the hardest thing she'd ever done.

"What?" Clipped and short, his voice raked over her senses, stroking her like a physical caress as she felt her sheath clench, felt more of the hot, silky wetness spill from her.

"Cassidy," she had to force herself to answer. "My name is Cassidy."

She was Cassidy Colder. She wasn't Cassandra Sinclair, no matter how desperately she wanted to be, how hard her mother and father—her step-father—had worked to give her that illusion. She wasn't Wolf Breed. She wasn't Dash Sinclair's incredible, amazing, intelligent daughter. She was Dane Colder's science experiment. The dirty little animal he'd helped create.

"A shower won't wash my scent from you." It sounded like a promise.

"Guess we'll find out . . ." Straightening, she'd almost taken that first step when she felt herself jerked around, her mate towering over her, glaring down at her, his gray eyes like thunderclouds as a warning growl left his throat.

That sound was the trigger.

It ripped through her, exploded through her mind and tore aside that veil of civility she was always so certain she possessed.

"Don't push me, Cassie," he snarled in her face, his head lowering, almost nose to nose with her.

Lifting to her tiptoes, she bit him. Her teeth snapped at the thin line of his lips, she tasted blood, tasted that hormone and lost control of the low, warning growl that left her own throat as she jerked back.

One hand latched onto his hair, she pulled his head down to get her fix. To pull in the hormone spilling from the glands beneath his tongue and allow the creature inside her to fully awaken.

The kiss was like a sensual explosion. It imploded inside her senses, laid waste to logic, to common sense, to the dreams, the hopes, the certainty she could overcome what she'd been created to be.

His tongue pumped between her lips as she licked at it desperately, allowed it to duel with hers, to spill the mating poison, to rush through her senses and jerk her on that wild, furious ride once again.

Long minutes later, dazed, drugged with the sensual heat, she pulled her head back. Retaining her grip on his hair she met the challenge in those wild gray eyes and the less-than-perfect features. As she stared up at him one broad, callused palm cupped her breast, his fingers gripped her nipple, tightened, and her head slammed back against the wall.

The sensations were terrible; they were exquisite. Agony and ecstasy slamming into the hard tip before ripping a line of sizzling electric heat straight to her pussy.

"Again." Her voice was strangled. "Do it again."

Easing the pressure, he did it again, this time harder, dragging a demented cry from her lips as his other hand slid between her damp thighs.

Damp because the slick moisture was weeping from her, spilling from the swollen lips between her thighs to the fingers now tucking between the folds to catch the silken heat.

"Come here, mate." Releasing her nipple and the desperately aching flesh between her thighs he lifted her to him, turned and sat her on top of the tall table.

Still gripping his hair she jerked his head to her breasts, her breathing hard, heavy, her chest tight with the screams she was holding in, the denials she so desperately wanted to give voice to.

"Suck my nipple," she demanded, pushing one enflamed tip to his lips. "Hard. Like you gripped it. Do it."

She watched him. Their gazes locked as he snarled then gripped the tip between his teeth and applied the painful, ecstatic pressure she needed.

White, strong teeth, curved canines at the side, a brutal snarl of lust on his lips.

His hands gripped her legs beneath her knees, jerked them up and forced her feet to the top of the table. With his teeth gripping her nipple, his tongue lashing it, his hand moved between her spread thighs. A second later a long, agonized sound of keening pleasure escaped her lips.

Two fingers pushed inside her, hard, deep. There were no preliminaries, no warning, just the sudden fullness and a firestorm of sensation tearing through her.

Her hips jerked, then bore down on the fingers as he sucked her nipple into his mouth, devouring first one then the other. Lips, teeth, tongue, suckling pressure and mind-consuming ecstasy. She didn't have to think here. She didn't have to consider what she was, what he'd turned her into.

"That's it," he snarled, lifting his lips as she fought to drive herself on his fingers. "Ride my fingers, mate. Look." He lifted enough to stare down their bodies, to watch her hips, to see the penetration of her body as she ground herself onto his palms. "Greedy baby. How much do you want? How much before you beg me to stop?"

Beg him to stop? She could take anything, everything he wanted to dish out.

"Go to hell," she cried out, but she couldn't help but watch as her hips pulled back, revealing the heavy layer of thick juices that clung to his fingers before she slammed onto them again, burying them inside her.

She froze for only a second. Before she could halt the downward thrust he added a third finger and pushed inside her even as she slammed her hips onto the penetration. She could feel her muscles clenching around the invasion, rippling with involuntary spasms.

"Enough?" She hated the challenge in his voice. Hated it. "Or more?"

His fingers curled, found a spot so sensitive, so explosively responsive that she couldn't hold back the climax that shot through her system. And it wasn't enough. It just wasn't enough. It only made her body hotter, made her senses more maddened.

"You bastard!" she cried out, her hands gripping his forearms, nails biting into his flesh.

Seconds later the thicker, hotter flesh of his shaft pressed against her, a hard spurt of hormonal pre-cum shooting inside her. His shaft parted flesh still highly sensitive, still clenching in pleasure and slowly—oh God, so slowly—began parting her inner flesh, penetrating her, filling her until she was certain she could take no more even as the hormonal ejaculations continued.

Dragging her gaze from the penetration she glared up at him. The hint of softening in his expression disappeared, the arrogance and challenge returned.

"Do it," she snarled. "Fuck me and get it over with. Go ahead, you bastard Coyote. Do your worst."

Ready to find
your next great read?

Let us help.

Visit prh.com/nextread